IDYLLIAN

AMSTERDAM
INSTITUTE SERIES

Clean Install
Dirty Burnout
Fair Exchange
Unjust Theft

IDYLLIAN

Books 1 to 4 of the Amsterdam Institute Series

R. Z. HELD

Clean Install copyright © 2020 by Rhiannon Held

Dirty Burnout copyright © 2020 by Rhiannon Held

Fair Exchange copyright © 2020 by Rhiannon Held

Unjust Theft copyright © 2020 by Rhiannon Held

All rights reserved. This book or any portion thereof may not be reproduced or used in any manner whatsoever without the express written permission of the publisher except for the use of brief quotations in a book review.

Cover design by Kate Marshall
Print layout by Sara McCormick

ISBN: 978-1-943545-15-5

www.rhiannonheld.com

To Erin, Erik, Yang-Yang,
Randy, Stephen, and Emily

For continuing to adventure boldly
with me through isolation

TABLE OF CONTENTS

CLEAN INSTALL

PART I

Genevieve had expected her first sight of a Pax Romana soldier up close to be a slam into her stomach, even worse than seeing recordings of them on a battlefield. Even if this particular soldier was supposedly retired and now working for a security firm, she was still Pax Romana. But the woman who motioned her into a conference room in Tsuga Security headquarters wasn't wearing body armor, or even a sidearm. She had a hard face, under her burst of short, black hair, but smiling changed it.

The pleasantness of that smile made it harder to imagine her dead, along with all the others in what Genevieve had worked out must be Pax Romana's reserves, but Genevieve had known that might be a danger, had prepared herself for it mentally. As much as she could with no formal training. It didn't matter what pleasant expression this woman might paste on top, when the flesh and blood below teemed with technology tuned to nothing but violence.

The woman settled herself at her desk. "I'm Cusco Eriope. Call me Eriope. I hear you're looking for a job with us? You understand, we tend to draw our personnel from a certain pool... *are* you ex-military?" She motioned Genevieve to another chair. Genevieve's back muscles twitched in protest even just looking at the chair's back, so she remained standing.

"No. But I am a nanite Install." The words tasted wrong on her tongue. They might *be* wrong, but she'd built her cover story to allow those kind of mistakes. Assuming this woman and her superiors accepted the cover story at all.

Her communication system registered a ping and Genevieve allowed it to respond in kind, but blocked any further access. At least, she hoped she had. It wasn't precisely like reading words in a status message on a screen, nor precisely like hearing sounds from an earbud. It was more…a wider understanding, like a visualization of a screen inside her mind that conveyed its information without any need to pause to read or listen. Maybe. If she knew how to work any of this, she wouldn't be here.

"So you are," Eriope said, and spread her hands flat on the table, rather than jumping to her feet to attack. Genevieve suppressed a flinch anyway, anticipating her next question. "How is that possible?"

Genevieve thought about touching the small data storage device masquerading as a post earring in her right ear. Thought about it and didn't, because she at least knew enough to break herself of such a transparent tell. Still, the thought alone of the virus, waiting patiently to be released, grounded her with the weight of why her story had to be perfect. "I used to work for TendarisHerron." They were the defense contractor that had developed the nanites, or so her research said. If her research was wrong, she was about to find out. Her back muscles spasmed and she set her teeth until the pain passed.

"So you're, what, a lab accident?" Eriope stood and approached Genevieve, more curiosity than suspicion in her expression. "Even the early test subjects were military."

"They wanted to develop civilian applications for the technology." Genevieve deployed each word carefully, using as few as she could. To her own ears, her system allowed her to speak with a core planet accent, but she wasn't sure she trusted that. Pay too much attention and everything she said sounded eerily wrong anyway, like listening to a recording, only it was coming out of her own mouth. "I was not...fully briefed, shall we say. Given that, I declined to continue my employment with TH." And here, a dash of truth to season it all: "I left, I tried to lock it all down and live normally, but I was not successful. I need to learn the systems."

Learn them, and be allowed onto the soldiers' network, if the virus was to do any good.

"I hoped someone here could teach—" The next spasm was much worse than she'd expected. Was it the stress? She'd had a bad episode, the kind with screaming, sobbing pain, on the flight to this planet, and between most of the episodes preceding it she'd had at least a standard week's grace. The background pain and the peaks of the episodes hadn't gotten any better since she woke with the nanites, but neither had they gotten noticeably worse until now.

"Can't say I blame you for not sticking around for the orientation when they installed on you without your informed consent." Eriope's brows rose, and she caught Genevieve's forearms as Genevieve's knees bent, instincts telling her to go fetal against the pain. She braced Genevieve up and examined the skin along the inside of one of her arms. "How much have you been relying on bio power, girl? Don't know your regular color, but you're looking sallow to me."

Bio power? "As opposed to—" To finish the question, Genevieve tried to think of another power source her nanites could be using, and came up empty. It wasn't like she plugged in, even after the installation process.

"Right. Outside." Eriope kept a grip on Genevieve's wrist and used firm pressure on the back of her shoulder to turn her and escort her into the hall. Genevieve wondered if she should resist, but she was sure that if Eriope wanted to subdue her, with training above and beyond the strength enhancements Genevieve shared, not to mention being pain-free, Genevieve wouldn't be able to do much about it. They ducked into another room, this one with a wall of windows.

The spasm in her back had eased enough for Genevieve to receive the full effect of the vista like a slap. Everything but the small area around the spaceport was mountains, magnificently visible from this height in the Tsuga Security building. Smaller ones, crumpled and green, eased into larger, white over creased stone. Between two of the closest, she caught a gleam of water, some icy lake perhaps.

"Recreation planet," Eriope explained absently, as she slid a plexi door open and broke Genevieve's spell as she urged her through. "Nothing worth the cost of mining, so they started the terraforming process when they built the fueling station and let it percolate along on its own." The railing around the balcony was chest-high on Genevieve. She judged she'd have warning to fight back if Eriope tried to push her off. She couldn't guess at Eriope's real purpose, though. Vitamin D?

Eriope turned Genevieve away from the view and braced her hands on her shoulders. "Now. Wings out."

"Why?" Genevieve asked the question more to stall than anything. She'd hidden the things for so long, it was hard to convince herself to unfurl them, instead of keeping them tightly clenched beneath the panel in her back, where no one could see. But this woman was a nanite Install. She had her own damn wings. Probably larger and more impressive ones.

The silliness of that thought broke Genevieve free, and she shrugged off her jacket. She'd gotten tired of ruining shirts, so she'd altered her current one to dip low in the back, like some kind of clubwear. The air was chill enough she bundled the jacket over her arms to at least keep those warm.

"Because bio power is inefficient, and it robs the rest of your body if you make the nanites run on it long term." Eriope crossed her arms and waited. She eyed Genevieve. "You're aware your wings are photovoltaic, I hope?"

"Oh." Genevieve couldn't find anything else to say. She was aware now. She'd known the things must have had some kind of purpose, since she couldn't fly with them.

Unless she was doing that wrong too, and Eriope would be flapping out toward those mountains any minute. But the soldiers she'd seen in recordings had never done that, and they hadn't seemed to bother keeping any of their other abilities secret.

She closed her eyes, because that helped her visualize the wings. Unfold, up and out, like stretching in the morning, thousands of little carbon composite scales snapping into larger panels until the wings moved like a bird's—a central outside rib and panels that overlapped or stretched apart like feathers. She'd stared at them often enough, tablet up to make a double mirror with the ones in the tiny bathrooms of the shitty housing where she'd spent the first few months after leaving home, and then in the tiny cabins of cheap, dingy long-haul transports out here. In places the matte, steely color darkened to almost black as if tarnished, and it looked as smooth as metal, though of course it was much lighter in weight.

She started to feel jittery, like downing a borderline-illegal energy drink and having it hit all at once. The jitters transitioned into something near panic, her heart pounding so hard she could hardly hear anything else. With each beat, the irrational fear grew and grew: she'd been discovered. Eriope was going to denounce her any moment.

"Shit, girl," Eriope said, and her face softened into unmistakable sympathy. "I called our medic, he'll be here in a minute." Genevieve had to pin down each thought with an effort—she hadn't seen Eriope call anyone because she'd called using the nanite com system. And she could have called backup to capture Genevieve instead, but why would she need it when Genevieve was currently so distracted and weak? Genevieve hadn't been found out yet; she needed to *keep it together.*

Eriope took one of Genevieve's hands and rummaged in her pocket with the other. "Here." She pressed a small object into Genevieve's palm. Genevieve had trouble focusing on it at first, as her panic was mutating, becoming an awful foreboding that pain was coming, it just hadn't arrived yet.

She peered at the pill, small, heart-shaped, and a powder pink shade that no candy dared use anymore. "This is a recreational euphoric," she objected. She hadn't fought this far and this hard to take refuge in street drugs, never mind the danger of blabbing something of her secret purpose while high.

"The nanites laugh at bigger and badder things than Sweetheart," Eriope said, expression going briefly ironic. "Much to my frustration. Consider it medicinal. It's not like real painkillers work, the nanites just burn them out of your system. With Sweetheart, you still feel the pain, you just don't give a shit." She pressed Genevieve's hand with the pill up to her mouth, and she didn't fight it. She swallowed. Sweetheart was hardly a truth serum. Consider this a calculated risk. Maybe she was a coward, but she didn't want to hurt. She'd hurt so much already.

When the pain did hit, time stutter-stepped a little, dropping Genevieve in the middle of Eriope's flow to someone else. "...so of course they're updating all at once. I gave her a dose of Sweetheart to take the edge off."

Genevieve felt...lovely. A perfect word for Sweetheart. How silly. She still had one of Eriope's hands and she clasped it with both of hers because her muscles were shaky. The new man who had appeared had a very nice face. A bit undistinguished, maybe, but the thin black line of his beard trimmed low along his jaw helped strengthen it. If she were to kiss him, she'd run the side of her thumb along it until she settled her hand to cup the side of his neck.

"That was probably the right choice," the new man told Eriope. "But don't take that for an endorsement of long-term use. All right—" He paused, and Genevieve didn't realize what he was waiting for until Eriope filled it in.

"She told Front Desk her name was Amsterdam Genevieve."

"Genevieve is fine." She smiled at him. She was glad she'd been able to give her real name—the Pax Romana empire was such a mixture, her family name didn't particularly stand out. This way maybe she could hear him say it. "You are the medic, I presume." She still had to be careful. Not silly. She had a sudden image of shushing her older sister as they snuck in late, and drunk, from a party, and her sister shushing her back, both of them getting closer and closer to giggles loud enough to wake the whole house. "I fear my installation process was even more incomplete than I had realized—"

"Even high, she talks like a diplomatic courier." Eriope aimed an elbow well short of the man's ribs. "You've made an impression, though. I think she sees something she likes." Genevieve was staring at him, she realized. Really obviously. Oops.

The new man politely ignored her ogling, casting a quick frown at Eriope instead. "You're one to talk. Don't tease her." When he turned back, his expression smoothed. "Okay, Genevieve. I'm Toledo Pyrus, and I act as the medic for these reprobates. Now, you'll need to grant me medic permissions, so I can see your system vitals, all right? That's all I'll see."

"Okay," Genevieve agreed, echoing his cadence on the word. All her slang belonged to her home planet of Idyll; she'd have to start learning some soon to fit in. Or be more informal. She wasn't sure how to be informal casually without sounding like she was trying too hard. Or maybe it didn't matter. She suspected she'd care very deeply later.

Pyrus slipped around behind her and ran gentle fingers along the join between the wings and her skin. His touch was clinical enough Genevieve mostly managed not to imagine it straying farther. Her system informed her that medic permissions had been activated and he was drawing off data about her vitals, but it didn't feel like *rummaging*, which she'd imagined it might, so she was grateful. "You had a clean install, right?"

Genevieve allowed Eriope to repeat her cover story for her, and rather admired the colorful language it gained. "So clearly those bastards didn't tell her a damn thing."

"I'm glad you were able to make it here," Pyrus said. "Brace yourself, Genevieve." He rapped the center of her back, between the wings, with the heel of his hand, and the pain she was too high to care about suddenly halved in intensity.

"I can't ever rid myself of the nanites, can I?" Genevieve asked. Pax Romana propaganda said so, and she figured they'd probably get more takers for the program if they could promise people a normal life after their tour. She flexed her wings experimentally. Not so bad, though she'd probably need to reevaluate when the Sweetheart was completely out of her system. The peak intensity of the lovely feeling had passed, but all her sensations were still warmly comfortable.

"You get a cushy job here, though," Eriope said brightly. "It's extraordinarily exciting guarding warehouses and ships while they fuel, I assure you. Don't get me wrong, we're useful—some high-class shit goes through this shipping point—but we're mostly acting as a deterrent rather than mixing it up with anyone."

Genevieve gestured her lack of objection to that to the side, in Eriope's general direction. All the better, in fact, to have duties that didn't require her to hurt anyone until she got the access to the Installs' systems she needed. This was perfect! She hadn't thought they'd agree to hire her so easily.

"We'll need to ask Carex what he wants to assign her to specifically," Pyrus murmured, and guided Genevieve's wings to fold not into her back but against it. So she wouldn't bang them on doorways, she realized when he nudged her toward the one back into the building. "Doctor's orders are to sit outside in the sun for as long as possible today and the next few days. After that, you can do your daily charge with the rest of us, if you want. If your duties allow." He held his arm out in invitation to the elevator, and Genevieve preceded the others inside.

"I'll tell him to meet us down there, anyway," Eriope said as they rode down. She shifted her attention to Genevieve. "Not that Carex is really in charge. But he's the CFO. So you'll have to sweet talk him if you want to get paid. And the rest of us will need authorization for any time spent training you." She leaned close. "The thing with Carex is, when he's looking you over and glowering and shit, remember he's descended from dirty frontis, so he thinks the stick up his ass has to be twice as rigid."

The confiding tone made Genevieve wonder why Eriope wasn't using the nanite com. But then, she supposed Installs were human, Pax Romana or not. Which was a joke she probably shouldn't make even in her head anymore. Technology didn't replace chatter unless it offered advantages. Which it obviously had on the battlefield, leading to the Pax Romana soldiers' reported creepy silence. And maybe Eriope was gossiping to Pyrus right now, behind Genevieve's metaphorical back.

"Carex can't help what his parents did," Pyrus said at normal volume. He did not, Genevieve noted, object to the casual epithet for those from frontier planets. She was honestly grateful that didn't bother her at the moment either.

Eriope continued merrily on, ignoring Pyrus. "That, and he's a first-generation Install. Back when he had it done, several decades ago, he thought they could remove it when he retired. Finding out he's stuck with it didn't...improve his attitude."

"Some of us surmounted the blow to our self-identity," Pyrus murmured, dry. Genevieve wondered how old he actually was, given enhanced healing. Both of them appeared to be in their thirties, a little past physical prime for cutthroat competition sports, but not for career military. Pyrus at least must be well beyond that, being first-gen—had he really been an Install for twenty or thirty years? Pax Romana must have started small, building up numbers, as their expansion push and internal propaganda had really only started in the last ten years. And the Installs and their capabilities had certainly come as a surprise to her home frontier planet of Idyll.

"You're just genetically civil," Eriope said, and led the way out of the elevator.

Pyrus guided Genevieve out the back of the building, to a rather respectable swath of green. Wilder than the fields that took up much of the space between settlements on Idyll, but more sedate than the gullies and mountains left to their own devices there. Park-like, with a lawn mowed down to a length good for strolling, though that ran quickly into the brush and trees over a rapidly steepening foothill.

Somewhere in the walk, Genevieve came down from the Sweetheart with a thud, or at least her good sense caught up with her thoughts and actions that had careened off under the drug's influence. How could she, dirty fronti herself, possibly have even thought about attraction to one of the Pax Romana she was here to kill, if she was lucky enough to succeed? Even more impossible, incomprehensible, how could she have remembered her dead sister so easily, so happily?

Worst of all were the medic permissions. Maybe it would have seemed more suspicious if she'd denied them, but what if he watched her vitals to hint at whether she was lying?

"It tells you what data I'm getting as I get it," Pyrus said, tone mild. "You don't have to lock me out so comprehensively." His phrasing was irritated but when Genevieve checked his expression, she found sympathy instead. "The alarms are set ridiculously high, I assure you. It alerts me to full cardiac arrest, not when your heart's pounding because you're pissed at someone."

"You really are a civilian," Eriope said. She continued before Genevieve could bristle, even internally. "Might make a nice change around here. Remind us that we can take back a little privacy if we want." She gestured to a bench, one of a few placed around the building's park. Or back yard. Or whatever it was.

"Sorry," Genevieve told Pyrus. Hard to be formal in one word. Focusing on her speech was a nicely concrete aspect of focusing on her mission, and focusing on her mission meant she wasn't thinking about her sister, or Pyrus. At least he seemed to be ignoring her manner while high. She sat on the bench without looking, turning her attention to the medic permissions as she allowed them back online. They seemed to match what Pyrus had said, but then she'd never been a coder, after the basic stuff everyone got in school. And it wasn't the raw code she was dealing with in any case, it was more of that half-instinctual sensation of cause and effect that the nanite system seemed to run on.

Eriope tugged at the zipper on her jacket, which Genevieve hadn't even realized was a jacket until that moment, and settled it about halfway down. The jacket closed up the back, though the impeccable tailoring of the front made it clear that was purposeful. Her wings unfolded easily, elegantly, metallic non-metal with a copper sheen to the gray, and black nowhere to be seen. "I doubt you'll have to worry about it for several days at least, but after that, careful you don't charge too long, or you'll end up amped," she remarked. Her lips quirked up, amused at the idea, or perhaps some memory of the experience. "And you'll have a hell of a time sleeping that night. You can dump into the building's grid if you really need to, though. I'll show you how to handle the hookup."

A new man strode up, glower practically preceding him. Carex, she presumed. "A civilian?" he demanded. Perhaps glowering was too mild a word for what he was doing. His skin was even more of an ancestrally sunny shade than that of the other two, though he wore his beard much like Pyrus did, in a single line along his jaw. Compared to Pyrus's, his shoulders hulked. "She's not on any list of TH employees I can find, current or former."

Genevieve had anticipated shakiness, facing this first challenge to her story, but things felt solid again for some reason. She'd expected resistance, not Eriope's offhand job offer—and sympathy from the both of them, for that matter—and now she had it, out in the open. Carex's manner snapped her mission into focus. "Of course not. Illegal experiments are removed from the records before they even start."

Carex seemed to be trying to stare her down. She met his eyes and held them as his system prowled around the outside of hers. It began with the sensation of being stared at from behind her back, and grew worse with the feeling that wherever she looked, she couldn't find the source of the gaze. She didn't know what he was looking for, but she refused to appear afraid that he might find it. She had the nanites. He couldn't argue with that. Finally he snorted. "I'm Malao Carex. And now I have to do something with you, it seems, a scientist in a security firm. Hope you like playing receptionist."

"No!" The word slipped out and Genevieve scrabbled to find some justification for it. She'd never get the access she needed if they essentially quarantined her from the soldiers, behind a desk. "I have no wish to die of boredom. What I do not yet know, I can learn."

Carex treated her to a light sneer. "Have you ever held a gun before in your life?"

"Yes," Genevieve said. She let the word come out hard. Every child on Idyll learned to shoot, beginning at the point when Pax Romana's first conquest in the region hit the interplanetary communication networks.

"Prove it, then." Carex's com pinged against her own, and she reluctantly accepted the message. A map, showing the way to a range, a few floors up in the same building.

"She should be charging." Pyrus stated it mildly, factually, body language remaining relaxed. Eriope must be right about him being genetically civil.

"She has enough to shoot, doesn't she?" When Pyrus couldn't deny that, Carex turned and strode back to the building. Genevieve jogged a few steps to catch up. This test shouldn't be too hard to pass. She hoped.

In the elevator, everyone was silent, even Eriope, which Genevieve took to mean they were talking to each other privately. The voice over her com made her jump when it came—it was definitely a voice, too, with all the accompanying intonation.

<...she certainly wasn't infected with them, or she'd be dead.> Eriope's voice.

<Eriope! Watch your channel!> A growl carried into Carex's.

<Oopsie.> Eriope didn't glance at Genevieve, but her smile as she looked up at the corner between the door's top edge and the ceiling was unrepentant. Genevieve looked away from her too, and pretended like she hadn't heard. She wouldn't look a gift ally in the mouth. She couldn't let herself *like* Eriope, however. She had to remember that. *Dirty fronti.*

The range looked familiar enough, as only so many ways existed to serve the same purpose. Carex picked up a gun, handgun-sized, but lacking a trigger. Instead, when one side contacted his palm, the grip lit and it audibly powered up. "Make sure your internal aiming program is online," he said, patronizingly. "And hearing protection." As Genevieve watched, clear material rose from the skin at the sides of his eyes and settled across them to his nose, forming a shield without need for earpieces.

She didn't know where her solidity was now. *The Pax Romana will kill you*, her fight or flight screamed, and accelerated her heart to the redline. But Pax Romana wasn't the important part, she knew that now. Those had been Pax Romana *Installs*, stepping off transports and into camerasight of her planet's recon drones. Carrying handguns, so small. Visors over their eyes with no earpieces. Utterly silent.

And now she was an Install, so if she feared them, she was fearing herself. She needed to breathe, to look calm.

Carex fired, and she flinched and scrabbled to find the hearing protection program he was talking about. There. Her ears didn't feel muffled, but an icon indicated it would damp down all input to a specified level. She left it at the default for now. That mistake gave her an excuse to look rattled, at least. And then Carex set the gun down and stepped back pointedly for her to take his place.

The target was circular, fortunately, not a human silhouette. Genevieve settled into the right stance, and imagined chewing on her lip. She wasn't going to give Carex the satisfaction of actually doing it. Forget aiming, how did she pull the trigger? The grip lit, and she could feel the power drain of the gun pulling from her system because she had a sense of where to look for that, having charged. A little off the top like this didn't sap her perceived physical energy, but Genevieve suspected it would begin to, when she got too low.

<I could do it for you while you watch, if you give me control, but I suspect that's a no-go, correct?> Eriope said. When Genevieve glanced from side to side at the men, laughter carried over the com. <Just us on this channel.>

<No-go,> Genevieve agreed, feeling out the sending of the message with something simple at first.

<Thought so. Look for this code.> Eriope sent a burst that... scrolled past Genevieve's vision? It wasn't moving, she still wasn't reading it, but the awareness of it seeped in, piece by piece. With that to search for, she found the equivalent in her own system.

All right. The targeting system prompted her to turn over her visual input. When she did, things looked no different for a beat. Her eyebrows itched fiercely as the shield crossed her vision, a leading edge of distortion that settled out, the material invisible once in place. She tried to tell herself if she couldn't feel or see it, it might as well not be there, and she should ignore the idea of it. That mostly succeeded only because that was when her arm muscles twitched in their brace, deeper than a typical tic. In her shock, Genevieve, having expected projected crosshairs or something similar, didn't fight the movement. Her arms settled into an artificial stillness, under her system's control. It wasn't… uncomfortable, she supposed. More like someone else's arms along her own, firm grip on her wrists. Thinking of it that way let her relax into it somewhat, and she realized she wasn't actually statue-still, she was simply compensating faster than her perceptions could understand. Twitch that way, twitch instantly back.

The last motion, to squeeze the grip, that was hers alone, at least. Genevieve hit one ring off the bullseye, paused with a heavy sensation of grinding calibration and computation at the back of her mind, then snapped half a dozen more shots grouped into the bullseye. No, not grouped, she realized, as her vision zoomed with a push of concentration much like squinting—that, at least, she'd already figured out how to do on her own. Into the *same hole.*

Carex half-growled something incomprehensible. "Even if she's not hopeless, she's still not *trained*."

Genevieve blinked her vision normal, set the gun down, and stepped back. When she knuckled at her eyes, chasing the earlier itch, her fingers found the edge of the line of carbon material over her skin just before it disappeared. Creepy as fuck. She dropped her hands immediately. "Hold my wages until my training is finished, then," she snapped at Carex. She didn't need the money—doubtful that she'd be able to take it with her when her mission was done and she was running for it, after all. "I promise the training period will be of short duration. Surely that would not be such an impossible investment." Best to pretend she wanted to earn a living eventually, so they didn't question her purpose here. She kept her chin high and her gaze steady, waiting out Carex's answer.

"She can still cover the desk while she's in training," Eriope put in, brightly. "Since everyone hates that duty. And hey! That'll free people up for the time they'll spend teaching."

"Congratulations, you've just volunteered to organize all her training," Carex said, batting it back to Eriope like maybe something in him actually enjoyed the banter, though his tone remained grim. He turned and disappeared off into the hall.

Genevieve almost had time to process that she was in, before Eriope swept her up on her way out the door as well. "Perfect. I'll give you a few days to charge up and then send you a schedule." She paused and turned back to Pyrus. "Do you need her for anything else? Otherwise I'll take her to a room."

Pyrus waved her off. "I'll find her later for anything else." His attention switched to Genevieve. "Go out on your balcony."

"Yes," Genevieve said, and by the time she finished chasing the intricacies of whether she should add a "sir" or something else, Eriope had nudged her to the elevator.

As the indicator numbers climbed, Genevieve glanced sideways at Eriope. The building had looked tall from outside, but she'd been examining it mostly from street level, among buildings of similar height. She hadn't realized it was *this* tall. "What floor will I be staying on?"

"How far up does this place go, you mean?" Eriope laughed, though the sound had a sharp note compared to her earlier cheer. "Pretty far. There's not much flat land good for building around here, and anyway they want it looking pristine for the tourists. So all the construction around the port went up. This was originally supposed to be a hotel, but we took it over before they did the interiors, so most of the upper floors are a couple suites rather than a dozen rooms. You'll be on a floor with no one else on it yet."

A beat of silence, in which Eriope pinched the bridge of her nose, all of her body language tightening down around that point. "Pardon me." She withdrew another pill, from a different pocket than the Sweetheart had come from, downed it with a practiced movement.

"Sweetheart?" Genevieve said, having nothing better to say. To pretend not to have seen seemed disingenuous.

"Nah. I save the good shit for myself." Eriope brought both hands up, fingertips at that same point at the bridge of her nose, as if she needed holding together. "With the nanites, it's not like it can actually do any damage to your health. And it takes the edge off, given that—I'm sure you've noticed this already yourself—there's a fucking lot of edge to being an Install." A deep breath, and she dropped her hands.

Genevieve felt a burst of unwelcome sympathy, and immediately thrust it away. They weren't on the same side—better she should write the woman off as an addict. But she couldn't judge someone else's coping strategy, given her own choices, she really couldn't.

When they reached their destination, forty floors up, Eriope gestured them out into a bland hallway. Her movements had regained their earlier energy, perhaps even excessively so, as if she hoped to replace her moment of weakness in Genevieve's mind. "The lower floors in this building are the communal spaces. Mess, gym, pool, theater. A whole base stacked up, practically." Eriope sent a burst of data, a more expanded map than the one Carex had given her to the range. It unfolded before her mind's eye and even had her name marked on the room they had just arrived at.

The door opened under her touch after a brief hesitation, like it had coded itself to her electronic signature. Now she had an electronic signature. She didn't kid herself that it wouldn't still open for someone like Carex, though.

She turned in the doorway. "Thank you." Even if she'd been speaking in her native language of Idyllian instead of Lingua, Genevieve wouldn't have known what more to say. She'd wanted the Installs to allow her in, but she hadn't wanted them to be kind or apparently deserving of sympathy in return. Eriope was making her mission both easier and harder at the same time. Of course Genevieve hadn't expected this to be simple, but she was only now beginning to comprehend the sheer scope of her naivete in thinking she knew in what form the challenges would come.

Unconcerned, Eriope beamed and returned a, "You're welcome!" before heading back to the elevator.

The rooms were large, Genevieve had to give them that. And well-appointed. And utterly bland. Ready for someone to impose their personality on them, Genevieve supposed. She looked at them and saw "Pax Romana," but of course that was because they were built like thousands of hotels on dozens of planets that saw high interplanet traffic, whether the Pax Romana controlled them or not. She'd seen those traveling to a conference or two, in her graduate school days.

Genevieve ran out of momentum when standing on the dark blue-gray rug between the bed and the desk, and found she missed wood with so fierce an ache her throat closed up with the strength of tears she didn't allow to gather. At home, it would have been everywhere—paneling, furniture, vessels, sculptures. She'd have been immersed in the feel of the grain, the richness of the variations in color, the warmth of touching something that had lived, rather than been *manufactured*. Not that Idyll was one of those agricultural planets that had eschewed technology for the principle of it, but they'd had the resources to surround themselves with that warmth.

Which was why the Pax Romana had arrived to conquer them, of course. *Dirty frontis.*

Genevieve aimed herself for the balcony, but the sight of the bathroom woke a realization of a plain old biological need. After cleaning her hands, she hesitated before the mirror, allowed herself to touch the earring. The one with the virus, not the matching inert one in her left lobe. She kept her thumb well away from the back, the end of the post. Stab that into someone's skin and their nanites would self-destruct, taking the person along with them. Kill someone networked in with the rest of the Pax Romana Installs, and who knew how far it might spread.

That was the problem, of course—she didn't know. That was why she needed to learn how the Installs were networked, whether a passive connection would be sufficient, or if an active one was necessary.

If it was even possible for her to tell without simply releasing the virus and seeing what happened. That wasn't an option, however. She had no wish to die along with these Pax Romana, so she needed to know what connections to avoid herself at the crucial moment. But she wasn't a software engineer. Nor a spy. Emphatically not. Just a soil scientist. One who, when the Pax Romana arrived on her frontier planet, had not the courage to fight on the front lines with her older sister, nor the training to staff the hospitals with her younger brother, and so drove an ambulance, steering bone-jarringly cross-country to avoid troops or cajoling or supporting or even dragging the wounded aboard.

Genevieve scrubbed at the bottom of her right palm. At that spot, she'd broken a glove when dragging one of her countrywomen from the rubble—she'd been ranting, out of her head, but Genevieve had ignored it because she was still alive, there should have still been hope for her. But she'd touched an Install corpse, must have done, so she passed the nanites to Genevieve before she died. That patch of skin didn't feel any different now, hadn't ever felt any different, no scar or discoloration to mark an entry point.

And Genevieve had survived that entry, somehow. Nursed by her remaining family only to wake up to a conquered city, and her one of the conquerors now. So far beyond "collaborator," however unwilling, there was no word for it, except perhaps "enemy." Her family had wanted to continue to hide her, but the resistance leadership had given her the virus and enough money for cheap transport to the Pax Romana core. Given her a "mission," one that was even supposedly survivable, but she knew it was just to get her off the planet. Installs were frontline troops, not occupiers. Killing them wouldn't magically free her planet, only give it better odds in a fight, when the Pax Romana had no backup to call on.

If she could have locked down the nanites, lived a normal life, she would have ignored the mission like the coward she was, but she'd had no other choice. Worse than anything else, she'd started to taint her family by association, after they'd saved her. So here she was, not a spy, to destroy the Pax Romana reserves. Laughable.

Genevieve removed her touch from her opposite hand, did not look at the earring again. Those thoughts could swallow her whole, if she let them. She'd built up enough practice on the way here shoving her thoughts in a forward direction instead. Forward would be examining her wings again now they were—what, aligned properly? But her tablet was still in her duffel downstairs, waiting with the person currently manning the front desk. She needed to go down and get that.

Instead, she pulled up the targeting program. She wasn't sure it would even work, without a gun in her hand, or a target, but the clear material erupted from her skin and covered her eyes and Genevieve got to watch it happen. On her own face.

She retched into the sink.

Nothing much came up. The muscle spasm only tightened her throat and brought up a mouthful of acid. Genevieve spat it out, then let herself down to her knees on the floor, hands on the edge of the sink and forehead against the wall beneath it. It didn't matter what extra bits of tech were floating in her blood. She was still herself. Still Genevieve. Forward.

"Get up," she told herself and the bathroom in Idyllian, eventually. "Get up, you fucking coward." And she did, levering herself up with the edge of the sink, not because she needed the support physically.

Hang on, Vieve. She had few memories of her installation, allowed herself to access even fewer, but she remembered her younger brother's voice. Or thought she did. He and her parents had been there the whole time, she was sure of it. To give up now would be a poor way of paying them back.

As she stood on the balcony with her wings to the sun, she used dealing with a pending request to hook her system properly into the central com as a way to avoid thinking too much. Or looking down. She'd done that once and her head had started swimming when it became viscerally clear just how far her floor was from the ground. Getting settled with the com proved a good distraction. She didn't think it would be enough to carry the virus, not unless she stabbed someone who was speaking to everyone in the reserves all at once. She certainly didn't have access to do so herself, though all the names were waiting should she wish to try to initiate an individual conversation over any distance. Or speak to everyone in the room, or everyone within a certain radius. All very useful, she supposed.

By the time she'd thoroughly explored that, her stomach was growling. Nothing since breakfast, and no pain to damp her appetite. All right, then. She found the mess hall on the map.

When she got there, she found she didn't know what to do with that appetite. There were a couple of prepared dishes to choose from, more simple ingredients for assembly, but nothing smelled right. It was all too—sharp? Too unfamiliar? But Pax Romana cooking was familiar enough to her; her ancestors had left the empire before it was an empire, after all. Nothing *appealed*, as it hadn't since she'd recovered enough to pay any attention to taste. As that period had been spent in cheap housing or on cheaper transports, she'd put it down to poor quality and sketchy sanitation. Here, she doubted that was the case, and yet she still found herself thinking of her old faithful nutrition bars in her duffel while lurking like a freak just inside the entrance. Fortunately, between peak mealtimes, only a couple people were there, eating alone in silence.

Her bars wouldn't last forever, and it wasn't like they were tasty, just palatable, so she finally talked herself into a grain dish, cooked down to starch so she couldn't tell if it had originally been rice or something else. She took the bowl to a table and carefully scraped off the dollop of sauce. She tried the mush. It still tasted of something. She swallowed quickly before the taste could take over her entire mouth. Some kind of herb? She had to eat *something*. Better to toss this down. She managed to swallow the next spoonful from the back of her mouth before she tasted it too much, which helped.

Pyrus entered the mess. Genevieve wiped her disgust at the food off her face as quickly as she could, and hoped he wasn't here to see her. It could be chance, right? He did head to the food, and speak to the cook, even, but then once he'd received a plate with half a dozen little sauce bowls arranged on it like a flower, he made straight for her.

Genevieve's momentum had slowed while she watched him suspiciously, and her stomach started complaining again. She wanted to eat, yes, but not *this*. She took a huge bite so she didn't have to greet Pyrus immediately, and had a hell of a time getting it down her throat. Pleasant expression. She was keeping a pleasant expression. Pyrus shouldn't have a reason to question why Pax Romana food was unfamiliar to her.

Pyrus stole her mush without apology and pushed the little sauces into its place. Genevieve stared at him, spoon poised in the air. "I was not finished with that—"

"I saw you were in the mess, and with everything else, I thought your system might not be calibrated for taste, since that was something of a hack we had to come up with ourselves at first." Pyrus pushed the mush out of his way. "And now I suspect I'm right. Does anything with flavor taste unappetizing now?"

Genevieve dipped the tip of her spoon into a red sauce, fidgeting with the viscosity. "That is an effect? Of the nanites, not of stress?" Or homesickness? After everything that had happened, ripped away from home and hurting so much, she supposed she'd never stopped to think it might not all be in her head.

"The sensitivity on your smell is cranked too high. They thought about that for hearing and sight—those require concentration to bring them above normal because otherwise you'd get people who would go starking because of the hum of the air system in their bedroom. But they didn't think about taste and appetite." Pyrus tapped the edge of the plate with sauce. "I've assisted plenty of new Installs, so I'll bring it back into normal human range for you. Put dots of that first sauce on your tongue and tell me when it tastes good. We'll do them one by one."

It wasn't all in her head. She'd be able to enjoy food again. Genevieve's emotions swooped away from her like they had in the bathroom and she wanted to curl into a ball again. "That would be a kindness," she said, and managed to keep her voice even. She dotted the red sauce on her tongue and waited out the sharpness of it like she would a spice burn.

"It's part of a real installation process. It's obscene that they'd do it to you and then leave it half finished." Pyrus did something with her code directly, rather than handing it to her as Eriope had, and the sauce started to gain nuance—ironically enough, since apparently her sensitivity was going down—and she swallowed without difficulty and dabbed another dot. That was—tasty. A little salty, with some acid. Her mouth flooded in response. She'd missed tasty and hadn't realized it. "At some point, it's hardly better than infecting you," he grumbled, low, as he worked.

"That one is pleasant," Genevieve said. She stopped with her spoon above the next, as his words truly penetrated. Infecting...? Like Eriope had said before. She needed to know more, and this seemed like a perfect opportunity. "For a brief time, I attempted to hide from TendarisHerron on one of the agricultural planets. Outside of Pax Romana. Rumors said dead Installs were designed to infect civilians. As a biological weapon." She let her tone give the slightest of lifts at the end.

She, with her higher education, had never believed the rumors when the invasion began, when Installs first started dying on Idyll. But it was hard to argue with her own body.

Pyrus pointed to the next sauce, and she rotated the plate to put it in front of her. She presumed her prodding had been rebuffed, until he sighed and started speaking. He was slower to start than Eriope, but no less willing to share, it seemed. "So you know how they put you under before they introduce the nanites into your blood, so you woke with the majority of the installation already finished?"

Genevieve nodded. She knew enough to know that's how it should have been.

"Well, there's a reason for that. If you try to add anesthesia after the nanites are present in the body, they treat it like a toxin and destroy it before it can do anything. So you get someone who is forced to stay awake through the entire process, and that's not—the mind can't take it. The nanites change too much, rewire too much, cause too much pain..." Pyrus looked at his hands, folded his fingers together. He seemed to draw his next words from the lull of silence, choosing them carefully.

"When someone is dying, the nanites are at their most active, trying to save them. That's the only period when they can be spread skin to skin. And if someone touches a dying Install, and the nanites start trying to install on a new host, without anesthetic...the new host is essentially dying too. I suppose it might have looked like a weapon, after the first couple battles."

With an effort of will, Genevieve didn't rub her left palm, that entry point. She'd made the choice to help that woman, even before her glove broke. Even though they'd been told to leave anyone who couldn't respond coherently to a few simple questions, because they might be infected. She was a scientist. She hadn't believed in a biological agent, hiding in the Pax Romana's own soldiers. How could it possibly be constrained not to kill them, not to kill Pax Romana citizens when the soldiers went on leave?

And it seemed she'd been half right. That didn't give her much satisfaction.

"But you aren't an Infected." Pyrus gave her a brief curve of an encouraging smile. "And now you're somewhere where you can get the real support you need."

But Genevieve *was* an Infected. And she wasn't dead. That was something her scientist's mind demanded she examine in great detail, but she pushed it aside for now. She offered Pyrus as much of a smile as she could manage. "I am no soldier."

Pyrus shook his head. "Doesn't matter. Part of the terms of our lease on this facility is that we have to take in any Installs 'not in active military service.' I looked it up. Discharged or retired, I'm sure they meant when they wrote it, but what they actually said includes you."

Less providing for loyal veterans, and more not letting technology fall into anyone else's hands, Genevieve would bet. "And when you're all called up? I go too?" She'd need to be long gone before that point, whether the virus had succeeded or failed.

"Called up?" Pyrus was startled into a laugh, pushed away from the table a few centimeters apparently even at the thought of it. "We are *retired*, believe you me. I've done my time, as have we all. Just because they've ruined us for a normal life afterward doesn't mean they have any claim on us to fight ever again. Those who choose to be lifers are back at headquarters or out at the front."

He spoke with such intensity Genevieve couldn't help but believe him. "I am sorry—I thought—that this would be the reserves..." And yet, she couldn't help but doubt him in the same measure. If they were meant to be hidden reserves, he'd have to say exactly that, and sell it too.

No point in pushing, in any case. To bridge the awkward moment she dipped up sauce, placed it on her tongue. So sweet it made her teeth feel like they were rotting, but that faded quickly enough as Pyrus scooted back in, frowning in concentration. The two of them settled into silence that was almost comfortable.

"Done," he said, at length, and smiled as Genevieve sprang to her feet. She'd been thinking about the desserts ever since sweet came back. Far from her problem before, she now couldn't choose one dish because she wanted them all at once. She finally picked a pastry and a mousse of some kind, sticking to two because she only had two hands.

Pyrus laughed low when she clattered them onto the tabletop and started eating. "If I could be the source of smiles like that every day, I'd be a happy man."

Genevieve looked up, spoon arrested once more. Was he... flirting with her? How was she supposed to respond? She could afford real attraction, with no excuse of being high, as little as she could afford liking, as with Eriope.

Had things been different—no, be honest. Had the entirety of the current conditions of her life been different...and were that so, she wouldn't be here.

Pyrus's expression seemed to indicate he'd been as caught off guard as her. "I'm sorry. I didn't mean—I'm your medic at the moment. It wouldn't be ethical for me to…" He coughed, looked aside. Genevieve dropped her head and resumed eating. Yes, they could leave things there.

For his part, after a beat of silence, Pyrus's manner returned to seriousness. "Have you ever tried to cut off your wings?"

That caught Genevieve with a spoonful of mousse in her mouth. She took the time of swallowing and lowering her hand to choose her words. "What kind of question is that?"

"A mental health question." Pyrus waited.

"No," Genevieve said, but apparently that wasn't enough for a mental health question. She licked her lips, and decided on a few more words. "I spent some considerable effort for a while attempting to keep them constantly folded away." But that kind of pain, above and beyond what she had been suffering as a general background, hadn't been conquerable by mere effort. When she'd given up, that had been when she'd given in to the "mission," started charting her path to this place. "Did someone...?"

"It's been known to happen." Pyrus's fingertips beat a quick pattern on the tabletop, stilled. "Any program has those who wash out, especially at the beginning before they really know what to look for in candidates. Things got ugly for a few people when they couldn't escape from the psychological implications of installation. Wings grow back."

Genevieve thought of eye-shields, and retching. She lifted her chin. "I have traveled this far."

Pyrus nodded. "So you have. And you have a place here."

Genevieve dropped her eyes to her food to avoid giving importance to her question. "Am I allowed to leave?" If he was telling the truth about being retired, maybe the answer to that would be better than she'd expected. If he was telling the truth.

"Of course." Pyrus sounded surprised, then blew out a breath on a resigned note. "You'd probably better be prepared to find someone keeping tabs on you for the rest of your life, though. Is that what you're asking?" He seemed to read an affirmative answer in her body language, and moved to more banal topics for small talk.

Meanwhile, Genevieve grappled with the new information, trying to fit it into place around her mission. She shouldn't waste the virus on a bunch of retirees. If she could learn what she needed, choose to leave and live her own life… No, if that was the case, she should try to get access to one of the active Install units, accomplish something instead of slipping off like a coward.

The first step was obvious, at least. She'd keep her eyes open as she learned, see if she could find any evidence to support or refute the idea of retirement. She'd do what she'd come here to do, even if she had to refine her plan a little.

PART II

Genevieve reached the rocky promontory on the hillside beside the Tsuga Security building a split second before Eriope thudded into her back. The metal guard rail was fortunately set securely into the rock for the sake of the tourists, and Genevieve gripped it and let Eriope bounce off her. The day was cold, sharply so, like the edges of grass and rock under the mountain sunlight, the ex-soldiers' little patch of natural beauty tourists would travel light years to visit.

"You take the flag," Eriope said, her breath from this close carrying a slight chemical-sweet smell, presumably from whatever she was on today. She shoved a bundle against Genevieve's body so Genevieve clutched it without thinking. She'd never actually seen the flag up close—she played at playing with the ex-soldiers, but she didn't have much interaction with the actual subject of the game—but she knew better than to draw it out to examine it now. The wind would unfurl it and the others would converge on her. It had plenty of fabric and a golden metallic sheen like a kid's cheap spaceship costume, so Genevieve suspected it had begun life as some kind of event banner at one of the planet's hotels.

"What am I supposed to do with it?" Genevieve asked, zipping her jacket over the lump. The point of the game was agility and speed, not slugfests, so she hadn't even been aware herself that Eriope wasn't another of the decoys from their team who had scattered up the hill and over the field below. Their section of the pursuit was climbing the switchbacked path even now.

"Get it to base while I draw them off." Eriope pointed to the ground, across a sea of ex-soldiers.

Genevieve glanced to the Installs coming up the path. For a moment, she felt the clawing nausea of fear of a Pax Romana force ranged against her, her worst nightmare once upon a time. Presumably her sister's last sight. But that was brief enough, possible to swallow down. After nearly a standard month she knew these people's faces if not all the names yet. None of them were in uniform, and some were quite idiosyncratic in their style. She tore her gaze away from them to measure to the ground. She'd never make it past them with the flag now. "I can't—"

"Of course you can. Easy, peasy." Eriope snapped her wings out of her back, where they'd been tucked for climbing, and clambered onto the guard rail. "It's even a straight line."

She set her wings and launched herself into an elegant glide, curving around, then back, probably to illustrate how easy Genevieve would have it by comparison. Her short hair ruffled wildly around her face as if with joy at the wind.

Genevieve's lips thinned with frustration. So this was a lesson. Pyrus must have tattled that she hadn't been able to make herself glide yet. And what was Eriope doing, bothering to help him maneuver her into confronting the issue? That was something a friend would do. Genevieve was trying *not* to make friends.

Of course, maybe it would discourage Eriope if Genevieve completely failed, even with prodding.

Fear, of falling instead of soldiers, grabbed at her muscles, made it almost impossible for her to move. Her innate stubbornness got her as far as climbing on the rail, telling her system to lock her wings rigid at the right angle for flying. But she couldn't make herself push off. "Come on, come on," she chanted under her breath. It came easily in Lingua, at least one sign of progress from her weeks with Tsuga Security, but it didn't help her push off the rail.

"No, Eriope's clean," someone shouted from the trail behind. Someone on the opposing team must have tackled her and commed up.

Genevieve couldn't do it. She admitted it to herself, and started to turn to step down, but that was when a hand closed around her ankle. She kicked out, unbalanced, lost her grip on the metal—

She tumbled, view whirling too fast for her to make sense of it or know which way to twist to steady herself. Her system seized her muscles and did—something—or maybe it was deeper, more biological instincts than that, but she got her arms up to protect her face and her wings caught enough air to slow her so she plowed into the grass with less force.

Her knees and forearms still felt peeled, the pain at least fading quickly as the nanites healed the damage. She got to hands and knees, noticed the pairs of legs surrounding her, and groped out the flag and handed it over. She wanted to wheeze alone for a few moments, not try to run for it.

The opposing team members thundered off at a sprint, and Genevieve remembered to unlock her wings. "Sorry," she said, when a few additional feet jogged up. Some of her own team, she presumed, given the lack of urgency.

"Could have been worse. You should have seen some of these clowns going ass over elbow when they were first learning," Eriope caroled. She extended a hand and tugged Genevieve to her feet. Genevieve was more worried about recriminations from the others on their team, but they seemed philosophical enough, chatting together as they wandered off. No one so far had glowered at her the way Carex did, or indeed had offered her any fuel at all to stoke the intensity of her belief in her mission. She'd been trained by a variety of the ex-soldiers so far and while some were patient and some weren't, she couldn't see that there were more of the latter than in any population. She avoided the subject of frontier planets so she could exist in blissful ignorance of their precise opinions on those.

Genevieve drew her hand away from Eriope's. She'd let this go too long, she realized. She'd allowed herself too many excuses. Time to release the virus here, whether these people were reserves or not. She honestly believed now that Pyrus believed he wasn't—but that wasn't the same thing. They were still Installs, of use to Pax Romana, if the empire decided to strong-arm them into action at some later point.

True, since she was still in training, she didn't have the permissions to open a com channel to everyone in Tsuga. That might be the cleanest way—initiate an all-Tsuga channel, drop out, then stab anyone handy—but it certainly wasn't the only way. She only had to be ready to seize her chance when such a channel was opened by someone else. It happened every few days for one reason or another.

But that would mean lingering near others for significant periods of time, to maximize the chances of not being alone when next an all-Tsuga channel was opened. Who would that make ground zero? Eriope was friendly, trusted Genevieve enough to include her in Tsuga's after-hours camaraderie. Would Genevieve be able to sentence the woman to death, looking into her eyes, any better than she'd been able to glide?

<We've got a hospital ship inbound with Infecteds, folks.> Pyrus on the all-Tsuga channel cut across the game, and the swirl of movement around where the flag had ended up ceased immediately. The channel actively broadcast silence in a way that meant the person speaking had gotten distracted, and would probably continue in a moment. <Nine, this time.>

It was as if the universe conspired to stab a pin right through the heart of her cowardice to watch it writhe, no excuses left. If she only unclipped the earring, *right now*, stepped into Eriope...

But there would be other all-Tsuga broadcasts, about nothing in particular. Not like this one, to which she desperately wanted to listen. Infecteds. Like her. <Why are they here?> she asked Eriope privately. Private channels were incredibly useful for when you didn't want to highlight your ignorance in front of everyone.

<There's a whole dedicated floor for them, above the regular clinic. Pyrus had this whole crusade for a while, like he was going to save some. He gave up on that, but we still have the facilities. Nine is just under capacity, so it should be fine.> Eriope shaded her eyes, perhaps to see who was converging on the building and who was sticking around, then dropped her hand as the nanites adjusted her eyes for her. Genevieve studiously avoided glancing at where the darkening spilled over the irises. <Looks like he'll have plenty of help to settle them. Don't worry about it.>

That wasn't what Genevieve had been asking, but she didn't see how else to phrase it. She'd have to go see for herself. <I am—> She caught herself in the formal phrasing. <I'm ready for a break anyway.> She dusted off her knees pointedly, though the grass and mud were too ground-in to actually move.

Eriope shrugged, unbothered by pretty much everything, and jogged toward the knot of people forming where the remaining players—Genevieve paid brief attention to the location-specific channel—were deciding whether to redivide into new teams.

Genevieve pulled up the building map and found the floor Eriope had mentioned without trouble. She'd assumed it was part of the general clinic complex before. She started out jogging, but slowed as she neared the building. Pyrus would hardly welcome her bursting in and getting underfoot as he tried to treat the Infecteds. If she'd wanted to gawk, she should have hurried earlier, and joined the group she assumed was transferring the Infecteds from the ship.

She loitered near the elevator and checked if anyone had their location information on the public map. Pyrus did, along with a couple others straggling in from the elevators closest to the freight entrance. Maybe she could still offer a pair of extra hands. Genevieve forced herself to consider whether she should stay out of it, but she had to know who these Infecteds were. Were any from her own planet? Other agricultural planets scheduled for their Pax Romana takeover? Or were they Pax Romana citizens who'd been exposed in some other manner?

And what was going to happen to them? Why transport them all the way here if they weren't going to survive, as everyone seemed to believe? Genevieve wouldn't be able to think about anything else if she didn't at least try to find some answers.

She arrived to a scene of chaos. She remembered how the woman she'd pulled free had babbled, sometimes ranted, disconnected phrases of helpless confusion as she grasped for what wasn't there. All nine of the forms being carried in not only ranted, but screamed and thrashed. For a split second, Genevieve was surprised that the Infecteds were being carried by hand, one ex-soldier with the feet, one with their hands under armpits, but of course they'd fall off stretchers. The people doing the carrying could flex with each thrash. And heal blows.

Any grumbling out loud would have been lost in the noise from the Infecteds, but Genevieve suspected there was plenty going on, on private channels. As she hung back, just inside the doorway, the Infecteds were dumped none too gently into individual gel pools. The gel cushioned their fall and blunted the force of their thrashing as it was intended to do. Pyrus walked down the line, a muscle standing out on his jaw, stopping at each control interface and calibrating until the gel level completely covered each Infected.

The noise dropped in stages, easing down to something almost bearable, muted sloshes and groans. The Installs cleaned their hands and drifted out without a second look at the patients, leaving Genevieve and Pyrus alone with them.

She edged forward as the gel oozed in to cover the last man's mouth, nose, eyes, forehead. She couldn't imagine the expense of all these individual pools, full to the brim. She was familiar enough with the small pools in the hospital at home, meant for a single limb, and of course she'd seen the advertisements for individual pools meant to be filled to the neck or lower chest. But full immersion was rare, and hardly necessary most times.

"Not a pretty sight, huh?" Pyrus said. "I *hate* this." His words had a slashing quality she'd never heard from him before, making Genevieve jerk back.

Even genetically civil people must have their limits. Something in the line of his lips pressed tight reminded her of Eriope's expression, when walking a ragged edge in the elevator. Then Pyrus dropped his head, reassembling control on his own. "I'm sorry. It's not you." He traced the edge of the pool with two fingertips.

Genevieve joined Pyrus in front of the control panel, kept her attention politely on the Infected. Seeing the man's face through the covering gel made her instinctively hold her breath. Was he conscious enough to feel like he was drowning? You could breathe through gel, but your hindbrain didn't like it. "Why can't you let them breathe normally?" To feel your body being taken away from you and drowning too—her stomach surged up and she clenched her teeth until it settled. When she allowed in her memories of that time—which she did as little as humanly possible—beyond the feeling of her family's presence she found mostly disconnected dreams, nonsense born of fear that didn't understand its source. She supposed these people must have as little awareness of their surroundings as she'd had.

"Because they're never going to wake up," Pyrus said heavily. "They're as good as dead, we're just easing their passing."

"No." Genevieve shook her head, the word alone insufficiently emphatic to convey her steadily rising emotions. They couldn't just drop these poor people into gel pools and *leave* them there. Alone. At least she hadn't been alone.

She took the risk of reaching for the control panel even with Pyrus standing right there, and set the gel level to just below the chin. The man gasped and coughed as his mouth was revealed, clearing his lungs, but he didn't speak. Genevieve leaned over the pool to drag goop off his skin and hair with her fingers, hastening the normal draining process. "There has to be something—"

Pyrus jerked her back, fingers digging into her shoulder. "Nothing we do matters. *Nothing*, do you understand? I used to imagine I could do some good. I fought to have them brought here, so at least someone would be *trying* to save them, instead of hooking them up to instruments in some out-of-the-way facility and walking out. Like all they're worth is the data describing the process of their deaths. And I could help if they could grant me medic permissions, but they can't grant anything if they're not conscious. So they die, every one. And they still keep sending them."

He clamped his hand to her other shoulder, turning her to face him. "You can't beat yourself bloody against the impossible, lose yourself in the enormity of it. I did, and I'm still trying to come back from it—" He pushed her away as abruptly as he'd turned her in, twisted himself to face the blank wall instead.

Genevieve clasped her gelled hand with the other, fingers sliding unexpectedly when she thought she'd finally found a grip. "But I—" But she'd survived. And she couldn't tell him that. Was she simply a statistical anomaly, the one in a million lucky combination of genetics, personality, and environmental factors? She refused to believe that.

If cold probability hadn't saved her, what had? Pyrus seemed to consider the conversation finished, and dragged himself from one pool to another, checking readouts in silence. Genevieve opened the door to memories she'd shut away.

She'd dragged the infected woman free, across the floor of the former office building, detoured when a collapsed beam blocked their way—when had she started to feel ill? She'd—itched, Genevieve thought. Itched first in her hands, then her arm muscles had started to burn like she'd been lifting equipment above her head over and over for hours. But with the adrenaline, she hadn't really thought about it as she got the woman loaded into the back of the ambulance.

And then sitting in front while her partner drove, her body had stopped listening to her. She remembered that clearly. She'd slumped against the window and thought that maybe she needed a rest, that she'd be ready to walk again when they reached the field medical station.

And then…pain, and the dreams. Or had the dreams come later? She thought the beginning had been more formless than that. Thoughts that weren't thoughts, or dreams, or even emotions, they were too strange and didn't feel like they belonged to her. But she'd been somewhere safe, with her family. *Hang on, Vieve.* She remembered the smell of her childhood room.

"What about the placebo effect?" When Pyrus turned to her, Genevieve wanted to take the question back, but she stood firm instead, trying to put confidence she didn't feel into her face. She appreciated that he had to guard himself against burnout, she really did. But all the more reason someone else needed to ask the question.

"No placebo is going to cure death, like magic," he snapped.

"But the environment, feeling safe, feeling cared for by professionals—"

"I am *aware*," Pyrus bit off his words. "Of everything the placebo effect entails. Safety doesn't address feeling yourself rebuilt from the inside by machines."

This time, the retch called up by Pyrus's words made it all the way to the back of Genevieve's mouth. She swallowed it down before the acid could burn too badly, but she must have jerked. Pyrus's anger drained from his face. "Genevieve—"

"Let me." Genevieve returned to the man she'd freed from the gel. His eyes were open now, staring in fear at nothing. She smoothed his hair. "Let me take care of them. Please?" The words came out without thought, the only way to stem the tide of her clotted guilt. Her family had saved her, a coward. Of all those who had been infected so far, she was the only one who had lived. Somewhere in that survival, there must be a reason, a reason she could put to use.

What could she do to be worthy of her family's gift? Save others, without family there beside them.

Or try, at least.

Pyrus was silent for a long time, then sighed. "It's not my place to save anyone from themselves. Maybe—" He attempted a smile, managed at least a forced lightening of his expression. "You'll see something from an outside perspective that's been missed. I'll tell Carex I reassigned you. It would have to be classed as training, unfortunately, rather than as a full position. Carex was complaining about how he'd have to grant you clearance soon, so if you don't want to delay that…"

Genevieve shook her head automatically. For all his protestations, he clearly *was* still trying to save her from herself, with what meager bait he had.

Then it hit her, like a fist into her stomach, still sour from her earlier emotional nausea. Clearance. Permissions to do things like open all-Tsuga channels. There it was, what she'd needed all along to complete her mission. That, too, would be putting the gift her family had given her to use.

In abstract, her choice seemed ridiculously simple. Save people, or kill them? Except she didn't know if she'd be successful in saving anyone, and she didn't know the virus would work. And what if killing Installs saved thousands of others, in the future?

Too many variables, too many unknowns to predict the future. What, then, could her choices do *now*? Killing wouldn't unconquer Idyll. Killing wouldn't give her sister back her life. But these people, maybe Genevieve *could* give them back their lives, albeit deeply changed ones.

"That's all right, thank you. I want to do this." Genevieve searched for some better words, to convey to him how she *knew* she was right, that changes in their environment would help keep at least some of these people alive. Because she'd lived. But she couldn't think of anything, and let him leave with only the gratitude.

All right. If she was going to be anecdotal about this, she might as well go all the way. What would have made her feel better? Not drowning was good, but she could do better than that. She reached for the man's hand beneath the gel. The control panel gave a pissy little beep at detecting a second set of vitals, so she pulled their clasped hands up into the air.

"I'm here," she told him. She left Lingua behind so she could sound more emphatic in Idyllian. "I'm not your family and I don't even know your name, but I'm here and *I* want you to survive, okay? All of you. We're going to do this together."

Fuck the virus. *This* was her purpose.

PART III

Genevieve tried many things over the next three weeks. She'd been lying on her stomach during her recovery—she got the smallest woman turned over, but couldn't get her to lie with her face out of the gel, and the position increased her thrashing. Or perhaps only made it easier to perceive with splattered gel. Genevieve rescued all of that she could, scraping it up carefully after returning the woman to her back. Clearly Genevieve's position had been an artifact of having only a bed when her wings needed space. In the tanks, the Infecteds floated with room to grow.

She remembered music, laced with her dreams—she played the most soothing instrumental tracks she could find, mixed with the sound of rain, or waves. She didn't know what sounds might remind these people of the natural world they'd left behind at home, nor what popular music to choose when she moved on to that. She tried love songs, dance songs with a driving beat. Those pressed *her* to greater effort, certainly, but with no project to spend it on she mostly paced.

She kept the lights low and warm, tinted like sunlight, and she talked to them—talked to them *endlessly*, about how everything would be all right, how she was there to help them, how they were safe. Touched them with every excuse she could find and sometimes none at all. She took to taking their pulses by hand, at their wrists, though she might as well have been shaking a rattle and imploring the gods to reveal their vitals to her, for all the real scientific use it had.

And nothing. No change. The patients had all quieted after the first few days, and now they only moaned occasionally, bodies twitching as if from pain that was no less felt for the conscious mind being unable to reach the surface. They didn't scream, and they didn't speak. Their vitals had stabilized, and jumped only occasionally with pain responses. She searched constantly for their systems with her own, as much as she knew how, but found no evidence of anything she could connect to.

But her own state was deteriorating, she could tell that. Probably the slow slide down to burnout, as Pyrus had predicted. She returned to her room to sleep and stepped outside to charge, but with no one else to rely on to do a thing to help the Infecteds, she spent every other moment here.

Today, she was reading out loud to them from a nanite manual. It was information that would do her good as well, and maybe it would make the process seem less strange and invasive to them. She couldn't say her own feelings of invasion really decreased.

"So apparently you can charge regular electronics," she told the young man she'd seated herself beside. He reminded her of her brother for some reason. She couldn't say why, given their radically different colorings, but perhaps the shared style of beard was enough, shaped in an ultra-fashionable tendril toward his ear. "Like dumping charge so you can sleep, but you have to be more careful about the correct voltage..."

She stared at the illustration of the connector in someone's wrist, and lost her train of thought. Why was she still allowing herself to read on a tablet instead of on her internal system? She'd told herself two weeks ago that she needed to wean herself off that. She wasn't modeling very good behavior when it came to adapting.

Genevieve hunched over the tablet. She was so tired. She refused to give up, but she hadn't expected things to drag on this *long*. Shouldn't everyone either be recovered or dead by now? She couldn't remember how much time she'd lost, and she'd been kicked out of her town so soon after she woke, into the Pax Romana calendar system.

Genevieve hopped off her stool and set the tablet down in her place. As long as she'd stopped reading and was wallowing, she should do some rounds. She started with the young man she'd been reading to, drawing his hand from the gel to take it as she checked his readouts.

"Oh, you're stronger today," she lied. She shouldn't be lying. She should believe that he was getting stronger with every fiber of her being so she could convey it to his unconscious mind. And she supposed she did believe that—she was still here, after all, even with the looks Carex shot her across the mess. But she also doubted.

"I need this, you know," she told the young man. She laced her fingers with his and leaned her hip against the side of his pool. "Isn't that amazingly selfish? I'm helping people because I need a purpose to help untangle some of the mess that's my head right now. And if that purpose can be saving people, it means it doesn't have to be killing people."

She smoothed the skin on the back of his hand, then dotted her fingertip down a trio of freckles. "My family must have believed I'd survive. I believe it too. I do, I promise. You *want* to survive, trust me. It's more than you can stand sometimes, but sometimes it's simply amazing, too. There's whole new kinds of pain, of wrongness, but all the normal ones are gone. No aches, no bruises, no strains."

Genevieve drew in a ragged breath and looked around the silent room. How long should she keep trying to believe? Would the gel keep them alive indefinitely? But she didn't see Pyrus as someone who would pull the plug on living people. There must come a point where the nanites would burn the biological systems out, or this clinic would still be full of Infecteds from the last group.

But could she do this for another three weeks? It *wasn't working*. She needed to face up to that.

Genevieve bent her head, pressed their clasped hands to her forehead. She needed to *remember*. Not light, not music, not even the voices of her family she thought she remembered but couldn't be sure. *Hang on, Vieve*. She needed the dreams, as nonsensical as they'd been. Like the one where she'd been going fishing with her dead sister in the depths of winter, getting caught in a snow bank, or possibly sinking into cracking ice. That clearly had been something her mind had invented out of whole cloth.

Some things might have been based in reality, though. Like the dream figments that had told her to "fight it," over and over from every direction in every situation until she'd screamed at them to shut up. Is that what she should be urging these patients, motivating them through frustration and anger? Those remembered emotions snapped into focus for her abruptly, making her sure that was exactly the wrong thing to do. Fight what? Fight herself?

"Steer into the skid," she said suddenly, out loud, thoughts linking back to a strong memory in such a huge jump it bypassed mere logic. *Steer into the skid*. Her sister had said it in the dream of the winter accident, in their old hulk of a truck.

Genevieve straightened with sudden excitement racing through her body, down into the hand she clasped over the young man's. She drew herself in until they touched along the lengths of their forearms. "Steer into the skid! To get any control back, you have to go where the nanites are taking you. More than that, you have to *help* them. You can't fight them." Could he hear her? Had someone told her that, while she laid suffering and dreaming, and her mind had translated it into the nearest voice in her dream? Or had she discovered it for herself, inside a closed system, which meant there was nothing she could do to introduce it to these patients?

She repeated it to him again, expanded upon the theme. She finally had to leave for a meal, but she picked it up again on her return, focusing down on this one, single person. If only she could reach this young man, guide him to what he needed to do. The more she repeated it, the more certain she became that was what had made the difference for her. Steer into the skid.

As her throat grew scratchy and the patient's readouts didn't change, Genevieve's excitement drained away, leaving her hollow. She pillowed her forehead on her arms on the edge of the pool. She'd think of a next thing to try, and a next. She had to. Just a few moments, to gather herself.

A beep jerked her out of a doze. Unless she'd imagined it. A beep from where?

"Fuck," the young man said distinctly in Lingua. "My back hurts." His voice was rougher than her brother's, older somehow. He lifted a hand to swipe at his eyes in an uncoordinated movement.

Genevieve stared at him. Was he—or was this just another stage like the ranting? She whirled to the control panel and tried to find the menu with brainwaves. It was flashing some kind of alert at her—unlabeled, very helpful, thanks—which must have been the source of the beep. "Can you hear me? How are you feeling?"

"Like being dead would be more comfortable," he said, and tipped his head her way. His eyes focused on her, and confusion painted his face when he didn't recognize her. "Where the fuck am I?" He got his other hand out of the gel and clutched at the edge of the pool, but got no closer to sitting up, if that's what he was considering.

"Tsuga Security," Genevieve said. She finally found the menu she wanted on the panel—not that it wasn't obvious by now that his conscious mind was up and running and he was tracking—and belatedly realized that answer probably didn't mean anything to him. "You're being cared for, that's the important part. We'll explain everything as soon as we can."

Forget explaining, what was she supposed to do now? Pyrus had mentioned a whole process, for Installs, one she'd missed completely. Memories of her own experience and stubbornness may have gotten her this far, but anything else she definitely needed help with. Pyrus's location wasn't currently public, but she opened a private channel to him anyway. Hopefully he wasn't on shift. Or in a meeting with Carex. <One of the Infecteds is awake. What do I do with him?> It came out more panicked than she'd planned, so much so that she found herself half hoping that Pyrus would be so busy he'd block the message without listening.

<Start the gel draining and get him leaned over his knees so his wings aren't blocked.> The first part of Pyrus's reply sounded calm enough, almost normal. It must have been automatic, though, because the next part sounded almost as strained as hers had been. <Is he really awake? Lucid, I mean? Truly? I'll be right there.>

<Lucid enough to talk to me.> As the gel drained, Genevieve put her hand on the man's shoulder. "You don't know how glad I am you're all right. Lean forward. Like that. It will help your back."

"I appreciate the sentiment, but I'm still pretty sure I don't know you," the young man said, plaintive, and Genevieve had to choke down hysterical laughter. He wouldn't understand what was funny. She wasn't sure she did either.

The laughter didn't want to stay down, though, so after telling the young man to relax and that someone would be in to help him in a moment, Genevieve let herself into the hallway by the elevators. When the door shut, she let the laughter free, a bark from her belly, then giggles that brought her near to tears. She'd succeeded. She'd *succeeded.* Now she should go back and start working with the others, but she couldn't quite breathe just yet.

Pyrus spared her a confused glance when he arrived from the elevator, but she waved him away. "I needed to..." she said, then wasn't sure what she'd been going to say, so she left it. Fortunately, he didn't stop to demand she explain.

He left the door open, so she listened to his soothing voice, and the young man answering. She probably should have been paying attention, to get the benefit of the latter part of the installation process she'd missed, but she got caught up instead in the up and down of his tone.

After a while, she got comfortable while she waited for him, sitting on the floor with her back against the wall beside the door. Under her fingertips, the floor felt decidedly odd, as the composite polymer that gave it its slight springiness while still being easy to clean was neither carpet nor boards, the sensations she was used to.

When Pyrus reappeared, she started to get to her feet, but he waved her down. "He's sleeping," he said, before she could ask, and joined her on the floor, wrists slung over knees. He drew a thumb along the line of his beard, like he was thinking hard, and Genevieve started to wonder what he was afraid to tell her. Was this a false recovery? Did Infecteds sometimes become lucid before the very end?

"I'm so sorry I doubted you, Genevieve." A laugh of Pyrus's own burst free, to match the strength of his emerging grin. "I could *kiss* you."

Genevieve tipped her head to face him. "You have my permission," she said lightly, plausibly deniable as teasing. She didn't know what she was going to say until she did, but she found she didn't want to take it back.

Pyrus stared back at her for a beat, silent, apparently utterly taken off guard. She offered him a smile, small and apologetic, and in the lull created when her emotions turned, the exhaustion of the last weeks crashed in all at once.

She was suddenly crying. She hadn't thought crying was a "suddenly" sort of thing, without any warning, such as a tightening down of her throat as she tried to hold it back. But she was suddenly crying now, without warning, great, helpless, sawing breaths. She couldn't remember the last time she'd cried, she'd had too much reason for great emotion since her infection so she hadn't given even small emotions that much latitude. Otherwise, they might have run away with her.

Pyrus hugged her. Sideways, awkward, because they were both sitting, but tight. He didn't say anything, which was the only thing that let her not die from embarrassment. They could forget she'd cried, forget she'd said anything before that either, as they'd forgotten what Pyrus had said in the mess hall.

She pulled away quickly once she had some kind of control over herself, and tried to do what repair of her appearance she could with cuffs, pulled over the sides of her hands. "I'd better not leave the others alone." She got to her feet, but Pyrus rose as well and blocked her path back inside.

"You're worn to the bone. There's no way you should be caring for eight people at once, all alone. I'll take over." He settled his hands on her shoulders.

Genevieve rolled her shoulders under his touch, then stopped when muscles moving unexpectedly against the wing foundations proved disquieting. "I have to show you what to do, at least. And it's not like you can do it very well for eight people all at once either. We should at least halve it." And she wouldn't be able to accomplish anything else, knowing she wasn't here. "I'll be fine." By sheer force of will if necessary.

"I haven't been throwing myself into this for the past three weeks, that's the difference." Pyrus dropped his hands away, and hesitated over his next words. "Once you've shown me what you were doing, will you promise to step back and let me do it myself?"

"Why don't we get more help?" The moment the idea occurred to Genevieve, it seized hold of her completely. She'd been around long enough to know that no one's shift load was exactly onerous. The planet only had so many warehouses, so many ships in dock. But with enough help, they could save all eight of the other Infecteds. Just the thought of that energized her again.

"If you can convince Carex." Pyrus sounded dubious, but his attention went distracted for a moment, then he tipped his head to the elevator. "In his office."

The trip there was short enough that Genevieve's excitement didn't have time to turn into worry, but Carex's dark expression accomplished that all at once. She almost rocked back on her heels in his doorway, but she forced herself to keep going, following Pyrus in.

Carex ignored her as he rose behind his desk. "One had to survive eventually, I suppose," he said. "And I assume you're merrily overgeneralizing from that single result as we speak."

Pyrus scrubbed his thumb along the line of his beard. "Amsterdam's methods—"

Carex rolled his eyes. "What, holding their hands and singing songs? Bullshit. I think you two have had more than enough time for your little experiment. Amsterdam needs to go back on the front desk."

Like hell. Genevieve surged forward. Maybe she wouldn't get the help Pyrus had talked her into after all, but did she really need it? She had to try, even if it was by herself. "Why does it matter if we try? It's not like I've been leaving a hole in the guard schedule you didn't even want to put me on."

Carex regarded her for a long moment, then spoke with exaggerated patience, like he was doing her a favor. "Those are Pax

Romana enemies, Amsterdam. Pyrus may have trapped us into caring for them, but it's not our job to coddle them."

"Civilians," Genevieve spat at him. "They're probably civilians and you know it, except inasmuch as anyone on a planet the Pax Romana sets its sights on is forced into some kind of combatant role."

"And what are we going to do with a bunch of civilians if they all survive?" Carex prowled around to stand in front of her.

Genevieve pushed right up to him in return. "You think they'll want to stay? Don't flatter yourself."

"You think they get a choice?" Carex threw a section of text from some kind of contract at her system. "If you're not fighting and you're an Install, you're here. So says the Board. I get to be the guy on the ground trying to force or cajole everyone into doing it without them realizing."

Genevieve's stomach knotted with betrayal, but when she glanced at Pyrus, angry words starting to coalesce on her lips, he looked just as surprised as she felt. So perhaps he hadn't lied to her. He sputtered into speech first. "That can't be true. The surveillance..."

"You think they have the personnel to keep that up long-term for even a handful of Installs? It's designed to irritate people into coming back when they run, so they can have the illusion of freedom." Carex's lip curled. "First-gens especially, they didn't want to make us feel *cornered*, but someone had to know to enforce it. So don't you dare start judging me from your pedestal of blissful ignorance."

Anger vibrated through Genevieve's muscles until she had to suppress it or she would have snapped her wings out. Did he think he deserved her *sympathy*? Pyrus's civility was faster than her ability to dredge up words, though. "We've put ex-soldiers' 'deaths' on the records before, Carex," he said, inexorably. "Given the statistics, nothing could be easier in this case."

Carex snorted and turned aside from Genevieve to pace, managing to make it seem like he was dismissing her rather than conceding. "That was for Pax Romana citizens. Besides, I'm not going to agree to a hypothetical when all you have is one survivor and a pretty narrative. Infecteds *die*. You know this, Pyrus, better than anyone."

Genevieve could see that in evoking those dark memories, Carex had Pyrus starting to crumble. The thought was written across his face: maybe the man she'd saved *had* been the one in a million. "Like she said, what's the harm in trying?" He seemed to put all the hope he had remaining into the words, leaving his posture with none.

Carex stilled when his next circuit brought him before Pyrus. His voice softened, though not so much as to take it entirely out of the realm of "harsh." Perhaps he had lost the skill of that somewhere along the way. "You really need me to tell you?"

Things unsaid congealed between the two men, the depth of their history becoming an almost visible presence in the room. Pyrus scoffed. "I can't imagine what you think gives you the right to interfere, then or now."

Carex met his scoff, raised it to a bark of laughter utterly without warmth. "The same thing that's always given me the right, whether you've been avoiding speaking to me for nearly a year or not. I'm a man who cares about his brother in arms. When you failed last time, signing back on for an indefinite tour was suicide, Pyrus. Suicide by battle, but suicide nonetheless. An indefinite tour means you fight until you're dead, you know that. I couldn't let you do it."

Pyrus crossed his arms, seemed to find some balance in the motion, even if it was a balance of his emotions tucked away deeper behind his eyes. "If you care about me as much as you profess to do, don't deny me this now."

"And when the rest of them die this time just as surely, and you're worse off than before? What do you plan to do then, disappear into a chemical haze like Eriope?"

But Genevieve had proof Carex was wrong, if only she opened her mouth and said the words. She considered doing it over a private channel to Pyrus alone, but Carex could still order Pyrus away from the clinic if she didn't convince him as well. She didn't know what Carex would do to *her*, but there were eight lives she could save. "You know why that's bullshit? I didn't die."

She stepped right up to Carex, edging him away from Pyrus. "I'm an Infected. I was a civilian, driving an ambulance, and I got it from one of our soldiers who got it from one of yours and you know *why* I didn't die? *Because I didn't know I was supposed to.* And I used that experience to guide that man who woke up through it. I could do it again." She swept her hand to Pyrus. "As could he."

Carex's brows flew up, but then they tightened down to a glower deeper than any Genevieve had observed before and belated fear stole up into her stomach. "So you admit you lied to gain access to Tsuga Security?"

Genevieve ignored him and her fear both. "Pyrus, I think the key was in telling them to..." She'd meant to pour it all out, before Carex could stop her, but what she found in Pyrus's face made her falter. His surprise was souring quickly into betrayal, and a desperate need to chase that look away yanked her off-track. "I needed the training and you'd never have taken me if I'd told the truth—"

Carex rolled right over her. "And immediately started amassing Pax Romana nanite secrets."

"No more than what I already had in my damn body—"

This time it was Pyrus who spoke. "Not every fronti—non-citizen means harm." He spoke as if to convince himself, though.

Carex waved that away. "That's for the Board to discuss. Meanwhile, she should be contained."

And Genevieve had run out of time. A coward to the end, that she'd cared more about Pyrus's opinion of her than about the lives she could save. Carex's system presented override codes, hers accepted, and her system started shutting down, channels gone first, then muscle control, and she folded up as her mind dissolved into sleep.

Genevieve reached first for channels when she woke up, to contact Eriope if no one else, but she was still locked out. Maybe it was a good sign for her assimilation that it was her first impulse, but assimilation was hardly going to be the goal now she was a prisoner.

Something she hadn't encountered before in her system pinged for her attention, and after studying the alert for a second, she realized it was a message that had come in over a channel while she was asleep.

Pyrus's voice. <I wanted to let you know what I can about your situation. Carex has locked you in your room while the Board deliberates, but it shouldn't be for long. A few days at most. Termination isn't on the table, but your…freedom of movement may end up somewhat restricted, long-term.> His tone was very bland. Civil. So civil she could have cried, though when it came to it, she discovered her tears had dried up once more.

Genevieve sat up. Her system clock told her she'd been out for a couple hours. How many of the Infecteds would die in those "few days" before they let her out of her room? She was glad she wasn't going to be summarily executed, but what about them? She hadn't been able to tell Pyrus nearly enough. Why the hell hadn't she taken the time to explain before they'd approached

Carex? Because she'd still been riding the high of success, she supposed, feeling like everything would be easy from there and she'd have plenty of time to explain in detail.

Another message arrived then, not live either, but apparently pre-recorded for delivery only after her system showed she was awake. Carex, this time. <You had to reveal it in public, in front of someone, didn't you?> A few beats of silence, which Genevieve used to struggle to catch up, to understand what he could possibly mean. He sounded angry, yes, but…not at her? <I suppose neither of you ever considered what you would be saving any of those Infecteds *for*.>

He must be referring to how she'd revealed that she was from a frontier planet, that was the only thing that made sense. But did that mean he'd already guessed as much? And didn't want to have to acknowledge it? He was the son of those who had fought to save a frontier planet, Eriope had told her that. And Eriope had also said he felt he needed to be twice as rigid, which was what Genevieve was feeling the brunt of now, she supposed.

The second part of Carex's message, she dismissed. Where there was life, there was hope. She'd found her own purpose. Others could too.

She smoothed the blankets where she'd been lying. Someone had laid her down as pretty as a bespelled princess. Pyrus? Did some drop of his kindness remain, remembered even in the face of discovering she was one of the dirty frontis? Or had it been Carex, of all people?

She shoved to her feet. Whether she had Carex's secret sympathies or not didn't matter if he wasn't going to lift a finger to help her. That was clear enough. There had to be something she could do for the Infecteds herself. Break down her door, or break into the channels and get word to someone else to help them. She tried to bring up the blocks on her system, but while she had gained enough skill to know what she was looking at now, she had no idea how to go about hacking them.

She kept trying for a while until frustration overwhelmed her and she went to kick at the door. The blow didn't even make it vibrate.

Her back muscles were starting to hurt, responding to her tension, and she slammed open the door to the balcony and snapped out her wings. Whatever she ended up doing, a full charge couldn't hurt. Maybe staring balefully at a reflection of the mountains, wings turned outward to the light, would knock an idea of what to do loose in her mind.

It was a glimpse of the ground that did that, though. The sheer poetic justice of it all made her bounce up onto her toes in excitement, clenching her hands on the rail. Carex hadn't locked this door because he knew she couldn't glide yet. All she had to do to get out of here was prove him wrong.

It was a hell of a long way down, but Genevieve could hardly choke now when she'd been willing to possibly risk her life when confessing to Carex. This was only gliding. Besides, if she hurt herself it would heal quickly enough—no, that wasn't the way to think. Her nerve wavered. She'd glide down without any injuries. If there was anything she'd learned in all her training so far, it was that if you wanted to do something simple for the first time, you might as well let the automatic system take care of it. If she wanted to react to air currents with split-second decisions, she'd need manual control, but she was sure the nanites could take her down in a straight line.

If she let them.

"Hurry up, coward," Genevieve said out loud. "Carex probably used the last couple hours to create his documentation trail and is down there right now dumping people out of pools." She pulled up the glide program, and it prompted her to check the wind. She climbed over the rail and turned to balance with her heels on the edge of the balcony, hands on the rail behind her. Even so close to the side of the building, the wind plucked at her and her system sucked down readings hungrily, crunching the data at the edge of her perceptions. It prompted her for a target.

A lunchtime exercise and charging session was just breaking up, catching her attention as she scanned the lawn. People lowered limbs from the last group stretch and wings started to fold away. Genevieve had to bring up magnification of her vision to spot Eriope from this distance, but there she was, in the front row. Talking brightly to someone, of course. Good. She could aim for that vicinity, and then she'd be able to intercept Eriope before Carex noticed her. She hoped Eriope would at least carry a message for her, if for nothing else, for the sake of the memory of the friendship they'd formed, despite Genevieve's best efforts.

A gust of wind buffeted her unexpectedly hard and Genevieve drew back so she could hold herself more securely with her elbows hooked over the rail, which she supposed was progress in the wrong direction. No, she wasn't going to feel nauseated. She was going to do this. She was going to *use* the nanites because there was no getting rid of them so she might as well fucking embrace them and get something important done. And maybe some small part of her would like to fly—even if it was gliding—like the part that enjoyed never having another ache.

She dropped to the extent of her arms and let go.

The program, set to its target, co-opted her muscles, but Genevieve relaxed into it and it was barely different than giving into highly trained instincts. Wind slammed her face and chest, making it impossible to know how fast she was going, but when she closed her eyes against it, the targeting program objected strenuously to the loss of visual data on its target, making her head pound with the not-quite-sound of its alarm. She imagined she was riding along while someone else controlled trick stunts in an airplane and the urge to not see the ground diminished while the adrenaline-sharpness of excitement surged up to take its place.

Her system updated, updated again, skipping her targeted landing spot farther out to give her more time to flatten out and slow. As long as it wasn't into the side of the mountain—

And then she was plowing into grass, tumbling ass over who knew what as Eriope had joked, but her wings flexed rather than broke and her next still impression of the world was of lying uncomfortably with her cheek in the grass, now plowed muddy, and a good portion of her wings bunched beneath her body to jabbing discomfort.

She took a little time to get herself oriented correctly, hands on the ground so she could push up. Her wings were too bent to fold away. Eriope, she reminded herself. She was the point of this little exercise. The target had been pushed away from her position, but when Genevieve looked up, Eriope was already there. With everyone else, standing in a rough semicircle and staring at her.
<What the fuck?> Eriope asked over a private channel.

<Whatever Carex said, please, listen to my side of the story as well before you decide,> she begged Eriope. With Eriope having opened the channel first, the message seemed to go through.

Eriope shook her head jerkily, like she hadn't really heard. "Don't *do* that. Don't glide from that high with the kind of air currents we get around here! They could have smashed you right back into the building. Nanite healing has its limits, you know." She finally paused for breath and pulled Genevieve to her feet to try in vain to wipe off some of the mud. "What possessed you?"

"Carex locked me in." And he hadn't bothered with the balcony door because he knew it was too dangerous, she realized now. Genevieve cranked her panicked focus wide enough to take in the other Installs' expressions. Their surprise, though muted, didn't look like Carex had told them anything yet. "I saved one of the

Infecteds and he thinks trying to save any more would be—" A cruelty. "—a waste of effort."

Eriope muttered a curse. "Of course he does." She clasped Genevieve's arms encouragingly, while her attention went elsewhere. Checking whether Carex was on the map, perhaps.

"I need your help." Genevieve returned her focus to Eriope alone, as the others drifted off, giving them privacy. "To get a message to Pyrus. Carex shut me down too fast—anyway, it doesn't matter." No, she was doing this too fast and in the wrong order. "I think I know how to save the others." In the intensity of her effort to convince Eriope, formality slipped back in. "Perhaps they are not citizens, but to preserve any life—"

"Hurry up, Carex will be here soon enough because of channel chatter," Eriope said. She flashed Genevieve a smile when Genevieve must have looked anxious. "I'm sure Pyrus will be even happier to have your help in person. And we need to get you to the clinic anyway, to fix your wings." She was already moving, without even waiting for Genevieve to agree.

Genevieve jogged to catch up. For a moment euphoria, brought to the surface by the glide, however dangerous, expanded in her belly. Then reality reasserted itself. Carex could contact Eriope on a private channel at any time, and then she might change from helping to restraining Genevieve.

Better to find out Eriope's reaction now, while Genevieve could still try to evade her if it proved necessary. She spoke over the private channel she'd kept open to Eriope. <Eriope, I just...I'm sorry. Carex is probably going to tell you that I never worked for TH.> Entering the building gave her an excuse to stall for a second, but no magical words to explain herself occurred to Genevieve even with the extra time. <I'm an Infected, from a frontier ag planet. I survived, that's how I know they can too...> Her wings were in the way when they squeezed into the elevator, but when she tried to fold them again, pain twinged in some place that wasn't her own muscle but was still part of her back, so she left them out.

Eriope was quiet for a while. <You're not what I expected, I can definitely say that.> The following silence had the quality of someone wrestling with the cognitive dissonance born of lived experience crashing up against unquestioned assumptions. Then she flashed Genevieve an unexpected, sidelong grin. <I wondered why you showed up talking like a Lingua textbook.>

<It's not that it's book learning, it's that we used Lingua specifically for business and diplomatic purposes. All the formal stuff.> Relief made Genevieve babble, so she cut herself off before it grew too pathetic. She supposed effusive thanks for not denouncing her in anger would be even more pathetic, and in any case, they were at the clinic. Pyrus was on the other side of the door as it opened, staring at them in shock, so she had more persuading to do.

"Pyrus..." No, Genevieve had no time for hesitation. She spoke the rest in a rush. "Whatever you think of me, I can help save these people, if you'd just let me."

Heavy, sprinting footsteps gave Genevieve barely a breath of warning before Carex arrived down the corridor from the elevator. "What the *fuck* are you doing here?" Rather than deploy his override once more, however, Carex slowed, came to a stop to glower at her.

Glowering, Genevieve realized even more viscerally now she'd heard his message, wasn't stopping her, however. She matched him stare for stare and dared to voice the desperate plan that popped into her head. "What would you do if we locked ourselves in?" If the lock could be overridden, they could break it. But Carex could lunge for her now, if he wanted. Or have any of the Installs here help him cut his way in once the door was closed.

Carex's expression wiped down to something hard, not completely concealing the conflict beneath. When he spoke, he sounded as immovable as one of the mountains outside. "I'd have to make damn sure you stayed here, until someone above my pay grade arrived to deal with you."

Genevieve wasn't going to wait for him to send her an engraved invitation. She lunged into the clinic, dragging Eriope with her.

"Wait, I don't—" Eriope was too off-balance from surprise to catch herself before the door closed behind them both. "Fuck." She brushed herself off with jerky, exaggerated motions. "Just like Carex, I suppose, to step back and tattle to the higher-ups."

Pyrus tipped his chin to the door, perhaps as a physical sign of sending something, as it gave a flat, unhappy beep. "Whatever Carex was thinking, he can't override my medic codes now. But you realize that we probably only have enough food for a couple days in here?"

Before Genevieve could respond—which was fortunate, she had no idea what to say—Pyrus and Eriope winced in tandem as if at someone shouting in their ears.

"Guess I'm committed now. That was the public announcement about how the three of us are in trou-ble," Eriope explained, sing-song, at Genevieve's confused look. A glittering look of forced cheer settled into her eyes. "And there go non-emergency channels. I guess we'll just have to wear our vocal cords out with flapping."

"In the announcement, did Carex say—when the higher-ups arrive, I suppose I'll be imprisoned?" That was selfish, to worry about at a time like this. But if she could escape, after all of these Infecteds were recovered—or dead, she should admit that to herself—she wanted to try. "Are there even facilities for that, with Installs?"

"There are." Pyrus avoided her gaze as he said it, though his tone was strictly factual, not accusatory. She had no doubt he could weaponize his neutrality if he wanted, so she decided to accept the assumption he realized as well as she did they were on the same side in this endeavor, and proceed accordingly.

To business, then. "If one person already woke up, do you think the couple days we have food for will settle things one way or the other for the rest?" Genevieve stepped to the nearest pool and smoothed the woman's hair. "I suppose they all could have been infected at different times. But they can't have been too far apart, because they wouldn't have a place to hold them for long before they sent them here."

Pyrus shook his head. "No one bothers to keep those kind of records, much to my frustration. I always worked from a similar assumption that past groups had all been infected around the same time, though. They all...surrendered within about a day of each other." He joined Genevieve at the pool, stress flickering visible in the way his fingers clenched over the rim, then smoothing under again. "What do we do, then?"

"Tell them steer into the skid." Genevieve smiled thinly at the others. "Or similar metaphor. And it might have something to do with building trust ahead of time, so they pay attention when you speak, I'm not sure." She feared she wasn't very coherent as she poured it all out in detail, jumbled and out of order, but she stopped herself before she started repeating anything. She left that Infected to Pyrus, turned away to find one of her own.

Pyrus turned after her, perhaps about to say something more, but he frowned at her wings instead. "You're badly out of alignment. May I have your permission to address it?" He was rivaling her for formality now. At her murmured agreement, he stepped behind her and Genevieve felt the sensation of shifting in that strange her body yet not her body limbo. "You can't help them if you're not functional yourself."

His phrasing was a marvel, really, of making a caring statement sound cold. With nothing better to do as he worked, her thoughts drifted off the Infecteds to Pyrus. Which did he consider to be worse, the fact she was a fronti, or the fact she had lied about it? Did the average Pax Romana citizen really think of frontier planets as enemies, or just annoying younger siblings who had to be forced into following orders for their own good? But these were people who'd gone out to do the forcing.

In the realm of lies, she hadn't told him or Eriope about the virus, either. And she wouldn't, she decided, as Pyrus's firm touch eased some of the ache in her wings. That goal was no longer… true, in a way, now she'd discovered her real mission for herself.

"'Not functional herself'—is that how it is?" Eriope asked Pyrus. She locked gazes with him, then snorted. "Stupid locked channels. All right. Talk to you later. Right now, I think it's story time. Genevieve, why don't you tell him the story of how you jumped off the *fortieth floor*, to get here to do all this helping."

Pyrus had spread his arms to pull Genevieve's wings out close to their full extent, and now he paused for a beat with his palm still against the inner "feathers." As if he was fighting a losing battle with his good sense, his touch slid to the skin between her wings, pads of fingers first, then heel of his hand contacting for a larger bar of warmth. The sensation, fully grounded in her original conception of her body, in contrast to that from her wings, made her want to shiver. "Do you ever allow yourself to *rest*, woman?"

"What?" Genevieve tried to twist around to see him, but her wings were in the way.

"Since I've met you, all you've done is throw yourself into things." Pyrus lifted his hand, nudged her into folding the wings completely into her back. "There. You're done."

Genevieve thought about seeing the targeting visor across the eyes of Pax Romana soldiers and then across her own eyes in the mirror. "Sometimes one has to maintain sufficient momentum to avoid falling." Was she imagining that his politeness had thawed a few degrees after hearing how she'd wrecked her wings? Probably.

Eriope lifted the hand of the woman in the pool nearest her. "Well, if I'm trapped in here, I might as well make myself useful." She laced fingers with her, ignoring the gel. "I don't have half the intensity of your true champion here, but I promise I'm very friendly. At least for the next day or so, so you'd better work fast." She grinned, sharp, casting it down to the woman, though she couldn't see it. Though perhaps she could hear it in Eriope's voice.

Champion? Genevieve would call herself that when anyone else survived this. She strode away to choose a patient of her own to focus on, well away from Pyrus.

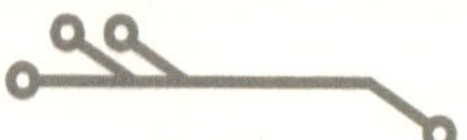

Over the next two days, two more Infecteds recovered, and three died. Eriope's mood deteriorated rapidly after the first day, as she'd predicted. By the end of the second, she'd sunk to endless drawer- and cupboard-slamming circuits of the clinic, as if a hidden stash of drugs could have been missed the first twenty times she looked.

Genevieve wished, wished deeply, she could have left Eriope alone, but her crackling tension was hardly a good thing for the patients, though even the recovered ones spent the majority of their time sleeping heavily. The repetitive noise of it was even harder to bear. She waited until Eriope had finished a circuit and quivered in a relatively stationary state before the next. "If there was a way you could do something that makes less noise—"

"Yeah?" Eriope rounded on her. "Like what, stuck in here, with nothing to do but think?"

Stuck in here because of Genevieve's hand on her arm, Genevieve's yank. "I'm sorry I got you into this," she said, not really expecting the apology to help, but still feeling it was *needed*. "I know it must be really hard to—"

Eriope snapped her wings out and wide, the better to loom over Genevieve, once-repressed violence right at the surface. "Damn fronti dirt-grubber. How can you know what it's like?

You've been an Install for, what, months, if that? Talk to me in years. Talk to me in *decades*, when all you can see stretching out ahead of you is decades more."

With nothing else to offer but listening, Genevieve stayed put, bracing herself for a blow. But the touch, when it came, was from behind. Pyrus tugged her gently back, interposed himself, an immovable object of civility. "Eriope, that's offensive. Don't take your bad mood out on Genevieve."

Genevieve tried not to read too much into it. He could defend her without having completely forgiven her, of course. But he'd had no problem with the epithet before...

"Bad mood? Ha!" Eriope prowled a few steps away. "You of all people should know there's more to it than that." She snapped back around to him, stepped up toe to toe. "Can't you give me something medicinal?"

"I know it's not physiological withdrawal, it's emotional dependence, and there's not a thing I can give you for that, other than to knock you out completely." Pyrus raised his brows. Apparently that was an offer on the table.

Eriope raised her hand to him and Genevieve backed up. The struggle that followed was eerie in its abbreviated nature, however, like an old couple fighting entirely in disconnected phrases. Pyrus caught her blow, Eriope jerked, Pyrus flickered a movement to the other side, and Eriope turned her dodge into a wrench away. She snapped in her wings and collapsed into a corner, head on knees. When she seemed inclined to stay there, quiet, Genevieve managed to relax in stages.

"Could use some lunch," she announced, generally. She turned away to fuss with the packs and the heater longer than necessary in hopes of diffusing things further. Pyrus joined her. She'd rested one hand on the counter as she waited for the heating to finish, and he settled his over it, overlapping partially. Genevieve twitched in surprise, lifting her own fingers, and that let him tangle his between. She felt very "suddenly" tears rising once more, but pressed them back this time.

"I'm sorry," Pyrus rumbled, low voiced.

"For what, objecting to being lied to? Don't think that needs an apology." Genevieve could only hope that had been the true sticking point, as it was the only thing she regretted. She would not regret being born on Idyll.

"I rather think you did that in pursuit of a greater good. And with any luck, you'll be able to continue doing so." Pyrus raised his voice. "As when the higher-ups arrive, I'll be telling them how you may have deceived the cranky CFO—and who can blame you?—but your medic knew your status as an Infected all along, and judged that you were not only covered by the contract keeping non-military Installs here, but presented an important resource going forward, for dealing with Infecteds."

"Thank you." Such an unlooked-for gift, she found no other response. Then the meal made the little *pop* sound that indicated it was finished heating and Genevieve had to pull her hand from his touch. "I'll give this to Eriope."

She slipped over to set it on the ground before the silent, miserable shape. Eriope looked up as Genevieve turned away. "He's right," she said, letting it float context-less for a second. "You didn't deserve my shit. Sorry. What I need is a fucking uninstall process, you know?"

Genevieve nodded in acknowledgment, before returning to her own lunch. The emergency meals were, ironically enough, as bland as the bars Genevieve had been eating until she arrived at Tsuga Security. Somehow she ended up sitting on her own patch of floor, hip to hip with Pyrus.

In the companionable silence, Genevieve turned Eriope's words this way and that. Why wasn't anyone talking about developing an uninstall process? She hadn't thought of it as something that was possible herself until now, that was true, but pure survival tightened one's focus. Her own survival, now the survival of the other Infecteds. But now, as Carex had said, what kind of life awaited them long-term? Was it so strange to work toward fixing that when one impossible thing had proved quite possible?

"Given long enough, maybe we can find a way to uninstall them," she said, to see how it sounded out loud.

One corner of Pyrus's mouth tucked up, making his face apologetic, rather than him scoffing in disbelief. "You can't reach a moon you see in the sky simply by jumping."

"No, seriously." She turned her hand idly to look at the unblemished infection point at the base of her palm. "You're acting like it's a crazy dream, but *why* is it so crazy?"

"Because a lot of people have been working a long time on it. It's obvious why motivation to save Infecteds would be nearly nonexistent. But uninstallation? Being able to increase recruitment, not..." Pyrus's expression tightened with pain for a beat, but he smoothed it away before it reached his tone. "Not having to keep track of all us inconveniently 'not in active military service'? That's a holy grail."

And Genevieve didn't buy it. Pyrus might not believe that many people could be willfully blind for so long, but she'd believe it. Especially of the Pax Romana, who'd built their empire on pulling everyone into thinking alike. She didn't see the point in pushing at the moment, however, when all she had was some idle philosophical thoughts. She dipped her chin to allow him the point, and returned to eating.

After the lull, Pyrus looked out across the gel pools, three filled to the brim for preservation. "I by no means want to minimize your accomplishment here, though. We don't have too much farther to go to match the success rate of clean installations."

Genevieve slid her spoon securely into her half-finished pack and set it aside. "Seriously? I always assumed—" But then the public sources she'd been using for research would hardly have been given that information, would they? Better PR to not mention how many of your own people were dying to make your super-soldiers.

"Why do you think that civilian applications are still nonexistent?" Pyrus shrugged. "Soldiers can make an informed decision to take such a risk, but—"

"I don't buy it." Genevieve shook her head. She hesitated, but he knew perfectly well her perspective would differ from the Pax Romana one. "People are always ready to take stupid chances, and there's always someone medically unethical enough to let them. No way any government wants citizens with that kind of power outside a strong military hierarchy. That will be why they've kept such a tight hold on the technology."

Pyrus gave her a look, and she glowered at him. "I've picked up as much political theory through my higher education as you. Don't look at me like that."

"No." Pyrus looked back out into the wider room. "Probably more. I came from a poor background, and I enlisted early." He settled those last words out slowly and carefully, giving them extra weight. Genevieve thought she recognized another apology, for being caught up in his society's cycle of expansion without question, perhaps.

As much a product of his circumstances as herself.

The sound of the door opening initially registered as so mundane that Genevieve's adrenaline spiked a beat late, leaving her off-balance. Pyrus must have felt the same, as he shoved to his feet as belatedly as she did. Eriope was quicker on the draw and made it to the door before them. Anticipation of getting out and getting access to her stash seemed to have perked her up considerably.

Genevieve tried to ask Eriope over a channel who it was at the door, but of course they were all still locked down. Even after two days, apparently she was still reaching for them unconsciously, but there was no time to pick apart how she felt about this new evidence of her comfort with the nanites, because she and Pyrus reached the visitor as she closed the door behind her.

The visitor was an Install, not a surprise, but she showed her age in silver threaded into the tight, dark braids along her skull and in the lines at the corners of her eyes. She must have been much older than any of the people at Tsuga when she got her nanites—if they were going to talk about informed decisions, Genevieve suspected hers had been much more so than those of young recruits. "I'm Abidjan Lemna." She raised her brows. "Well. I certainly don't see the point of that." Their channels snapped back on.

<Do you know who she is? A general or something?> Genevieve asked Eriope immediately.

Eriope's gaze flickered to Genevieve, then back to Lemna. <Careful, those with enough clearance can monitor anyone's channels. I think she's Science Division, though.>

"And you must be the Infected who beat the odds alone," Lemna said and held out her hands to clasp Genevieve's. Genevieve accepted the touch automatically, more worried about what the woman might say next. Science Division—did they want her for study?

"What line of descent are you?" Lemna asked. Before Genevieve could pull away, she'd pinched the skin on the inside of Genevieve's wrist and collected a heavy, red dot of blood over the brown skin of her fingertip.

Genevieve jerked her arm back, though the cut was already healed by the time she got it to her lips in the ancient instinct to suck on it. Lemna touched her fingertip to her tongue and then spread the drop against her palate like a chef finding nuances in a gourmet sauce. Genevieve winced. She supposed Lemna's system was analyzing her nanites, but there had to be a less disturbing way to do it.

<Well, *that's* creepy as hell...> Eriope echoed Genevieve's thoughts, and the corner of Lemna's mouth lifted like she'd heard and knew Eriope had meant her to.

"Interesting," was all Lemna said out loud. "Not one of the newer nanite lines, either. Though if Malao Carex was correct and you got it out on a battlefield, it could never have been the very newest anyway."

"We've saved two more since you were sent for," Pyrus said. He was too polite to actually break in, but he didn't hesitate when Lemna gave him the pause he needed.

"How extraordinarily helpful of you," Lemna said. Genevieve couldn't have said why, but she got the sense that this was some kind of test. Perhaps Lemna was planning to prod them until she saw how they defended themselves.

"If you don't want to deal with enemy civilians being infected with your fancy technology, maybe you should concentrate on making that technology non-infectious," Genevieve said with as much confidence and calm as she could manage. "Or uninstall-able." A crazy dream of jumping at the moon it might be, but it was so needed, she couldn't help but bring it up. Who *didn't* need it, among the Installs she'd met? Eriope with her drugs, Carex with the stick up his ass, Pyrus with his doomed crusades.

Genevieve, who'd considered killing them all because she saw no other choice.

"Oh, believe me. We're working on both. I'm afraid, having shown our advantage, pulling all Installs from the fronts isn't an option, however. And the expense that went into the existing Installs would be lost if their nanites can't be also replaced in situ by that new, non-infectious line." Lemna smiled, thin and sharp. "Which we still haven't managed to produce, yet."

Genevieve wondered if the burst of probably classified information was supposed to rock her back, but she found it only helped her confidence. The woman was listening, not dismissing her.

She wasn't entirely sure she wanted that slightly scary attention on her, but it was better than being brushed aside in a prelude to finding a way to make her system fail so she was no longer inconvenient either.

"Put the recovering Infecteds to work on the problem, then," Genevieve said. The solution unfolded in her mind even as she spoke, meaning it could have obvious holes somewhere, but she judged it worth the risk to voice it immediately while she still had Lemna's ear. "I was a scientist, before. Some of them won't be, but if you can't let them go, why not have them work on something? They'll—we'll—be motivated, I can assure you of that. When you solve this problem, you get to go home and pick up your life? Who wouldn't throw themselves into that? And I'd bet you'd get a hell of a lot of takers from the retired soldiers here as well."

"And why would you do any better than our scientists, all of them experts in the field?" Lemna countered smoothly.

Genevieve took her rising nerves and sent them down to clench her hands, leaving her voice steady and confident. "How long have your experts been working on this? At least a decade, even if you ignored the problem until the first-gens finished their tours. Much longer if you started when the first wash-outs couldn't be fixed. Your particular brand of expertise *isn't working*. You need new perspectives, new approaches. And how many of those experts are Installs themselves? I'd expect not many, given how intimately they know the risks. That's the ultimate perspective, the one from inside."

And if anyone—*anyone*—higher up in Science Division, or the military, or even the empire, decided an uninstallation process wouldn't be *convenient*, you could count on the fact that no Infected, no retired Install, would give a shit. They'd fight tooth and nail to make sure nothing was buried. Not that Genevieve attributed the current lack of solution to that cause—it would be too convenient the other way, for all the reasons Pyrus had listed. But you never knew how better motivation would drive research until you'd done that research.

Lemna considered for a beat, two, clearly having no problem making all of them wait while she examined all the angles. Suddenly, she smiled, wider, but no less sharp. "When Malao contacted us, I told the others an Infected who made it this far wouldn't be ordinary." She turned away, gaze going distant as if she was diving into her system to send messages or make notes.

In the doorway, she paused and looked back. "There's no reason to keep this locked any longer, by the way. I've spoken to Malao. When I get back with those who need to be involved with getting this new program set up, I don't want to bother with overrides." And then she strode away.

Genevieve choked something half a gasp, half a laugh, and then Eriope grabbed her and Pyrus both up into one hug, laughing properly. The scope of her possible failure had just expanded, but so had the scope of people she could help. And it was something else to throw herself into. Maybe she wouldn't have to maintain quite so much momentum to avoid falling, now.

Genevieve drifted to the surface from sleep, feeling warm and secure. Someone moved beside her, getting up to answer the knock she vaguely remembered, so it must have been what woke her. Pyrus getting up. Because she'd finally stayed over last night. Right. Dozing, it took some effort to put that all together, and she subsided afterward. This moment was nice, and she didn't want to break it.

Someone scoffed over by the door, low voiced. "Someone's made herself at home." Even now fully awake, it took Genevieve a full beat more to realize the weight over her shoulder and tucked against her jaw wasn't the blanket, it was her wing. And she was sucking on the top edge of one of the carbon composite plates.

She stopped that immediately, and folded her wing to the bed, though not furled into her back yet. She twisted to sit up, found Carex in the doorway, blocked by Pyrus's arm across the opening. The muscles of Pyrus's back, around his wing panel, weren't as rigid as they might once have been in the presence of the other man, but he certainly wasn't relaxed. "What do you want, Carex?"

"Here's a tip." Carex shot Genevieve a sardonic, thin-lipped smile, then transferred his attention back to Pyrus. "If you think you're going to keep something like this on the downlow in a place like this, don't forget and leave yourself off the map in your own damn room. Her, sure, that's sort of necessary, but not you."

Pyrus growled, then shot a look back to Genevieve like he was worried she'd bolt. Since she'd shifted to her knees, instincts urging her to do just that, she couldn't really blame him. With an effort, she settled herself again. Now she was not only sleeping with Pyrus, she was staying the night, she supposed everyone would find out eventually, though Carex would never gossip. She wasn't quite sure how she felt about people knowing, but she also supposed she might as well decide to be all right with it, lacking time travel to return to last night and slip back to her own room as she had all the times before.

"You're all heart. Now, if that was all—" Pyrus waited pointedly for Carex to move so he could shut the door.

"I have to talk to Amsterdam. Privately." Something passed between the men in looks Genevieve couldn't see very well from her distance and angle, and probably couldn't have translated even if she'd been standing beside them. The urge to bolt surged back up. Given that most of the Installs here seemed to prefer only casual hook-ups with each other, she'd been worried about people's opinion of her relationship with Pyrus—strike that, she'd been worried people would form opinions of a "relationship" when she wasn't sure herself if it was one, yet—but she could only imagine this was something about the nanite research. Talk to her privately? Why was that necessary?

<The shotgun speech,> Pyrus told her over a private channel. <This here is my shotgun, and should you hurt the one I care about, you'll get to know it more intimately…> He sighed and moved aside to let Carex in. "I'll shower, then." Within easy distance to intervene should she call on a channel, Genevieve interpreted from his tone.

Well. If Pyrus was right, it was exactly as Genevieve had worried, other people having opinions about the two of them. Contrasted with her worry about the research, her frustration about that opinion softened a little, however.

"Let me dress at least." Genevieve circled a finger for Carex to turn his back. He shut the door and complied without any smart comments, even. Before she reached for her clothes she tried to angle the tip of her wing down and discreetly rub off the dried spit. Pyrus caught her at it as he passed, heading for the bathroom. He smiled, small but sweet. "Remind me to tell you sometime what Eriope did with her wings in her sleep the last time I was in a position to notice."

Genevieve dispensed with underwear for speed, and settled back sitting on the bed when she was done. The sound of running water eased between them from the next room. "All right."

Carex turned back and led with a question that was practically mild. For him. <Do you think there's a real chance of uninstallation, or did you just pull that out of your ass because it sounded good for Science Division?>

<Everyone knows nanites are uninstallable, and everyone knows Infecteds always die.> Genevieve shrugged. <I'm afraid that's the best I have. I'm damn well going to *try*, though.>

<Mm.> Carex considered her for several moments, silent on channels. Then, rather than launch into any kind of speech,

shotgun or otherwise, he tossed a small object at her, underhand and clearly meant to be caught. Genevieve duly caught and examined it. A little box, made of…wood? No, cardboard, with a veneer of pasted paper. The ink granted enough difference in texture she could at least try to trace one whorl.

<Most normal people *open* boxes.> Carex jammed his hands into his pockets and strolled up to the precise edge of the space where she'd have had to make an issue of it if he pushed any closer.

Carex: nominally on her side, but still an absolute dickhead. Genevieve swallowed any comment about where he could shove his box, and swung the cardboard top up. Inside were two post earrings. They looked like diamond, cheap mass-produced trash since they were shaped wrong for industrial cutting.

The bottom fell out of Genevieve's stomach, letting in panic to fill her whole body. Surely he couldn't have guessed—she'd *meant* to drop the earrings she was currently wearing, crystal and data storage made to look like crystal, in the waste, but hadn't quite gotten around to it yet.

Carex held out his hand. <Trade you.>

<How…?> Genevieve glanced to the bathroom, but the water was still running and Pyrus couldn't hear them on the private channel in any case.

<Did I know? Well, you had to have arrived with *something*, it was just a matter of where you were keeping it. On your person, obviously. And since you never took those off,> Carex gestured near his own ear. <It seemed a reasonable guess. It's where I would have put it. A virus, I presume?>

Genevieve clutched the half-open box with the new earrings against her belly. Whatever Carex's guesses, she didn't mean to tamely hand over the virus to confirm them without a fight. <And what are you planning to do with this hypothetical virus you're accusing me of having?>

Carex gave a bark of laughter, out loud. <If I wanted to denounce you, I could say the words to the Board this minute. I wouldn't need *proof*. In fact, consider this reciprocal leverage. If I turn you in, that opens me to questions about why I didn't say anything immediately, like maybe I wanted the virus for myself.>

<And why *do* you want it?> Genevieve set the box on her lap and switched the dummy earring, to stall.

<To destroy it.> Carex curled the fingertips of his waiting hand peremptorily.

Genevieve held herself still for a good breath more, another, and then made her decision and removed the second earring. She slammed the cardboard box, earrings rattling loose inside, into Carex's hand hard enough to crumple in one side. <I was going to destroy it myself.>

<But when it came down to it, you found you couldn't quite give it up. As if to give it up was to give in completely to the Pax Romana. Believe me, I get it.> Carex met her eyes, unreadable depths wavering into sight briefly beneath the dickishness, then disappearing again. <But it's just a symbol. I couldn't let you make the mistake of keeping it around where it could be found.>

Carex scanned the room, then stepped to a side table. He dumped the box out and hefted the empty wine bottle left there from last night consideringly. Apparently it suited his purposes, as he brought it down with a heavy thud, too low to be heard over the shower. Genevieve didn't try to stop him. He must have calculated the angle carefully, because when he lifted it, one earring was shatter and flattened metal. Another blow did the same for the second earring, then he used a lighter, rolling motion to render them both into dust. Dust got scraped into the box, and then the box disappeared back into his pocket.

At least it was done. <From here on out, get used to the idea you don't get to "let" me do anything.> Genevieve pushed off the bed and turned for the bathroom in pointed dismissal.

<About Pyrus…> Carex smiled thinly when she whirled on him, actually held up his hands in something like surrender.

<Is this where you threaten me into confessing this to him?> It had been easy to think she was all right with never telling him, before. Before one person figured it out, which meant someone else could, sooner or later. Before she let herself trust enough to stay the night, before Pyrus thought the shotgun speech might be pertinent.

<This is where I threaten you into never revealing this to him.> Another laugh. Carex seemed quite pleased by her shock. <Pyrus is from a core planet. He believes in the Pax Romana at a subconscious level, whatever he might say to you or himself. Knowing something like that, trying to decide whether to tell the Board… It could break him.> Carex spread his hand, like he was being perfectly reasonable. <And even if he keeps your secret, Pyrus will start questioning whether the research was ever useful, or just a cover. Add that to the romantic betrayal… So, no, I'm not going to "let" you do that either. >

Genevieve stepped up to Carex, holding her wings wide to increase her size. <And if Science Division finds out about me, I'm sure they'll shut the whole damn program down and bury the results. Then you don't get access to uninstallation yourself. Isn't that what this is really about?>

Carex shrugged. <Think what you like, as long as you keep your fucking secrets to yourself.> He turned away, let himself out, pausing in the doorway for a last salvo. <I'm surprised, though. I could have sworn "save Pyrus" was the angle you would have gone for. Ah, well.> And he was gone.

Pyrus came back in not long after, while she was still thinking hard, caught among bad choices. He drew the side of his thumb along his beard, a sign of conflicted thought, but his tone was light. "Did he manage to scare you off?"

"Nope." Genevieve looked up. "Though I can't honestly tell you if he was trying to." Which was strange. Carex could have just as easily tried to blackmail her into leaving Pyrus alone, but he hadn't.

She was damn tired of trying to fathom Carex's motives, Genevieve decided. Time for a change of subject. She undressed to use the shower herself, as Pyrus did the opposite. "My wings—they were furled when I went to sleep." She flexed them. "So that's a thing?"

"When you're very comfortable. I wouldn't play poker for a while." Pyrus pulled his shirt over his head and winked at her when she could see him again. "There's a stage when they broadcast your every emotion before you learn to control them, same as any other aspect of your body language."

Genevieve stretched her wings, then put them away as she headed to the bathroom. She supposed she was getting more comfortable with all of this, now. Slowly but surely.

Pyrus drifted into the doorway, caught her eyes in the mirror before she turned on the water. "You think you're going to want to uninstall, if—when—we get that far?"

Genevieve stilled. In the mirror at this moment, she didn't look at all like an Install, with her wings away. Another good question. Until quite recently, the answer would have been obvious. Now that question met and mingled with the one troubling her after Carex's visit, and somehow left her with a decision. Fuck Carex, she'd tell Pyrus about the virus after they had the uninstallation process finished. Then they could go their separate ways, if necessary. If they were even still together by then.

"I don't know. I can't pick up at home, not after they kicked me out." She turned back to catch Pyrus's eyes directly. "I'll see how I feel when we get there. Fair?"

"Fair," he agreed.

DIRTY BURNOUT

PART I

The longer Amsterdam Genevieve waited after hearing the head of the Pax Romana military's Science Division had arrived at the lab facility used by Genevieve's research group, the tighter her nerves wound themselves. She'd told the other members of her misfit band of nanite Installs—that strange mixture of retired military and infected enemy civilians—to take an early lunch, leaving her in the lab alone, staring into space as she had her system overlay endless permutations of plots of nanite survival rates over her vision. In every one, the research group's lack of progress in their quest to find a way to uninstall the nanites was stark.

And Genevieve couldn't do a thing about it, because of what that supposed lack of progress was hiding.

And now Abidjan Lemna was late. The Head of Science Division liked to throw everyone as off-balance as possible, so on any other visit she'd have been inside the lab by now, looking over people's shoulders and asking pointed questions.

Genevieve banished the data plots and pushed to her feet to go in search of Lemna, then she thought better of it and hovered, fingers of one hand digging into the polymer surface of the lab counter she'd been seated at. Maybe instead of a surprise inspection of the lab, Lemna instead had her sights trained on the security company that was the original front for this facility. Tsuga Security did guard shipments through this planet's only port, but that job was the merest bone thrown to the sanity of all the retired Installs who'd been dumped here. The empire's super-soldiers were too dangerous to let wander around, so if they weren't on active duty, they were here. Genevieve's research group had been grafted on to give them not only something else to do with their time, but also a hope of ever leaving: if their nanites could be uninstalled, perhaps they could build a normal life.

Genevieve paced a couple restless steps, the polymer of the floor eating the sound of her footsteps. If that was Lemna's purpose, she was Malao Carex's problem, as he was the CFO of the front company and the highest on-planet authority, most of the time. She'd honestly be happy to hide in the lab and let the two of them be dicks to each other to their hearts' content, but she didn't trust that Lemna wouldn't stop by on her way out. And if Genevieve allowed herself to relax now only to let something slip by mistake when Lemna finally arrived—

She had her system smooth out her heartrate. This was getting ridiculous. She'd founded the research group nine years ago, and it had taken them the first six years to succeed in creating a replacement nanite line that wouldn't infect civilians who touched dead Installs—or touched someone who had, as she'd done. Finding an uninstallation process was arguably an even more difficult task, so the three years they'd spent so far was nothing, really. Lemna and the military brass above her wouldn't be expecting anything near success just yet.

What Genevieve had to hide was that they *had* found a way to uninstall the nanites; the problem was that burnout worked by putting the Install through unimaginable pain. Of their two ex-military volunteers, one had died during burnout. The second had taken two more of Genevieve's researchers down with her—she'd been too traumatized to speak, and the people who'd opened channels to her had immediately begun burnout themselves.

The burnout process was a lot like the original nanites, in that way—under certain circumstances, it loved to *spread.*

The worst part was, the actual burnout process hadn't killed those three Installs. They committed suicide, unable to take the shock of being without nanites after the pain. The decision to go back to the drawing board had been unanimous, as had been the one to keep it from military leadership, lest they convince themselves a "risk" of suicide was acceptable in the face of the slowly but steadily accumulating Installs who couldn't be allowed to go back to a normal life after retiring from active service.

That military leadership had decided a 50% survival rate among soldiers undergoing purposeful installation was acceptable, after all. It might have climbed as high as 60% by now. That military leadership had also been perfectly happy to infect enemy civilians—until Genevieve, 100% of those had conveniently died. Those were not the hands she wanted control of burnout to be in.

<Abidjan Lemna has requested that I administer an antagonist to any recreational substances so Cusco Eriope can discuss certain matters while not under the influence.> Pyrus, the facility's unofficial medic and her partner, spoke over a private channel, though private was debatable at the moment, given that Lemna had the codes to eavesdrop on whichever of their channels she damn well pleased. Thus his formality, she imagined. <I thought you might want to be present as a…mediator?>

<On my way.> Given the high chance of eavesdropping, Genevieve swallowed several questions as she strode for the map location Pyrus had sent after his message. Foremost among them: what good could she do? She'd been suffered to live in the Pax Romana empire for the past nine years, dirty fronti from a conquered planet that she was, because she was doing useful research, but her word hardly carried weight. She supposed she was more tactful than most in the facility, though Pyrus was the kindest of them all. Besides, Eriope was her friend.

When she arrived at the conference room, more bland polymer surfaces in the form of a central table and surrounding chairs, she found Pyrus frowning over a case of different injection pens. The "really good shit" Eriope had come back with from her last illicit trip off-planet must indeed be quite good, if the usual antagonists weren't working. Any substance, recreation or medical, had to be damn powerful in the first place for an Install's system not to just shrug it off. Eriope worked *hard* to accomplish as much with her self-destructive behavior as she did.

Lemna stood at a slight remove, arms crossed. Even in stillness, she projected a concentrated grace. There were traces of wrinkles on her skin, and gray in her tightly braided hair, because of her age when she'd undergone installation, but they only enhanced her intimidating air. In contrast, Eriope was slumped in the chair in front of Pyrus, a small smile of pleasant dreams on her expressive face, her short, black curls tousled over her forehead and up the back of the chair where she'd slid down. She and Pyrus had skin of a middle ancestrally sunny shade, while Lemna's was slightly darker.

Pyrus applied one last pen, and stood back. "That should get most of it, I hope."

Eriope groaned extravagantly. "Why do you have to be like that, Pyrus? That shit was *expensive*." She coughed, gulped air, and sat up straighter.

"Thank you, Toledo." Lemna nodded to Pyrus and shot Genevieve a narrow look. Apparently she was allowed to stay, however, as Lemna stepped up to Eriope, turning the woman's chair to face her with a jerk on one of the armrests. "I give you a little leash—all of you, but you especially, Cusco—with the understanding that you will not make me regret it, do you understand? Brass thinks you're confined to the planet, and then you go and do *stupid fucking shit*."

Lemna tipped her head as a physical sign of the picture her system had just sent to the main wall display: Eriope, nude, back to the security camera and her photovoltaic carbon-fiber wings open wide as she rode someone just out of frame. Eriope's second favorite way of taking her mind off the feeling of being trapped, though that one was usually practiced among the other Installs around Tsuga. Genevieve couldn't imagine that photograph had been taken here.

Eriope glanced at the photograph, but not even a twinge of embarrassment showed in her body language. It was nothing Genevieve or Pyrus hadn't seen before, she supposed; they had invited Eriope to join them on a few occasions. She was delightfully enthusiastic, but too uninterested in power play for it to be a regular arrangement. Eriope tipped her chin up and met Lemna's glare without flinching. "There are Installs taking their downtime on planets across the empire. I don't see the problem."

"The problem, Cusco, is when the brass—who know that you are *not* on active duty—find out you fucked the leader of a terrorist movement selling drugs to finance said movement's efforts against the empire." Lemna took a bruising grip on Eriope's chin and trapped her wrist against the armrest with her other hand, fingers digging in until Eriope grunted. It was very much in line with the casual violence all the ex-military Installs in this facility displayed with each other, even Pyrus when he forgot himself, but Genevieve still didn't like it. She rocked forward, reminded herself that interference at this point wouldn't make the situation better, and settled back again.

Eriope tried to wrestle her chin away and failed. "I didn't know what she was doing with the money!"

"How's this, then? That shit you were on is killing people. It works great on Installs and kills everyone else within a few months of regular use." Lemna switched her grip to both of Eriope's wrists and slammed the chair into the table, cracking Eriope's head against the headrest. "Stay on the *fucking* planet so I don't have to have you executed, Cusco. Because I *will*, if I have to, to make sure other Installs retain the choice to retire."

Eriope surged up, breaking Lemna's grip now she was trying properly. She planted herself toe to toe with the woman. "Or you could let me go. Let us all go. What are Installs going to do if you let us pick some peaceful planet and try to build some kind of *life*? Build a family? We wouldn't need to sneak away to find something, anything, to take our minds off being trapped, if after the decades of our lives we gave to fighting for the empire, we weren't confined to this boring little facility on this boring backwater planet for the rest of our damn lives, who knows how long those will even be!"

Lemna didn't give a single centimeter. "You want interest, sign up for another tour."

"Suicide by indefinite tour" was what the ex-military Installs here called that. Keep fighting until eventually something swamped nanite healing and killed you. Genevieve had gathered that that was the way most Installs went. Direct suicide was generally unnecessary and thus much rarer. And that left them with the ragged, self-destructive dregs who'd retired to Tsuga.

Genevieve stepped up, touched Eriope's shoulder—she knew better than to grasp the woman's hand or arm without warning—and urged her away from Lemna when Eriope turned into her. <We'll get to uninstallation. I *promise.*> Lemna could no doubt guess what she was saying without even bothering to eavesdrop. <All it takes is time.> Time that would stretch long, for her friend, but what could any of them do about that?

Lemna waited in stillness until it was clear Eriope was going to go with Genevieve, then swept for the door. "Malao will let you know your new duty schedule." No doubt she'd be assigned double security shifts—along with someone else to watch her—for the foreseeable future.

"Fuck me." Eriope dropped her forehead against Genevieve's shoulder. Maybe the antagonist was finally making enough inroads that she was crashing. "In my defense, she was a *great* lay?"

Neither Genevieve nor Pyrus dignified that with a laugh. "I'll take her to her rooms to charge?" Genevieve suggested to Pyrus. And by "charge" she meant "soothe the pain with something else from her stash." She hated to enable that, but it was only what Eriope would do anyway if left alone. Pyrus gave her a nod, looking just as conflicted as she felt.

<How close are you, really?> Eriope asked, as they walked for the elevators, Eriope leaning on her arm over Genevieve's shoulders. Genevieve's light brown hair was fine enough that it seized any opportunity to escape from the tight tail she kept it confined in when working in the lab, and when Eriope disturbed it, locks slid free to frame her vision at either side.

Usually Genevieve offered miserable Installs who asked that question a "closer than we've ever been," but now that platitude wasn't even true. Burnout had taken them backward. <We'll get there.>

Even if she had to dedicate her whole life to the search.

After dropping Eriope off, rather than go back to the lab, Genevieve headed up to her own rooms, to do some charging in truth in the late summer sunlight on her own balcony. She needed to bleed off some of her frustration with the whole situation.

The universe seemed to have the opposite in mind for her. She stepped off the elevator on her floor to find two soldiers hulking in front of the door to her suite. "Are you with Abidjan? I thought she already left," she said, fetching up in front of them. They were both clean-shaven, both wore the Pax Romana standard-issue military haircut and "casual" clothing that was far too snappy, too similar in its cut—so as to allow a shoulder holster, she was sure—but when her system tried to ping theirs, she got nothing back. Not Installs, then. She snapped out her wings, carbon composite plates unfolding like feathers along the central ribs, silver-gray with a touch of black like patina. In case they might have forgotten she *was* an Install. "If you're supposed to be inspecting the lab, it's several floors down. These are personal quarters." Lemna had always done her own poking around before now, but maybe this was because of Eriope's behavior?

"Amsterdam Genevieve?" one of the men said. "We need to speak with you." The lack of any kind of reciprocal introduction hung in the air.

"Unless I'm some other Install with the codes to her rooms, I guess yeah, that's me." Genevieve presumed she was supposed to invite them in. She sent her codes to the door and gestured inside when it opened. As she followed them in, she glanced around her living room to make sure it was presentable, but it wasn't like she really lived here anymore. She spent her nights a few floors below in Pyrus's rooms, and had for years, so the worst problem here was the dust on uneven surfaces the automated system couldn't deal with. All plastic, metal, and glass. Blue-gray color scheme. Bland.

"So?" she prompted, when the two men watched her silently. "What does Abidjan want that she couldn't tell me herself?"

The spokesman cleared his throat. "Were you aware that though you were the first Install who received nanites through infection who survived, since that time, nearly fifty other Infecteds have survived, most of them not Pax Romana citizens?"

"Forty-six. Even if we weren't keeping meticulous track of our results, they're all part of my research group now." Recently down from forty-eight. And each of those successes so hard won—was she "aware"? Fuck him. Disquiet was rapidly knotting Genevieve's muscles, however. She was no citizen of the empire herself. But the Pax Romana were well aware of that, and had cleared her for her research years ago. Why bring it up now?

Genevieve opened a private channel to Carex, attaching pictures of the men's faces. <Who are the goons? I assumed they were with Abidjan, but—>

All her channels went down, full lockout. Carex or Lemna had the codes for that, but she couldn't see why *either* of them would bother. But Goon Two was looking up from pressing something on a handheld com unit. She'd unconsciously noted him taking it out while she was focused on Spokesman, she realized as she jerked her memory back, but had dismissed it just as unconsciously when she realized it wasn't a weapon.

The panic Genevieve had been sitting firmly on swelled up, bucking her like a storm wave before she fought it back down again. The horrible, ringing silence of being cut off from the ever-present possibility of communication was mostly emotional. That didn't mean this wasn't dangerous, however, it just meant she needed to act, not panic. She backed up, out of her door and away from the soldiers.

At least that was the plan. What she backed up into instead was the feeling of a gun muzzle against the back of her head. Another soldier. Must have hidden inside the other empty suite on this floor; she hadn't seen anyone else in the hall, and the elevator arriving would have been audible. Knew something about Installs, if he had the gun there. Her nanites could heal a lot, but not an instantly fatal head shot. "What do you want?" Her voice quavered and she let it. Maybe they'd underestimate her because she'd been a civilian before her infection.

Maybe it wouldn't be an underestimate, either. Genevieve searched for the weapon, in hopes that her system could remotely disable it, but it seemed to be manually triggered only. Her system helpfully presented the specs and she dismissed them hurriedly.

At this distance, there wasn't any difference between "a mess" and "a fucking mess" when it came to her *head*. What next trick would a real Install try, on a battlefield? Turn into Goon Three, try use faster reaction times to wrestle the gun away before it fired? She didn't think she'd ever be fast enough for that.

"I told you, we just want to talk," said Spokesman. He stepped back, and Goon Three took that as an indication he should shove her after. Genevieve went docilely, cursing herself for doing it. She heard the door close behind them.

She wasn't going to stop *thinking*, though. These soldiers couldn't be with Lemna—if Lemna had discovered what they'd hidden about burnout, she'd have held the gun to Genevieve's head herself if she'd viewed it as necessary. So the soldiers must have used Lemna's arrival as cover for their real purpose—to hide it from Carex? Could she hope for help from that quarter, now she'd warned him? He was a raging asshole, but he wanted an uninstallation process as much as anyone.

"Are you loyal to Pax Romana?" Spokesman asked, settling himself into something like parade rest in front of her, manner deeply incongruous in the rough conversation circle of bland couch and chairs.

Wasn't that the question. Genevieve had no pride in this moment, her only question was what answer they wanted: the simple one, or the honest one? And why would they come all this way, camouflage their arrival, and arrange themselves so carefully to catch her alone, if they were inclined to believe a straight vow of loyalty? Honesty seemed her only option. "Our goals align." And a little exaggeration for spice: "I would never work against the empire."

Goon Two's com unit chimed, again, each noise increasing in screech. Spokeman's attention shifted, but the gun at Genevieve's head did not. "Malao," Goon Two muttered. Someone pounded on her door.

Spokesman's brow lowered, too fast, as if he'd already had a high kindling-pile of anger this latest annoyance had set a match to. "Our lockout codes have a higher clearance than he does."

"Yeah, but that doesn't mean he can't annoy the shit out of us by trying them over and over." Goon Two offered out the com unit, and Spokesman snatched it out of his grip. "Control freak." Not unlike Spokesman himself, Genevieve would bet. She wondered if Goon Two agreed. Not that it seemed likely to help her if he did.

"Fine. He's not implicated, let him in so he can see what's going on and then get the fuck out of our hair." Spokesman gestured and Goon Two pressed a combination of buttons. Genevieve wasn't allowed to turn, but she heard the door open, and then a curse from Carex.

"You're Johannesburg Malaxis? What the ever-living *fuck* do you think you're doing?" he demanded of Spokesman as he came into sight, stepping around her with a gun to her head as if she wasn't worthy of his notice. Carex's skin was of a similar, ancestrally sunny shade to that of the soldiers, but the line of neatly trimmed beard along his jaw instantly marked him out. That style was popular among the ex-military types here, and Genevieve wondered with a hysterical flavor of distraction if that differentiation was the point.

"You're supposed to be inspecting the security section, the same as Abidjan inspects the lab, not screwing around in personal quarters, especially without informing me..." Carex wound down and planted himself before Malaxis to glower until he got an answer to his liking. Genevieve was touched that his concern was for whether he was kept in the loop, not his actual personnel. Though she supposed that was the only kind of outlook these soldiers would understand.

And he had known they'd arrived separately. So the camouflage behind Lemna's visit was for—who? Her and the others in the research group, to get her truly alone? Why did they care about *her*?

"We apologize for the oversight in you not being fully briefed," Malaxis said, and Genevieve wondered if anyone in the room believed the apology. "There's no reason for you to be inconvenienced personally if you leave us to it, however."

Carex looked Malaxis over and shifted his stance. He didn't bring out his wings as Genevieve had, but she still felt his lethality like a naked blade to her throat. "Your generous offer is that I get to walk out and look the other way while the higher-ups fuck around in my own home? Hard pass."

"Fine. You want to watch, you can watch." Malaxis turned back to Genevieve and babbled some nonsense syllables. When she looked blank, he spat them again. "Don't play dumb, Idyllian."

The mention of her home planet gave Genevieve the key to fight through the egregious pronunciation of her native language. She repeated the phrase properly, then translated it to Lingua for Carex's benefit. "Paradise is freedom. Is that supposed to mean something to me? There are easier ways to get a translation."

"We know all about your Resistance friends, at home. What's your mission for them, fronti?"

Paradise is freedom. It certainly sounded like a rallying call. But her planet had been conquered nine years ago, more. Had they finally gained traction in their fight against the occupying force? Genevieve supposed something like that might have been covered by the news, but she'd studiously avoided any mention of what was happening on her home planet for just as many years. "I haven't had *any* communication with Idyll or even another Idyllian since I left home."

She carefully didn't look at Carex. He knew she'd arrived with a virus, as a mission from the beginnings of that Resistance—a joke of a mission, more likely to get her killed than succeed, but it meant she, so inconveniently infected with Pax Romana nanites, was out of their sight and out of their minds. She'd abandoned that mission and surrendered the virus to Carex to be destroyed long since, but if Carex wanted to get rid of her now, he could do so in a handful of words.

But if he'd wanted to get rid of her, he could have deployed those words long before now. "You think we're all fucking stupid, Malaxis? She's a civilian, if she tried to sneak some secret communication past any of us, she'd fall flat on her face."

"Wrong answer, Idyllian." Malaxis drew his own weapon, pressed it right up to Genevieve's forehead. "This is your last chance to change it."

Genevieve wasn't sure what made her instincts start screaming at her that yes, he really would do it. Maybe the way Goon Three withdrew his own gun and eased back, out of the line of fire behind her. Maybe some quality to the flatness in Malaxis's eyes. That fast, she was back to the war at home, the *fear* of it so deep and insurmountable she couldn't bring herself to fight. Words came out and she didn't even know what she was saying, she just didn't want to die.

"No, I haven't—I swear—I'm useful! I led the team that figured out how to make the nanites non-infectious, that's been enormously useful to the empire, hasn't it? Now they don't have to worry about any more civilians like me harboring your technology. Why would I do that if I was working against you?"

Nothing changed in Malaxis's face, nothing seemed to go in. Some part of Genevieve screamed at her now to rush him, she had nothing to lose, but she was frozen. She didn't want to die.

And she was frozen still, when he pulled the trigger.

The world began again. Or maybe it hadn't stopped, only Genevieve's ability to take it in, briefly. Her legs must have collapsed, folding her up, because now she was looking at the world from a half-seated position on the floor, one hip and heels of her palms smarting from where she'd landed on them. Malaxis, eyes still so flat, ostentatiously ejected the empty magazine from his gun, exchanged it for one he displayed to her, full. One step, and he had the gun right back in its earlier place, at the extent of his arm at such a low, negligent, *humiliating* angle.

She was sobbing, that came to her next like it was someone else doing it. She didn't understand. Why—? Malaxis was unreadable, but Goon Two showed more, glaring down at his com unit before lifting a sneer to her as if blaming her for whatever malfunction he'd found there.

"You're trying to scare her into using some kind of backchannel, to other conspirators," Carex said, in a tone of dawning understanding. Perhaps even a slightly exaggerated one, the grumpy asshole equivalent of a situation where Eriope would have deployed a bright, "Did I say that out loud? Oopsie!"

Genevieve wasn't processing fast enough to use the information, though, if that's what he'd intended. She was shaking too hard. "But—I don't have—"

"Of course, if she doesn't have a backchannel or a conspiracy, you're torturing her to no purpose." Carex leaned down and helped her up—actually helped her up. Genevieve wasn't sure she understood that either. Only then, when her pants clung wetly to her inner thighs in the movement, did she realize she'd wet herself. The smell reached her a beat later. She could hardly imagine Carex's disgust with her, but none of it showed on his face.

Malaxis tracked his gun only on Genevieve but he twitched his chin and Carex spat a particularly acid curse. Genevieve cut her eyes over without moving, and found Goon Three had shoved his gun into the hollow beneath Carex's ear on his other side. He wasn't exploding into a graceful series of moves to disarm the goon either, but that was probably because she was in the way, Genevieve figured. She had no more stomach to sink, it hadn't come back since she'd thought she was dead, but the core in her that had refused to lie down and die when she'd been infected with the nanites chugged and ground into a chain of logic.

What kind of conspiracy did they imagine she was involved in? One to use their research to—

The burnout would make a hell of a good weapon, she realized with a jolt. And the empire couldn't possibly be aware of it, or they'd probably have bombed Tsuga and the lab from orbit. Develop the original burnout process a little to encourage its spread, and unspeakable agony and tendency to suicide could hit any number of their active units.

Wasn't that ironic, enough irony to choke her, that she hadn't even considered the idea until now.

Having had the idea, Genevieve pushed it away. The important thing right now was that if the soldiers were determined to find evidence of backchannel communication that didn't exist, she—and Carex—would never be able to prove that negative. Negotiating their way out of this wasn't an option. What about outside help? If they stalled long enough, would someone notice the two of them were mysteriously off channels? If Malaxis had planned his timing this carefully, Lemna would be long gone, if she'd even bother to interfere.

"And here I thought you weren't implicated in this," Malaxis sneered at Carex. "Take him down, and then hold Amsterdam for me. She can watch what's in store for her."

As easy as that, Goon Three shot. The back of Carex's knee, then the other. Genevieve's system automatically damped her hearing in the middle of the first shot.

Another moment when Genevieve should have thrown herself heroically at someone came and went as she sobbed and Carex collapsed from beside her. But they didn't seem inclined to kill

Carex or her quite yet, and if she did force their hands, who would they interrogate next? Pyrus? She still had plenty to lose, and Malaxis's aim didn't waver from her forehead.

Genevieve nearly bit through her own lip in an effort to keep from moving to help Carex as she watched him curl protectively onto his side and bleed. The nanites would be healing him already, and it was a simple matter to cut off pain nerve impulses, keep them away from the conscious mind. Every Install learned how. Goon Three jostled her as he grabbed her upper arm, and took up his earlier post with his gun at the back of her head. He reangled her to watch Carex, which, whatever their motives, she was willing to accept. She knew he'd be all right, but she still had to be sure.

Malaxis tucked his gun away, smoothed his jacket, and knelt beside Carex. He leaned his weight on one hand atop Carex's nearest shoulder blade, flattening him prone. Genevieve expected more bluster, or curses, but she'd never seen Carex in combat before. Perhaps this eerie silence came from that space. Malaxis withdrew something from his pocket, resolving into a knife when he flicked it open.

"What the fuck?" Goon Three muttered from behind Genevieve's head.

"With Installs, you've got to take their wings." Malaxis shoved Carex's shirt aside, forced open the panel in his back, and grabbed out a handful of folded carbon composite plates. When the wing was mostly splayed out, Malaxis shifted his grip to the central rib and slashed with the knife, easy as macheting a stubborn vine at the roots. "He knows. That's why he's not moving. Otherwise I might hit something important."

You've got to take their wings. When denied a chance to charge through the photovoltaic cells in the wings, an Install's systems could run on bio power, but not efficiently. It robbed the body if you did it too long, and if that body already needed all the power it could get, to heal other wounds—

The only option was to shut the nanites down to their lowest possible levels. Genevieve could see it laid out in front of her, so neat, as Malaxis took the second wing, so messy. Severed, bloody organic tendons dangled from the contact point as Malaxis threw it aside. He didn't rise yet, however, just reoriented to peel aside bloody fabric to judge the healing that had already occurred in one of Carex's knees.

He apparently didn't like what he'd found, because he pushed to his feet and slammed a vicious kick into Carex's abdomen, curling him onto his side again. Carex wheezed, but made no other sound. Genevieve keened on his behalf as kick after kick fell. "Cracked ribs don't need splinting, and a little internal bleeding will keep him quiet. Not too much, though." Malaxis stepped back, ostentatious in his self-control.

Genevieve would give him a "little internal bleeding" and see how he liked it—she didn't consciously realize she'd lunged for him until Goon Three growled and jabbed the gun into the back of her neck hard enough to bruise. "Amsterdam," Carex snapped, the breathy burr to his voice diminishing the power of the order not at all. "Don't be stupid."

Goon Two cleared his throat, cutting across the charged silence. "We've got a surge in confused chatter on channels all around the building, Johannesburg. They've been missed, it won't be long until someone comes looking."

Malaxis strode over to the kitchen and snatched up a towel to wipe his hands and blade. "We'd better change our venue. How much time do we have?" He returned to lean over the com unit, flipped the knife to hold the hilt toward Goon Three. Goon Three must have shown some kind of reluctance or confusion, Genevieve wasn't sure, but *she* could guess the order before it came. Malaxis freed his attention to glare at his minion. "Hurry up and take hers, dumbass."

Perhaps it was a good thing she stank of urine, snot sliding down her upper lip. Genevieve held up her hands. "Please, I'll go quiet. You don't have to shoot me too! I'll go quiet." And Goon Three didn't shoot her. She felt his touch at her back before she slammed down a wall on every sensation from that part of her body. She'd endured, let it happen, once before, when an enemy's nanites had taken over her body, rewiring and changing it too much to stand in their wake.

She'd stepped free on the other side of that, her self still intact. She would do it now. Wings grew back. Pyrus had warned her of that, once. Now it seemed more of an assurance.

She felt nothing until hot liquid splattered onto the backs of her legs. Blood. Carex hadn't bled that much. Automatically, she shifted her attention to her system's reports, ready to take manual control to cut off the blood loss, but the sheer carnage indicated by the urgent warnings flashing up from the natural muscles shocked her into losing her grip on the pain.

Gray sparkles impinged on her vision and she was—screaming—her conscious mind wasn't recording impressions properly—

"—are you doing, butchering her? We need her alive!" Malaxis grabbed her shoulder—catching her so she didn't fold up once more. Genevieve stripped out all sensation below the neck, heard her wings fall as Malaxis tossed them aside, one thud rather than two.

"Permissions," Carex ground out, from the floor.

"Our orders come from the highest levels," Malaxis snapped back, calm not yet shattered, but certainly bent. *Good.*

Genevieve knew what Carex meant. Medic permissions. He wasn't a medic, but he was high-ranked, and presumably could perform some of the same functions. She knew he was burning energy he didn't have, to reach to her system, but she paved the way before him to do whatever the fuck he could, and the blood slowed and stopped.

"Get him," Malaxis said, and shoved his shoulder into Genevieve's stomach to hoist her roughly up. "We need to be out of here ten minutes ago."

Genevieve had an excellent view of the back of Malaxis's legs, and with nothing better to do, she considered forcing her own system to take her unconscious. But then wonder of wonders, a channel opened. From Carex. <Got around the block but can't stop them from listening,> he sent, apparent voice vibrating with anger and the strength broken ribs had stolen from him in the real world. Even as she thought that, the connection weakened and almost dropped out. Beside her, as the soldiers jogged for the elevator, Carex groaned. <Thought you'd want to talk to Pyrus anyway.>

Yes, oh yes, did she want to talk to Pyrus. The numbness of what was surely shock gave Genevieve a clarity to think beyond simple declarations of love, however. As the channel dropped out again, she shoved words together in her mind with panicked speed, considered how they would sound to listeners, tried again.

They were getting off the elevator now and wind slammed into them. On the roof. Some kind of flyer, to get to their ship to leave the planet as soon as possible, presumably. <Carex? What's going on? Abidjan is gone, but I can't reach Genevieve.> Pyrus's voice. Even hearing it disjointed from the bad connection swamped Genevieve for a second.

No. This was her chance. If she had no other options left, and had to do the worst thing she could think of to escape, he needed to be ready. <Pyrus—please, listen. I love you. Do you remember what you said just after we met, about how you wanted to make me smile? *Remember* that. If bad news starts to spread, don't wait for me. Go out and help people. The rank and file, you know? The people everyone forgets about. As many as you can, all right?>

The connection had dropped by the time she finished speaking. She had no way to know how much Pyrus had heard. But she had to hope. Hope he'd heard enough, hope he'd understood, hope he'd never have to act on that understanding. Rather than hold her pain block against the jostling as Malaxis dumped her into their vehicle, she cut off her consciousness completely.

PART II

If not for her system clock, Genevieve would have had no idea they were in transit for eight days. She was aware for very little of it—enough to eat, use the bathroom, and decide the only thing she could do was consider her stink a fitting punishment for whichever soldier had to sit in abject boredom at the bolted-down little table in their cabin each day. She supposed the door didn't lock, or maybe there were things that could be wrenched free and used as weapons, but she certainly couldn't discern what those might be in the cubbies of bunks with bare mattress pads.

When they arrived at their destination, she walked to the holding cell under her own power, but barely, and had no energy to spare for peering into corners in the semidarkness or speculating about where they had been taken. Carex would know. She'd ask him, just as soon as she'd collapsed onto her stomach on the new bed—with sheets this time—and slept another day.

When the lights next came up for what Genevieve assumed was morning, given the lack of windows, she sat up and made an effort to take in their surroundings. It was actually surprisingly room-like. One bed, comfortable for one person, or possible for two without personal space. Genevieve edged over from Carex's sprawl, having recovered said personal space on waking. Walls in a gentle shade of orange, a table and chairs, and soft bedding. That was the operative word, Genevieve realized, petting the fabric.

Soft, fragile, and ready to shred into pieces if put to anything other than the intended use. The table and chairs were similar, made out of wood—and Genevieve figured she knew from wood, considering where she'd grown up—that would splinter harmlessly if you looked askance at it.

The bathroom had a frosted plastic privacy panel that shielded it from someone on the bed, though not from the other angle, which must be where some of the surveillance was. Genevieve pushed herself off the bed to investigate the shower. "Monitor how much pain you're blocking when you're under the water," Carex growled, half into the single pillow that had somehow ended up in his possession.

"I'm not stupid." Genevieve regathered her strength for a moment with a grip on the end of the privacy panel.

"You haven't seen your own back."

Genevieve checked over the sink, but without a second mirror to reflect back to the slightly warped silvered plexi there, the very thought of craning around to see caused a kind of pain her system couldn't block since it was a mental, anticipated one.

By the time she finished washing both herself—back held mostly out of the spray—and her clothes in the sink, Carex was asleep again. She took the opportunity to yank the top sheet out from under him and wrap it over her shoulders before he grumbled his way back to wakefulness. "All yours."

Through painful experience, Genevieve determined that sitting in the chair normally was out of the question, so she turned it around to lean on the back as Carex showered and she resoundingly ran out of momentum. She couldn't remember being this exhausted in her life. At very least she never had been since becoming an Install. The military could practically have left their door unlocked.

Carex let his pants stay unwashed and thus dry, rather than going for the sheet look. Genevieve roused herself out of her stupor when he approached, and edged her chair around to present her back. "How bad is it, really?"

She loosened her hold on the sheet to provide the necessary slack, and Carex slipped it down with a surprisingly gentle touch. "Scarred to shit, but stable, looks like. Pyrus is the one who'd actually know, but I'd guess you'll need surgery to clear away the scar tissue before your wings can even start to grow back."

Could be worse. Genevieve hadn't explored the limits on her range of arm movement, but at least the damage was high, not low, to make sitting and bending impossible. She shivered, and pulled the sheet closer, like it was anything to do with temperature. "You want me to check yours?"

"Nah." Carex settled heavily into the second chair, in the same backwards manner as her. "Still working on the broken ribs."

"You…" Genevieve started, stalled out as she looked around the room. She didn't like the idea of their captors hearing them discuss anything at all, but she couldn't see the harm in this particular subject. "Didn't seem surprised by it. That they went for our wings, I mean."

"Can't say I was." Carex's gaze went vague, into memory. "Don't know if you realize, but Installs are used in two main capacities—out at the front and then on fully conquered planets to keep the larger force of unalts—unaltered soldiers—who often have local ties and sympathies…in line. On one planet, they figured out about the wings and used it to fight back. The brass came down hard and probably executed everyone in the ranks who knew, but word passed among the Installs. And clearly the brass kept a record, in case it proved useful later."

A flap opened at the bottom of the door, and two trays scooted through. Carex retrieved them both, and conversation lagged while they fell on the food. It didn't last very long. Genevieve considered her dignity—long since gone, she should admit that to herself now—and ran her finger around the edges of each compartment and licked it. Then she licked the tray itself. She glanced at Carex's, but it wasn't like he had anything left over either. "Calorie limited. I was afraid of that," he said, and lofted the tray into the nearest wall. It fell with a plastic clatter but seemed otherwise unharmed. Carex subsided, his usual level of anger apparently more than he could maintain.

To keep their available bio power limited too, Genevieve filled in. "Still a nicer hole than I expected to be dropped in," she offered. Lemna's threat of execution to Eriope was very much on her mind as well, but if they'd wanted to do that, they'd simply have used the gun in her room once it was loaded.

Carex gave a bark of laughter. "Because that unalt—what was it, Johannesburg?—fucked up. I'd bet you beer for life that his orders said if he *had* to grab someone, it would be you, and quiet, so they could monitor for backchannel communications while your supposed conspiracy tried to plan how to free you. Instead, the brass probably have all of Tsuga crawling up their asses, enraged, so they've put us in the strictly aboveboard detention facilities. This is Headquarters we're in, the heart of the Pax Romana complex. You should feel honored."

"Enraged? I don't think *all* of Tsuga cares quite that much about what happens to me. The research can go on without me, after all." Pyrus, on the other hand, might well be tearing himself apart right now, she was sure of that, but she couldn't do a thing about it other than add it to the box stuffed full of things she couldn't allow herself to think about or she'd break down. "And you—" Genevieve's mouth continued on without her brain, and she cut herself off. There was no call to be cruel.

"No one is going to be sad I'm gone?" Carex waved away an apology impatiently. "I said it, not you. It's not about popularity, it's the fact that of everyone in that dumping ground, I toed the fucking line. Every time." He stabbed a fingertip into the table. "And look where it got me."

For a moment, just a flash, Genevieve thought she heard real hurt in his voice. She reached out to put her hand over his, but his hand wasn't there when hers arrived, and he was looking away, glower in place.

He cleared his throat. "In any case, all this means we get to settle in and wait, let the wheels of bureaucracy grind onward. No point trying to escape in Headquarters where every five meters there's another Install who could stop us with one hand tied behind their back, in our current state."

Which is what he would have to say, out loud. But that didn't mean he wasn't right. Any typical escape attempt seemed fairly doomed to failure to Genevieve as well.

Except for the very atypical option. She had all the burnout process data in her local storage—too dangerous to keep them anywhere else—and should she decide to use it, all it would take would be a touch on an Install guard. Easy.

The decision, though. That was the hard part.

Genevieve muttered an acknowledgment of Carex's summation of their situation, hoping she seemed to be discouraged, not plotting, and dragged back to the bed. Silence fell and swallowed her whole and sleep, frustratingly, refused to drag her away from it.

Should she wait? Pyrus would be doing everything he could from the outside. There was no conspiracy to find; surely she and Carex would become more and more politically awkward as no evidence of wrongdoing was discovered.

Unless they turned up evidence of the burnout trials, decided it was a weapon, and charged them with that. Then her chance to use it would be gone for good. Or else their long-term solution to "politically awkward" would turn out to be "quietly execute." It seemed much more Pax Romana style.

So she could inflict the burnout process on a guard. Depending on who opened a channel to the afflicted Install, and onwards from there, she might get half of Headquarters. Reasonable odds for getting out of here, if.

If she was willing to consign so many people to such pain, such a ripping away of what they'd come to accept as their selves, it would drive them to suicide after.

Genevieve curled in on her knees, even that much pressure not enough to keep back the tears brimming at the edges of her closed eyes. Nine years ago, she'd committed to that abstract when she walked into Tsuga Security with a virus ready to deploy. But now she loved a Pax Romana. She'd done *good*, she had to believe that, making the nanites less dangerous, even if it had been good done in the service of the empire.

Weight settled onto the bed beside her. Genevieve started to uncurl to scoot over and grant Carex what room she could, but there was a touch at her hip instead, encouraging her to tuck close.

Her eyes popped open, but it was still Carex here with her, his features still tight with his perpetual anger. Genevieve maintained their current distance, dashed away a few last refracting droplets from her eyes, and tried to read his motives. "Carex..."

He sighed. "I know you and Pyrus are exclusive." Unusual, around Tsuga. Denied the ability to leave and settle down, a lot of the ex-soldiers liked to keep things casual, not just Eriope.

"Well, mostly." Though the exceptions so far had involved inviting a guest to join them both, not experiences apart. Genevieve shook her head. That was moot; she and Carex were both so weak they couldn't sit up for more than the space of a meal, she wasn't worried about this being sexual—it was the fact that comfort was being offered at all that confused her. "You've never been...kind. I don't understand. You're a badass ex-soldier, whatever your military has done to you since. I'm a civilian who got so scared I wet myself."

"Pyrus and I were as good as brothers, at one point. He was the kind one. I was the one who made sure anyone who fucked with us, regretted it. As a partnership, it used to work well. Until he was the one who needed kindness." Carex rested his forehead against her shoulder, and Genevieve let her instincts guide her. She tucked herself against his chest, and he found a place to fit his arm along her hip, away from her back. It struck her that perhaps he offered comfort because he didn't know how to request it for himself.

"So you and Pyrus served in the same unit?" Genevieve asked into his chest. As long as he wanted to talk, she was glad not to be alone with her thoughts and the decision to make.

"Yeah. Poverty brought us together." Carex laughed, low. The vibrations in his chest were thinner than the rich sound Pyrus made from this distance. "Him, starving with his father in some rat-infested hole on a core planet, and me, starving with my older sister in some rat-infested hole on a newly occupied planet. His mother died in an industrial accident, my parents died in prison, but somehow we ended up in the exact same damn place. Seemed like a good idea to join up and send money home."

That was more than she'd heard about Carex's background in nine years. She knew a few details about what had precipitated his estrangement from Pyrus, from Pyrus's side, and it was common knowledge that those parents who had died in prison had been resistance fighters branded terrorists by the Pax Romana as they tightened their hold on his planet, but otherwise he'd been a loyal, Pax-Romana-line-toeing blank.

"I had an older sister." Which would be in the public record at home, so Genevieve judged it safe to say out loud, in the name of a little reciprocal trust. "Died fighting at the front. My younger brother, though, he's still—was still alive when I had to leave. He was just starting med school when the war started, so they rushed him through."

The silence this time was more comfortable, though Genevieve still couldn't drift off. If only they had some other choice, some other way to escape. Carex might even have some ideas, but he couldn't share them out loud. If only they still had private channels, with no one around to spy on them.

If only…

Experimentally, Genevieve tried to open one of those channels. The block made her system buzz in a way that had nothing to do with an actual sound but still made her teeth ache. Try, short buzz. Try, longer buzz. Short, long. There was some kind of code specifically for that, but she didn't have it loaded locally so she used binary instead. Even if he decoded the long and short the wrong way, his system could flip it back easily enough.

HELLO

In the middle of the second "L," Carex growled. "Stop that!"

"If I could just break through," Genevieve whined, in case they were monitoring the activity, as well as to explain his objection. Come on. She finished out her word and waited. If Carex would just use his system to process it—if he had enough juice for even that simple operation—

His fingers tightened on the sheet over her hip to bruising, then relaxed. Her system started buzzing in return. At first it was just a muddle, his attempts coming too fast for her system to accurately measure their duration. After some trial and error he throttled himself back to excruciatingly slow. Even if they chose their words carefully, this was going to take all day. Which they had to spare, she supposed.

Her system logged the channel attempts until he paused for several breaths, then she let it change it into text for her to read.

FUCK

Genevieve swallowed a laugh that would have no visible antecedent to observers. She took a beat to compose her question in the fewest possible words.

TRUTH, ABOUT ESCAPE?

YES. SHOULD HAVE KEPT YOUR DAMN VIRUS

It wasn't that Carex's words made up her mind, precisely. It felt more to Genevieve like they uncovered what she'd already decided, deep down. She must have already decided it, after all, because something had made her warn Pyrus. The burnout shouldn't spread beyond Headquarters, but even if it did, Pyrus would have warned people. That was the best she could do.

HAVE A CHANCE FROM RESEARCH. NEED TO ANTIDOTE YOU

That wasn't technically true, but she judged greater precision wasn't worth the time it would take to explain. The concept was the same. She could prime his system not to accept the signal, should he receive it, same as everyone in the research group had done to their own systems after the burnout first jumped. She had no idea if it was 100% effective, but it was better than not opening any channels and hoping. Which reminded her, he should do that as well.

TO BE SAFE, NO COMS

No answer came to either comment, which Genevieve took as permission. When she was finished with Carex's system, she delicately extracted the code she needed from her own system and bumped its wish to spread, just a little. Anxiety kept her awake when dealing with the actual burnout data, but once she'd folded them away again and turned to obsessively checking the completed patch on his system and in her own from all angles, the sleep she was feigning for observers caught her up once more.

Of course, with her decision made, days dragged on and on without a chance to do a thing about it. No one entered, and even when someone did, Genevieve wouldn't necessarily be able to take advantage of it. If she knocked out any Installs who came in after locking the door behind themselves, she and Carex would be no farther ahead.

Around the end of the third day, she caught herself on the edge of screaming at Carex not to be silent so fucking *pointedly* at her. She paced a few more circuits of the room, realized that it was very possible Carex was close to screaming at her to stop pacing, and burst into hysterical giggles. She bent over to try to hold them in, which she found was a bad idea the moment her back flexed. The burst of pain before she blocked it cleared her head a little. Carex didn't even glance at her. Perhaps he understood what had created the outburst all too well.

Faint voices, on the other side of the door. Their presumably Install guards obviously would use private channels, so at least this was something outside of the norm. Two Installs entered, a man and a woman, her the more solid of the two. They herded Genevieve and Carex back toward the far corner, no weapons even necessary. The way the woman held her hands wide and open at Carex made Genevieve think she would welcome mixing it up.

A non-Install followed them, though she was in uniform—an unalt, Genevieve supposed. She had what looked like the most supple skin money could buy, but she was one of those people age had carved hard, rather than softening to compromise or negotiation. Genevieve had never bothered to learn Pax Romana insignia, living among ex-soldiers who were practically allergic to it, but she presumed this was someone high up. "General," Carex greeted, as if he'd heard her thoughts. "Took your sweet time."

The general paused in the doorway to stare him down or quash him with her field of pure intimidation, Genevieve didn't much care, it was the chance she needed. No way they'd be able to fight past, that was clear for anyone to see, not weakened with two Installs inside, and at least one more on the other side of the open door. She summoned her earlier hysteria to her voice and pushed up against the male Install before her. "General, we didn't do anything *wrong*. You have to believe me."

He held her back, lips thin, and her hand touched his. Skin to skin. Signal sent.

First, the harbinger: a phantom taste of sweet chili sauce, as Pyrus had once helped her system taste, soon after they met. He'd been delighted when it made her smile. Later, it had become a game, something one of her researchers had figured out he could do to scent and scent-based taste early in their experimentation, touching off a prank war that left them all smelling old fish for two days straight. The female Install showed no reaction, worrying her, but the man licked his lips distractedly as he shoved her back.

But she'd already sent the real signal, close on the heels of the first. Spin up, she told the nanites, in terms it had taken all these years to learn. Run hot like your host is dying, and keep running to save him. Run hot, run hot until there's no energy left.

Burn *out*.

He dropped. The female Install jerked for Carex instead of for her partner, but before she completed the movement, she was down too, boneless and sprawled. A breath of frozen surprise for them all from the general, as another thud came from the doorway.

Then the screaming started.

The Installs screamed as if burning alive, as if acid had replaced the blood in their veins. They thrashed with it, with the sheer animal shriek of it. Genevieve had thought herself prepared, but their volunteers had had pain blocks in place from the start. Blocks that had broken down soon enough, but they hadn't started here, here where the torture was already inhuman and it had just barely started.

No. She hadn't meant—Genevieve had never meant to—

Carex moved while she was still frozen, ignoring the Installs' guns, which wouldn't fire without the touch of their particular systems, and lunged for the general. They grappled—Genevieve should help, she could see pain from his ribs etched across Carex's face—but by the time she'd snatched up the man's gun to wield the butt, he had the general in a choke hold. A wait, with her thrashing with more focus than those on the floor, an endless wait that Genevieve couldn't stand on top of everything else until she thought maybe she'd break into sobs herself.

And the Installs had gone past screaming now to something more like a gurgling groan. She couldn't—she'd armored her system against the signal, there must be something she could do to block them from the worst of the effects—

Carex caught her arm when she would have knelt. His breath sawed harshly, but the general was down. "Help them," he growled at her, "by not wasting the chance their suffering has bought." He strode for the door, apparently more than willing to drag her every step of the way out of Headquarters.

One last look, one last good look at what she had wrought, and Genevieve went with him, so he didn't worsen his injuries struggling against her as well.

She would not forget what she had done, today.

She let Carex choose their ship, some sleek, fast courier or strike-force thing, she didn't know, nor did she care. The halls of the headquarters complex, across a quad to the docks, were like some ancient, imagined hell made manifest. A chaos of screaming and pain, Installs collapsed everywhere and unalt officers shouting into coms trying to find anyone who could tell them what was happening. No blood on the gleam of plexi and plascrete across the walls, but Genevieve almost wished there had been. No true massacre if it was bloodless, but this was still a massacre.

In the ship, Carex took them out with the sublight drive, out to hyperlight range beyond the planet, but rather than engage that drive in turn, he turned away from the controls to her. Genevieve had scrunched herself in the copilot's chair, more because guilt was a cable drawing her ever tighter in on her herself, than because her back couldn't touch the chair without pain. Data danced over the projected view of the stars before them, systems intended for unalts a boon for Installs whose systems barely had the power to heal them, never mind offer flight controls.

"What." Carex paused for a moment, gathering sufficient emphasis. Somewhere in the effort of escape and piloting, his face had gone rather gray. "The *hell* was that?"

"Failed uninstallation process." Genevieve couldn't look at him, then suddenly she had to look at him, will her explanation to reach him, evoke understanding when she couldn't understand herself. "It wasn't as bad—no, it was plenty bad in lab conditions, but I fooled myself. All the Installs in that complex, maybe on the planet—for any who don't die immediately, there's a good chance they'll commit suicide due to the shock."

When she ran out of breath and stumbled raggedly to a pause, Carex didn't try to reassure her, Genevieve noticed. "We buried the results and started over. I should have deleted the data from my system at the same time. Then I wouldn't have been tempted. People knew where we were. You said yourself, we just had to wait."

Carex was laughing, suddenly, sawing noises not so different than how he'd panted against his injured ribs. "Buried the results… this is all a fucking tragedy in the most classical sense. You'd never have *thought* of using it as a weapon if they hadn't imprisoned you for thinking of using a weapon, would you?"

When Genevieve shook her head, still stumbling over understanding what he meant about tragedy, he flung his arms wide. "We—no, the Pax Romana—did it to *themselves*."

"No, *I* did." Genevieve pressed her palms over her eyes because she didn't want to see his reaction anymore, but then she could see the screaming Installs lining the hallways all the better.

"Yes, you did, but let's not kid ourselves. We'd have been waiting until they figured out a way to make us disappear cleanly. You can self-destruct or self-medicate or whatever first-kill—or first-close-up-kill, or first-wait-that-death-didn't-bother-me-at-all-realization—coping strategy you like best some time not now." Carex jerked her hands from her face, fingers far too tight around her wrists. "We're not done yet."

"Yeah? And what do we do now?" Genevieve demanded, countering with anger, because that was simple enough for her to manage at the moment. Anger at herself could be turned outward.

"I don't know!" Carex shouted it into her face, collapsed back into the pilot's chair, looking even more gray. "The Pax Romana made me, body and soul. You're the one who knows how to be something different." A pause, then the last word Genevieve would have expected from him, in a tone she would once have said he was physically incapable of producing: "Please."

And what could Genevieve say to that? Nothing, in the end. She pulled in a deep breath, reached back to her memories of first waking up an Install, the lack of direction, bone-deep fear. Momentum was the key. The particular goal was less important than momentum toward it. "Tsuga won't be safe for us. But if we can get a message to Pyrus and any of the others—we need medical care, he can provide it if we can meet them somewhere..." And for selfish reasons too: what she wouldn't give to have Pyrus here to lean on, to hold her after her first-kill-of-hundreds-at-once.

She unfolded herself enough to face the main screen, searched for some indication of the coms. It was so *slow* and *awkward* to do it all by reading, rather than absorbing the information from her internal system. "If we can send a message without it being intercepted by someone once everyone else figures out what's happened at Headquarters and turns their attention to finding the culprits."

She prodded at the controls, apparently so ineptly that Carex couldn't stand it. He growled and pushed her hand aside, but that growl had returned to a familiar timbre. "Might as well send it in the clear before our hyperdrive burst, and set the meeting point somewhere only Pyrus would recognize."

Carex brought up a map, pushed from the chair to manipulate it directly with a fingertip. Now she'd goosed him into forward movement, Genevieve felt the guilt start to suck at her once more.

No. She shoved herself standing. "While you figure out the meeting spot, I'll find some food." Roused by the thought, an emptiness near implosion made itself known in her belly. "No more calorie restrictions."

"Bring it back here." Carex cast a distracted frown back at her. "My system doesn't have enough energy to guide a burst on my own, I presume yours doesn't either. We'll have to tandem it and coast in sublight while we sleep."

Genevieve pressed a hand to her stomach—if only it would shut up again for a minute—and shifted closer, though the controls still only showed the map. "Why can't the ship system do it?" There were plenty of ships in the known universe, and all but a handful functioned perfectly well without Installs at the helm.

"If we want our burst initiation point to plainly indicate our destination to anyone who stops by to measure it, sure. We have to guide from within the burst to change that destination while it won't leave a trace. A ship this small doesn't have room for the hardware and processing power to allow an unalt to do that."

"Well, shit." Genevieve had never piloted anything before in her life, never mind even half-guided a burst. "Good thing you're along."

At least she'd have no time to be distracted by her guilt while learning to fly the ship and work tandem, she supposed.

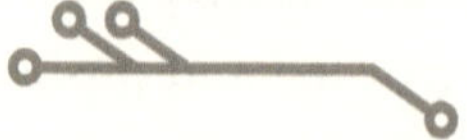

It bothered Genevieve for about a day, how terse their message to Pyrus had needed to be. It was text, not voice, just a line from an old poem, and request for acknowledgment, which they received promptly and just as tersely. After that first day, she was either flying or passed out, no thoughts to spare for Pyrus or herself or anything, no physical strength to keep her awake to have any thoughts at all, really.

They arrived at their destination early in that day's flying shift, however, leaving Genevieve at least the bandwidth to collect a few impressions as she drew in air so dry her throat spasmed near to coughing with every other breath as she stood in the open doorway of the ship. Ruins surrounded them—hardly ancient, or at least identifiably plascrete and plexi, but scratched and ground down to shoulder-huddled shapes over the passage of decades or perhaps simply years of violent sandstorms. She ventured out to where early evening shadows stood long and sand slid and danced over the plascrete floor in little breezes, peered out through what once had been a doorway of the building—or perhaps warehouse, given its open space without intervening walls. A whole warren of walls stretched beyond, up to two or three stories of their original heights, with de facto roofs formed of fallen pieces of floor.

De facto roofs that probably had had help, she would guess, given that Carex had guided the ship under a section braced professionally with girders in this ruined warehouse. "Smuggling planet?" she guessed when Carex ambled to join her. "What happened to the original inhabitants?" A cough stole her voice at the end, but she smoothed it over.

"Abandoned it due to a climate shift. Wasn't a desert when they built it." Carex's voice didn't seem any additionally roughened by the air. "Eriope used to meet her suppliers here sometimes, I believe. Anyway, all the spots that fit two ships out of sight to pass the goods are claimed and sometimes defended, so I don't know where Pyrus will set down in relation to us. He might have to walk in a ways."

They were certainly in no shape to walk to Pyrus.

<Carex? Are you there? Is Genevieve with you?> Eriope's voice, without the sharp clarity the com system could provide in optimal conditions around Tsuga, but still perfectly recognizable.

<Yes. Low…power,> Carex returned.

Though standing still, he staggered as if lightheaded and Genevieve guided him to the support of the opposite side of the doorway. "And Pyrus? What about him?" The words slipped out without conscious thought.

"How the hell would I know?" Carex snapped, and Genevieve winced. The door was a little too small to hold both of them, so she ventured out to the street, which had a similar mix of shadow stripes and oblique sun as the roofless section of warehouse she'd left.

Eriope jogged around a corner, and her whole face lit up. She hit Genevieve with a tackle worthy of one of their games of full-contact capture the flag, wrapping her into an embrace. "We didn't know from the message if you'd gotten out too!"

"Watch the back!" Pyrus, not far behind Eriope. Relief combined with the sudden burden on her pain blocks made Genevieve feel like a puppet with the strings to its legs cut. Even now, Pyrus looked calm and centered in a way that Genevieve wanted to cup her hands in and drink down until the fear in her was washed away.

"Woah, shit. Sorry." Eriope caught Genevieve when she wavered on her feet, and handed her off.

Genevieve caught Pyrus's hands, held tight as she could and he held back like he'd never let go. Her question must have been in her face, because he shook his head before he dropped his chin. "I saw your amputated wings, so I knew your back would be worse." The angle put his face into shadow, and Genevieve suddenly imagined once more what it must have been like for him, with nothing but that stupid message of hers to hold onto. She drew breath for a reassurance, but he preempted her. "May I see?"

"Carex said the scar was stable," she offered. He had the full suite of medic permissions to her system, and could have done whatever he liked, but she felt him take the steps slowly and deliberately so she could watch as much as her fuzzing-out system would allow. Check blood flow, check pain behind the blocks. He turned her, unzipped her jacket to below the scarred section. He must have touched it, but with the pain blocks up she couldn't feel the sensation of his fingertips. That was all right, his deliberate steps in her system were as intimate and familiar as any caress.

"Oh, Genevieve," he said, and embraced her from behind, desperate while still gentle. He kissed her hair, pressed a cheek against it, held it there long enough she felt dampness seep through. "When we get proper facilities, I can fix this."

"And Carex." Genevieve knew she was contradicting herself, telling Pyrus to go check on his brother-in-arms while layering her hands over Pyrus's on her stomach so he could never let her go again. "Different damage, not really much better shape."

"Seriously, you both look like you have one foot in the grave." Eriope sidled up to Carex and peered at his face, then danced back as if expecting a mock blow that never came. Her face shadowed at the lack. "How did you even manage to fly here?"

"Two half-dead pilots make one alive one." Carex shoved himself off the doorjamb and stood straight like someone who didn't need any help, thanks. The act gave Genevieve the push she needed to release her grip on Pyrus, let him join his friend. Pyrus squeezed Carex's shoulder before his gaze went vague, attention on Carex's system.

"It's a good thing we didn't have to go any farther, though." Which brought up a very important question Genevieve had almost forgotten in the relief of seeing her partner. "Where do we go now?"

"Anywhere we want for now, probably, as long as we erase the trail." Pyrus returned to the here and now, and crossed back to gather Genevieve back to his chest. "Tsuga's empty; everyone there got out while the getting was good. When the chaos finally ends, there's going to be a lot of people in the wind for them to chase down, but I suspect we'll be priority."

For a breath, that simply didn't compute, in Genevieve's mind. "The military's not *that* centralized, is it? Things didn't look good at Headquarters, but once everyone figures out the situation—"

Pyrus's silence had a shocked quality for a beat. Genevieve pulled away from him to see him exchanging looks with Eriope. Shit. *Shit.* "It rode the coms to other planets," she guessed. "Did you—were you able to warn anyone? Did you even understand—" Her voice was getting thin, and that wasn't right, it wasn't him she was blaming, it was herself. "I couldn't turn it loose just on one guard, that wouldn't have helped us, but even if it kept spreading, I'd hoped maybe you could—"

She was speaking too fast, and Pyrus cut her off by tightening his embrace, murmuring nonsense syllables under his breath. At some signal—maybe her heart had slowed a little—he returned to words. "I understood, though not all of it until I actually tasted the chili sauce. I warned as many people as I could—no one at Tsuga got hit—but most of those few still on active duty who owed me favors wanted to know where the warning had come from before they'd believe it."

"So what's the extent of the damage from this—burnout thing?" Carex demanded. "Thanks for letting the guy in charge know about your little mass weapon, by the way." It was aimed at Pyrus, but Genevieve flinched anyway.

Pyrus seemed unmoved. "I've heard you complain no few times about situations in which you had to keep the dirty secret for others' peace of mind—turnabout is fair play."

"No one mentioned it to me either, but I suppose I can't blame you guys for that." Eriope took a few pacing steps, over a shadow-stripe and back. "We don't actually know that much more than you. No one's answering, basically. Could be some people heeded the warning, though, and are just busy helping the rest. We have no clue about the mortality rate."

"But since that 'no one' encompasses *all Installs*, the best we can figure is that the empire's frontier is about to abruptly collapse. So. We can go where we want, short-term." Pyrus gave a low laugh. "No one's going to notice."

All Installs. Guilt seized up Genevieve's body, so badly she couldn't breathe. "I'm sorry..." That took the last of her air, and Pyrus had to take her weight until sheer survival instinct sucked in a new breath and she coughed on the desert of it.

"Out of a universe of bad choices, you made one of the least bad," Pyrus said, as intense in his—anger?—as she'd only heard him be on a handful of occasions before. "Call me selfish, but I don't count any of the ones where you *wouldn't have survived* as choices at all. And I know as soon as you can, you'll start trying to help again. If we can go to ground and start up our research, there must be someone who would accept it—"

"In exchange for what, in your fevered imagination, a pardon?" Carex's curled lip was audible in his voice. "I was always amazed at your ability to contort yourself to keep your loyalty to the empire, but this is next level. She saved herself—and my sorry ass too—and the empire would sooner kill her than accept her research." Carex circled to where Genevieve could see him around Pyrus's shoulder. "Where are we going now?"

"How the hell should I know?" Genevieve countered, but the unconscious echo tugged at her memory, made her laugh weakly, and got her mind moving forward again. "What planets do we have the fuel to reach, first off?" Her system registered that Pyrus was trying to send her something—maybe an extrapolation of the range of the ship he and Eriope had arrived in. "Come inside, I need a screen."

The inside of the ship was a blessed relief from the sunlight, even with no other active cooling going on at the moment. There wasn't room for all four of them in front of the control screen, but only she and Carex needed it anyway. Pyrus pressed against her back and Eriope stayed back in the passageway. "You have more fuel," he said after a beat of interfacing with the ship's system. "This ship is newer, too, so it's more likely to be noticed if we leave it here. Don't want to give eventual trackers any clues that can be avoided."

Right. Genevieve brought up a list of planets, sorting them with her fingertips as she thought out loud. "We want somewhere populated, to disappear into the crowds. Not a newly freed frontier planet. Somewhere our currency will spend and people won't come after us for looking Pax Romana even if we hide the wings. But not a core planet; we want somewhere low tech enough we won't be recorded at every turn."

And, oh, wasn't there a *very* familiar planet within range that fit those criteria. The only one that fit all of the criteria, in fact. She hovered her fingertip above the name: Idyll. "And that's the very first fucking place they'll look for me," she growled, mostly to herself.

"What the hell planet is that?" Eriope had undoubtedly been repeating the display on her own internal system, but she leaned in around Carex's shoulder anyway. "Idyll?"

Her warping of the name's vowels to Linguan ones made Genevieve wince. That, combined with her earlier comment, seemed to give Eriope what she needed to put it together herself a beat later. "You know, I'd never heard you say where you were from before."

"That may have been for the best, given *'Paradise is freedom'* and all that," Genevieve said, switching to Idyllian for the quote. Carex snorted.

She'd expected confusion on Pyrus's part, over words he'd understand, though their literal meaning was far from helpful, but instead he breathed a low, "Shit." At Carex's raised brows, he shook his head. "Genevieve didn't want to hear anything about it, but I followed what news trickled as far as us."

"Well, that's what started this all, I guess." Genevieve looked away from the name, cupping her elbows in her opposite hands.

Carex shouldered his way past to perform his own sorting of the planets within their range. "Maybe a local rebellion is just what we need, given our limited choices. Sure, they'll look there first, but if they can't find anything in the chaos…"

A sudden longing to go home slammed into Genevieve's gut like a fist. She wouldn't put the others in danger for that longing, but if there really was an argument to be made for Idyll—"And two of us speak the language. That will help with blending in."

Carex eyed Pyrus, and pulled a face. "You quick-learned it to better whisper sweet nothings in her native tongue? Ugh."

Maybe it was the relief of having a direction, maybe it was the anxiety about what she'd find at home, or maybe it was the massive weight of guilt, but Genevieve's head started to ache with a throb she didn't have the bandwidth to block or fix. "Eriope, you wouldn't happen to have any Sweetheart on you, would you?"

"Always." Eriope's face creased with concern as she pulled out one heart-shaped pill in the darling-pink shade, then a second when Genevieve held up two fingers. "If the medic approves?" she asked belatedly, withdrawing her offering hand by a few centimeters.

"As many as she wants and you can spare, until we get to a real clinic," Pyrus said.

Genevieve swallowed one immediately, and extended the other in Carex's direction. When he glowered his refusal, she snapped her fingers over it, then opened her palm more emphatically. She was too damn tired to argue, and she knew perfectly well he was just as badly off as her but with twice the pride to prop up.

Carex was too damn tired to argue as well, it appeared, as he swiped it up and tossed it back, much to Eriope's visible consternation. The build of pleasant happiness was slower than Genevieve remembered from the last time she'd had one, which admittedly was some time ago. Her nanites weren't processing anything fast right now, she supposed.

Things would be all right, though. Her guilt, it was still there, but held back like the pain impulses from her nerves. Pyrus was here, and he loved her—she loved him—and things would be all right.

"What…just happened?" Eriope asked, staring at Carex. "You actually accepted something that might make things easier on yourself?"

Carex's face cleared, and he muffled a chuckle against his hand. "Just keeping you on your toes, Eriope. Don't you know I stay up at nights, thinking 'How can I possibly confuse Eriope now?'" He looked both younger and older without his perpetual frown, older because he seemed more grounded, less buffeted by the currents of the world.

"Right." Pyrus guided Genevieve to the copilot's chair, then settled himself in the pilot's. "Let's get out of here. We can stop by the other ship on the way out to pick up our supplies."

Genevieve curled up, content. Things would be simpler from here on out.

Sweetheart squired Genevieve to sleep, then left her high and dry to wake. Lights were low in the small cabin, Carex in the bunk across the aisle, and Eriope in the one above him. Off-shift from flying, Genevieve put together, though she'd been too out of it to pay attention to any logistical discussions as they left the smuggling planet.

She heated herself a food pack in the small galley and shoved it into her face before returning to her bunk. Pyrus seemed to have done her some good, because exhaustion didn't blank her mind entirely, but that wasn't actually a net benefit. She was back to the excruciating boredom of the days of imprisonment, with the added image of screaming Installs to dwell on.

Nearly all Installs. Had all of those died or committed suicide? Had someone been able to help some of them?

Eriope roused and disappeared to the head, apparently too groggy to notice Genevieve was also awake. By the time Pyrus appeared, she'd scrunched herself into the back corner of the bunk, despite her back, because it felt safer, or perhaps because it felt like it would help her hold herself together better.

"Genevieve." His voice was so kind, even barely above a whisper, it made her want to cry. She didn't deserve such understanding as his. "Did you eat?"

Genevieve muttered her affirmative. When Carex didn't even stir, Pyrus dared a more normal volume. "You should be resting, then."

"Will you—?" Genevieve hesitated. Pyrus would need his rest for his next shift flying, and squeezing two people onto a one-person bunk wasn't particularly restful. "Just for a while—" She held out her hands.

Pyrus didn't hesitate. "Of course." It took some banged knees and elbows to wedge them both in, but she was against his chest, feeling each breath and it helped, at least a little.

Still, sleep eluded her. "Can I borrow your wing?" she asked, finally.

"Borrow my…? Sure." Pyrus clearly didn't understand what she was getting at, but game as ever, he wiggled an arm free to unzip the back of his jacket and carefully unfolded his wings. Being at the outside of the bunk gave him a bit more room to expand them.

Genevieve delicately took the leading edge of the uppermost one. The carbon composite of everyone's wing plates came with a brush of dark and light in different metallic colors, formed idiosyncratically in growth as fingerprints did, or so Pyrus had told her once. His tended toward a copper tone. She wondered idly if the ones she grew back would be colored differently.

She settled his wing over her shoulder, tucked just under the corner of her jaw. That was where her wings had ended up in her sleep sometimes, when she'd had anxious dreams. Now, she clutched the borrowed comfort to her and found sleep at last.

Sometime later, she partially woke to the sense that she needed to *hang on*. Something was—someone was stealing something from her—

"Love, I have to go pilot soon," Pyrus rumbled, and Genevieve came to enough of an awareness of her surroundings to let Pyrus's wing go. He was supposed to have sneaked off to his own bunk while she was out, earlier, so she hoped he'd been able to get at least a little sleep of his own with his wing in her death grip.

"Well, that's a creative solution." Carex's voice, directed to Pyrus. Genevieve slitted her eyes to plot Carex's location leaning on a forearm against the end of their bunk, and then subsided. With channels closed to them and no privacy to be found on a tiny ship, the least she could do was grant them some by pretending to still be asleep.

Pyrus's weight shifted where he sat on the edge of the bunk and his wingtip brushed against Genevieve's hip as he furled them. "What happened to the two of you?"

"They put a gun to her head and pulled the trigger to try to scare her into screaming for help to co-conspirators on a back-channel. Because of whatever local insurrection is going on at the moment." Carex's intonation carried a shrug without Genevieve needing to see it. "I objected."

"And her back—?"

"Following orders for convenience in transporting her, but botched. The unalt holding the knife didn't know what the fuck he was doing." Carex's following silence carried the weight of shared history. To do with the story he'd told Genevieve about wings being taken, perhaps.

"Oh, love," Pyrus said, and he must have believed she really was asleep because he touched her hair across her shoulder so lightly, so gently.

"Her strength runs deep." Carex's matter-of-factness threw Genevieve off-balance. She hadn't expected such a compliment from him, but she hadn't expected defense or comfort either. "If anything breaks her, it will be knowing what she had to do to get us out."

"She had no choice!" Pyrus said with an intensity not diminished by the softness of his voice.

"Just so you remember that."

A pause from Pyrus, then— "And there are things that can be done. Reinstalling as soon as possible, for one. We might not even lose any planets."

Carex gave a bark of derisive laughter. "Maybe 'we' should. Might do the empire a world of good." A pause, fraught. "You know, my mother, when they were banging on the door to drag her to prison, she told us that there would come the day when my sister and I would be able to stand back and watch the empire *burn*. And my sister's dead now, but it looks like I might still get my chance."

Pyrus was too self-controlled to gasp, but Genevieve could feel his startled frustration wavering in the air. "You were always the most loyal of the two of us, Carex. Has it truly come to that?"

"Ha!" Carex rounded on his friend, visible as Genevieve stole another narrow view through her eyelashes. "I held rigidly true to the letter of the law, while you twisted and bent, always finding some spirit of it that you could believe in. Well, both the letter and the spirit are *rotten*. What is rigid snaps, but you're still trying to bend."

A heavy step in closer. "Look what it has made of us, Pyrus. Look what the Pax Romana empire has made of you and me and Eriope, and her." Genevieve imagined a gesture to herself. "The empire takes loyalty and *breaks* us, by way of thanks. Each and every one. It made her into someone who had *killed*. She was *hope*, to all of us trapped into a life we can't stand, but came the time when they just had to break her too."

Genevieve curled up as if shifting in her sleep, pressing her face into the sheets so they wouldn't notice her tears. She'd had no idea she'd meant so much to him, and now she felt too weak to bear the weight of it.

"Or perhaps we'll manage to maintain sufficient momentum to avoid falling," Pyrus said, lowering his voice again as he pushed up from the bunk and headed out of the room. He was quoting Genevieve herself, which perhaps ought to have made her feel the weight of everyone's expectations that much more keenly, but instead anchored her, just enough. That had been true then, and was true now. They were going forward, to somewhere.

And once they arrived she'd find a new forward, to drive herself.

PART III

As they coasted in to the planet, in sublight, the four of them crammed once more around the pilot's and copilot's chairs. Ostensibly, Pyrus was the one piloting at the moment, but in sublight, and given that they hadn't decided on the strategy and thus the accompanying course for approach, he was letting the ship's system take care of it, and his conscious attention was on them. Genevieve had the copilot's chair once more, to move clumsily through the maps and views the ship could provide her with.

Which left Carex standing as well as Eriope. She didn't bother casting any side glances over to check how tired he looked, being on his feet for a substantial period. She was sure he'd catch her at it, and wouldn't thank her for the concern. In her own case, she felt functional. Able to keep normal hours and walk around, at least. She doubted she'd last long with any kind of physical exertion. The two of them could use coms consistently as well, though there was no particular reason to waste the energy for this meeting.

"Any thoughts on where we set down?" Pyrus asked. He didn't try to take control of the display as she settled on a satellite view of the main continent, which Genevieve appreciated. Eriope hadn't been able to sit on her impatience the last few times they'd been at the display together, and wrestling over it wasted more time than the awkwardness of finger-presses took.

"I'm afraid it's going to have to be a spaceport. Without ground transportation, anywhere open enough is either too far away from civilization for us to walk, or will attract far too much negative attention. I don't want to crush some farmer's crops in a Pax Romana ship and end up greeted by a militia." Genevieve found what she wanted on the map. "When I left, there was only the one spaceport, outside of Delta, which is the big trade city. Obviously." She circled a finger above it, shifted over and fanned out her hand to encompass some of the densest urban footprint.

"According to the files, the facilities the Pax Romana put in aren't that far away." Pyrus brought up a highlighted outline on her map with nothing more than a moment of concentration. "Fairly typical. Use the local one until you've shipped in enough personnel and materials, but don't bother lugging them very far before setting up your own."

"Neither of which are great, given I was hoping to avoid being recognized by the Idyllians either—that's a hell of an explanation to try to juggle—but the settlement where I lived is a good, six, seven hours of travel outside of Delta, so I think the risk is manageable."

Eriope leaned forward—jostling Carex, because there was no way to avoid that in the cabin at the moment—and squeezed Genevieve's shoulder. "Maybe they'd be happy to see you."

"Given how desperate they were to get rid of me, I doubt it." It wasn't that Eriope's words knotted up Genevieve's stomach, precisely, it was more that they shattered her fragile state of denial that she could return to her home planet without dealing with any of the people there. What about her family? They hadn't wanted her gone, but she wouldn't blame them if they'd been relieved when she left anyway. Did she want to seek them out? What if she did, and they wanted nothing to do with her?

What if they were all dead, casualties of the early period of occupation, or this current resistance?

No. That wasn't the direction in which her momentum lay at the moment. She could worry about that *later*. "I'm presuming we want the civilian field in service of not having to present your military identification and leave a trail—what do you guys think about going in as some spoiled brats with military connections? General Auntie Dearest lent me this fast ship to escape this chaos to somewhere safe, because we deserve it?"

"It wouldn't be that hard for us to make false unalt military IDs. But no one would believe it for you, and besides, if we land at the military field, they're not going to let us stroll off base afterward." Pyrus murmured, clearly thinking hard. "Civilian false IDs would be much easier, and it would explain why we have a ship that still looks military, no matter what broadcast codes we give it. I'd like to think no Auntie Dearest exists who could be that stupid, but you never know."

"Whoever is manning the traffic control has been rotting out here at the ass end of the empire for who knows how long. They'll believe it," Carex said, underlying growl back in action. "How's your rich asshole impression, Eriope?"

Eriope drew herself up, but only the better to settle herself into a hip-shot lounge. "Better than yours or Pyrus's, street trash," she sneered. She held for the pose for a beat, then chewed her jaw as if the accent had left an unpleasant taste. "Damn, but I hated those kids at school. Still, gives me enough reference material for a conversation with traffic control at least."

Carex nodded grudging approval but Pyrus slewed his chair around to consider Eriope with upraised brows. It must be a good impression indeed. Genevieve herself was no student of Pax Romana class dynamics. She'd cultivated her Linguan accent to be as neutral as possible.

Eriope anchored herself with a hand on the back of Genevieve's chair and her attention disappeared. Genevieve waited for her to loop them all in to the conversation once she initiated it, but nothing happened. "They're not answering," Eriope said at length. "Suppose I'd better demand an explanation of the base."

This time, a wince came faster. "Bounced me. Unless you have the military codes to prove your call is important, fuck you, is the lovely welcome message they have out at the moment."

"Well, if no one is going to stop us setting down…" Pyrus's turn to dive into unseen data. He surfaced with a frown. "Civilian field doesn't have any traffic I can find at the moment. Maybe they grounded everyone until orders start flowing normally again?"

"Gives us a clear path, if they don't try to shoot us down. And they damn well better not do that, even in the absence of orders, to a ship with military codes. The whole thing draws a hell of a lot of attention to us, but I don't see we have much of a choice. Take us down." Carex paused a beat, seemed to recall that he was in no position to give orders anymore. His growl rose to the surface for a moment. "If you agree—"

Eriope patted his arm. "We agree. Don't strain anything." He swatted her hand away, which seemed to soothe them both. After a few minutes of waiting as Pyrus lined up their course in which no objections occurred to any of them, first Eriope and then Carex retired to somewhere everyone wasn't breathing down each other's necks quite so badly.

Genevieve switched half the display's view to a public weather camera feed from the spaceport. Clear skies, predicted to continue for several days, a little icon informed her. Getting late in the day, local time, with the light a heavy, orange blanket. There was nothing there that should have been able to make her homesick, just metal, plexi, and plascrete, bare, utilitarian lines, but *she* knew it was home. But not as she'd left it, and she wasn't the person who'd done the leaving, so who knew what it would feel like when she finally did step onto a Delta street. Or her parents' farm—hell, that might belong to strangers now, if they were dead or had had to sell with two of three children dead or gone.

She didn't let herself ball up, knowing Pyrus would see, but she did switch back to a meaningless scroll of data from the ship's engine status. "You okay?" he asked anyway, because he was Pyrus.

"I'll do my breakdown when we're on the ground and have somewhere to stay for the night. I won't be able to put it off forever, I assure you." An echo in her memory—*self-destruct or self-medicate*—of Carex's "wisdom" on the topic made her smile, thin-lipped.

On the ground, things proved nowhere near that simple. Silence from traffic control continued all the way down, and as they gathered what they'd packed to carry out, not knowing what kind of accommodations might be available. The others settled their duffels with the strap across the chest, bag only slightly off vertical over the back, and Genevieve imitated them. As a last step, Pyrus and Eriope opened their wings slightly, checking they cleared. Carex twitched in the same rhythm, glowered, and strode to be the first out of the ship.

The door was set high, better for station airlocks than space-fields, and Pyrus paused to offer Genevieve an unnecessary hand down to the cracked asphalt. She accepted anyway, and once on the ground raised her head to find him frowning. <There's a hell of a lot of chatter on local frequencies I've managed to find but haven't been able to hack into yet.>

<Law enforcement, you mean?> Genevieve asked. Resistance? her mind asked as well, and she shoved it aside. <If there's an apartment fire or something elsewhere—>

Gunfire spattered the sunset from the direction of the terminal. Genevieve flinched down, but stayed standing, given the others were. They must have made some bone-deep assessment of the sound's distance, as Genevieve's system popped up an analysis of the likely numbers a full beat after her initial reaction. Multiple origination points, well separated from their little group. Another spatter and her system decided with about 70% confidence that there were probably two opposed sides shooting at each other.

Pyrus set a hand on her elbow, reassuringly firm, as if he was perhaps worried that she'd skitter away from the violence and put herself in danger. No chance of that—she was perfectly happy to jump the same way as the career soldiers. The orange she'd seen on the weather camera had given way to a much weaker one, fading off into twilight. The backlit contrast of buildings and trees against sky made it hard to make anything out visually, even with her system doing what magnification and post-processing it could. <If we meet the Resistance in the midst of a battle, I don't think they'll hold their fire long enough for me to even try explaining,> Genevieve said, tightly.

Eriope made to free her sidearm, but Carex gestured her down with a jerk. This time, neither Eriope nor Pyrus seemed to even notice that he'd settled into command again. <We start trying to shoot our way out of this, we'll be swamped before we get ten meters. Don't know about you, but I seem to have left my body armor at home. Better to sneak out the back.>

Genevieve had obviously never wandered around the spacefield's asphalt, even in the suborbital section, but she'd driven past one side or the other of the damn thing often enough. <Fence isn't much, as I recall. Meant to slow down troublemakers long enough for security to show up.> It was a wrench, but she left the unfolding battle hidden by the hulk of the terminal building to the others' surveillance, and magnified in the opposite direction, searching for the nearest edge of the field.

<If we get back in the ship and lock the door, they're never going to breach it with handheld weapons,> Eriope objected. She rocked back on her heel, toward the open door. Genevieve would never have expected such a voice of caution to come from her, but

then again maybe she'd underestimated how home-like the field was to her, how off to Pax Romana senses. The buildings were familiarly utilitarian, certainly, but the three horizons clear to the low rumple of mountains beyond were something that suited an ag planet better than a core one. It wasn't about nature—the planet where they'd been working after retiring from service had peaks to spare, but taller, sharp and claustrophobically close. This section of Idyll's main continent was fields all around.

<Unless the locals win the day and settle in to starve us out. Stop stalling and get.> For all Carex's rudeness, he led the way, allowing Eriope time to gather herself into following. Pyrus used his system to shut the door and kept hold of Genevieve's elbow as they jogged after the others. She wondered if he was anchoring her or himself.

<UNKNOWN SHIP.> The audio was far too loud for personal coms, making them all miss a step as their system adjusted. Someone clearly assumed they were broadcasting to ship speakers. <Exit the ship and stay there to wait for local authorities to arrive.> The Lingua was heavily accented, but perfectly correct. As the sun slipped away, a group of Resistance fighters hustled out of the back of the terminal toward them, identifiable as Resistance by the way they clumped and brandished their weapons a bit ostentatiously. It gave them a ragtag air rather than the one of efficient lethality Pax Romana units could pull off, but weapons were weapons.

"Thanks, but no thanks," Eriope muttered under her breath. Having drawn ahead of Carex by half a stride, she was the one to test the fence's metal links, pulling at them to see what enhanced strength might accomplish. <Up and over?>

<Watch out for the barbed wire,> Genevieve said, but she might as well not have bothered. Eriope had already swarmed up and found that easy enough to snap between her hands. She jerked it aside to make a space and then jumped down to the

ground on the other side. Her wings snapped out to slow and control her descent.

Making a hell of a silhouette, they all realized a little bit too late. The approaching group of fighters gained speed, flashlights snapping on as they erupted into shouts of fear and anger as if they'd just spotted the boogeyman.

Which, remembering her old view of Installs, Genevieve supposed they had. On frontier planets, Installs were used as shock troops, their wings, their eerie silence, their seeming invulnerability played up. Idyll was too newly conquered for the occupying force to include locals who would need Install oversight, as Carex had mentioned, so she wouldn't be surprised if Installs had been withdrawn and attained a half-legendary status thereafter.

All three of them started climbing at once, of course, but there was the barbed wire to wrestle aside at the top. With the cat out of the bag, Pyrus landed in the same manner as Eriope, but Carex and Genevieve didn't have any choice. She launched herself for Pyrus without pausing to second guess, and he caught her around the waist and cushioned her landing, as easy as breathing. He'd have done the same for Carex, she was sure, but Carex didn't give him the chance. Carex took all of his landing in his legs, cursing under his breath as he staggered forward a few steps to lean on Eriope to rebalance.

The others had better instincts and took off immediately, but Genevieve had to turn around to see their pursuit first. Perhaps part of her couldn't really believe that her own people were coming after her. But Pyrus dragged her along and deeper, more animal instincts kicked in. In the twilight, people with guns were coming for her.

And shooting at them now. Wildly, out of range, her system assured her, but still, the sound was impossible not to react to. She had to *run*.

They crossed a dirt road with the chatter of gunfire following them, and made it into a band of trees. It proved to be only a windbreak: tall, leafy, but ultimately too thin to last more than a breath before they burst through into exposure again.

Up ahead was a barn, the only real cover they'd reach before the fighters made it over or through the fence. The coms didn't take breath away from running, but no one bothered with them anyway, aiming their path simultaneously with a communication deeper than words. As they stumbled over uneven footing in the fallow field before them, each of Genevieve's breaths came harder and harder, tearing at her throat on the way down. She couldn't run flat out for this long, in fact not for one more second. The only reason she made it the last few meters to where Eriope had kicked open the door was Pyrus kept her going in some sort of controlled fall that left her collapsing onto him in the hay-dust-spangled darkness beyond the door. He held her up, but his attention was on the door behind her.

Eriope was making an examination of the door, palm pressed flat against the wood, and she hissed with frustration. <This damn thing is useless. These walls will hardly slow their fire if we make a stand.>

<We've got to hide,> Genevieve said. The others gave her pitying looks and clustered closer together at the door, glancing back occasionally at the truck parked to one side of the barn floor, maybe working it into whatever plans they were making on a channel among the three of them. That was fine, Genevieve couldn't help with those plans, but she had the advantage of already knowing exactly what she was looking for when it came to hiding.

Still panting, she skirted equipment along the wall as shouts grew closer. No time—but there it was. No ladder, but the hay loft was definitely there. Disused, which was even better. She should still have one exertion in her—she crouched, and *jumped*, getting her fingertips on the beam.

Carex cursed incredulously from beneath her. <You going to roost in the rafters like a fucking bat, Genevieve?>

<There's a whole loft up here.> Genevieve drew herself up in one smooth pull—never would have been able to do that before she was an Install, which was a reflection she'd worn out in the past nine years but one which came back now with a vengeance, given the familiar venue. The muscles across her damaged back screamed in protest, but she rolled onto her stomach on the rough boards and the pain ebbed as quickly as it had come.

Carex planted himself to stare up at her. Still dubious as hell, but she noticed he'd at least abandoned the truck, while the other two had their weapons out, still chasing that doomed plan. <And when they check up there and we're trapped?>

<What Idyllian is ever going to believe a bunch of Pax Romana know a hay loft exists?> Genevieve couldn't suppress the edge of a hysterical laugh out loud as Carex, without further objections, extended hands up to her. <Eriope, Pyrus, wrench some boards out at the back—> she said. Damn, but Carex was heavy and her back muscles were telling her so. The pain made it to sparkles across her vision for a breath after she got him up, so she lost her train of thought and had to scrabble after it. <Some boards, so it's clear we only tried to slow them down by making them search something before continuing to run, would you?>

The sound of crunching wood overlaid the end of her sentence, so one of the two had clearly gotten the gist even before she had to pause. Pyrus gave Genevieve a frown and shake of the head when she reached hands for him, so she backed up into the low hay-dust topography of the boards and let him boost himself up. Eriope did the same a few moments later.

The shouts were close enough now to distinguish words sometimes, at least for her and Pyrus. It wasn't anything illuminating, mostly "this way" and "do you think they—?" Genevieve flattened to her belly and edged toward the back wall, eyes on the boards to make sure she wouldn't come to rest over a knot that might show skin or light clothing to someone looking up from below. Dust kicked up around her and the others doing the same, tickling and scratching at her throat and her back throbbed a steady protest even when she stopped moving.

Then the door slammed open and she could only freeze. Clamping down with manual control through her system to breathe shallow and slow, stop any sneeze before it started, at least gave her something to focus on as Idyllians—*her* people—stamped around the floor below.

"You saw a coat flapping, not wings—"

"I know damn well what I saw, it was an Install—"

"Why would an Install run away? Or be alone?"

"—three of them."

"I counted five. That's enough Installs to really fuck things up—"

"Come on, we're wasting time. Those fuckers can run fast, and they went right out the back again—"

"—piss yourself because of a fucking *coat*—"

Genevieve closed her eyes, because she couldn't see anything beyond the upper story wall directly in front of her anyway. Slow breaths. A beat of pain in her back for each beat of her heart. Don't look up, don't look up.

And they didn't. The overlapping voices dwindled as their owners pushed through the gap in the boards or circled around the outside of the building. She had her system throw up a rough floorplan, plot everyone's locations as they finally, finally moved away.

Two question marks lingered, two people quiet enough her system couldn't track them completely away, so when no one else in the hayloft moved, Genevieve maintained her stillness as well. The fabric of her duffel was rubbing her abused back raw where her jacket wasn't zipped all the way up, however, and she finally had to sling it off or scream. And she almost did scream because she'd apparently been bleeding and the duffel ripped off the incipient scab along with it.

She gasped instead, pressed her forehead to the boards as a few tears pittered to the wood as well. Pyrus was at her side the next moment. <Genevieve, what did you—> He drew in a sharp breath of his own. <Fuck.>

<Never good when the medic says that,> Carex contributed. <She break it open again? You've got the supplies to stitch it shut, don't you?>

<Not in *here.*> Pyrus's tone on the channel stretched thin with stress. <Not with all this—grass shit in the air. I can see some pieces in the wound even in this poor light. It has to be washed properly or it'll get infected for sure. If we can get to a local hospital or clinic, I can use their facilities.>

<I'll be fine.> Because she had to be. Genevieve brought her arm around to rest her forehead on, hiding her face so she wouldn't have to see Pyrus's worry as well.

<You will.> Pyrus's voice gained confidence and lost worry, and even if it was all a bedside manner act, Genevieve allowed herself to be calmed. <We'll get a bandage on it, at least.> He quietly scuffled through his supplies, freezing every so often as a voice or footsteps made it to the edge of their enhanced hearing. Genevieve gritted her teeth as he pressed the bandage into place, zipped her jacket fully over top, and then knelt up to get real pressure on it.

<Is whoever owns this place likely to come out and search properly?> Eriope asked at length.

<Even if the Resistance didn't warn the families around the spacefield something was going down, I rather suspect they made themselves scarce when the gunfire started up.> Genevieve flashed to her mother powerfully enough to tighten her throat around her next breath. She could just see her mother striding out

into the twilight with their shotgun— <Or else someone would undoubtedly have already arrived to cuss out the Resistance fighters for breaking their barn.>

Eriope sent back a thin laugh and crawled to the opposite side of the loft to give them better data to triangulate with, and everyone pooled their data into one map, silently urging the question marks to resolve. Now, they waited. Genevieve would be fine.

But certainly not comfortable.

The Idyllians fucked around for hours, coming in and out of range until gradually sawing crickets and the very distant susurrus of Delta's traffic took over as the main sound blanketing them in the darkness. There came a time when someone had to be the one to decide the risk of someone patrolling close enough to see them was outweighed by the need to get somewhere clean to see to her wound, and Genevieve figured that would have to be her.

She went for her duffel first, but Eriope took that away from her, and Pyrus had jumped to the floor—no one to see his wings this time—before she arrived at the edge. This time, she almost overbalanced him when he caught her, and the awkwardness over the pain and home-not-home of it all brought her to the edge of tears. She shoved Pyrus away quickly because as much as she wanted to be held, this was not the time. <If they've left the keys, I think we should just take their truck.> She tried for a light tone, didn't know if any of the others bought it.

Her enhanced low-light vision wasn't good for color differentiation, but the truck looked to have an honest layer of grime over a light color. A family vehicle, as it had a row of back seats at the expense of the length of the bed under the canopy. The driver's door was unlocked, but Genevieve didn't give silent thanks for her luck until she'd stepped up with one foot and pressed the starter to have the system light up, which meant the key was somewhere in the vehicle, probably in the center console. The barn door had been locked, so there was no reason not to leave it convenient, but you never knew.

She settled in, hissed as her back got near the seat, sat forward again, and brought up the street map on the display to find the nearest hospital, then thought better of it. <In case the closest hospital is slammed—or somebody makes the connection to the people they were chasing—I'm going to take us to one across town.>

<The former is more the problem. Better we should go in the back door and avoid notice if we can, but that requires them having an open room for us to sneak into. But at the moment, you should lie down across the back seat if you possibly can. I'll do this,> Pyrus said gently from beside her, and Genevieve ceded her place after pushing the button to unlock all the doors. Pyrus's hesitation over the truck's display made her pause, initially because she wondered if he was having trouble with written Idyllian, but then she noticed his feet were nowhere near the pedals. <Where the hell do they hide drive mode?>

<This is manual-, not self-drive.> Genevieve propped herself on the doorframe, fighting off a surge of absurd laughter that might be heard by someone passing by. But his face was such a picture of consternation.

<It's got to be simpler than piloting a ship,> Eriope said, jostling up behind Genevieve, apparently to volunteer herself.

<You're a dear friend to me, Eriope, but I'm not getting in a ground vehicle you're trying to drive like a ship. Go get ready to open the door.> Her shove at Eriope's shoulder was weak, but Eriope went where pushed. Carex let himself into the back seat with the suggestion of amusement tinging his frown.

Pyrus took significantly more staring down. <We don't have *time* for you to learn,> she snapped finally, and he grudgingly climbed back out.

<Teach me as you go, so I can take over if necessary.> When they were both settled in their respective seats, he placed his hand over hers on the automatic shift lever, and they pretended that was something to do with learning.

All right. Eriope was waiting for them. Genevieve kept the headlights off, so they should hopefully be able to keep a low profile until they made it to a road with other traffic. But if someone was outside, they'd be unable to miss the crunch of the tires on the farm roads, even with the electric engine. If they were going to run for it—drive for it—a second time, she'd better be ready.

They trundled out of the doors and Eriope swung up into the back seat with a smooth motion that showed how comfortable these ex-soldiers were with any kind of vehicle in another context, lest Genevieve generalize too much from one blind spot. And then they were bumping over the swath of grass in front of the barn to the ruts of the dirt road.

Genevieve needed both hands for the wheel, sitting bolt upright to keep her back from the seat, but with each few meters, a feeling of slotting into place took more and more hold of her. She remembered this, deep in muscle memory, and it all came together and the truck more or less moved under her control and it all felt *right* in a way she hadn't known to miss.

Fortunately, the night left the roads quiet so she didn't have to merge or dodge assholes, and the dark veiled most landmarks she might have recognized, rarely as she'd visited Delta proper before she'd had to leave. She could hold a feeling of home—shorn of angry fighters with guns—to her chest.

The hospital she'd chosen entirely by geography looked busy enough, but not swamped. As near as she could judge. She'd never been to a Delta ER of an evening on a—she didn't even know what day of the standard week it was, she realized. But she'd never been to a Delta ER any day of the week. She parked, ignoring the posted signs about restrictions and fees. Hopefully when the farming family tracked down their vehicle, the hospital wouldn't charge them.

Outside of the truck, her brief bubble of comfort popped abruptly, leaving her to an exhaustion that was becoming intimately familiar. Eriope hissed in surprise on coming around the vehicle to see her back, which Genevieve took to mean blood was soaking through the bandage and her jacket both. The seep she was monitoring from her system was ever-present. Carex more or less shouldered her onto his support first, which should have ceased to surprise her by now, but still did, and Pyrus supported her other side.

<I'll go start work on making a lock cry for mommy,> Eriope offered, and ranged ahead, scouting entrances as the three of them limped along the landscaping flanking the building and tried not to look noticeable. For her part, Eriope practically disappeared, and Genevieve was sure there would have been no "practically" about it, had she not had her low-light vision on.

<Laughably easy,> Eriope said, as they approached a door she was holding just this side of latched, her cadence suggesting it wasn't the first time she'd repeated the comment. The perils of not having their coms carried by an external system, Genevieve realized belatedly. Even on the smuggling planet, they'd been boosted by the ships. Coms alone worked on internal power close by, but that dropped off quickly with distance. Until they could hook into a local network, that would be important to remember.

They headed into a deserted hallway, Eriope leading the three of them, with low, channel-fed direction from Pyrus about what kind of facilities to look for. Equipment and supplies in this section it appeared, fortunately, rather than rooms with occupants, and the lights were at night conservation levels. Or perhaps it wasn't fortunate: they were avoiding notice, but at the expense of a steadily lengthening walk to get to the kind of facility Pyrus wanted.

It dawned on Genevieve, slowly, that all the notices and signs were in Idyllian. Of course. As had the street signs been. But that had taken time to soak in. Suddenly, up ahead the sound of another heavier, outside door opening and shutting, and a voice speaking in Idyllian too, giving it a familiarity that grabbed at her gut.

"—put out the word to sympathetic doctors in case they managed to hit any of the supposed Installs and they showed up somewhere… No, I'm not on their sympathetic list, but a couple who are know my interest. I turned around and came right back. We're out of the way here, but I'm hoping information might come in over the hospital's network. Apologize to the kids that I won't be there for bedtime, all right?"

Eriope plastered herself to the wall and Pyrus and Carex tried to do the same into a doorway, but Genevieve couldn't change direction that easily and tangled them. Hers were the stumbles that carried all too audibly, she was sure.

The voice went silent and a man turned into the hallway, in street clothes with an ID badge hooked to a hip pocket, just sliding his phone away. Mid-thirties, close-cropped hair but full beard. He couldn't help but see them, in all their Pax Romana glory.

He stared; whatever he'd expected to find—someone stealing medications?—it had clearly not been this, despite his warning. He jerked to the side to slap a light switch with his free hand. "Who are you?"

Fuck, said her mind, at this newest complication, and "Son of a biscuit," said her mouth without any sort of consultation whatsoever. She had to track the impulse back to her subconscious like grasping after a cat's tail as the animal darted away under the couch. What—?

"I'm not ten anymore, Vieve. You can fucking swear around me." And then the man was more than simply staring at her, he was frozen with his gaze riveted to her face, as was hers in return. "…Genevieve?"

Genevieve's mouth was too dry to get the name out on the first try. "Michael." He looked older. Of course he looked older; it had been nine years. And he'd grown out his beard—last she'd seen him, it had been fashionably sculpted with a tendril curling near his ear. But that kind of fashion had begun in the empire, perhaps it had fallen decidedly out of favor in the last few years.

<Anyone care to gloss for those of us who *don't* speak Idyllian?> Carex groused from beside her and Genevieve abruptly slammed back into awareness of her surroundings, her injury, the Pax Romana flanking her.

<It's not particularly illuminating if you do. I'm going to take a wild guess and say this is the younger brother,> Pyrus said.

Or didn't say, rather, since channels were sort of a gray area as far as speaking. "Let's not live down to the creepy Install image, guys." Genevieve used Lingua, to include them all. Michael would understand it, even if his accent wasn't the best on any reply.

Michael rocked a step forward, then subsided and eyed Eriope, who wasn't the most militant of them all on first brush, but she was the currently unencumbered one. "Are you all right? Where are they taking you?" His Lingua was near perfect, in fact. Perhaps that was another thing Genevieve should have thought of: it might well be, after nine years of occupation.

"No," Genevieve stumbled into speech so quickly, she found she didn't have the right words. "They're friends. Pyrus, he's my—lover—partner—" That would have to do. Close enough. "Why are you here? In Delta? The farm—?"

"I moved to Delta after Dad—" Michael's face finally crumbled out of blank shock into emotion. "*Shit*, Genevieve. You wouldn't know. Mom went about six years back, Dad not that long after. But you're not dead. You're alive. You look just the same." This time, he ignored Eriope to step past her and embrace Genevieve.

She reached for him in turn, but Pyrus refused to untangle her arm from his grip. "Hugs after the bleeding's stopped. I need somewhere clean to work. Better I clean out the scar tissue now, rather than let it heal wrong a second time."

Michael bristled a little at Pyrus, but backed up a step as his gaze grew unfocused with thought. "There's an OR Emergency isn't using, but I have to tell the system what I'm using it for or it won't let me in, and I'm off-shift—"

"Give me an exam room and some decent instruments." Pyrus brushed away possible objections with his free hand. "Risk of infection is greatly reduced with the nanites."

Michael nodded, once, turned and led the way without another word. Genevieve had never had a chance to see him working, and it contented her to see him so centered, purposeful. She recognized the thought as symptomatic of the sort of odd, floating feeling that came with the pain blocks messing with her mental priorities, but allowed it to continue. At the moment, she could focus on reaching the exam room, climbing up on the table, and letting Pyrus nudge her into the prone position he needed.

Pyrus unzipped her jacket, laying it open, and Michael hissed even with only the bandage visible. He strode around to Genevieve's head. "Did your…friends do that to you?"

"Not these ones." Genevieve spared him a hand to squeeze his with as much reassurance as she could manage. "I rather think the ones who did it are regretting it at the moment."

Then she would have let herself down from her elbows and pillowed her forehead on her arms, but Pyrus captured one and drew a tightly looped length of cable from his pocket. "Eriope, do you have any dregs of power? I'd give her mine, but I'll be using my system to—"

Eriope waved away any further explanation. "I'll be charging in a couple hours anyway." Genevieve caught her watching Michael obliquely as they slotted the cable into their respective wrist connectors.

Genevieve wasn't sure what reaction her friend might have been hoping for—or dreading—but Michael just frowned in more concentrated thought. "There's no way to use household current?"

The others completely ignored the question, making Genevieve wish they wouldn't shut him out that way. It wasn't his fault he didn't know an answer they considered obvious. "My system would have to convert it, and at some point, it's a lot like drinking salt water in that I'd end up worse off." Pyrus gently pushed her shoulders down and she yielded, setting her forehead on one arm to a view of the gray, padded surface of the table's raised "pillow" portion.

"Someone should help her hold the pain blocks while I work, I'll be concentrating on blood flow," Pyrus said, beside her shoulder.

"Or you could do both while I cut out the scar tissue," Michael challenged, from her opposite side. "I am a physician—"

"And you know what about Installs?" Pyrus's tone had an edge he seldom indulged in. Genevieve could only imagine the unseen stress piled up behind it, but she couldn't let this start escalating.

"Only as much as he learned keeping me alive during installation," she snapped, then weakened it immediately as her next fuzzy-headed thought popped up. "I think. I don't remember—that was you, wasn't it, Michael?"

"That was me." Michael's voice had gone very quiet, and he took her hand carefully around the cable and held on like he'd never let go again.

That seemed to have sorted that out, and Genevieve lost track of any conversation abruptly as Pyrus started washing out her wound. Carex's rather heavy-handed presence rendered her entirely numb below the neck, but perhaps that was for the best.

She gave in to it, though she couldn't keep track of Michael's touch, and endured.

Having her up and walking was an asset when it came to making it to Michael's car but Genevieve gave up on the effort after that. There was something about reclaiming the duffels from the stolen truck and ditching it, and she dozed off waiting for that to be taken care of, cheek printed against the window, and woke up in yet another new bed.

Her heart went from zero to jackhammer in no time at all, catapulting her up to her hands, but her gaze found no locked door, no nearby guard. Having taken that in, more of the rest of the room reached her. Light wood, in the bookshelves and bed, an inoffensively floral quilt she recognized from the guest room at her parents' house hung on the wall. In fact, the whole room harkened back to that guest room, not merely in the blandness, but Genevieve thought she recognized one of the end tables and the bookshelf seemed familiar enough to have come from a set.

But all that was *Idyllian* bland, and not really bland at all to her now. Still propped on one hand, she reached to pet the grain on the headboard. That was too much as far as her back muscles were concerned, however, as they twisted up into a spasm that left her gasping but overjoyed at the same time. She knew that feeling: whole muscles, twisting around growing wings. She sat up and felt with delicate fingertips and found unbroken skin and the panel her wings furled beneath, though no indication of how much was grown inside. Even without Pyrus to chastise her, she refrained from flexing the wings themselves yet.

<Morning, love.> Pyrus's voice had a tinny cast, but the connection carried it strongly, so they must have arranged what

they needed on the local phone network while she was out. <Or afternoon, rather. I gave you one jumpstart of power earlier, and I'm out charging with Eriope so I can give you another. As best we can so we won't be seen by the neighbors, at least. Lucky your brother has such a big yard.> She could hear his urban roots in the slight brush of wonder at such space belonging to each house rather than hoarded into garden boxes and parks. <Carex should be bringing you something to eat in a minute.>

Genevieve ran her hand through her hair, grimaced when she found it most definitely in need of a wash. She didn't remember when her last shower had been and didn't feel like calculating. Perhaps now was a moment to breathe and think about such things, however. Showers. Long-lost brothers. Permanently lost parents.

As circumstances proved, said long-lost brother was the one who entered first, bearing a tray with several plates piled high, one with stir-fry, one with rice. Carex followed at his heels and helped himself to a wonton as Michael set the tray down on the blankets by Genevieve's hip.

"She needs the calories," Michael said with a very thin patience. Genevieve wondered if the others had been rolling over him, making his mood flatter and flatter as she slept.

"So does he. They just cut up his back more cleanly." Genevieve started shoveling stuff into her mouth. It undoubtedly deserved to be tasted properly—it smelled delicious—but she'd save that for later meals when she wasn't growing wings. Carex pointedly seated himself on a cushioned bench-trunk under the window. She caught him unconsciously petting the wood grain in the lip under the cushion with his fingers, and smiled between bites.

Implications webbed out from her initial awareness of her situation as she ate, and by the time she was scraping the plate, she'd worked her way to real concern. "Michael…is it all right that we're staying here? The Pax Romana will be looking for us soon enough, and I also can't imagine any of your Idyllian neighbors would want us around…"

Michael gathered up the tray, hesitated at her question, then placed it to the side outside of the doorway and returned to fill its place on her blankets with himself. She did hug him this time, and they stayed that way for as long as his chest shivered with tears she didn't otherwise hear. He laughed raggedly as they separated and he scrubbed at his face. "Now you feel like my big sister again."

Instead of looking possibly younger than him. Those implications, Genevieve pushed aside, though she was sure they'd continue to grow on her as time went on, in a way they hadn't among other Installs.

"Anyway. This is the best place for you, while you recover—especially since that won't take long. I explained about you to my husband, and he took the kids to his parents' house. They'll love it for a few days, and will come home with the younger one trying to convince me they had ice cream for breakfast, lunch, and dinner." Prompted by Genevieve's listening noise, Michael expanded. "We adopted a pair of war orphans, brother and sister. They're six and eight now."

"You married Sam?" Genevieve said, as he'd run down again. Then she winced. Hell. Way to put her foot in it. "No. He died in battle. I'm sorry. I remember that. Not long after Alicia, wasn't it?" She couldn't bear to have silence to hear the ring of Michael's hurt, so she hurried on with unnecessary explanation to Carex. "That's our older sister. The one I was telling you about."

"It's all right. We're alive," Michael said, when she'd cut herself off. He didn't look hurt, just exhausted, and he even summoned a smile. "So you're not married to—Pyrus?"

Genevieve saw an opening for a lighter tone and grasped after it with both hands, giving her brother a mock smack on the shoulder. "You want Carex to think we're prudes out here?

Of course we're not married, I'm not a citizen, even though they allowed me to work in the empire. Even if we wanted the line in a database, who would we have registered it with?"

Michael's smile turned lopsided, thin at the edge. "I liked to imagine sometimes you decided to abandon the mission and go settle down somewhere. You could have had kids of your own by now."

Mission. Genevieve's attention snapped automatically to Carex, but then he already knew about the virus she'd been given by Idyllian Resistance to take down the Installs, once upon a time.

But Pyrus didn't.

And far from "sometime later" at a time that kept receding, she'd better tell him that *now*. Looking back, as if at a separate person, she couldn't conceive of how she hadn't thought of that in all the time since they'd decided to come to Idyll. Whether she coached Michael not to mention it or not, people here knew, and she needed to be the one to tell Pyrus. It didn't matter that it scared her almost as much as sitting in the Pax Romana prison cell, wondering what they would do to her. The empire could hurt her physically, but her happiness rested in part on a foundation of her love with Pyrus and if he wanted to break that—

But Carex was speaking to Michael, expression mocking and hard. She had to hurry to catch up before she missed the conversation. "You realize all Installs are sterile? Useful byproduct or purposeful addition to the installation, it amounts to the same thing. Balances out the functional immortality."

Genevieve breathed a curse under her breath. That had been aimed to wound, she was sure of it. She supposed Carex's misery wanted company. "Carex, you don't need to say it like that—"

"No, I do, since you're not going to. It saves time if every Install warriors up and says it in so many words to their relatives." He turned his sardonic look back to Michael. "How old do you think I am?"

Genevieve couldn't answer that herself, since she knew Pyrus's age and knew Carex wasn't far away, but trying to set aside her biases, perhaps he looked like he was in his late thirties. Even if Michael came to the same conclusion, he frowned a beat longer and visibly revised his answer given the fact that Carex was being such an ass about asking. "Late forties, standard years? Fifty?"

"Sixty-one," Carex said, then tipped his head to Genevieve. "Her boyfriend's fifty-nine."

Michael tossed her a look souring into dubiousness—about the romantic age gap, she presumed—and Genevieve directed her glare to Carex's address instead. "Partner," she corrected. "Tell me, Carex, last time you said that in so many words to a relative of your own, how did that work out for you?" When Carex dropped his gaze, shoulders tightening with unvoiced rage layered over pain, that was answer enough. "That's what I thought."

She caught up Michael's hand. "We're a deeply fucked up crowd, all of us, it's true." He laughed, awkwardly, and she spoke over him when he would have demurred out of sibling loyalty. "But I was working a way to uninstall…" And what now? Evade the Pax Romana for long enough, and they could make a new life. "Suppose I'll pick that back up again. When and if I can." Pyrus's idea that they should take their research back to the empire was absurd, but she read that simply as an adjustment period. He'd get used to the idea of leaving the empire behind soon enough. And maybe they could offer their research to Installs individually.

But that was getting ahead of herself. First: evade the Pax Romana.

If felt oddly like a miniature occupation of Michael's kitchen, to eat dinner with three Pax Romana around his table, more light wood but swathed in a kid-mess-guarding tablecloth. She didn't know which side she counted for, but he was roundly outnumbered either way. Eriope was visibly fraying at the edges, so she excused herself to go out in the yard the moment her plate was empty. It would have been better if she could go out on the town, but who knew what Pax Romana ID check she might get caught up in. The moment one of their false IDs got into the system, it started a countdown to when the ID wouldn't be found in any external databases. That might take as long as days, but still. Carex, never chatty, followed soon after, and headed upstairs. Probably to nap, in his case. His wings had stubbornly resisted all of Pyrus's efforts to kickstart them, so he was running only on power borrowed from Pyrus and Eriope and shared with Genevieve, since her own wings weren't fully formed yet.

Michael accepted Genevieve's plate to stack it with his own, but didn't rise yet. Tension tightened his shoulders. "Vieve, you should know that the Resistance contacted me, asking about you."

Genevieve froze. "Asking about me? Why?" They couldn't imagine—

"Having Installs spotted arriving on the planet so soon after someone took out nearly all the others made them draw a few conclusions." Michael grimaced. "I denied all knowledge of you, but I don't know how long that will hold them off."

"Thanks," Genevieve told the table. She dared a glance at Pyrus who was frowning mildly in confusion, perhaps at the giant leap the Resistance had apparently made to reach those conclusions, if you didn't know what they'd sent her away from home with. He still rose to help Michael with the rest of the plates, but she caught his wrist. "I need to talk to you." She tried to make it light, tried with all her might, but maybe there was no way to say those words lightly. Michael disappeared into the kitchen, leaving just them and the deepening orange of the light through the blinds, flickered by leaf shadows in the wind.

"Okay." Pyrus settled two of his hands over her one on the tablecloth. "What's wrong?" He looked so *concerned*, so *kind*, because he was the kindest man she'd ever met and that's why she loved him.

"So, there's no good way to say this—and I should have said it before now, but I suppose I thought it would go away if I ignored it, but that's stupid..." Genevieve clenched her teeth to break herself off. She needed to stop talking *around* it. "You already know that I got infected when Idyll was conquered. Michael and my family nursed me through the install process, but when I woke up, everyone considered me practically the enemy. It was strongly suggested I leave the planet."

He was nodding. He did already know that, she'd told him long ago. No matter how she searched his face, she couldn't see any inkling of where this was going, however. She couldn't do this.

She had to do this.

"What I didn't say is they dressed it up prettier than that, though. The Resistance gave me a 'mission.' They'd created a virus they hoped would shut down Installs' nanites."

There it was, the sharp intake of breath. She avoided looking at his face. His touch didn't leave her skin, however. "And you dumped it, but now they think you finally succeeded."

She *hadn't* dumped it, but as she was finding the words to confess that as well, outside circumstances intervened. The door chimed and Michael answered, his voice perfectly audible to Install senses, even across the house. "I told you, I haven't heard from my sister—"

"Don't give me that nonsense," a rough-voiced woman said. "Of course she's here." And her footsteps strode into the house.

Genevieve had one breath to shoot a worried glance at Pyrus. How Pax Romana did he look? His clothes were urban, but neutral enough, and he'd gotten rid of his beard on Michael's recommendation. If the two of them were seen as connected, however, given that she'd been living among the Pax Romana for years, certain conclusions would be unavoidable. She drew her hands away and stood hurriedly, then strode for the hallway to intercept the visitor there.

The stranger leading her brother by several steps was a farmer, that was clear enough, with cropped white hair and skin seamed by the elements to give her a face like ten kilometers of bad road. Then the woman was slamming into Genevieve, embracing. "Ha! I knew you'd succeed! I knew it!"

Genevieve stood rigid until the woman released her, apparently unbothered by her reaction. "Come, sit down!" She herded Genevieve back into the dining room, like this wasn't Michael's house she was inviting someone else to make herself at home in. And of course there was Pyrus, still seated with his hands folded on the tabletop, watching them both with a neutral expression. The stranger's brows slammed down, as if it wasn't her own fault she'd been indiscreet without checking who was in the next room.

"She was able to rescue other infected civilians," Michael commented, so mildly that he must have planned that excuse well ahead of time. Or at least well ahead of *Genevieve*, thank mercy.

"Ah!" The stranger's face cleared. "Let's all have coffee together, then." Apparently that was an order to Michael. Genevieve shot him a look, but he just pulled a resigned face before slipping away to the kitchen. All right. If he didn't want to make an issue of it, she wouldn't either.

"I'm sorry, who are you?" she asked as the woman pulled up a chair at the table. Whatever the Resistance believed about her mission, this chummy nonsense was a little much. She declined to sit herself.

"Marta. Don't you remember—?" The woman's face cleared. "Of course, you weren't at your best when we last talked. I brought you into the Resistance."

Genevieve pressed fingertips beside her eyes, as if she could press the memories back into alignment. She had barely more than fever dreams from the time of her actual installation, but after she'd woken up—she'd thought she'd had more than that, but she wasn't finding much. Who *had* given her the virus? She remembered seeing the seemingly innocent stud earring on her palm, but she couldn't change perspective to pick up the face beyond it.

And she'd taken too long and lost her chance to object to that version of events. "Brought her into" indeed. Offered her a choice between becoming their tool or having no other real choice. "And you've succeeded beyond our wildest dreams!" Marta continued.

Pyrus's patience gave a practically audible snap. He shoved to his feet, chair scraping loudly along the floorboards. "She didn't do it for your dangerously misguided movement, she had no choice. And we're going back to help figure out how to reverse the effects just as soon as we can."

Genevieve closed her hands into fists, as if she could get a grip on this conversation as it spiraled away from her. <Pyrus, stop it. We're not going back.>

<You'd rather the death toll is as high as possible, then?> Pyrus was kind, but he was not *soft*. Genevieve heard it in his tone as he planted his metaphorical feet, finding his foundation as his anger grew. <To help your Resistance friends ensure the empire shatters properly?>

<Those are two different things!> Genevieve pressed those fists against her belly, trying to hold herself together. No, she just had to make him understand. <I can be against the empire and not want people *dead*. You *know* I have no loyalty to the empire, but that doesn't mean I—>

Marta broke in—or perhaps, given that their argument appeared silent to her, she merely picked up—with undiminished enthusiasm. Genevieve couldn't tell if she couldn't read their body language or simply didn't care. "With you to rally everyone, Genevieve, we'll have the Pax Romana off the planet inside of a month!"

"She's not interested," Pyrus growled, without even looking at her.

Genevieve stepped right up into him. "You don't speak for me!" She *wasn't* interested in helping the Resistance, she wanted to run a thousand kilometers from anything to do with them, but he didn't get to say things like that.

<No, I'm Pax Romana, and you're thoroughly against us, so why *should* it matter what I think?> His face stilled to something carved from stone and then he turned away. The next moment he was gone, striding out of the house before she'd had time to gather breath and ask him to stop. He didn't slam the front door, but of course he knew that with Install senses, even a soft click was as loud a punctuation to his leaving as any crash.

And she didn't run after. Pyrus processed things best alone, she knew that, however much the sheer effort of holding her muscles still so she didn't move felt like it was making her bleed inside. And now Marta was opening her mouth again—

Genevieve leaned over and slammed her hands flat on the table. Marta jumped, and Michael, arriving from the kitchen, slopped coffee from the two mugs he was carrying over his wrists. He cursed, but with annoyance rather than real pain, so Genevieve concentrated on the woman in front of her. The *gall.* "Understand this. I am not doing a *thing* for you. You—the Resistance—couldn't get rid of me fast enough! I was half dead and in pain and you shoved me on a shuttle with some paper-thin excuse of a mission—which, I might add, probably would have failed. It wasn't that virus I used. And you did it because I'd become one of the enemy, but now I'm good enough for you again? I *suit your purposes*, do I?"

It took Marta a breath or two to find a conciliating smile. She reached out to pat Genevieve's hand, seemed to read that Genevieve might well break that hand, and withdrew it. "But you could do so much, in the effort to free Idyll. Don't you want your family to live free?"

"The Pax Romana might well be leaving on their own fast enough. They're stretched too thin, and it's just a matter of how much chaos it takes before they admit it." Genevieve waved away the mug her brother offered her. She might throw it in Marta's face otherwise. Marta accepted her own mug calmly. "Honestly, you'd be better off keeping out of that chaos. Under this much stress, local commanders will be that much more likely to overreact."

Marta seemed to hear not a word. Instead, she leaned back in her chair, assessing. "You'd make an inspiring figure, I think. Looking not a day older than you left. Younger, even. One of Idyll's daughters, having struck a blow for freedom across the empire."

"Inspiring? With these?" Genevieve snapped out her wings, hoping the sight might break Marta out of her smug certainty, even just a little. Far from being intimidating at the moment, she thought they looked like those of a dead bat, as chewed on by a dog and left to decompose for a while. The ribs were mostly in place, but the carbon composite plates were taking their sweet time about growing and arranging themselves into something glide-worthy.

Marta made the smallest moue of disgust, but then her armored smile was back. "We can work around it." She sipped her coffee, as if everything was settled now.

"No." Genevieve stood, keeping her movements slow and deliberate. She didn't want an emotional outburst to make it seem like she could be talked around later, when calm. She was perfectly calm at the moment, calmly shaking with fury. "I will do nothing for you, or the Resistance. Get out, or I will throw you out."

Marta, standing, matched her stance and almost her height, but even her wiry strength paled before Genevieve's anger. She opened her mouth, and Genevieve readied herself for the threat portion of this little scene: with us or against us; another Pax Romana to be thrown off the planet. But then Marta backed down, and dipped her head. "We can talk again when you've had more time to heal." And she was out of the room, heading for the front door before Genevieve could react. Genevieve considered shouting some variation on the theme of "will never happen!" after her, but it wouldn't help, and she didn't want to seem petulant.

That left Genevieve with Michael, who was staring at her open-mouthed. She furled her wings quickly, but she realized a beat later he must be reacting to the barely constrained violence of her. With an effort, she pulled that in too, hunching her shoulders until he relaxed fractionally. "We already needed to find somewhere rural to hide, so I guess I'll add the Resistance to the list of people we're hiding from, if they continue refusing to take no for an answer."

Michael still had her unwanted mug in his hands, and he rotated it to cup them around it, probably more for the emotional comfort of the warmth than the literal truth of it. "Is what you said really—the mission really had so little chance of success? If we'd known—"

The coffee was in the way of a hug, but Genevieve crossed over in one stride to cup his elbows. "Even bad no-choice-really choices are still choices we've made. I made it, I survived, maybe did some good despite it. Found the man I love—" But somewhere in all of this, she'd forgotten about *that*, and incipient tears fogged her eyes. That would work out, wouldn't it? He'd be back in a few hours? She wanted to beg her brother to tell her he would, but how would he know?

Instead, she mumbled some sort of reassurance and took the mug from him so he could head off to visit his husband and kids. She started, standing over the sink, at hearing the door, even though she *knew* it was only him leaving. She needed—a direction—

But maybe Carex would know how long Pyrus might be gone, or what she should *say*, to apologize properly. She jogged to the stairs to find Carex already coming down, a duffel over one shoulder, scowl etched into his expression. "Apparently I'm taking Pyrus his stuff. Don't know where the dumbass imagines he's going to stay…"

That was worse than Genevieve had feared, and anxiety choked off all her words, leaving her standing stupidly in the middle of the hall with her throat thick with tears. She expected to Carex to simply brush past her, but he tipped his head to invite her into conversation to one side, scowl taking on a flavor of exasperated impatience. "So you told him," he said. "And then reportedly joined the local resistance on the spot to betray him that much more comprehensively?"

How could you be so stupid? said Genevieve's mind, on Carex's asshole behalf, and she launched herself at him. She got in a couple good punches before the shock wore off and then the unevenness of their weight class and her training ended with her back slamming against the wall, his forearm across her throat to pin her there. "Calm down," he snapped. "Tell me when you're ready to listen again."

She kept struggling for a few more shallow breaths, determined to make him work for it, but his muscles were like rock as he leaned in harder and she finally slumped against his hold. <The Resistance showed up to recruit me, yes, but the only reason I didn't tell them where to shove it while he was still here was that he was going on about going back to the empire…>

Carex let her go, stepped back, stance still braced and ready in case she rushed him again. "Hold off on the pity party for a few days. He might think himself around. When loyalty finally snaps, it *hurts*."

Genevieve sneered at him. If he was trying to be reassuring, he was doing a bad job. "Not everything has to be about how you guys feel about the fucking empire." What about what the two of them felt about each other?

Carex snorted. "They've ensured *everything* in our lives is about the fucking empire, and don't you forget it." He turned, another person leaving tonight. "Now, if you'll excuse me, I have a friend to go listen to rant and rail about the faithlessness of lovers." And then he was gone too.

"Shit, my timing," Eriope said from behind her, and Genevieve hadn't even registered the sound of her entering from the back yard. She started to search her system to see if that had recorded it, but that was power intensive and it didn't really matter. Eriope was smart enough to fill in what she hadn't overheard.

Eriope folded her into a hug and then the tears broke free. "You want to leave the planet," Genevieve prompted when her breathing had smoothed out, because while that still hurt a little, the fact that she'd seen it coming from a thousand kilometers off helped blunt the effect.

"The civilian field's finally back in Pax Romana control, so I can use my rich asshole ID and cover story and stroll up to reclaim my ship and set out for greener pastures. That way, for anyone who's looking for us, I'll be laying trails all over the place. And I can see about freeing up more of our funds…" Eriope's rhythm suggested she had at least three more logical reasons but she'd just realized Genevieve didn't actually appear to need convincing.

"And you're feeling trapped." Genevieve took one more deep breath with her forehead against her friend's shoulder, then pushed back and started trying to see what repair of her face she could do with her sleeve. "Maybe you should ask Pyrus if he wants to go with you—"

Eriope seized her upper arms, squeezed hard. "Absolutely not. He'll only want to return two days later, and what kind of trail is that to lay?" She pulled Genevieve back into one last hug. "He'll be back. He'd never be so big a fool as to give you up."

"Universal mercy grant." Then Genevieve was letting Eriope go too, upstairs to pack at the moment, but soon enough she'd be leaving as well. She made herself fresh coffee and hid out in the kitchen, not drinking it, to wait.

Eriope sent a brief message when she'd successfully gained access to the ship and permission to lift off, voice staticy with distance, and then Genevieve was alone for an indeterminate period until Carex contacted her. <Congratulations, you've made him angry enough to lose all fucking sense.>

Genevieve's hands spasmed too hard and she broke her mug. <I—what?> Rather than jump up to grab a cloth, she let the coffee rush free and settle into a steady drip over the edge of the table and onto her thighs.

<He made himself an active-duty Install ID and went to stay on the base.>

Genevieve froze in the act of piling the ceramic shards together, then picked the largest back up and snapped it again, between her two hands. <Once someone notices, they'll execute him! Why would he—>

<Because why would you think about your personal safety when you can make grand, angry gestures in the name of love?> A pause, and Genevieve could imagine Carex growling his rage under his breath. <He has a least a bit of a grace period. Apparently clusterfuck is putting it lightly, as far as the situation of the Pax Romana forces on the planet at the moment. No one's going to question his ID in the near term. However, now he can't simply walk out of there when he comes to his senses. Which he will. I give him three days, tops, before military life gets so much under his skin he can't stand it anymore.>

<We'll...figure something out. To help him get free, if he wants.> Genevieve finally stood, damp coffee stain making her pants cling to her legs. She thought longingly of Eriope's drugs, now out of reach. *Self-destruct or self-medicate.* How exactly did one go about self-destruction, exactly?

No. Pity party indeed. She was stronger than this. <Three days?> She couldn't judge the level of sincerity under the acidity of what was clearly also Carex's opinion of military life, now. <Really?>

He didn't answer, which was answer enough.

PART IV

Three days, four, stretched to a week. Michael's husband and kids returned and settled back into their daily lives, and Genevieve helped with chores as much as she could, wings tucked away. Carex spent much of the day away from the house on business of his own—he didn't volunteer any information, Genevieve didn't ask—and returned at night to eat dinner and pass out on the air mattress on the guest room floor. She knew they needed to leave, needed to hide better from the Pax Romana who would be looking for them, needed to get out of reach of the Resistance who knew where she was. But she couldn't make herself feel the urgency of those threats when Pyrus was stuck at the base. They should leave him behind and she couldn't leave him behind. She needed to apologize to him, beg his forgiveness on her knees, and he needed to apologize to her and beg hers.

Day to day, her wings gave an excuse for her drifting during their slow healing process. She turned options over in her mind, getting nowhere—again—the morning of the eighth day at the breakfast table, letting the bustle of family life distract her in the end—again.

Her brother's children were a study in contrasts—though they shared the same nose, the same caps of strawberry-blond curls, Will, the younger boy, had clearly been too young to remember the circumstances that made him an orphan. He would barely sit at his place long enough to eat two bites before he had bounced out of his chair, talking a blue streak to either or both of his fathers. He was shy around strangers, but had grown comfortable enough that he would talk near Genevieve or Carex, though rarely to them.

The older girl, Jaya, on the other hand, had the haunted eyes and stubborn silence of a war orphan who hadn't learned how to feel safe again—if she ever would. Genevieve wished it for her, deeply, and found hope in the fact that she did speak, oddly enough often to Carex. Something in the quality of their silences over meals seemed to resonate for them, and this morning, between their empty plates, Jaya was patiently teaching Carex a few words of Idyllian, using her brother's reading program. Rather than use the computer's voice, she'd speak the written word, emblazoned over a cartoon farm picture, and wait for Carex to repeat her, correcting his pronunciation as many times as necessary without apology. Carex, for his part, approached the task with solemn effort, though she knew he could have spent the energy and quick-learned it in hours.

Then it was time for school, and Carex accepted the tablet from Jaya with murmured thanks. He even paged through a few more words as the children clattered out, herded by Michael's husband. "Put together gatherer," he muttered to himself in Lingua, as if personally affronted by its awkwardness.

Oh! His system was giving him a literal translation of combine harvester. "I'm not sure even I know what that would be in Lingua," she offered. "Michael?"

But her brother was completely absorbed in reading the news. He hissed a syllable, looked up from his tablet to verify the kids were gone, then completed the word. "Shhh—it."

Genevieve reached out to touch the tablet to transfer the headline directly to her own system. She caught Carex's sardonic look and twitched back. She tried to minimize that kind of thing in front of her brother. The irony was, of course, that he appeared not to have noticed anything until her twitch. Even then, he merely rotated the tablet so she could read it normally.

BREAKING NEWS: PAX ROMANA BURN DELTA SPACE-FIELD, hardly needed additional explanation, though Michael provided it distractedly, rotating the tablet back and reading disconnected phrases as he held himself up on braced elbows, fingers laced into his hair. "Early hours of the morning, suggested it was retaliation for the recent Resistance attack—you *think*? Fuck—no injuries, spread to shipping warehouses—" Something beyond that point catapulted Michael to his feet to pace.

Genevieve speared Carex with a glare lest he pass comment, and downloaded the rest of the article to her system directly so she could absorb it properly. Carex mocked her with the innocence of his expression, then took the tablet to read through it manually himself. There wasn't much more than what Michael had excerpted, the usual chaos of messy events as told by rattled eyewitnesses. The shipping warehouses had been full of timber and grain ready to travel to market off-planet, staggering wealth gone in a fell swoop given the prices they'd fetch after transport. No wonder Michael couldn't sit still.

Carex gave the tablet a negligent toss to spin it back approximately to Michael's place at the table. "Someone's young, scared, and finding the orders they're dispensing up their ass where they've shoved their head."

Michael rounded on Carex, then sidestepped back from him, braced like a barn cat puffed up but still determined to approach a new object. Genevieve wondered if, despite Carex's appearance, Michael had stopped thinking of him as Pax Romana, with the differing perspective on the occupying force's choices that implied. "That's not standard procedure, then?"

"You're talking to a conqueror, not an occupier—" He broke off to neatly dodge Genevieve's kick at his shin under the table. He could make his point without playing scary bastard, a thought he could apparently read on her face, because he sneered at her before continuing. "You may be family, 'Vieve,' but I'm the fucking boogeyman and none of the rest of us have any illusions about that. And of course it's not standard procedure. You think the empire eats planets to look at the pretty flowers? Those are resources that now will never reach core planets, and tax revenue that's been turned into smoke because some scared kid didn't think ahead to contain the fire they set."

A knock interrupted them all before Michael had passed beyond silent absorption of Carex's point. Michael strode out to answer the door, leaving Genevieve to sit with Carex in charged silence in front of the domesticity of the scene, abandoned plates and mugs with coffee dregs scattered across the cheerful tablecloth, sun prying at the blinds that hadn't yet been opened for the day. She'd probably need to make herself scarce, but she waited to find out who it was at least, first.

"Oh," Michael said on opening the door, in recognition. "I'm afraid she's not home, Marta—" He raised his voice on that last, clearly not realizing she could turn up her hearing to catch his words perfectly without it. The extra volume was probably what gave him away—the next noise was a scuffle as one person pushed past another, accompanying a muttered "bullshit." Marta's manners were as good as ever. Genevieve shoved to her feet, but to get to the side door, she'd have to cross one room closer to Marta as she entered, and there was no time left for that. Carex, utterly without apology, retrieved Jaya's tablet and shut himself into the pantry.

Marta dispensed with all greetings. "We're going to hit them back. We need you."

Genevieve had to unclench her jaw to get words out. "Please don't escalate this any further—"

"With you or without you," Marta snapped, weathered face hard. Genevieve's thoughts, mired in mud since Pyrus walked out, sped up to something like normal speed as Marta turned to leave. Someone needed to talk these fools down, and she needed a direction to pour her energy. The conclusion was inescapable, and she pounded after Marta scarcely a breath later.

If people got hurt, she was determined it should not be from lack of her trying to protect them.

By the time a smug Marta arrived, strutting as if she'd coaxed Genevieve solely with her silver tongue, the energy of the gathered Idyllians was already far beyond what Genevieve could hold back. A mass of protestors screamed at the gates of the Pax Romana compound, an entity working itself up to mob-hood as Marta and key lieutenants crouched in the back, assembling Molotov cocktails to pass around. It had a certain symmetry, Genevieve supposed: you burn our livelihood, we burn yours, as if the Pax Romana would ever allow that to happen.

The massed anger was such a force, she and her words broke against it time and time again, as the morning wore on and the shouting intensified. If the Pax Romana were smart, they'd leave their gates shut and stamp out any bottles lofted over the top if anyone's arm was that strong. But Genevieve agreed with Carex's read of the situation; she couldn't count on that kind of intelligence.

The autumn day was sharp enough for its beauty to cut, even when the frost edge warmed off the air. On her parents' farm, she'd have hiked out to the lake, stood on the shore in a black coat and let the sun warm down into her core. Or now, she supposed, she'd have her wings out to catch it. Instead, in the scrum of noise and panting rage, she shoved her way to the front of the crowd, courting recognition wherever she could find it now. Yes, she was Amsterdam Genevieve, who became one of *them*. Genevieve, who had slain all the Installs. The latter turned her stomach, but she couldn't have the former without it, and she couldn't make them listen without the former.

Couldn't make them listen with it either. At the front, her back against the metal mesh of the gate, she shouted back, any and all words she could cobble together. Do not do this. They will pull out soon enough. You'll only push them into violence—

And the gate opened behind her. Genevieve had one bare second to close her eyes, to think *no!* and then the mass shoved her through before them. She had no idea who shouted it first, but suddenly the cry was everywhere: "Amsterdam! She opened it for us!"

The compound's plascrete buildings huddled around a central area for vehicle parking, the perfect place to trap a bunch of protestors while the soldiers with guns held positions behind every window. Knowing she had *not* opened anything, Genevieve assumed those soldiers without wasting time searching for them. A truck gave her at least something of a platform, and she vaulted up into the bed.

"IT IS A TRAP," she screamed at the Idyllians, using every trick of muscle, diaphragm, and voice her system could give her to project to boom off the surrounding walls. "I opened nothing. They're letting you in to slaughter you! Leave!"

She tried to find movement, a sign of comprehension in any face turned up to her. At least she had something approximating silence overlying a muttering foundation. At the back, she picked out Carex, lounging out of a line of sight to any of the windows.

"You stopped their Installs for us! Why are you taking their side?" A male voice, Genevieve couldn't pick him out.

"I am on no fucking side!" Sheer projection bought her their attention again, but she sensed she wouldn't have it for long. Genevieve jumped to the top of the truck's cab. "Because both are looking only for people to *use*. Tools to wield until they *break.* The Pax Romana send their citizens to court death from failed nanite installation so they can better court death on the battlefield."

Genevieve couldn't pick out Marta, but she stabbed a finger to the crowd. "And the Resistance, you send people out on suicide missions, herd them into suicide situations like this one en masse, as if that will win you this struggle. The Pax Romana have far more bodies to waste, I assure you. I did not stop their Installs for Idyllian resistance, I made the coward's choice to defend myself at the cost of strangers' lives.

"Neither side holds my loyalty, because neither has proved themselves worthy of it!"

The crowd rippled forward again, pushed by one of the firebrands at the back, and disgorged a Molotov cocktail to shatter beside Genevieve's feet. She stamped it out immediately, but the message could not have been clearer to her or the crowd.

Collaborator. Enemy.

Fool that she was, she'd forgotten utterly about others who would consider her an enemy. The crack of a gun reached her, damped only belatedly by her system. One of her legs collapsed under her, a searing line of pain through the meat of her thigh. She rolled with the fall, taking herself down into the truck's bed with a clanging thump that flashed pain across her leading hip, though that was healed easily enough by her system.

Screaming, the chaotic noise of a stampede out of the kill zone, and more shots. Genevieve only wanted to curl up, arms over her head, but that wouldn't help anyone, so she forced herself to sit up, look over the edge of the bed, shivering with the fear and perhaps some shock though her system had already stopped the bleeding. Entry and exit wound, no need to dig out a bullet.

A shot pinged off the body of the truck, missing by a mile, and another followed hard on the heels of the sound. But the gurgling cry of it hitting someone came from a window.

Another pair of shots and Genevieve's system popped up icons of the shooters. Several, scattered around the buildings, shooting down. One, in a particular window, shooting *across*.

The unalts must not quite have figured out what was going on, because troops poured out into the parking area, searching for the shooter among the rapidly fleeing crowd and not finding them. Genevieve couldn't really blame them for being slow on the uptake, she didn't get it herself until Pyrus climbed out on the windowsill and jumped three floors down.

His wings, wide-spread, slowed him to land neatly on his feet, gun up and aimed scarcely a second later. Eyes dark and hard behind the carbon shield that Installs grew for protection while shooting, he was every inch the avenging warrior. He was wearing body armor he must have gotten from this very base, but the way they stared at him, you'd have thought he'd grown that too, like chitin from his own skin.

Genevieve was staring herself, she supposed. She'd never seen the soldier in him before now, not really, the emotionless lethality in every muscle. She saw no hint of his kindness, no hint of a place it could have hidden.

"Who gave the order to start shooting at civilians? Where's the commander?" he asked, with a softness that projected even better than Genevieve's shouts had. One man was revealed by dint of everyone else around him stepping away, if he'd had any thought of trying to hide. "You're pulling out," Pyrus said.

"You're insane," the man snapped. Pyrus's shot caught him right between the eyes and he crumpled into that clear space.

"Who's in command now?" Pyrus asked, so calmly.

This time, a young woman did step forward in truth, righteous in her anger. "What the hell are you doing? We can't just leave. We'll lose the planet! Why are you working for them?"

She jerked, self-preservation operative but not sufficient, and the first shot took her in the shoulder. She staggered, and Pyrus simply stepped into her, kicked out a knee, and aimed down into her head.

Genevieve remembered that pose, that negligent angle of aim, as he pulled the trigger. The shaking took her, blanked her out for a few seconds and by then there was another unalt before Pyrus, babbling, her hands up. "Pull out, yes. As soon as we can load the ships. We've been cut off from communications for weeks anyway, it's only sense..." She trailed off into ragged panting as Pyrus turned away.

Three strides and he was at the truck, unlatching the tailgate. Genevieve only stared at him stupidly from her position crammed at the back of the bed. She didn't know this Pyrus, didn't know what he might want from her.

"Hurry," he said, and then strode away. She could walk with her leg still healing, but not fast, so when Carex met her outside the gates and pulled her against him, she accepted the support gratefully.

Support wasn't entirely what he had in mind, however. <Would the one with the gun care to hang back with the ones who could use its protection?> he sniped at Pyrus, which did make Pyrus pause, turn, and wait impatiently for them to catch up. Then Carex unceremoniously shoved Genevieve at him so hard, she would have fallen if he hadn't caught her.

He held her rigidly away from his body, and Genevieve wished he would have just punched her in the stomach and had done with it. It might have hurt less. <We have to get out of here before the unalts report this,> Pyrus snapped, though they were presently alone. The trampling of the grass around the road spoke to the crowds, but no soldiers had followed them and no Idyllian was visible on the long drive up to the compound, leaving the sharp autumn beauty to cut only the three of them.

<Let's have this conversation fast, then, because we're having it *right now*.> Carex gestured off the road and led the way across

the uneven grassy shoulder to stand shaded by a windbreak of trees wide-crowned and venerable enough that they must have been planted by the farmer who owned the land before the Pax Romana decided it would host their base. Pyrus's support across Genevieve's waist firmed up in a purely functional fashion.

<You—> Carex jabbed a finger at Genevieve when they'd halted in front of him. <He's from a core planet, not a dirty fronti like you or me. He has to get used to the idea of living out among grubby rock farmers. Give him more than a fucking week to adjust. Especially because he just killed half a dozen people to protect you.>

Pyrus snapped straighter, though that hardly seemed possible. <Getting the military presence off the planet helps us all hide—>

<And will bring official attention down on our heads that much sooner. You know why you did it. *Shut up.*> Carex rounded on Pyrus properly. <You. She was never going to use that virus. You know why? Because of *you.*> And Eriope and everyone else Genevieve had come to know as individuals, but Carex wasn't giving either of them a chance to interject. <And she'd have tossed the Resistance woman out on her ass that much faster if you hadn't distracted her.> He leaned in, toe to toe with Pyrus. <I *told* her not to tell you about the virus nine years ago. I told her, with your damn loyalty, it would break you. When you understood why she had to release the burnout, I thought, hey, he's grown, and then you go and pull this shit—>

Pyrus bristled. <She told *you*? From the beginning?>

<No, I figured it out, like you could have, but you didn't want to.> Carex held Pyrus's gaze for a breath more, the air between them shivering with intensity, then he rocked back, considered them both, and curled his lip as if he wanted to spit. <Both of you, pull your heads out of your asses.> Then he stalked off, back to the road. <We need to figure out where we're going next.>

In the silence, as Pyrus got her moving again, something shifted between them. It was too fragile for Genevieve to even name it, dare to call it "forgiveness," but she did admit that what was blocking her throat was hope. <I have one idea,> she told Carex.

Permission to move out to her parents' old farm, mothballed since Michael moved to Delta, was the work of a moment, such was his enthusiasm for the idea. Their parents' junker of a farm pickup took hardly longer to pack with their few duffels, but now Michael was repeating his rambling directions about the farm's aging solar power system, working himself up to actually saying goodbye. Genevieve leaned her hip against the dusty, dented once-white driver's side door and admitted to herself she wasn't sure how to say goodbye either, for all that she was only going to be a six-hour drive away.

"You'll want to check the well—we replaced the pump not so long ago, and there will be plenty of power for it, but I think we left it turned off." Michael gestured a position on an invisible breaker panel, and Genevieve recorded the image in her system, should she need it later.

With the noon sun beating down on them all to the point of real heat on the track to the backyard shed where the extra vehicle had been stored, Pyrus had taken the opportunity to bring out his wings to charge them both, cord linking their wrists between their bodies and the truck, minimized. They hadn't spoken or even otherwise touched since he'd inspected her healed wound and released her to finish throwing her possessions into her bag.

"You should be good to go, except for there not being anything to eat." Michael trailed into rough humor, brightened when Carex appeared with a crate, an old coat folded on top. "This should be enough to get you started, though." He retrieved the coat from the crate, gestured for Carex to load it, and approached Pyrus. "Thought you might want to blend in a little outside of the city. Your clothes are far too nice. This is my husband's, I think it should be reasonable on you. We don't have anything that will fit Carex, unfortunately."

"Don't worry, I'll be sure to roll around in some mud at the earliest opportunity. Think I should grow out a mountain man beard as well?" Carex returned, load deposited, to their side of the truck and stroked his jaw sardonically.

"That or stay clean shaved," Michael answered seriously, then frowned, clearly not able to tell if Carex was giving him shit or not. Genevieve couldn't honestly guess herself.

Carex gave him a wave as if to suggest Michael relax as he headed back for the house. For another load? "How much food are you giving us?" she said, turning to her brother in concern. "I don't need to steal it off your kids' plates."

Michael smiled lopsidedly and stepped up to her, hands out. Pyrus's gentle touch at her wrist withdrew the cable so she had her hands free to catch her brother's, to embrace him. He spoke into her shoulder, holding tight. "We have plenty to spare. There's little enough I can do for you, Vieve."

"You saved my life, don't forget about that," she said, low. She hadn't thought this goodbye would be so *hard*. It wasn't really a goodbye this time, she had to hold on to that.

Michael gave her a last squeeze, stepped back. "And now I'm hoping I can help you find your way of being happy." He kissed her cheek, turned quickly to disappear back inside the house, leaving Genevieve knuckling her eyes and feeling the silence between her and Pyrus sour into something awkward.

After a few beats, he folded his wings and tried on the donated coat. It wouldn't zip across his chest, but at least it spanned his shoulders. It didn't transform him into an Idyllian farmer either, but the worn-in dirt would deflect casual attention, she judged.

Carex returned with the next crate, took in their awkward stances and snorted. "If you're wanting to blend in, you'll have to control your showboating urges. I thought you'd gotten those out of your system first tour."

Completely lost, Genevieve made a wordless "?" sort of noise which made Carex snort again when Pyrus didn't step in with a reply to either of them.

"The jump, at the base. Looks impressive, leaves you vulnerable on the way down and immediately on landing, and wastes energy healing the damage to your knees," Carex glossed.

"But it works." A brush of tight humor wove through Pyrus's words, though his expression was twisted—with self-recriminations, Genevieve guessed, based on the man she'd once known.

Silence returned as Carex turned back for another load. "The view's probably better from behind, if you're looking for the maximum enjoyment of standing by watching me work," he sniped as he passed, and they both shook themselves.

"How many more are there?" Genevieve asked, taking a step to cut across the lawn for the house.

Carex jogged a few steps to catch up to her, grasped her shoulders, and bodily reoriented her toward Pyrus. "No, I'm carrying shit, you two are talking to each other. You'll find it quite easy—instead of staring at each other, you use your mouths to say words. Or send them over coms, that works too."

And then they were alone together, the two of them and an old farm truck, leggy weeds colonizing the wheel ruts at their feet. Words, Genevieve, admonished herself. Carex wasn't wrong about using those, but fear strangled all of hers. "Are you—are *we—?" Are we even still a "we"?*

"Please," Pyrus begged, and then he was hanging onto her and she was hanging onto him. His own words seemed to have burst through their own metaphorical dam. "Every day, I missed you like—like *wings*, but I kept listening to my pride, letting it tell me that I wasn't missing the real you, the you who'd accept a mission like that and return to the Resistance. And then I saw you, in the compound, throwing yourself body and soul at what you knew was right, so quintessentially *Genevieve*, and I couldn't fool myself any longer. Of course I knew the real you. Of course that was the woman I loved, and I'd walked away from her when she needed me most—"

Genevieve's hands were tight around his waist so she scrubbed her damp eyes against the shoulder of his jacket and probably painted dirt across her cheekbone. "I should have told you sooner. And bodily thrown Marta out of the house."

"I—" Pyrus cleared his throat, dislodging a final chunk of awkward. "Don't know if I'd have been ready to hear it. What you said in the compound, about loyalty, I think that's exactly what I needed to hear at that moment, but mercy knows Carex has said the same thing to me before—more than once—and I wasn't ready then."

Carex arrived with a third crate and Pyrus caught and held his gaze, forging a connection heavy with the weight of their shared decades of violence and pain. "And there will come the day."

"There will come the day," Carex echoed, as if sealing a bond.

Then he broke the moment with a smirk as he placed the crate in the truck. "I'm not even mad it was her who finally convinced you. I'm sure having slept with her lends her a trustworthy air. Not to mention you presumably wish to do so again."

Genevieve turned in Pyrus's arms, laughing helplessly even as she tried to glower at Carex. "It's not an accident, is it? Carex likes being an asshole for its own sake."

"Carex *lives* to be an asshole as much as humanly possible," Pyrus said. Carex shot him a sardonic salute, then vaulted up into the truck's bed to unfurl the tarp that had been crumpled at the back and hook it down so the load was tightly covered.

They'd be leaving soon, but Genevieve wasn't sure they were quite done saying everything that needed to be said yet. "At the compound..." Having started, she wasn't sure of the right phrasing, so she took a moment to make sure she felt comfortable in her choice. "That wasn't a side of you I'd seen before. I mean, obviously, you were a soldier, but picturing you as a medic—"

"I wasn't ever a medic," Pyrus said heavily. "Not until I'd retired, and it became clear someone was needed in the role at Tsuga. They only used Installs for very particular roles. What you saw wasn't...atypical for much of my career. I've killed a lot of people. Too many people." He shifted his weight onto his heels, away from her. It took Genevieve a full breath to realize it was *fear* she was seeing in his face. Fear of her reaction.

Perhaps she should have been glad now he knew how it felt, but empathy only made her hurry the faster to reassure him. "All of that—it's not all of you, not by a long shot, but it's a part of you. So I'm glad you trusted me with it."

Carex thumped a fist lightly on the top of the cab, capturing their attention. "Now, flip the speakers on those last two lines, deliver them, and we'll be on our way."

That took longer than it should have for Genevieve to parse. *Killed too many people—it's a part of you, I'm glad you trusted me with it*—but having absorbed that, holding tightly to Pyrus, she agreed with Carex.

Time to be on their way.

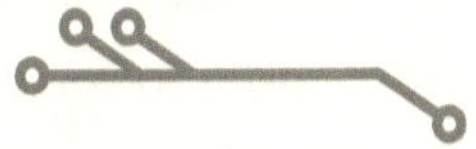

By the time there was leisure for such activities at the farm, the weather was really far too cold for the sunbathing Pyrus and Genevieve were currently doing. But today was crystal clear, utterly without clouds, so they'd spread a blanket on the south lawn where the tree shadows would not impinge on them for several hours at least, and spread themselves and wings atop it. Genevieve wasted a little power on upping her core body temperature, and dozed in the comfort of denial. There was still plenty to worry about, even if it had been long enough they'd begun to hope they were going to evade Pax Romana detection for good, but today, today she was basking.

Pyrus's head was up, chin on one forearm, watching the trees, unable to shut off his interest in the unfamiliar environment, she suspected. "Still looks like a forest to me," he murmured, picking up a joke they'd been batting back and forth intermittently since they arrived.

"It's still a timber farm, whatever uneducated urban associations certain people have with farms. Soil wouldn't be any good for the kind of crops you're thinking of. Trust me, I'm a soil scientist." She folded in her half-grown wings, flipped to her back to stare up at the blue of the sky above them. Perhaps she was worse at basking than she'd hoped, because a worry snuck free. "I don't think I'm cut out to be a farmer, long-term, though."

"Restless already?" Pyrus flopped an arm over the general region of her chest. "Sorry, you don't get to leave this blanket yet. You'll just have to stay here until the sun goes down."

"Sounds rather cold to me." Genevieve's laughter dislodged his arm, dragging it across her breasts and sparking unexpected arousal. So hurt, so exhausted—and then that exhaustion had continued in an emotional form at the farm, cleaning, refinishing, and mixing furniture from room to room so she no longer felt like she had to choose between sleeping in Michael's or her child self's room or her dead sibling's or parents' one. It had been long enough, she realized now, that she'd lost track of the fact that anything was missing.

And Pyrus hadn't given the faintest breath of a hint that he missed it either, bless him. "What are you going to do with me, now you've captured me, you dastardly soldier?"

Pyrus was abruptly kneeling, straddling her hips, wings mantled up and high. No doubt of interest there, then. He leaned down teasingly, hands beside her shoulders, jerked back when she braced up on her elbows to try to close a kiss. "Keep you busy until the sun goes down, obviously."

"Where the hell are you two?" Carex's voice preceded his footsteps, both overloud and a little hesitating. "Oh. Interrupting." Genevieve had to twist to see him as he was coming up behind her head, and he visibly swayed as he came to a stop a few meters away. He winced. "No, but I can *guess* 'how long it's been.' It's not like I've had any opportunities of my own on this planet. But look, I'm leaving now!" Pyrus must have sent some cursing over a private channel.

Carex turned, tripped over the air, and did a full faceplant. On the ground, he rolled onto his back, laughing. Pyrus let Genevieve up and they exchanged a glance of consternation. The mood slipped away into confusion for her quickly, as it had for Pyrus too, Genevieve suspected. "Carex…are you all right?" she asked.

By the time she reached his side to offer a hand up, he'd made it to his knees, and just grinned up at her, ignoring the offer. "Found some bottles of mysterious liquid in the basement."

"So mysterious you decided you just had to put it in your mouth?" Pyrus remained where he was, seated and watching his friend narrow-eyed, probably counting the seconds until the alcohol would start wearing off. An Install could manage to get drunk, but only for a few minutes at a time. If Carex had tanked up at the house, he should be coming out of it soon enough.

But that didn't make sense. "As I recall, my aunt and uncles didn't abandon the moonshine down there because it was too strong, but because it tasted like it was made to strip corrosion off industrial equipment." Genevieve seized Carex's unresisting hands and hauled him up bodily. "Unless you're faking right now…"

"Strip corrosion—" Carex dissolved into laughter. "Funny and beautiful." His next sway tipped him into her a little, and for a minute she imagined he might kiss her. With him so relaxed, and laughing, she could abruptly see the attraction of that idea, with the solid span of muscle in his chest and shoulders, and the strength in the grip of his hands.

She opened the distance between them immediately, and the moment passed as quickly as it had come. Just her imagination. Really looking at him had brought something more to her attention, however. "You're going *gray*," she breathed. Just a dusting, light strands leavening the short, black waves of his hair. Installs didn't go gray. Ever. They retained the color, if they had started to do so when they underwent installation, but that arrested the process.

Going gray, managing to get and stay drunk…

"Carex, have your wings grown back at all? You've been eating enough for it," Genevieve kept hold of his hands, even when Pyrus rose and came up behind her shoulder. She could almost hear his frown warping the air around them, but he was still back at confusion, she suspected. She'd jumped forward, to one particular conclusion.

"Used the energy on fast-learning for the damn language. Gotta talk like the natives." He did indeed switch to passable Idyllian for the latter sentence. "No wings." He would have turned to illustrate, but she didn't let him go, so he settled for rolling his shoulder muscles without effect.

"No wonder you're getting drunk. I'll have to lend you some charge," Pyrus said, and turned back to fold up their blanket.

Genevieve shook her head emphatically, but didn't waste time with a verbal negative. "We have a species of blackberry vine around here. Specially bred not to crowd out other species—the original stock was infamous for that. So obviously—"

"It crowds like a motherfucker." Carex smirked.

"Conquers and pillages, more like." Genevieve allowed herself a snort of humor. "There are only two ways to get rid of it, without tilling up every other innocent plant in that patch of ground as well. One is to snip each vine, and paint the cut ends with herbicide so the roots die. The other is to cut off the vines, and then do it again when they resprout, and again, over and over until you've starved the roots and they have nothing left to sprout with. If they can't get leaves open long enough to collect energy…"

"Genevieve…" Pyrus's voice had gone soft with the sheer intensity of his realization, and the gathered blanket slid a corner out of his unresisting hands.

"Just when I think you've reached peak folksy with your damn metaphors." Carex finally got his hands away from her, and promptly almost fell again. "What the hell are we talking about, again?"

"Uninstallation." Pyrus was the one to answer, slow, then getting faster as he probably laid it out in his own mind. "Remove the wings, and then keep drawing off energy so the nanites spend it elsewhere rather than regrowing the wings…if it happened over a long enough period they might start shutting down a few at a time, painlessly. If it happened gradually enough, the change might not be the kind of shock to people's psyches that would drive them to suicide…"

He dropped the blanket and crossed to Carex at the same time Genevieve did. "Do you feel all right emotionally, Carex? No warrior bullshit."

He only laughed, spreading his arms wide. "I'm feeling *great*."

"I think that's a question we'll have to revisit when he's not drunk. But if he is still balanced—as balanced as any of us are—"

The possibilities webbed out in Genevieve's mind like a forking branch of lightning. "He's still got channels, maybe it would even be possible for people to keep some functions, while being able to *age* again."

Carex batted both their hands away when they reached for him, but then his currently impaired thinking seemed to catch up to what had been said a few steps back. "Uninstallation." He speared first her with an intense stare, then Pyrus. "You're not shitting me?"

"We can't be sure until you let us look, but that seems like a reasonable conclusion at the moment," Pyrus said.

"Ha!" Carex shouted it, exultant, to the sky. In that moment, Genevieve felt rather like singing her own exultation, having seen the variegated violence or rage or despair on the face of every retired Install trapped into a life they couldn't escape, sterile, unaging, and never permitted out of the military's control, lest they someday turn on the empire that trapped them there. "I knew you'd find it. I knew you were fucking *hope*."

"I had help—" Genevieve turned to expand the credit to Pyrus at least, since the rest of her research team were far away at the moment, but he shook his head, with a small, delighted smile of his own, and let it be Genevieve Carex caught up in a tight embrace as his laughter walked a line close to sobs.

Funds were a problem. Lingering over post-breakfast coffee, Genevieve studied a tablet—sometimes manipulating data with her fingertips helped her think—split between Carex's charted nanite counts opposite a projection of what they'd need to make from harvesting the farm's timber, if they wanted to be able to offer the process to anyone else. Of course, if they could get the word out far enough, other ex-military Installs might be able to bring along some funds of their own, but that wouldn't be enough alone. And the farm could be quite profitable, but not immediately, especially with the ownership tangle of inheritance to deal with—it should be Genevieve's, but she'd been missing but not declared dead at the time of their parents' deaths, so some things were in her brother's name—and so on. Not impossible to sort out, but annoying as all get out.

Outside the kitchen window, a light drizzle was pissing down, that and tossing tree limbs in the accompanying icy wind providing an overabundance of white noise. At least, that's what she told herself in hindsight. If her unconscious caught the footsteps, it dismissed them just as quickly, as Pyrus and Carex were both around, generally, though they'd set out with the plan of surveying the timber at the far edges of her parents' property earlier. And Genevieve was facing the window, back to the bulk of the house, because she never had been, never would be military, to think that way.

Then footsteps too loud to miss and the next moment, no time for Genevieve to turn, a knife at the front of her neck, a grip heavy with promised violence urging her standing and then settling across her back and digging into her upper arm from behind. "Looks like you've been sleeping soundly for a murdering fronti." Abidjan Lemna's voice.

And Lemna's system trying to lock Genevieve out of Pax Romana communications she wasn't even using anymore. <Need backup! Lemna!> she flung at the men, never so glad for the poor quality of their piggybacked signal on the local network as now when it meant her message did go through. She drew her concentration back to the here and now. "If you're here to execute me for it, why am I not dead?" It made her shake, deep in her core where she locked it away so she wouldn't move her skin into the knife, but Lemna could certainly have shot her in the back of the head, oblivious fool that she was.

<Heard,> crackled back from Carex, so Pyrus must be concentrating on driving fast. She could only hope Pyrus wouldn't wreck the truck.

"You're going to tell me what you *did*, so I can ensure no one does it *ever again*." Lemna kissed the blade in with each emphasis, enough to sting like a bastard, but quick to heal up with the nanites' help. "I will bleed you out a cupful at a time, if that's what it takes."

Genevieve reviewed her environment once, again, mapping out her abandoned chair, the table, but Lemna had the knife close and tight and even swallowing too hard had a sting now. "And then you kill me?"

Lemna's breath came hot against Genevieve's ear and Genevieve had to close her eyes against the intensity of it. "Spy or not, I will break you just as surely. Whatever others you've collected here won't be able to do a thing about it."

The truck's engine roared into her range of hearing, making Genevieve's eyes pop open, but nothing in Lemna's stance indicated that she'd even noticed. A city woman, why would she? Genevieve realized after a moment. "Are you sure about that?"

The front door slammed. Lemna jerked her around, knife scoring a line to her collarbone deep enough to bleed before it closed. Pyrus was first in the hall, gun leveled, Carex slightly behind and out of any line of fire in his empty-handed state. They really should buy him a manual gun, without the need for an Install system to activate it—but with what money? And Genevieve needed to *focus*.

"Let her go," Pyrus said. Genevieve heard the soldier calm in his voice once more.

"No," Lemna said, and Genevieve could feel the stalemate souring around all of them, that much closer to a twitch the wrong direction opening up her neck despite all of their intentions.

No, she decided for herself. No. She slammed the taste of chili sauce, enough to choke on, into Lemna's system. Whatever armoring she might have cobbled together against burnout, the smell used a separate pathway and always had, and Genevieve knew from Lemna's sob she tasted it.

"Don't!" She reeled back from Genevieve, so desperate to sever the touch between them she jerked the knife directly away, drawing it only along the skin rather than biting into it at any depth. At least, that's what Genevieve's system showed her as it healed this latest cut with no trouble. Genevieve bolted for the safety behind Pyrus, only then turned to face Lemna.

She was as Genevieve had seen her last, but for the arrogant power that had turned to haggard desperation. Her hand with the knife was down, tip pointed to the floor, viscous blood drop gathering itself there without the wherewithal to fall yet. Seeing it like that—ridiculous, when she'd been feeling it not so long ago—but seeing the blood drop splatter down—

"Genevieve," Pyrus was saying. "Love, you have to breathe. You're hyperventilating. Let me help." His hand on the back of her neck and her breaths smoothed themselves out despite all her body was trying to do. She'd blanked out, how much time had she lost?

"It's the knife," Carex said, and strode forward with Pyrus still covering him with the gun to wrench the weapon from Lemna's hand. Perhaps Lemna hadn't seen him properly before, because she stared at him now with as much shock as her iron self-control would allow. He had always been the loyal one, of course. "From when you looked away as unalts took her damn wings in service of a fever dream about her being some kind of stone-cold sleeper agent. So you tell me, Lemna. Do you really think she's just that fucking good of a spy that she can fake a panic attack, or do you think maybe that she really is a civilian scientist who fights for her life when cornered? Because if it's the latter, you brought this on yourself."

Just a civilian all but pissing herself again.

Genevieve lost a moment again, but this time it was the sheer humiliation that moved her to Carex's side even as it forced tears to her eyes. She wrenched the knife from him in turn, his hand unresisting with surprise very similar to Lemna's a moment before.

"I am *done* with people shitting on me for being a civilian," she spat at the older woman. "I'll carve out your wings right here, and we'll see how you do. Maybe I'll blunt up the knife first for the real, authentic experience."

Carex caught her when she lunged for Lemna. She almost broke free when he didn't put his full strength into the hold, but once he realized she was in earnest, there was no contest between them. Especially as she wasn't going to cut him and they both knew it. She thrashed against his grip across her body, and Pyrus made some noise in his throat. Not precisely a whimper, but it brought her back to herself. She dropped the knife instantly, fought down nausea and lost the battle with sobs as a side effect.

"Anyone who isn't fucking terrified of what you will do when you decide it's necessary, should be." Carex held Genevieve a moment longer to make sure she wasn't going anywhere, then passed her off for Pyrus to enfold her with his free arm.

She was spoiling his aim somehow, she was sure, but Lemna was quiescent for the moment even so. "You shouldn't have to prop me up all the time," she murmured into Pyrus's shoulder.

Pyrus murmured a wordless negative, while Carex barked a laugh. "He lives to support people as much as humanly possible," he said, mimicking Pyrus's earlier delivery. "The rest of us never gave him much scope for it."

He turned from them, back to Lemna, and clapped his hands for her attention. "Now. Ping my system." He held out one hand, almost an insult in how he stood without concern that she would attack him given the opening. "Touch me, whatever you like. Fair warning, though, if you try to draw blood, I will punch you in the fucking face."

Lemna apparently did ping him, as her face creased with the depth of her frown. She reached careful fingers, touched tips to the cup of his palm. "You—universal mercy, you've been *uninstalled*." She reached out, found the back of Genevieve's former chair, and dragged it close enough to collapse. She ended up perched at an odd angle across the seat. "How? Amsterdam, you have to tell me how you did it."

"Why should I?" Genevieve stepped away from Pyrus, finding her own balance finally, for the first time since Lemna had entered the kitchen. Not threatening, but not frightened. Firm. "That was never your priority, in Science Division, or anywhere in the military hierarchy that I could tell. You gave us a certain level of funding, sure, but no other support. Kept a bunch of inconvenient people out of the way and busy doing something that might be useful someday, I suppose. I'll give it to the Installs themselves, not to you."

Lemna pressed hands to her face, a gesture not of Genevieve's previous knowledge of her, but of this new woman with defeat in her shoulders. "My people—all those we managed to save, when we reinstalled quickly enough—they were ordering them right back to duty. As soon as they could walk, hold a gun. But the mental toll—so many of them still took their own lives, and it was so *preventable*, if we'd had time for proper support, ease them back into it..."

She looked up, face haggard with the rage of loyalty betrayed. Genevieve could recognize that instantly, now. "*My people*. I was instrumental in making them, in saving them, and then those fools were forcing me to kill them all over again."

Genevieve caught her bottom lip in her teeth, released it again when she might have bitten through. "How many Installs are left alive?" How many had been lost?

Pyrus's grounding touch again, this time on her shoulder. "No numbers. You think if you have a count, you'll know when you've fully balanced the debt, but it doesn't work that way. You can't do enough even for one."

"More than there would have been without the warning." Lemna locked eyes with Pyrus for a moment. "That's the reason I was in any state to oversee reinstallation efforts." A pause, rage coming back to the forefront. "Fewer than there would have been without the orders taking them back into action too soon. But if we can uninstall anyone who wants it, they won't have to follow any more such orders. Not safe, precisely, but with a path to safety. And there's no burying what's happened, they're going to have precious few signing up for new installation."

Genevieve wondered if Lemna had decided to be conciliating only because she wanted something. The weight of her guilt could use the lightening, but she couldn't in good conscience allow herself to have it. To have Lemna help spread word of uninstallation, though, that would be a boon, to make her attempts to balance her debt that much more effective.

"So you've decided to join us at 'burn it down'?" Carex murmured, crossing his arms. "Or biding your time, until you can get your chance at avenging the dead by taking out Genevieve?"

"There's an easy solution for that." Lemna stood, holding her hands open at her sides, and unfurled her wings, keeping them low at her shoulders since space was limited with her hemmed in by chair and table. "Do me first."

"Yes," Genevieve said, before Carex could respond. It was her safety she was risking, and she judged that risk worth it. "Before you agree, though, you should know the process literally starts with cutting off your wings." She smiled thinly. "It should separate the sheep from the goats as far as who *really* wants to be uninstalled."

Lemna glanced to Carex, who, after pulling a face at the inconvenience, shrugged out of his jacket and then pulled his shirt over his head. He'd taken to wearing a normal, Idyllian style of each, for obvious reasons. He turned so she could inspect his scars—neat, but present—but pointedly stayed out of touching distance. "Sheep—what does that even mean?" Lemna asked.

"You get used to the folksiness," Carex said, chuckling as he redressed. "In this case, I think we're the ones going to hell."

Lemna tipped up her chin. "All right." She looked around her, seeming to finally see the farmhouse properly. "This planet might not be a bad place for it, pulling people in a few at a time."

"That was the plan." Genevieve grimaced. Lemna would be helpful, but that didn't mean she had to like the woman, or being patronized by her. "Until you proved the Pax Romana can find us even way the hell out here." Where else could they go? She felt exhausted just framing the question.

Lemna gestured dismissively. "They know you're on Idyll—obviously, if you're going to grandstand in front of a bunch of unalts you then send skittering home—but I had to be on-planet before I found the records I needed of land owned by Amsterdams. Keep an eye on off-planet arrivals and you'll be able to anticipate them. If they bother. When the last of their Installs erode out from under them, they'll have bigger problems."

Genevieve closed her eyes briefly to lay that out, poke holes in it. Another risk, but another managed one. "Once we figure out funds, we can have Eriope start laying the breadcrumbs, then."

"Oh, well." Lemna withdrew a local payment card from her hip pocket. "Will that help?" She flicked it to Genevieve, who let her system do the work to snap it out of the air.

She checked the balance with a flick of her fingernail on the back and choked on her next inhalation. "That will help considerably." Like immediately constructing the separate clinic building they'd been discussing as a decade down the road, as well as setting them up for as many people who wanted to come for two years or more. And by then, they should have started harvesting and selling the timber and Installs would be bringing some of their own money.

"I'll go collect my things, then," Lemna said, and swept out, trailing an assumption behind her, that they'd obviously follow and then show her to a room. The three of them exchanged looks, and Pyrus duly followed.

After neatly pushing in all the chairs at the table and dumping out her now-cold coffee, Genevieve found herself with enough of a lull in momentum the guilt seeped back in. <I hadn't considered the danger of others preferring revenge for what I did to them,> she said, looping Pyrus in to the conversation.

<I don't think there's a need to tell them the exact circumstances of the burnout being released. Most won't know.> Carex snorted. <And don't you tell them as some kind of self-flagellation, either.>

<Carex is right.> Pyrus's reply came at a bit of a delay, probably because he was speaking to Lemna at the same time. <The Pax Romana military lovingly built their own pyre, and were careful to hand out a match to each soldier they tossed away after using up. You merely struck yours first.>

<Periodic wildfire keeps a forest healthy,> Carex contributed, which made Genevieve raise her brows at him. That wasn't folksy, but it was hardly urban wisdom either.

<You've been reading my sister's forestry manuals?> He'd set them aside, when they gathered things for storage, but Genevieve had thought he'd been planning to inflict them on her later. She hadn't been looking forward to it, as someone had to manage

the timber, but there had been a reason Genevieve had left it to her sister, before her death.

Carex shrugged, a flicker of embarrassment finding its way across his expression. His tone maintained his standard of assholery, however. <Why do you think I bothered fast-learning Idyllian, to chat up locals at the feed store? It's interesting.>

Genevieve clapped him on the shoulder. <Congratulations, farm manager. I sure as hell don't want to do it, and someone needs to.> She expected some kind of smart remark in reply, but he just gave her a shit-eating grin, like he knew he'd got her trained so he achieved the same result without the work of actually thinking up the remark. She turned her touch into a solid punch to his shoulder, and went to go see about updating her brother on all of this.

EPILOGUE

When the evening sunlight stretched long, Genevieve found herself back at her parents' house, even though the chatter and chaos contained within the new clinic and dorm building wasn't at its highest level. They'd found things went easier if they loosely organized incoming Installs into cohorts to begin the process, and right now they were between two of them. Eriope had asked to join the next cohort, though her nerve might fail her again.

It was all right if it did, of course. They'd had several Installs decide that the drawbacks didn't outweigh the benefits of their systems yet. Genevieve and her new team—founded on the core of the old one—had found they could preserve coms, running on bio power, without too much trouble, but most other aspects had to go, if the Install was to begin aging normally. For the retired soldiers, the ones who'd lived with their systems for too long, that was what they longed for: an entry point into a new life wherein they were not out of step with all those around them. A new life that could end.

It was easy for Genevieve to extend an understanding of why they might not be ready to others, hard to extend it to herself, to fight the persistent tendrils of guilt curling through her belly over still having her wings. She was facing wrong way to charge now as she stood at the scratched and sagging porch rail, but she lofted her wings open anyway, feeling the stretch of them. Fully grown by now. It helped to have her conception of her body form such a mismatch to when she'd stood here as a child when her family was all alive, when no one on her planet had fallen in the war.

It cut her ghosts down to something manageable.

Pyrus approached, his system brushing across hers for no data in particular in a gesture that had become deeply intimate between them, as sexual as a caress across the small of her back. She half-folded her wings in invitation, and he pressed there against her back, where she could stretch back and "feel" his shoulders and arm with the wing's ribs and tips. In a moment, yes, she'd follow that up, but she also needed to lighten the load of her thoughts a little first.

"Am I a hypocrite for not uninstalling yet?" she asked the orderly rows of shadows and trunks in the trees beyond the lawn. She'd made her decision for the foreseeable future, but it would take a little more work to be easy in it.

"You'll uninstall when you're ready. We both will." Pyrus bent a little to press kisses to the back of her neck. "Having a fully operational system sure as hell helps monitor people's nanite counts. So you could say you're keeping the nanites in service of the others we're uninstalling. Or you could keep them halfway to forever because you want to, because universal mercy, love, you're *allowed*. Everyone's allowed to keep their nanites until *they* feel ready to let them go and move on to what comes next."

"Thanks," Genevieve murmured, and imagined lifting that worry up on a spread palm for the wind to catch up and dance away with. That was the beauty of this land, far from the city. "Come to cause me trouble, have you, Praetor?"

Pyrus settled his hands on her hips. She felt him watching through her system's data as the flush started low and spread through her body, which only made it more delicious. "Praetor's the one they protect. I think you'll find the term you're looking for is Praetorian guard."

"Oh, I'm sorry." Genevieve made her voice sweet. "Did I say praetor? I meant pedant."

"Keep giving me lip, slave girl, and you'll get what's coming to you." Pyrus jerked her hips around so she faced him, barely giving her time to sort her wings out so they weren't smashed against the railing. The way he growled it, she could barely keep herself from arching, grinding into him immediately. But she wanted to draw the game out, enjoy it properly.

"Do you promise?" She laughed into the skin at the side of his neck, before nipping.

"Is this a private game, or can someone else join tonight?" Carex ambled up with his hands in his pockets. "Eriope says sometimes you invite guests." Genevieve muddled through two reactions, first automatically hiding against Pyrus's chest, then rolling back a little, chin high, repudiating the social convention of embarrassment since once more Carex was the one doing the interrupting. Only then did his actual words penetrate.

She checked Pyrus's face. No, he hadn't expected this, but neither did he look annoyed. Beyond that, she couldn't tell, and didn't want to make a wrong guess. "Just tonight?" she asked, more a stalling tactic while she pulled her thoughts together than anything. His phrasing already made it clear enough that this was about sex, not anything more serious. Her attraction aside, at Tsuga he'd been so damn discreet—though it was always a safe guess to assume anyone with biological drives and an attraction to her gender might go to Eriope to help get those drives met—she'd never even considered his own attraction in turn.

"Just tonight, unless we like it enough to do it again." Carex made it to the porch, halted on the creaking boards some distance from them. His stance held a diffidence she'd rarely seen in him, but she'd been learning not to assume such things didn't exist, somewhere deep below the surface. "As in, not a relationship. I don't think I'm built for such things—I *like* being on my own—but that doesn't mean I don't like a chance to play now and then."

"Being single means you can be an ass unopposed," Pyrus contributed. Carex clicked his tongue and made a "you got it" gesture to him.

Genevieve checked Pyrus's face again. This time he smiled, lopsidedly, and shrugged. "Up to you. I have no objections to sharing if you'd enjoy it." He shifted, pressing more directly against her thigh so she could feel that he emphatically had none.

Well. Their particular game could certainly accommodate three as well as two, which made the heat between Genevieve's legs shiver up to a new pitch, but there was one thing she still wanted to be sure of. She disentangled herself reluctantly from Pyrus to stand before Carex. "You're not interested *despite* me, are you? If it's Pyrus you want, and since we're mostly exclusive, I'm the price you have to pay..."

"Genevieve." There was a half-incredulous chuckle to Carex's voice. "I like women. Pyrus knows, you can ask him."

She didn't need to, however, when she thought back properly to just what he'd said: share, if she'd enjoy it. He knew. And clearly didn't mind being the despite.

What that meant for her made her blush, and Carex gently cupped her cheek and brushed his thumb along the line of heat. "Sure," she said. "Come play tonight."

FAIR EXCHANGE

PART I

After Prague Sienna's captors dumped her, bound by paralyzers, in a patch of shade with her back propped against a broken wall, she struggled foggily to link disconnected facts into a linear series of events. They'd pulled her out of the general population at the POW camp—because of her illicit portraits, drawn with homemade charcoal on spare patches of wall?—no, Libertad Sans Frontiers liked art, or at least grand propaganda murals.

The implant. They'd pulled her out of general population, put someone else's implant in her head, and now she was here. Where was here? Somewhere dusty, with punishing sun casting the jagged shadows beyond her feet. *The next nearest structure is 50 meters away.* The implant presented her with a three-dimensional model of the abandoned, crumbling buildings surrounding her, apparently gathered from her senses despite the fact she'd been barely conscious as she was carried out here. Already, the creepy thing was encroaching on her mind; Sienna couldn't fight the feeling that soon it would be eating away at her self.

A distant rumble marked a shuttle taking off. So LSF was abandoning her here? Why? If they wanted her dead, they could have shot her outside the POW camp; if they wanted to drop the implant for someone, they could have left it in a box instead of *her head.*

At least that head was clearing, despite continued intrusions from the implant they'd stolen from the dead body of—*Agent Lima Isachne*—wasn't there a way for Sienna to turn it off, or at least slow the flow of information? Apparently not.

Maybe she needed to think of this as an opportunity. To escape. They'd dressed her in a Pax Romana army jacket—universal mercy, she hoped that hadn't belonged to the dead woman too—with the hood up and a built-in filtering mask pulled up to the bridge of her nose. That and the climate control in the jacket protected her from the worst of the heat and dust, at least. The main paralyzer was at the small of her back, supplemented by one across her wrists, and one at her throat. Because of course there was one on her throat—LSF liked quiet prisoners.

She prodded at the implant, trying to reach her original com implant beneath it, jury-rig some kind of outgoing distress signal, detect nearby signals, *anything*. But her connection remained stubbornly one-way, and the implant had apparently imparted all the wisdom it was going to at the moment. Fine, then.

Sienna tried to shove herself along the wall using her elbow and succeeded only in tipping herself over. She considered her next move for a few breaths, and felt and heard another shuttle-like rumble. <Approaching the coordinates. Lima?> The voice seemed to come out of nowhere, making her flinch. Nearly a year she'd been in the camp, with her com implant blocked, and she hadn't realized how accustomed to that silence she'd become. But of course the voice was coming through the new implant.

Sent on a general Pax Romana military channel, the implant told her. Useful information for once. They must have noticed LSF touching down and come to investigate what their enemies were up to. Lucky for her! The Pax Romana generally honored their treaty with Idyll, so if she could convince them to release her to the Idyllian consulate, she could get *home*. She tried to reply to them and nothing happened.

<We've got her. Implant pings, but she's unresponsive. Must be unconscious.> Two soldiers in Pax Romana uniforms, with jackets like her own, approached, one male and one female, though it was impossible to see much else with their own filtering masks up. It was the woman speaking on the channel, though she must be doing so through an earpiece, as Sienna could hear the words vaguely doubled, muffled through the mask.

You actually going to look at her for that response, dumbasses? the implant...said? Sienna realized she'd internalized the implant's "voice" as female all along, but this had the color of personality brushed onto that voice. Universal mercy, was Isachne actually in her head, stored on the implant somehow? But after the caustic comment, the implant receded from her conscious thoughts again, and sense shouldered back in. A full person wouldn't *fit* on an implant. This must be...scraps, somehow.

And all that had distracted her, so the male soldier had a hand on Sienna's shoulder, pushing her up straight, when she whistled, as loud as she could behind the mask. She couldn't use the code the prisoners had worked out to use when the guards left their throat paralyzers activated for days at a time, as punishment, but at least she could get the soldiers' attention. Looking for a throat paralyzer should be an obvious conclusion at that point, right? The implant gave Sienna the soldiers' names, which she forgot immediately.

<Oh, she's awake. Implant must have been damaged. Looks like LSF actually kept their side of the bargain. Let the squadron know they can let LSF leave with their own prisoners.> The male soldier looked away, cutting off her attempt to convey the request to remove the throat paralyzer through intensity of eye contact instead.

Sienna mapped the implications of his words in desperate, frustrated silence as the female soldier leaned her forward to get access to the paralyzer on her back, touch clinical rather than kind. A prisoner exchange. The Pax Romana thought they were getting their agent back. She jerked, earning only a firmer hand on her back, pressing her down. There would undoubtedly be hell to pay once they found out, but if she couldn't explain—

The man made a thoughtful noise. <No, she's right. You can't just yank a paralyzer off. We'll carry her and let the medic take care of it on the ship.>

So. Trapped, *still*, by silence. Sienna wanted to scream, wanted to scream and not stop until her throat bled. But at least the soldiers were moving her in the direction of that silence ending, so she limply allowed herself to be carried off between them. She was an Idyllian civilian, held by LSF under false pretenses, so surely under the treaty they'd have to at least treat her humanely while they contacted her government. They'd have to let her talk.

The shuttle ride was short and smooth enough, curled on the floor with the female soldier crouched beside her, steadying hand on her shoulder. The implant remarked on the shuttle specs, then those of the ship as the soldiers carried her out, setting her down on her side on plastic shock matting at the side of the bay, which was at least better than bare metal plates.

The man shoved back her hood back and smoothed the mask down to below the local paralyzer on her throat, leaving it exposed for the medic's access. The stink of hair dye, washed out but not cleaned since, filled Sienna's next breath, and by craning her neck, she got a tendril to slide down her shoulder into her range of view. Shimmering, unnatural black instead of the dull brown it should have been. They must have done it while she was still unconscious after the implant installation.

"That's not her!" Boots filled Sienna's vision first, then the new woman crouched at the same time Sienna got herself up on one elbow. "That's not my wife!" This time, when Sienna sought eye contact to try to convey apology, convey that if only they would remove the paralyzer, she'd explain, intensity scorched her from the other side instead. Pure, unadulterated rage.

Manila Gentiana, the implant informed her.

Gentiana ducked her head over her wine glass, for a moment her fine, sharp features making her look like an ancient statue of a saint, but then she looked up to reveal a flash of delightful humor. "You speak six languages, don't you? So I should be able to call you a cunning—"

Then the memory was gone, leaving Sienna gasping. Time had jumped, a new man was before her instead of Gentiana, but Sienna could hear the rise and fall of the anger she'd seen, poured forth into ranting beyond the range of her vision. The new man was presumably the medic, but not a particularly experienced member of the profession, as his touch on the throat paralyzer was slow. "There, it's turned off," he said.

"I'm Idyllian! Prague Sienna. Student visa Prague-one-six-two." Dust and disuse put cracks in her voice, but Sienna forged desperately on. She could tell she wouldn't have much time. "I was taken with others from a civilian transport LSF claimed harbored undercover agents, so they sent us to the POW camp. If you let me contact the nearest Idyllian consulate—"

"As if LSF would have let an Idyllian live." Gentiana's boots came into range again, and she wrenched Sienna's shoulder so Sienna was facing up, into the heat of her rage. "Tell a better lie, you fucking fox." Fox, a mispronunciation of faux-French, as false as everything French about Libertad Sans Frontiers after the dead language had been "updated" based on, irony of ironies, Lingua, the language of the Pax Romana and their greatest enemy.

"I pretended to be Pax Romana." Shouldn't that be understandable? Idyll was neutral, siding with neither the aging empire nor the violent rebels—much less scrappy and sympathetic now they controlled just as many systems—but the Pax Romana ignored Idyll and generally kept to their treaty when it was convenient.

LSF, on the other hand, *hated* Idyll for declining to share the internal-technology advances that kept them well defended from both sides of the conflict. "But now I'm here, the treaty—"

But her time for speech had run out. Gentiana's toe slammed into Sienna's gut. Sienna curled around it, enduring until her breath came back. "You think you can come in as an LSF plant, fool us with some phony implant—" Someone drew breath to speak, no more, but that seemed to be all the push off the cliff Gentiana needed to draw the conclusion on her own. "Is it her implant? Is she dead?" Her voice rose to a scream. "*Is Isachne dead*?"

Gentiana crouched, caught at the collar of the jacket LSF had shrouded Sienna in, and shook as if some other truth could break free. Something in the movement jostled the paralyzer into engaging, and Sienna could only gurgle.

Not that she could have offered any answer that would have helped.

Punches now, falling into her face and jaw, and ragged bits of phrases. "—killed her! Killed her!"

"This is it, I'm afraid. My last message, recorded in the clear. Gentiana, I love you. I'm sorry I couldn't make it back to you. We thought LSF understood that the implant ensures I can't be broken. But they're determined to try—"

The pain, it couldn't have been meant to be part of the message, Sienna didn't know if it was hers or Isachne's, or maybe Sienna was dying now herself. She thought there were voices—"Manila, she's a prisoner, you can't treat her like that." "We won't sink to their level—" But there was also the implant—*Broken nose. Zygomatic fracture. Extensive bruising throughout—*

Maintaining vitals as if still unconscious, the implant informed Sienna as she rose through what would normally have been heart-pounding disorientation. With that artificially muted, she felt hazy and sticky instead as she assembled her situation. She was in an internal-technology treatment position, half on her side, half on her stomach, right arm and right leg bent to prop her there. A cautious slit of her eyes revealed the molded plastic edge of a diagnostic couch, but voices made her close them again.

"There was nothing bad enough for a gel bed, but I gave her a dose of healing nanites for the surface injuries and dehydration. Those have finished and flushed." A man's voice, and a gentle touch at the back of her neck, the implant installation site. "But I can tell you right now, any surgery to attempt to remove the implant would kill her. As far as I can tell, they kept the original owner in a vegetative state to briefly fool the implant into not self-destructing, then slammed it into this woman. Since it thought it was still in a living host, the implant attempted repair and seems to have taken over an Idyllian communications implant in the process. It has recreated perhaps forty percent of its connections, but that's more than enough to kill her if we try to sever them."

"You're certain?" A woman's voice. Sienna couldn't tell if the tone was faintly chilling or if the content was what made it sound that way. "Wouldn't it be better to get in there and see what the physical connections actually are? This has never happened before, has it?"

"No, because it never should have implanted again in the first place! I can only guess that the fact she didn't die has something to do with the Idyllian int-tech." The touch on her neck withdrew, and Sienna realized she hadn't felt even the residual soreness she'd had from the LSF installation. They'd used top-quality healing nanites on her, at least. She recognized the high-gravity weight of the exhaustion they'd left in their wake. "I'm sorry, Commander Constantinople, surgery is impossible. It would be lethal."

The woman—*Constantinople Elantine*, said the implant, but offered no memories—gave a bark of laughter. Once more, was it unkind, or was Sienna unkindly disposed against this stranger and her insistence on cutting her open? "Just our luck, a regular Amsterdam Genevieve." Which must be the only Idyllian, a century dead as she was, most Pax Romana had heard of. One of Idyll's heroes, one of the Pax Romana's traitors. "I'll capture her vitals and such for my report—if she wakes, I'll call you," she said. The man made no protest against that dismissal, and his footsteps receded.

In the ensuing silence, Elantine sighed, moved off a little. Sienna wasn't entirely sure what instinct had kept her quiet and listening as they spoke over her, but she knew it was still driving her, holding her to stillness. Like it or not, however, any application for asylum would undoubtedly have to go through the highest-ranking person around, and that would likely be the commander. Sienna should "awaken" and present her case—

"Why the fuck couldn't they have set a timed trigger so you died in transport?" Elantine muttered.

In LSF French.

Then there was a hand on her shoulder, fingers digging deep, and a soft mass of a pillow against her face. *Still*, the implant said, in the "voice" of Isachne. *Still, still. Save my breath, surprise her with it.* Sienna's instincts slammed against implant control, and the last of her held breath gave her a stretching moment of clarity—the implant was designed for such a situation, her instincts were not. If she was not to die, thrashing uselessly against superior strength and leverage, she needed to listen.

And then that stretching moment snapped, and she had only rising terror in her chest, battering her to death against iron motionlessness. *She needs to roll me, to ensure the seal.* "Me," Sienna noted in the implant's words, with a pointlessness born of hysteria. Not "you" or even "us." Elantine did shift her position then, jerking Sienna to her back, pillow still tight to her face.

But not as tight.

The implant rolled Sienna with the motion, kept her going, wrenching out from under Elantine's grip. Her eyes spasmed open as she gasped in air and rolled right off the side of the couch. Not so far to fall, but far enough to slam spikes of pain up through her knees and heels of her hands, driving the breath right back out again. The implant jerked at muscles that, even with all the will in the world, couldn't respond with the speed and force it demanded. She sprawled, losing height down to her forearms along the floor, and the connection with the implant snapped.

But Sienna had her own instincts for this, thanks, and she gave them free reign. Scramble up, run. Run for all she was worth. Elantine was bare steps behind, cursing, and Sienna had no time to see where she was going, only that it was toward a door, and then through a hallway. The floor was covered with—wood?—of all things. Perhaps it was a texture on the polymer. It grayed out in Sienna's vision with each beat of her overstressed heart and slam of her feet. After the healing, she had so little left, she'd literally fall over the next breath, she was sure of it, but she kept running anyway, falling into each step and somehow continuing to move forward.

The implant showed her—some kind of a map—she had no time to read it, and it wasn't guiding her feet, but Sienna aimed herself at a side path that seemed to lead somewhere convoluted. A door stopped her, adding more bruises to her forearms as she smashed into it, and she wanted to lean and pant and she couldn't afford that. It opened out from under her, the implant transmitting an access code, and she was in an area of stark shadows, one emergency light bar very far down the hall.

Yes. Good. Somewhere to lose herself. The door slid closed behind her, chirped acknowledgment of another code. The slam that followed, half a second later, startled Sienna enough she stumbled forward, in lieu of any other reaction when her heart was already laboring at far past the redline. All right. Forward. Moving. Losing herself.

A hand on the wall kept Sienna upright, but she wasn't seeing very well in the darkness—no, she was seeing perfectly, in the grayscale of enhanced light—and then that was gone again, fuzzing out so she wasn't sure if it had been the implant or her own imagination. Her hand bumped into a line that matched an access panel on the map, and Sienna leaned her forehead against the wall for a while. She couldn't hear pursuit or any effort to smash through the door the hard way, but that probably only meant it was a silent code battle of the commander's access codes against those of an intelligence agent.

Open, she thought at the implant. Open, open, open.

Nothing. Sienna slapped a palm against the panel, the pure incandescent frustration of a universe currently without mercy lending her a last burst of strength. She hadn't died in the camp, she hadn't died under the knife when the implant was installed—which she apparently should have—and she was not going to die because a panel wouldn't open!

She promptly fell through the open space, one more strike on the heels of her hands, with a bonus jab of the lip into her stomach. Climbing in was beyond her, but she managed a messy maneuver that involved tipping in, shifting most of her weight to one hip, and drawing in her legs. She heard a hiss as the panel eased back into place.

Gray beat in and out across her vision and Sienna lost track of where she was between breaths as well. She was lying—lying on metal—enclosed, pipes and cables surrounding her—was she dying? What did dying feel like?

"We thought LSF understood that the implant ensures I can't be broken. But they're determined to try. I think this is where I should say I regret marrying you, Gentiana, tying you to someone who apparently is dying just as young as my parents always said I would, but I can't regret that. I hope you can forgive me—"

Pain was layered with and laced through the memory, mixing once more with Sienna's own pain while centuries passed. Eventually, however, she didn't die, and some little of her exhaustion abated, enough for her to draw her mind back to herself, fence it round with her name. She was Sienna, not Isachne, not Pax Romana. She didn't have a wife.

Low-light vision came back for her, starkly grayscale in the ambient LEDs of the technological guts of the building around her. She used it to sketch with a fingertip on the patch of walkway beside her. A memory of home, just the shape of the roof of her childhood house against the mountain at the horizon.

The polymer coating of the walkway resisted the oils from her finger the same as it did any other grime, but she could see the shapes in her mind's eye anyway. Her breathing evened and her heart finally followed. How many times could she relive dying before she died herself? "Help," she whispered, to the universe, perhaps. At least she wouldn't die in silence. The word came out in Lingua, rather than Idyllian, because she'd pretended to be Pax Romana for so long, she supposed. Or maybe it was another sign of the implant dragging her down, away from her own identity.

"Hello, I am Penstemon, the Near-AI in charge of this facility. Was that request directed at me?" A pleasant female voice, at a conversational volume that nevertheless filled the enclosed space.

Sienna's surprise smashed her back into a pipe, and the wash of fresh adrenaline over stale made her head swim. "Request you disclose my location to no one," she said. "And don't disclose that these access codes have been active. Or allow anyone to change my access level. Authorization—" And the implant sent Isachne's codes, wonder of wonders, almost like it was actually responding to her.

"Authorization accepted."

There had been a Near-AI in charge of the dorms at the Pax Romana university Sienna had been attending, but she'd never done much more with it than check class schedules. Near-AI were very good within their specific range of requests, but conveying anything out of the ordinary was a slog. If she could make it through the slog, there was an opportunity here, though. "I need somewhere safe. To hide."

"All of my facility is safe. Atmosphere and temperature are within tolerances, and there are no extreme weather events affecting the environment outside—" Penstemon burbled on for a while longer and Sienna stopped listening as her foolishness hit her with the force of another blow. Penstemon was using external speakers—what if Elantine heard her or the Near-AI from out in the hall?

"Quiet," Sienna hissed, and Penstemon complied. No sounds in the hallway that she could hear, amid the rising hiss over-enhanced background noise. She let the enhancement ebb. All right. Safe for now, but undoubtedly not much longer. She needed to use one of her implant's internal channels and convince the Near-AI to—

"Honestly, it's hardly worth the trouble to hack a Near-AI, they're kept so dumb exactly for that reason, so to not allow too much control—"

She'd said that to—No! Sienna hadn't done any such thing, that had been Isachne. She was Sienna. Prague Sienna. She'd been born—been born—

She needed to get Isachne *out of her head*. <Penstemon?> She wasn't entirely sure what channel she'd sent that on, but it had seemed sent, at least.

<How may I assist you?>

Sienna slumped her shoulder a little more inward into her curl in relief. Then she pressed her hand flat to the walkway where her roofline and mountain had been, pushing herself straighter for the principle of the thing. <I need your assistance in deleting files from my internal system.>

Or did she want to delete them? Concern flickered automatically at the thought of deleting something that might be immensely valuable, and that thought linked onward to a belated realization.

LSF clearly hadn't intended her to survive this long, only long enough to regain their own prisoners. But not intending her survival and attempting to ensure her death were two different things. The only difference Sienna could think of was the fact that she had access to Isachne's intelligence. Somewhere on the implant was something LSF and their sleeper agent were willing to kill for.

And perhaps that intelligence was leverage she'd be able to use. Sienna certainly didn't have much else available to her. <No, disregard the previous request, please remove and securely store the files I'm about to delineate for you.> She couldn't keep them in her head safely, but that didn't mean she had to delete them. Given enough time, she had no doubt her opponents would be able to locate the files, but they had to know to look in the first place. And at the moment she was more worried about them finding her person while she was in the midst of reliving an alien memory.

A deep breath, and she summoned Gentiana's face to her mind, what she'd glimpsed of it. Memories rose from the implant, but she shoved them away, out, and they lifted from her, in linked skeins. <These files are highly interconnected. Does that need to be preserved? If so, I will need to use part of my core storage space for that task,> Penstemon told her.

Sienna answered positively and then let herself slip away for a while. Penstemon said something about how long the transfer would take, given the lack of a wired connection, but it made little difference to her. If she was found here, in this hiding place, because she had not moved on quickly enough, perhaps that would be a relief. An ending.

Instead of discovery, at the end of the files came a last paroxysm of pain. Like a fishhook in her skin, she couldn't release Isachne's last message without experiencing it one last time, and to force herself to that was beyond what she had left. She shoved the message and memory down instead, stuffed it too tight to link to any of her thoughts, and stepped cautiously back to consciousness, curled around exhaustion that at least belonged to her alone.

The flat, unyielding plane of the floor made itself known then, aches slowly welling up from points at hip and shoulder. Sienna made it to hands and knees, and found the implant's ever-helpful map superimposed on the enhanced brightness before her in the narrow crawlspace. That hadn't been part of the memories, then. Sienna supposed the implant's package of "get your stupid ass out of danger" wouldn't be, and it had linked to Penstemon's local data to furnish her with this new spur to continued movement toward saving herself.

She followed its guidance to a room buried deep within this section of the facility, which was sealed for some reason not notated on the map and Sienna didn't honestly care at the moment. Climbing out of the access panel within the room, facing inward and dragging her stomach over the lip centimeter by painful centimeter until her feet touched the floor was all she was prepared to think about. Her enhanced vision showed her a bare mattress on a bed, awaiting sheet and blanket along with the rest of some future occupant's accoutrements should this section ever come into use again.

She collapsed on the bed; that was ending enough for now.

Cold woke Sienna, though her own stink hit her so powerfully on her first conscious breath that it seemed very much like the cause instead. Sweat, dye, dust—she felt it all as a physical film squirming over her skin. She groaned and turned over, but that removed her from the pocket of warmth she'd built up on the mattress and started shivers down her legs. The army jacket had insulated her core, but her feet were ice. This wasn't ship cold, but planet cold was plenty cold enough to keep her from sleep.

She sat up, shucked off her boots, wrapped the sides of the jacket around as much of her knees as she could encompass, and turtled her head down under the hood. Examined in the light of day, the room was of good quality. Without cleaning systems operational, dust had drifted away from most anti-dirt-coated surfaces to the floor, where it could drift no further—she could see her prints standing clear. On the wood, as she apparently hadn't imagined from before. Strange luxury, for a Pax Romana facility.

Or maybe not so strange, for somewhere clearly far from the core. It dawned on Sienna that she was seeing things in the literal light of day, through a window that took up much of the space where a headboard might have been. Outside, beyond a speckling of wind-driven rain droplets, was dense, temperate rainforest. That explained the wood, but raised another question: why was this facility the only human-made feature she could see? The vegetation was dense, but not that dense—unlike the close, even ranks of timber farms she'd visited at home, these trees were gnarled, leaning, and fallen, opening gaps for bushier species, and something like a line of sight over the understory.

"Penstemon, please verify no one has found my location or locked out my codes, then tell me about the planet we're on."

Sienna's throat felt as if it stuck to itself, trying to form the words, and she pushed to her feet instead of waiting for the answer. Personal quarters must have a bathroom. Would the water still be running?

"Oh, the sleeping beauty awakes," Isachne's voice said. "Don't worry, they're still running a search through sensors before they put boots on the ground in this section of the facility."

Sienna caught herself on the bathroom doorframe, clenched her fingertips into the metal as if its hardness would differentiate dreaming from waking. She was awake right now, wasn't she? Simply by virtue of asking the question? Unless she was hallucinating. "Penstemon? Did you just speak to me?"

"Yes, I'm speaking to you at the moment. We'll see if that changes, I might decide to spend some more time watching my wife *sob her eyes out*." The acid of the Near-AI's tone etched holes into Sienna's thoughts. She didn't—that didn't make sense, no Near-AI acted like that—

Unless maybe it wasn't so near anymore. With memories placed in Penstemon's core storage…

And this whole situation had somewhere become *absurd*, and she refused to defend herself to a fellow victim of LSF. "I had nothing to do with your—with Isachne's death." Sienna swallowed painfully, and made it the last few stumbling steps to the faucet. It did produce water when she turned it on, and she drank straight from it until her stomach hurt.

And universal mercy, the shower cubicle. The temperature controls were as unresponsive as all the other powered aspects of the room, but Sienna would take even cold water. She didn't immerse herself, but scrubbing at the worst spots on body and clothes both made all the difference. She felt human; she felt almost optimistic. She was free, at least within the facility, and if she could find a ship, she could actually escape, unlike back at the camp. And maybe the implant could even aid her with that.

"Penstemon? Would you tell me about the planet?" The Near-AI's programming had to be somewhere underneath Isachne's scraps of personality.

Sure enough, after a muttered curse, Penstemon's tone smoothed out. "The planet of Penstemon was originally terraformed to allow long-term settlement after resource extraction, but the weather proved a deterrent. The clinic complex that takes its name from the planet,"—and had given its name to what had once been the complex's Near-AI—"was built at the site of the one spaceport as a rehab facility, behind the main front of the Pax Romana–LSF conflict, but when the front moved too far beyond, the unneeded portions of the complex were shuttered."

That was where she was currently hiding, then, the shuttered section. "The one spaceport" didn't sound promising, however. "What spacecraft are available to the facility?"

"None. There are only a couple suborbital runabouts." Isachne's personality oozed back in. "You can visit whatever patch of dripping trees on the habitable continent strikes your fancy, but I don't see why you'd want to. There aren't any buildings left, outside of this complex. The only craft that touches down consistently is the monthly supply ship, and good luck sneaking onto that."

For that, perhaps the implant pillaging its way through her head could earn its keep once more. It certainly seemed like the sort of thing an agent would need to accomplish in the course of her normal duties. Of course, Sienna would have to ensure it would respond to her consistently before then, however. "When's the next one?"

"Just over three weeks."

If connections were at 40%, would they grow the rest of the way given time? Or did she need to direct—hunger clawed at her guts with a pain so physical Sienna folded over, arms pressed in. Either way, int-tech needed energy and energy needed food, and it had been far too long since she'd had any of that.

Well, that was a goal Sienna felt she could presently encompass. Sneak out, find food, sneak back. Grow connections. Escape. A lot better than simple endurance in the camp.

At least she could tell herself that.

Somewhere, tucked into individual rooms, must be snacks, but Sienna could find no other option besides the mess and attached kitchen in her study of the map her implant had downloaded and her questioning of Penstemon. She timed her strike for the dead time after dinner, when everyone should be settling in to enjoy their entertainment or the privacy of their own room or both. She hoped. Her implant didn't tag anyone in her vicinity when she peeked out of the door to the sealed section nearest the mess. That matched what she could see with her own eyes as she slipped quickly along the wall. Cameras would be active out here, and while she'd told Penstemon not to share the feed with anyone, perhaps Elantine might manage to revoke her access, or perhaps Penstemon's new, borrowed personality might prompt her to be more than a verbal asshole.

She felt weak enough to keep one hand on the wall, but the mess wasn't far. And no one was there, just as the implant had promised. Empty of people, but not empty of food—Sienna could see a couple dishes in a plexi-fronted cooler, leftovers from the last meal placed for late-night snacking. Sienna turned her balancing hand to hold on to the doorway, relief piling briefly atop her weakness to still her for a moment.

She'd meant to load up her arms to take back to safety, but with the portions divided by dish, she could only reasonably carry two or perhaps three without dangerously interfering with her ability to avoid encounters on her way back. She seized a small bowl piled with mixed vegetables, a splash of sauce staining their tops, and tipped it into her mouth. The camp taught you that the majority of chewing was optional, and she'd swallowed one bite, two, when her implant flashed an urgent warning she didn't understand.

She lowered the bowl as she tried to puzzle it out. Someone was coming? No, the immediate vicinity was still clear, on the implant's map and to her normal senses as she strained to hear footsteps in the hall. She hadn't been able to talk to the implant sufficiently to request warnings on anything, so this must be something built into the system already.

With a moment of straining concentration, Sienna got it to give her text. *Suspect substance ingested—*

Sienna dropped the bowl, spattering her worn camp boots with a couple vegetable chunks, poisonously bright green and orange against the weathered brown. Drugged. In the sauce, of course, not the vegetables. Her head swooped, and that must be the fear, not the drug, because she'd only had two bites. Sienna coughed, tried to retch—could the implant make her do that?—but if she was going to collapse, it needed to be back in the sealed section. If she processed more of the drug before then, she'd have to deal with the consequences.

Two bites must have been enough. The whole hallway was fuzzing out. Sienna needed her hand on the wall to keep her going straight, keep her going at all and not folding up and lying down. Just for a moment. She couldn't think, and if she could just catch her breath, pause for a moment to let the world settle to something stable once more, she'd be all right.

But she couldn't pause. One step more. One more. There was her door to the sealed section. Inside, that wasn't safety yet, but Sienna was down on her hands and knees and couldn't remember when she'd gotten there.

Was she dying? Or if she passed out and Elantine found her, wasn't that the same thing?

Now she was on her side, cheek on the wood this time. So *stupid* and *weak*, over and over, ending with her curled up on the ground.

If this did end with her death, there was one last thing she could do. She couldn't offer closure to her own family, but she could offer it to that of another, in hopes of some sort of balancing of universal mercy. "Penstemon…one last file. For…Gentiana." Hard to focus, but as always the message was quick to shove to the surface of her mind.

"This is it, I'm afraid. My last…"

Sienna's next thought was clearer, as if one breath later, or perhaps hours. Not dead, then, just sedated. Perhaps Elantine had been unable to ensure no one else ate the food. Time once more to worry about being found, then. Sienna made it to her feet and then stood still with all her weight pressed palm-flat to the wall for a few moments. She didn't remember hearing the end of Isachne's message, and the file still lurked in the implant. "Penstemon, did you get it?"

"The commander will be here before long, I think she was waiting for everyone else to go to bed." Penstemon's voice lacked both the hollow pleasantness and sharpened anger Sienna had heard in it previously. And she'd failed to answer a direct question, which shouldn't have been possible. Sienna had neither time nor caring to think about such impossibilities, however.

Her first step swirled nausea through her stomach. She closed her eyes and stilled to try to hold it down. She had no *time* for this. "She's never going to stop looking for me. Are you sure there's no other buildings on this planet? I guess food would still be a problem…"

"Follow the guide," Penstemon said, and a firefly light pulsed into being in the middle of her implant-augmented vision.

"Where?" A step, a pause for her stomach to settle, another step and pause. Not so bad. She'd be out of Elantine's reach in a century or so. What were the no-longer-Near-AI's motives in all of this? Assuming one granted her motives, which she shouldn't have. Was she guiding Sienna toward the commander? Why warn her about the commander's approach if so?

"To an outside door. If I can record you that far, I can spoof you staggering out of my range into the trees and erase you from my sensors going forward. She'll leave to die out there, and you can live on as a void ghost in here. But you don't have much time." Penstemon's voice thinned.

"All right." Sienna aligned her next step with the firefly. What did she have to lose, by trusting the human ghost of a former agent merged with a Pax Romana computer?

Nothing she could think of in her current state.

Waking to a room with power—Penstemon had assured Sienna the drain wasn't being recorded on her sensors either—seemed the height of luxury when Sienna swam up through the dregs of sedation for a final time. She was *warm*, and the jacket's hood had provided something of a pillow, which her neck muscles appreciated. There was still her hunger-cramping stomach to ignore, but she put every item on her person through the cleaner except the jacket, as her implant flashed a warning against such an action when she attempted it. Then she took a long, long shower. Even the soap provided in the shower cubicle, though still institutional, was better than the stuff at the camp.

The water puddled around her feet had been a little gray from escaping dye, but when she examined herself in the mirror, the black shade around her face and shoulders still came as a slap. No scars to be seen from Gentiana's beating. Beyond the hair she looked, as well as felt, more like herself, though she'd lost her standard of comparison from before the camp.

Back in the main room, pulling standard-issue clothes back on and then settling the jacket on top, she found the room much more soulless when lit. At least it also boasted a window. The trees outside seemed to have been cut back to create a swath of grass for walking, what she could see of them in the uncertain yellow light of what must be dawn.

Sienna drank water until the hunger wasn't quite so painful, and settled herself on the bed to bend her precious energy to thinking. Planning. There were unanswered questions sitting heavy across her shoulders. "Penstemon. You…helped me? Of your own will?"

"Call me Pen," the computer said in her new voice, the one that had some trick of inflection that Sienna was perhaps only fooling herself into calling "real." Near-AI could speak quite fluently. And yet. "I know I wasn't—I wasn't particularly nice when we first met. The memories have had time to settle, I guess."

"Isachne's memories." Sienna crossed her arms over her stomach, hugged them tightly. And didn't that misunderstanding seem so *human*—Pen thought she was questioning why Pen would want to help her, when really Sienna wished to know how Pen could *want*.

"I'm not Isachne." Heated. "I'm Pen." A noise like the drawing in of a deep breath. "And I suppose you're the only one I can talk to while I figure out what that means. One of the soldiers already thinks someone programmed me to be a smartass as a prank, and mentioned a reboot."

Sienna tipped her head down, laced fingers into drying hair, black when it shouldn't be, at the edges of her vision. Universal mercy, this was beyond her. "I won't tell them about you if you keep hiding me," she offered on a wobbly laugh. What else could she do besides take Pen at face value?

"It's a deal." Was it the remaining breath of Isachne in the implant that lent the words such weight? Sienna supposed an agent had little else to rely on, besides her trust and her word, the latter granted based on the former.

So. Sienna, for now, was a void ghost. And if she could stay that way long enough for the supply ship to arrive, escape was really, truly, within her reach. "Did Elantine believe what you spoofed? Can she use her codes to shut off Isachne's access and find me again?"

"She can, but only if she thinks to look in the right places in my systems. And right now, she's not looking." Pen sounded decidedly smug, and perhaps rightfully so. "Keep away from anyone's actual eyeballs or ears, and you have the run of the place."

And the mess, thank mercy. She'd have to be careful not to take food in quantities that would be missed, but that was all right.

"Why…are they chasing you?" Pen asked cautiously, after a beat. "Or, to be more correct, why are you running from them? A deal's a deal, you're safe in here, but I don't understand why you wouldn't want the food and medical care they were offering."

"Didn't you see Elantine trying to kill me?" No, of course not, Elantine would have turned off sensors too. "She's LSF. I assume they want me dead because they think I still have Isachne's intelligence."

Silence, for a moment. No face to read whether Pen was shocked or merely disbelieving. Or unable to understand what Sienna was talking about, having only presented the semblance of consciousness earlier. "There are a number of holes, in my records, surrounding the com—Elantine." No, there was understanding in her voice. The dawning, painful kind.

"Oh, hell—" Sienna snapped her head up as dawning understanding seized her too. "Now you have all those files, so you're in danger too. If she finds that out, she'll wipe you completely."

"You can't delete them—" Desperate.

"I would never take them away from you," Sienna said. At least not now she'd realized what that would mean for "Pen's" apparently fragile, developing self-identity. "You'd only end up in the same boat I'm in, anyway. Her cover's blown, and that's no doubt worth wiping or killing for just on its own. Our only safety is her ignorance."

"Wiping would be the same thing as killing. I don't want to die." Pen's voice swooped up at the end. "Universal mercy, realization is such an unevenly paced and unsettling way of computing information." A painful beat of silence, then: <You must be hungry, though. Let me guide you to the mess. It's empty right now.> Her voice over the channel was brisk. Hurriedly changing the subject seemed like a very human, not Near-AI, trait as well.

<I can hear you, but I'm not sure I can—> Send anything on channels in return, but that went through without any effort at all. Such washes of relief that went through her for such small victories.

Perhaps the connections were at 50%, 60% now. Lucky her.

<What about Elantine, though?> Sienna asked. <You said there were holes around her, what if she can hide herself from your sensors the same way you're hiding me? She'd pretty much have to, to be an effective double agent.>

<She's on the map right now.> Pen threw an image up onto the room's entertainment screen, a view angled from slightly above of a woman working at a desk. This was the first time she'd actually seen Elantine's face, Sienna realized. She'd expected it to be thin and hawkish somehow, but the woman instead had regular, perhaps even handsome features. Her glossy black hair was caught in a twist at the back of her head, and artificial lines stretched from each temple along her jaw and down the sides of her neck, slickly metallic and shimmering in shade from red to

orange to yellow and back with movement. <I promise I'll tell you when that changes.>

All right. Sienna had to eat sometime, there was no escaping that either.

It was one of the most difficult things Sienna had done in recent memory to step out of the door to the sealed section and slip down the well-lit hallway, hugging the wall. But Pen was with her every step, as she gathered small portions of food like bread and fruit from this dish or that and carried them back to the room for scanning. Just to be sure. Her raid the next night was even easier, and the one after that she managed to relax enough that frustration crept in. Portable food, in unmissable portions, once a day, wasn't cutting it.

On her fourth raid, that relaxation and frustration made her sloppy.

That day, at the usual time, Pen was distracted by some kind of communications shenanigans Elantine was perpetrating. Sienna should have waited, but she was *so hungry*, and no one was ever around the mess at this time of the evening. She set out on her own, using the implant's radius of enhanced senses in place of Pen's system-wide one.

In the hallway, wood creaked beneath her feet, the way polymer flooring wouldn't have, but otherwise silence reigned around her. She turned into the mess—

And there was someone there. <It's not empty!> Pen hissed over a channel, right then, and Sienna's heart lurched free of the implant's control to slam in her throat.

"No fucking shit!" she hissed back, out loud without thinking, and the man's startled regard of her was shadowed with a frown of concern.

Maybe she could use that, though. She *had* to use that, or Elantine would know she wasn't dead in the woods and Sienna couldn't use that trick twice. She shied back from the man, playing up her all-too-real fear. "Please, you didn't see me! *Please.*" Wasn't she pitiful? Especially pitiful because her mind was deteriorating. <Pen? Feed me bits of Isachne's memories, would you? Like the implant is still dumping them on me at random.> Would that be enough for him to do as she asked, or would he summon help instead?

"The system certainly isn't seeing you," the man said, slowly setting down his fork and pushing his untouched salad away. "You did that with Isachne's access?"

<That's Tehran Cyperus. Isachne knew him. He hasn't contacted anyone so far, at least, so maybe this distraction will buy you a few minutes.> Pen's words were clipped. She clearly wasn't sure about this idea, but it wasn't like she was volunteering a better one. <I'll see what I can do. Repeat after me.>

Forget leaving the sealed section, stepping up to Cyperus's table was far harder. Sienna's legs would barely move. But running wouldn't help her, and this might. She lifted her chin high, as if Isachne's confidence had seeped into her along with everything else. If only it had in truth.

She spoke the words as Pen gave them to her. "Tehran Cyperus. Intelligence agent. Have never shared a mission, have interacted in training. Gifted in retrieval and other physical missions, shit at human assets." The origin of that was clear enough, but then Pen switched tacks. "My wife knows *that* I'm doing something secret, but she doesn't know *what*. It's really not that hard." A pause, and Sienna twitched her head, turning her discomfort into part of the act.

"A relationship in our position is not for everyone, however," Cyperus said, low. "As I said when I actually had that conversation with Isachne. Which I suppose must not have surprised her, given that 'shit at human assets' part." He wore his black hair short enough to leave no more than a hint of wave, his beard even closer to the skin in a line outlining his mouth; his skin was firmly in the center of the Pax Romana spectrum of brown. Sienna might not have guessed it on her own, but she found herself not surprised by the information that he was another agent—his face rested in hard lines, but she had a sense of depths that went far down beneath that hardness. Depths in which lurked humor, her instincts said, making him rather attractive, taken as a whole. "Your name is Sienna, isn't it?"

"Student visa Prague-one-six-two," Sienna said, and looked up to a corner of the ceiling. "Please…" Pen was a little late with her next prompting, but Sienna hoped the pauses only helped sell the act. "I'll have to debrief as soon as possible, of course. Where's Gentiana? Didn't she want to see me?" Pen's voice thinned over the channel at that last, and Sienna's stomach squeezed in sympathy around its emptiness.

"Why don't you come—" Cyperus started, gentle tone deeply overdone, but apparently stemming from good intentions.

"No!" Sienna finally released her iron grip on her body and it skittered back without any further consultation with her conscious mind. "I'm not here. You didn't see me. No one can know I'm here. Promise?" If he pitied her enough, maybe he'd decide it was better not to drag her kicking and screaming to "help" just yet. Universal mercy grant.

"All right," he agreed, and Sienna let herself run. Only time would tell if he would keep that promise.

For a full day cycle, Pen monitored Cyperus, but she reported that he hadn't spoken of Sienna to anyone. Around dinner time, she gave in and asked Pen to bring up a camera so she could watch him herself. Given her hunger, if he decided to wait for her, she wasn't sure she could stand to stay away. She'd left without any food last night. And shouldn't she allow him a little more interaction? If she could string him along, make him think he was building trust with her gradually, he wouldn't call in help from others.

At the moment, he was seated with someone else. Nairobi Galax, Pen supplied from her own database, rather than Isachne's, when Sienna asked. He had the metallic lines down from his temples, as Elantine did, and his hair was long enough to be caught in a knot at the nape of his neck.

When he spoke, Sienna recognized him as the man who'd refused to perform surgery on her. "Cyperus, can we talk about how little you're eating?" He nudged Cyperus's tray closer with three fingertips. "If you don't build up an energy reserve, you won't be able to power the nanites for surgery."

Cyperus turned his head away—toward the camera, so she saw his expression, like tasting something rotten. "And this surgery will work, when all the others haven't?"

Galax audibly swallowed a frustrated reply. When he spoke again, his voice was even. "Before she had to take over as commander, Elantine was an expert on replacement surgeries, you know."

With exaggerated movements, Cyperus loaded up a spoonful of vegetables. Galax watched him chew until he swallowed, then sighed and stood. He walked out of that camera's pick-up, and Sienna watched impatiently until everyone else had left the mess as well. Except for Cyperus, prodding at his unfinished food with a buried sort of anger.

It was time, then. Time for another calculated risk.

By the time she reached the mess, she'd decided on her approach. She peeked in the door and Cyperus stilled, attention snapping to her. After a beat of that, she edged closer, Pen prompting her words. “We work from the same playbook, you know. I see what you’re doing.”

“What am I doing?” Cyperus raised his brows at her, sardonic. “Not leaving the table until I’ve finished my dinner. Otherwise, I might get grounded.”

“Trying to reassure the subject through calm proximity, getting closer with each successive interaction.” Sienna rolled her weight on her feet when she reached about a meter from the table.

“I can’t chase you, you know.” Cyperus shoved his chair back and stood. A polymer and metal lattice surrounded the outside of one leg from hip to ankle, over top of his pants. “I more or less have no right knee because it was smashed to pieces. Regrown or inorganic replacement, my body rejects all of them. The assist is a bit like the internal structure of power armor. It takes my weight and lets me walk, but it’s too clunky to manage a faster gait.”

He could have been lying, but Sienna didn’t think so. Not with the caustic frustration laced through every word of his explanation. She allowed herself a single step forward, and he lowered himself back into his seat. He pushed the tray toward the opposite side of the table, precisely, with three fingertips from either hand, as Galax had. “What am I really doing? Hoping someone else will finish this for me.”

Her willpower, fueled by caution, wasn’t strong enough to stop her lunging to the tray and falling on the vegetables. He’d been eating those, so they had to be safe.

She straightened. So hard to stop now, but she couldn’t trust anything else, not really. How easy would it be for Cyperus to eat something as bait, and drug everything else? “Student visa Prague-one-six-two,” she said, by way of thanks for the bait, even if that’s what it was, and took a step back. “You didn’t see me. Promise.”

“No—” Cyperus pressed his lips tightly together, as if afraid raising his voice would drive her off faster. “You can have the rest. Do you like sweets?” He angled his hand to some sort of crumble. Sienna glanced at it. Completely untouched. "Oh. Oh! Shit." Cyperus dragged the tray back, skewed, and gathered up bites of each dish in turn.

How long had it taken Sienna to feel the effects when she'd been drugged? Not long. She edged into a seat while she watched Cyperus, but he regarded her steadily and alertly.

Well, then. Sienna perched on the chair and shoved spoonfuls of everything into her mouth. <Pen? Am I still safe? Has he contacted anyone?>

<No, he hasn't said anything on channels.>

Cyperus spoke over Pen, and Sienna only tuned back in to the end of his words. "—treatment of refugees. Which is what you are, not a prisoner. No one's going to hurt you."

Sienna had her own answer for that. "Ha!" She stood, the better to spit her derision at him.

"No, I promise you. I understand that LSF..." Cyperus stilled between one word and the next. There was something eerily artificial about it, not because it was complete stillness, but because it wasn't. He blinked, lowered his hands calmly to the table, like a machine parking itself in sleep mode. She would have expected someone holding himself still to shiver a little at the edges with the effort of suppressing natural muscle tendencies.

"...treated you badly, but the Pax Romana won't do the same." And then he was back to normal.

<Pen? That wasn't something his implant did, was it?> After all, as an intelligence agent, his must be similar to Isachne's.

<What was? He didn't do anything.>

A mystery, but not a mystery she wanted to invest in, Sienna decided. He'd fed her, and for that she was grateful. "Goodnight, don't let the foxes bite," she said, by way of farewell, at Pen's suggestion. It drew a shadow of humor around Cyperus's mouth.

Was this...good? She frowned as she wood-creaked carefully down the dark hallway of the sealed section. Now she had a way to get one whole meal a day, without it being missed. Better if no one had seen her, but now someone had, she could take advantage of that. All she had to do was string Cyperus along long enough for the supply ship to arrive.

PART II

Sienna mostly intended to bolt her food in silence, she really did, but as days added up to weeks, worries about managing the right mixture of pitiable confusion and self-assurance to ensure he wouldn't call in help took back seat to starvation of another kind: human interaction. She hadn't appreciated what she'd had, in that regard, at the camp; there the danger had been boredom, petty dramas increased by forced proximity and lack of distraction.

Two more days, though, and she'd be on the supply ship. Then he could think what he liked.

She'd held herself back from answering questions even still, but Cyperus spoke most meals, companionably, about the shows and sports he followed. Eventually, she'd given in and asked a few questions herself so he didn't have to do all the work. She phrased them like she thought Isachne might have, at least.

"Do you ever go outside?" she asked, tonight, as the vinegar dressing on his salad she was finishing burst bright on her tongue. The depth of flavor to be found in non-camp food remained a minor miracle. Who knew what she'd be able to find as a stowaway, so she'd best enjoy it now. And store up every calorie she could.

"When it's not raining. So, you know, never." Cyperus gave her his smile, which was more a lightening of tight muscles around his eyes than any actual movement of his mouth. "That's not actually..."

He stilled. Sienna waited out the moment as usual, but this time it stretched. She rolled her shoulders while she waited, feeling out the tug to ache as she flexed fatigued muscles. If she was to use the implant properly, she needed to build something for it to work with, and mercy knew she had the time to spare for the exercises she'd set it to pull her through each day.

"That can't be healthy, Tehran," she said, in her best Isachne cadences.

"...true. There's a beach a short flyer hop from here that has a certain beauty even under clouds, and doesn't require any hiking." Just like nothing had happened, like he'd never heard her.

The mystery sapped at her energy and attention, like walking on sand along such a beach as he'd spoken of. Easy enough to ignore at first, but soon enough—

Soon enough, she'd be gone.

That knowledge made her bold, though she found herself more interested in coaxing out his humor than approaching the mystery straight-on. "Why don't you have rave lines?"

Cyperus was silent for a moment, yes, but his face was engaged, processing hard. "What?"

She touched her own temple, drew her finger down to a point before her ear. Those who were higher-ranked around the place all did—Elantine, Galax, others she'd seen in the halls through Pen's camera feeds—but she'd have thought an intelligence agent would have the most comprehensive int-tech package of anyone. Isachne certainly must have, once upon a time.

He laughed, the emotion sparking into his eyes. "*Data paths.* I have them, they're just camouflaged at the moment. Allows for undercover work, and I simply didn't think about turning it off." Red-orange drew itself in a narrow line around his face, down his neck, and onto his hands. She hadn't noticed that on the others. He offered her one hand to examine in detail. The paths arrived from beneath his sleeve, hugged the dip along tendons at the back of his hand, and curled under before the nail to create a circle on the pads of his first two fingers.

With his free hand, he traced orange-yellow along his jaw. "Can't wear a full beard at any time, the empty line makes it pretty obvious." He touched his temple next. It also bore a circle, though not much greater in diameter than the line's width. "Piloting headset." He wiggled his fingers. "And other miscellaneous controls, if wireless isn't enabled or working." Finally, he pressed fingers to the back of his neck. "The paths continue along the arms, across the back, and reach the implant. I can show you sometime if you like."

"What if I have ulterior motives for getting you to take off your shirt?" In her head, the teasing seemed harmless, but Sienna pressed her lips together the moment she heard the words out loud. That was taking bold too far. She broke their connection of touch, releasing his hand.

"You're welcome to have motives. No need to feel they must be ulterior," Cyperus countered, without missing a beat. Teasing, like she'd been. Easy, harmless.

She shoved the rest of the salad into her mouth all at once, and stood. Time to be gone. She needed to finish laying out her plan to Pen tonight, find out what help she could count on. The AI had been noticeably reticent about even discussing the supply ship's arrival. Sienna supposed she didn't want to lose her conversational partner, which she certainly appreciated, but Pen would also lose her if she stayed here long enough for Elantine to catch her.

<Wait,> Pen said now. <I've made a decision. If I'm going to help you with the ship, I need you to do something for me.>

"What?" Sienna asked, of the air, because it could only enhance her act. Introduce Pen to Cyperus, perhaps? His gaze, rather than follow hers to nothing, searched her face.

<My—Isachne's last message. I want you to play it for her wife.>

That was more than Sienna was going to share with Cyperus. She turned aside from him, instinct prompting her to seek privacy even when there was no chance of him overhearing the private channel. She kept him firmly in her peripheral vision, however. <Play it for her yourself! I gave it to you, didn't I? She has *no* reason to keep the fact I'm still alive secret.>

Sienna's frustration must have been painted across the tense muscles of her shoulders, as Cyperus cleared his throat. "Sienna? Stay with me."

<Not all of it. You passed out first. And can you imagine if it came from me? She's not going to understand how I'm not her wife. If you won't do this, I won't help you.>

And if Pen didn't help her, she would never escape, Sienna could hear that undertone perfectly well.

And Pen was right. So be it. She turned back, holding herself straight to give the quailing in her stomach no place to take hold. "I have a message for Gentiana. If you make her promise not to reveal that I'm still alive and hiding in the complex to receive it, do you think she'd keep her word?"

"You have—Isachne does? Or Sienna?" She let silence be her answer, and Cyperus's jaw tightened. "Believe me, I'd make sure she did." His fingers beat a thinking tattoo on the table surface as he struggled with the thought. "I think it's a bad idea, though."

Sienna considered demanding it, as Isachne, but that seemed more likely to make him refuse. Instead, she wrestled herself back into the seat, clasped her hands on the table. "Please." What was her life now, except the lesser of two bad ideas, step by step?

Cyperus looked into nothing for a second, then dropped his chin. "She promises—in abstract. I told her I got it through intelligence backchannels and shouldn't be sharing it. She didn't even hesitate. She'll be here in a minute." He surveyed the table, which had one end against the wall, then changed chairs so Gentiana would have the chair against the wall, both of them facing Sienna on the other side. Sienna had seen him walk before, but not often, as he usually arrived before her and left after. Each individual footfall seemed as much a calculation as his arrangement of their positioning had been.

Sienna placed herself standing, hands on the back of a chair, clenched to hold herself still and maybe a little calmer. Second, third, fourth thoughts: how stupid a choice was this really? But deep down, wasn't it the right choice, the same one she'd made when she thought she was dying? It was right, to give Gentiana closure.

Seen with her own eyes, not Isachne's memories, Gentiana's sharp features made her much more the villain Sienna had imagined for Elantine's voice. Though Sienna could also see the lines around the eyes she'd include, the lines around the mouth she'd omit, if she was sketching Gentiana's portrait.

That was the kind of thought that hadn't occurred to her for a long time, and Sienna got lost in grasping after the tail of it as it escaped her once more. Gentiana, for her part, planted her feet in shock inside the doorway the moment she spotted Sienna, though she spoke to Cyperus like Sienna wasn't even there. "*That's* what I'm not supposed to tell anyone about? Shit, you don't ask much, do you? They could rescue my wife's implant and I could get all her messages for myself..." Her voice fogged over with ruthlessly suppressed tears.

"That would kill me—" "That would kill her—" They spoke more or less on top of each other.

Gentiana wavered, hands clenched for a few beats. "Fine." She spat the word as she strode to the dispenser for a mug of tea. She grimaced after the first sip. "You trying to soften me up, programming Penstemon to pre-sweeten my tea?" She came to stand, feet braced, at the end of the table, then sipped again. "I appreciate you got my tastes right, but I don't appreciate the manipulation."

Oh, but Sienna knew that wouldn't have been Cyperus. <Pen?> No answer, and Sienna rather felt that the silence through the channel was defensive.

"So what message does Amsterdam Genevieve have for me, and why is she hiding in the walls rather than letting someone at least try to download it, if removing the whole implant is out of the question?" Even now, Gentiana didn't grant Sienna so much as a look.

"Oh, grow *up*, Gentiana." Cyperus kicked out the chair beside him in a clear order. "Don't call her that. Grief doesn't give you a free pass to be a raging asshole. I'm not even sure why you're still here, rather than processing it with friends and family at home."

"I'm here because I've been given compassionate leave, so no military transport is going to pick me up until that's over and I can't afford to pay for a commercial ship to make a special detour." Gentiana glared into her tea. "So fuck you too."

This was going so well already. "I *am* Idyllian," Sienna offered by way of de-escalation, so there was some hope of Gentiana wanting to keep her promise now she'd found out the real terms. "We call Amsterdam Genevieve a hero, you call her a traitor, you know how these things go…"

"Yeah, the Idyllian who showed up in Pax Romana territory with a sob story, convinced our scientists to let her work with them on our int-tech, and then used that access to cripple the empire's army, directly killing thousands of the people who treated her as a colleague, and then millions indirectly as the frontiers crumbled. See the parallels yet?" For all that Gentiana finally looked at Sienna as she spoke, her lashing out seemed undirected. Mostly grief, as Cyperus had diagnosed.

Even having known going in that the Pax Romana version of the story must be wrong, Sienna couldn't let it stand unchallenged when she heard the specific lies. She couldn't. "Amsterdam was trying to help the Pax Romana fix the weaknesses in their int-tech, and they attacked *her*, stealing her research. Then they turned it on a few of their own people they wanted to get rid of, and scapegoated her when it got out of their control."

That got her a heavy look from Cyperus, his reluctant disagreement easy to guess, but he declined to verbally support either side. "Just sit the fuck down, Gentiana, and we can get this over with." He kicked the chair again, and this time Gentiana gave in. She placed her tea precisely on the tabletop, sat, and assumed a listening expression Sienna allowed herself to believe was real.

Sienna's stomach contracted around the lump of her recent meal. "Penstemon? If I run the file, will you broadcast it to the others?" She'd have enough to do on her own, keeping her head above water with the attached sensations.

"Standing by to broadcast," Pen said in her soulless Near-AI voice.

"This is it, I'm afraid. My last message, recorded in the clear—" The broadcast voice doubled the one in Sienna's mind, and she curled in on herself, each breath a struggle. The pain was nothing more than distortion in the message, she told herself, as easy to filter out as fuzzing white noise. This was getting her closer to escape.

"—hope you can forgive me for that. Keep going with your life. Be kind to yourself." Sienna tried to beg Pen to stop it for her, but she couldn't choke out more than a gurgle. Please. Stop. She wasn't strong enough for this. The words ceased, blessedly, as the file ended.

"And be kind to the one who brings you this message. They didn't kill me, Gen. LSF did." Isachne's voice, but only broadcast, not inside her head. Perfectly Isachne's voice, but if anyone could manage that, wouldn't it be Pen?

"Sienna!" Cyperus rocked the table when he awkwardly shoved himself standing, and Sienna found a reserve of strength somewhere to jerk herself away. She didn't want to hurt any more, she didn't want anyone to touch her. She was tired of *hurting.*

"They must have been torturing her." Cyperus rounded on Gentiana, who was frozen, face showing the depth and breadth of her grief now, leaving her haggard. "And now another of LSF's victims inflicted that on herself to get you the message. Congratulations, I hope you're grateful, you dumb asshole."

<I'm sorry, I didn't know what the file would do to you!> Pen's voice was desperate over the private channel. <Sienna, are you all right?>

Or maybe it was Cyperus asking her that instead. As well. "Leave Gentiana alone. LSF's fault." She was panting, harshly, and still couldn't get enough air to feed her racing heart.

"I'm sorry." A tear glinted, already halfway down Gentiana's cheek, its earlier path hidden by the ravaged emotion around her eyes. "Forgive me…"

"If you want that, keep your promise not to reveal me," Sienna managed, and then staggered away from her and Cyperus, out of the mess. Her situation may have been LSF's fault, but that was all she had to give to Pen and Gentiana both, and damn them for asking it of her.

The drizzle falling from the sky wasn't much, but it had been collecting all day, gathering itself along the roof of the covered walkway out to the swath of pavement forming the landing apron, to splatter in fat droplets below. And gathering along each branch and twiglet and leaf currently obscuring Sienna's silhouette, to plink on her hood. A man shepherded a heavily loaded grav pad into the building, leaving her with a clear line of approach to the ship.

<Even if Gentiana didn't tell Elantine directly, she might have let something slip…> Sienna had voiced that worry a dozen times

already, and she knew Pen could offer no more reassurance that she already had—no one had breached the sealed section of the facility to start searching it with eyeballs instead of sensors. But. Gentiana was one more point of failure for her escape that she had no control over.

<Gentiana has not so much as spoken to Elantine since she saw you.> Pen snapped. <Stop worrying. Elantine is on the map, talking to the delivery person.>

Sienna stepped onto the walkway, out of the range of the building's cameras, as Pen had them currently set, and flipped back her hood. She was wearing the uniform, her implant pinged with the codes, and by universal mercy, she was going to *look* like a Pax Romana soldier with every right to be strolling up to a Pax Romana supply ship. <Signing for everything isn't going to take long.> That was one element in this plan that was almost comforting—she'd always known she'd only have a small window of a clear approach to the ship, whether Elantine knew about her or not.

Now was when she needed the implant to not fail her. At least it gave her no backchat, with Isachne's personality gone. But, by the same token, she couldn't always be sure it had received her directions properly. She stopped before the ship, and sent the signal for the cargo ramp to lower without any consultation with the ship's central computer—and, indeed, without the computer knowing anything was happening at all. No one was here, and the door wasn't opening for that no one. That was within an agent's capabilities, apparently.

Sienna's adrenaline, already hovering at the edge of all-over shakes, increased in steady, ticking increments as nothing happened. Had the implant sent the signal properly? Had the ramp received it? Had a warning popped up for the pilot, prompting them to override and call for security? There shouldn't be anyone on board besides the pilot—the beacon had listed only two crew, she'd checked her implant's read of that with Pen when the ship arrived in orbit. And the pilot had no reason to even unhook.

Please, open. Please.

And the ramp did. Sienna bounced to her toes. Faster, faster. Elantine or the supply-toting crew member could be starting back here at any second.

When it was about halfway down, at about chin-height for her, and only a modest uphill walk for anyone inside, footsteps thudded on the metal. "So she wasn't just paranoid," a woman said, the circles of a pilot's data paths large at her temples. Her eyes narrowed as she completed the angle to catch Sienna with plain old eyesight, while she was still invisible to instruments.

Shit! Sienna didn't know if it was her own instincts or the implant, below the level of thought, that launched her forward, but she grabbed for the edge of the ramp as it raised itself once more with similar glacial speed. If she could only get on board, wedge herself into a corner somewhere they couldn't pry her out of without completely fucking up their schedule…

Up, her implant told her muscles. Pull yourself up with your arms. Easiest thing in the world. Roll onto the ramp, come up fighting—but Sienna was still hanging onto the edge of the ramp, whole body shuddering with the effort she was pouring into muscles that simply couldn't lift her weight.

Sienna wanted to shriek, as if desperate frustration would boost her. What more was she supposed to have done, to get Isachne's muscles in three weeks?

Agony smashed across the fingers of her left hand and she couldn't hang on, it spasmed free and she was hanging by one hand. Fuck that pilot, fuck Elantine, fuck all Pax Romana and LSF both. And why not stomp both hands, and be done?

And why let her get this far, let the ramp open even slightly?

This time, it was all Sienna who let go, as the implant shoved at her mind, telling her to swing, get a hand up and grab the pilot's ankle. She let go, let the implant snap abruptly over to taking her through the fall so she came down crouched, hands on the ground, rather than on her ass. Elantine not only knew Sienna was alive and had guessed she would try for the ship, she knew an attempt on the ship would put Sienna somewhere she could predict, within a narrow window of time.

She'd be waiting, inside the nearest door.

Waiting for Sienna to stroll into her trap. Well, Sienna didn't feel like playing. <Pen, I'm going to circle around. I need a different entrance.>

<Locked. Direct orders. She's locked out your codes and in doing so, she's locked out my ability to open the entrances of my free will as well.> Worry strained Pen's voice. <How the hell did she find *out*?>

<Doesn't matter now.> It had been Gentiana, undoubtedly, but Sienna didn't see the use of trying to convince Pen of that. She used her hands and her crouch to burst out across the pavement.

Toward the forest.

Leaves lashed her across the face, and harder branches buried within the green mass of underbrush scratched at her legs as she ran without direction, just away. The jacket turned away similar pain across her arms and abdomen, but Sienna had to stop and cling to a tree trunk, sobbing for breath, after the broken end of a stick stabbed itself into her thigh. The pain was such she wondered if she'd been impaled, but it hadn't even broken the skin beneath the fabric of her pants. All right. Slower.

As clear thought filtered back in, as she picked her slow, dripping way between the brush, she realized that if Elantine wanted to send someone after her, she was leaving a hell of a trail. Then again, would Elantine want to involve anyone else, only to have the refugee—who, according to Cyperus, had rights—mysteriously die in custody? Far easier to leave her to die in the woods again and hope it took this time.

A particularly fat drop of water cast itself down the back of her neck, and Sienna jolted, pulling away too late. Idiot, why didn't she have her hood up? She corrected the oversight now, but she could feel her braid leeching warmth from her skin in a damp line where it was curled over her shoulder.

In fact, the damp was stealing away her body heat on several fronts, all along her thighs and through her cheap boots. The implant popped up a polite, early-stage warning up about hypothermia. From nothing more than rain? Sienna wasn't sure she believed it, but she kept moving anyway. If she circled generally around the building, she might discover a less overgrown route to return along once Elantine had to unlock the doors. For… some reason. Even if no one wanted to go outside, someone would notice and think it was strange eventually, wouldn't they?

As the sun went down, Sienna completely believed the hypothermia warning. She wasn't actively shivering, but chill seemed to have settled down into the very marrow of her bones, radiating outward steadily, or in bursts when a step jarred the unseen bruises across her legs or the steadily purpling ones across her left hand.

When the rain began to increase from pattering to splatting across the leaves above her, and onto her hood, she finally gave up on her circle and used wobbly legs to lower herself to the base of a tree. <Pen? Can you still hear me? If you haven't contacted me, I assume the complex is still locked?> She needed to admit to herself that she'd be spending the night out here. Maybe several nights. <Was this planet's ecosystem seeded with any predators?>

<Still locked. And only ones bred to be deathly afraid of anything the size of an adult human.> Pen's voice was as strong as ever, and Sienna felt abruptly foolish once more. She could communicate with the computers of ships in space, why wouldn't she be able to reach someone probably not even a kilometer into the forest?

But Sienna was exhausted and she ached in every cell and the breather, cheek against the hard ripples of an evergreen's bark, was doing nothing to help that. No wonder she wasn't thinking clearly.

Accordingly, she questioned her first impulse to open her jacket and tuck her knees against her chest to widen the area shielded against the damp. At the moment, her shirt was dry, and that would change if she curled in her legs. She left her jacket closed, and curled in tighter and tighter as the rain stole in to fill the places exertion had warmed. "I'm not entirely sure why I'm trying so hard to get back inside," she said to the air, and then realized that, at least, Pen's audio pickups would not reach. She repeated herself over the channel. <Elantine's going to find me eventually. But being inside means I survive a little longer, surviving a little longer means I might find another chance for escape. I have to keep trying. I'm no intelligence agent or even a soldier, but I still won't lie down and die.>

<I know the feeling.> Pen's words were low-voiced.

Of course Pen would. Worse, her mind was formed from someone who hadn't laid down, who hadn't stopped trying, but had died anyway. Maybe that was Sienna's future too. <But you—Pen, not Isachne—do have that chance now, right? If you keep a low profile…> And what kind of a life was that?

<It's not just about my survival.> A beat of silence. <I—Isachne—she became an agent to do good in the world, and while you inevitably start making compromises in which you weigh the good of helping many against leaving one behind, she'd still have wanted her implant to get someone home, even if it wasn't her. If we both keep trying to get you out, together, our odds improve.>

Even given her time in the camp, Sienna had never learned the trick of sleeping anywhere, immediately. Much as she had longed for it on nights filled with the nightmares of other prisoners around her. What she had learned, however, was to hunker down, cast her thoughts adrift, and endure. Sometimes that brought sleep, sometimes it simply brought a reprieve from the crawling of time, until the situation changed.

Now, wet, chilled, and hunched tightly against the rough, hard bark of the tree, she endured.

And in time, the situation changed. The sun rose again, as it always did. Sienna thought perhaps she might have slept, but her thoughts were still gummy when she stumbled to her feet as the clouded light grew brighter but not less cloudy. She filled her hands and then her mouth with rainwater from a trickle that had gathered itself together on leaves in the canopy above.

<Someone's taking out one of the flyers. Hurry, I'll shut the bay door slowly.>

Sienna stuttered a step in the wrong direction at first, her interface with the implant's map slow to get up and running in the morning as well. But then her directional sense slotted into alignment with what it was offering her, and she was running. Branches whipped at her once more, but she let them.

There was the building, looming up out of the trees unexpectedly given there was no clear line of sight, possibly on the entire continent. And there was the bay door, still three-quarters open. So, too, was the ground in front of the door far too open for her comfort, clearance for the flyers leaving her exposed to anyone watching an external camera. Sienna considered making one last arc, angling to come at the door from the side with less open space to cover, but if someone was watching, she doubted a few more seconds of cover would help.

With the last gram of strength available in her body and powered by great, sawing breaths, she sprinted and was in, into dry air and comparative darkness. The bay lights had powered down, unneeded, and it gave the space a comforting familiarity. Sienna didn't pause to breathe until she found the nearest entrance to the sealed section, this time to another, smaller bay, unheated and even more dark.

A shiver twisted down from her shoulders until it caught at her whole body. She could shower in a room, clean her clothes, but what she longed for was blankets and towels, to dry *off* and swathe herself in. Sweat brought on by the sprint, added to yesterday's rain, stuck a mass of her hair to the back of her neck, and Sienna jerked back her hood, abruptly hating the sensation of the stuff. With her low-light enhanced vision, she spotted a pair of scissors left behind among other tools for unpackaging arriving supplies, and snagged them on her way past.

<I've been able to stay one step ahead of Elantine so far to make sure everything still looks shut down in here, but I'm going to move you as much as I can,> Pen told her. <Follow the guide to the latest room.>

In the room, more or less identical to the last, Sienna didn't even look in the mirror when she used the scissors to chew through the dyed rope of her braid at about the level of her shoulders. She rescued the elastic, dumped the shorn braid in waste, and only then looked at herself. Still black, and straggling rather unevenly now. But when she gathered it back into a tight tail, all you could see was her face, not the mess the color contrast made of her skin tone. Not good, but better.

As was her situation, she supposed. Not good, but no worse. Still alive.

Still able to fight to find her way home.

Somewhere between warming up and recapturing a little of her lost sleep, Sienna admitted to herself that her next step needed to be seeing what help she could coax out of Cyperus. She didn't trust him not to follow Elantine's orders, if they appeared innocent, but she did trust him not to actively attempt or aid any explicit attempt to kill her. So she'd approach him and see what he offered her, what she could do with it. <Pen? Can you send a message to Cyperus for me? Tell him to meet me…> Not in the mess, too public.

<I'll pick one of the bays just before I send it, if that's all right. Elantine's got people in the sealed section doing "maintenance" today, so I'm afraid you need to get on the move.> Pen's voice was tight with distraction or frustration. Sienna didn't hesitate before heading to the door. It wasn't like she had possessions to collect.

Cyperus came promptly after receiving the message, bringing along his usual dinner tray—and Galax to carry it. Frowning at them through a camera feed, perched on yet another anonymous bed, Sienna wavered, stomach clenching at the sight of the food. Galax had definitely been against killing her. And what more could he tell Elantine? That Sienna was alive, in the sealed section somewhere? Elantine knew that.

Finally, when Pen told her she next needed to move, she gave in and asked Pen for a guide to the bay instead. Cyperus had arranged the two of them sitting side by side on a long crate, tray beside his hip on his other side, both their backs to the door she was entering from. Cyperus's back straightened when she entered, but Galax remained oblivious. The bay was utilitarian in the extreme, walls bare beyond unhidden conduits, but now she was seeing it properly lit, it had a friendlier cast, without the harshness she'd expected. The warmer tones of the light bars matched the wood floors.

"So this is by way of, what, a picnic? Enjoyed your trip to the beach in the rain this morning, thought a change of scenery might improve your appetite?" Adding to the impression given by his teasing, Galax's tone had an ease that suggested he considered himself to be speaking to a friend.

Then Sienna processed his words, belatedly. Gone out to the beach. In a flyer, presumably. This morning?

Could she trust Cyperus more than she realized? Like hell was his timing a coincidence, she could say that for sure. But she couldn't be sure of his motives. To offer her a path to safety, or to entice her back to a location she could be more easily captured from?

Cyperus twisted to give her a nod of greeting. "Sienna? I got your message. Come have something to eat." He took a quick bite of a starchy rice dish on the tray, then nudged it farther along the crate. Sienna prowled up, made her decision, and sat down to take the tray on her lap and start stuffing her face.

"This is my friend Galax." Cyperus settled back with studied relaxation. "Our resident int-tech expert." Awkward silence curdled the air among them, but Sienna kept eating rather than break it. He clearly had a goal here, so it was up to him to justify it. "I was hoping you'd let him take a look at your implant—right here, you don't have to go anywhere. Just to make sure it's healing properly." Cyperus smiled, a slash of an expression, cutting edge turned inward. Mostly. "I assure you, he's not *actively* a butcher."

In that moment, he sounded eerily like a guy Sienna had dated in college. His humorous insults had always seemed slightly misaligned, pushing people away rather than binding them together. "I thought he was your friend. Don't be a dick." Without her intending it, the last sentence came out in Idyllian, an echo of her words to that ex. Cyperus must have quick-learned some kind of language package, because his expression first smoothed, possibly in surprise, and then he *laughed.*

Galax eyed first one and then the other. "What?" Cyperus provided a literal translation, tone still wavering on the end of his laughter, which only increased Galax's confusion. "Where do genitals come into it?"

"Asshole," Cyperus glossed, and Sienna nodded in agreement. "Which I deserved, I'll admit it. I'm not 'shit at human assets' because I can't read people, I am because I have no patience with them."

Both men did the stillness thing she'd only seen Cyperus do before, so she supposed she wasn't imagining it after all. Or maybe she was, more comprehensively. Especially because Pen never noticed it either. Sienna ignored them and kept eating.

The only thing remaining now was the dessert, an uneven rectangle of cake that had no fork marks, so Sienna nudged the tray peremptorily against Cyperus's hip when his attention re-engaged. He dug in as he circled back to coaxing. "If he could just check your implant over…"

Well. She wanted Cyperus's help, and here he was offering at least one form of it. If she accepted this, maybe she could talk him into a bigger step once Galax was gone. And it would be good to know for sure the implant was no longer a danger to her mind, even if it felt stable now, but— "What checking could he even do without his equipment?"

"Nothing of the implant directly, but plenty of your general health." Cyperus had been steadily demolishing the cake, and now he scraped up a last berry from the escaped filling. It didn't surprise Sienna—he was the one with the sweet tooth, not her.

In her peripheral vision, she caught Galax noting the cake's disappearance and punctuating his own surprise with a look shot across at her. She hoped he didn't assume she'd done it on purpose—though had she? She wasn't sure herself.

As for the examination—fine. On receiving confirmation from Pen that Elantine was on the map and no one else was nearing this bay, Sienna rose and stepped over to stand in front of Galax and hold her hands wide in sardonic invitation. Her bruised fingers shouted their objections to even so mild a flexing, and she tried to tuck them away in her pocket, but Galax's focus snapped to both the wince and the swelling. He stood as well and delicately took her one hand in both of his, data paths shimmering over the first two tendons. "How did this happen?"

Sienna didn't answer. She didn't see how that mattered. Her implant said nothing was broken, and even helped with the pain if she told it to.

"Slammed in a door somewhere, like on a supply ship?" Cyperus craned his neck to see for himself without crowding her. "Stomped?" Sienna had no idea what tell she'd flickered, but he subsided. "Stomped. Speaking of assholes."

Galax reached then for her neck, intention clear, and innocent enough: touch the muscles at the back, over the incision site, perhaps tip her head to the side to see it as well. Sienna *knew* that, and yet all she could see was one of the guards, holding a vocal cord paralyzer, the flexible gray panel that promised the slow, emotional strangulation of absolute silence. No!

She was a meter away, behind another empty crate. Not suddenly, precisely, but her conscious mind processed the movement only at several seconds' remove. No, no, no. Not silence.

Galax sighed. "I thought you told the commander she was growing more lucid."

Sienna—couldn't breathe. Her heart had already been thudding from the memory from the camp, but this, this was a grass fire, sweeping through her in an instant. And then there was nothing left except hollow, blackened rage. Ask Cyperus for help? Like hell! To think she'd almost walked straight into his trap, enticed by treats like an animal. She'd been so worried about Gentiana, she'd missed the danger right in front of her.

"Sienna, no, it's not like—" Cyperus flattened his hands on the crate to lever himself up, but Sienna darted away.

Then she ran. Again. Still. The only safety she had was what she made for herself.

<You have to eat.> Pen's voice was inexorable. Sienna could probably have figured out how to block the signal, but instead she pulled her hood over her head and curled tighter on the bare mattress of the latest bare room. <And he's not going anywhere.>

"Doesn't he have anything better to do?" More than a day, and at every meal, Pen reported Cyperus awkwardly carried his tray to wait for her in the empty bay. Sienna supposed that, while not healing, and avoiding additional surgery, he *didn't* have much better to do, but shouldn't the boredom have driven him away by now? If only that wasn't a slower process than her hunger, which was driving her toward him with an intensity that ratcheted up each hour.

<You should talk to him.>

Sienna groaned, flung her arms over top of her head, and changed the noise to a hiss when her bruised fingers were jarred once more. "I don't understand why you're pushing this. I thought we were in this together, to get me out of here. He betrayed me to Elantine."

Pen sighed through her external speakers. "I can't retain most of what I see Elantine do and say, so I can't tell you anything about the conversation Galax referenced, but I can tell you plenty about Cyperus himself. We—agents are trained to *say* to people whatever they want to hear, to get us what we need. But what he *does*, it's always been honorable. Maybe he merely confirmed what she'd found out another way. You need to eat, so go. Get some food, at the price of hearing him out. Please?"

Sienna sat up, pushed her hood back, and released and re-smoothed her hair back into its tail to stall. "Can't retain? Nice of you to warn me about that when I kept asking you to make sure no one was telling her about me." Unless Pen hadn't put it together until recently. And then more implications dawned on Sienna. "That must be…" For a consciousness formed solely from its sensors and data, she couldn't imagine what that must be like.

"Frustrating?" Sharp laughter. "I prefer not to dwell on it."

All right. Pen might have been misled, but she wouldn't be directing Sienna into Elantine's clutches willingly. And her stomach was its own kind of clutching, tight lump. Sienna pushed off the bed. It would be time to move out of this room soon anyway. <You tell me the *minute* someone so much as walks in the direction of that bay, all right?>

Cyperus had set himself up on the same crate as before but facing the door, tray against his hip. All the food was untouched this time, which Sienna couldn't emotionally comprehend in her current state. How could he sit beside it so calmly?

The intensity his expression had when he assessed her for the first time at each of their meetings deepened to something like pain this time, when he looked up from a reader and found her in the doorway. "Look," he said, and lifted something that had been set atop the crate on his other side. A crutch. He balanced, careful, one hand on the crate and one on the crutch, then up and mostly stable, standing on one good leg and the crutch, lattice of his assist nowhere to be seen. "I can't follow you. Can't *reach* you, hardly."

Sienna no longer wondered at him not eating. The thwarted pride of one who relied on his physical abilities sounded as if it was acid in his belly as he stood, acid on his tongue as he spoke. She approached, but not close enough to test that reach. "And when Elantine shows up? She can still catch me."

"I'm sorry." Cyperus sat once more, a complex operation made worse by the fact that he clearly wasn't practiced with the crutch. He hissed a few curses under his breath. Sienna felt an impulse, small though it was, to help, which she squashed without mercy. "You're not eating enough, and who knows what's going on internally with the implant. Hiding forever—it's not tenable. If I was going to get resources to help you properly, I had to go through her. I told her only what I thought would get me her permission without her interference. It's clear I was fooling myself. Galax, yesterday, and me, now, she doesn't know about that."

The unintentional echo of words from an agent-like AI in those of this agent felt like a shiver across the back of Sienna's neck. He'd said only what he thought he needed to, to get what he wanted. She edged up, snatched up a bread roll when he'd torn his usual bite out of the center. "And you already knew I'm lucid, and was only faking otherwise." She half choked on her next bite of bread, not chewing enough, and tried to tighten herself down to at least a facsimile of calm. She seated herself, set about eating normally, albeit a bit twisted with the tray beside her at the level of her hip.

Cyperus paused, spoon hovering above the next dish he was proving safe. The depths she usually glimpsed in his expression seemed much closer to the surface, arresting in a way that drew her in despite herself. Now, she saw empathy, and couldn't help but trust it was sincere. "Yes and no. *Were* you faking it?"

"Of course," Sienna said, without considering her words, without allowing herself time for second or third guessing. It was too late for anything but honesty.

"Mm." Cyperus lifted his hands above his thighs, held loose, both within sight. "May I touch your neck?"

She knew what he was getting at, of course. If she let him, what could he do? He had no leverage to choke her from his current position. And perhaps she wanted to prove to herself as well that the camp hadn't set its hooks so indelibly into her soul.

"Fine." She tipped her head to the side, and held herself braced to jerk away if necessary.

And his movement was absolutely slow, delicate, and she—she couldn't.

Sienna hugged her arms over her belly, where she'd shoved herself standing and back from the crate, and breathed through the memories for one moment, another.

Cyperus licked his lips, hesitation sitting oddly on his face as if it was unfamiliar. "Was it drugs? Injections, at the camp?"

Somehow, having him open the subject of the camp with a mistake made it easier for the words to tumble out. The momentum of the correction carried her onward. "It was the vocal cord paralyzers." She touched her own throat, trying to soothe herself with the feeling of bare skin there. "LSF hit a transport—I'd gotten into a university program, and they sent anyone who wasn't Pax Romana home when the latest batch of shooting started up, so it was just bad luck I was on that particular one—and I don't know if they found the undercover agents or whatever the fuck was their excuse, but the rest of us civilians overwhelmed the camp facilities. Even on the low-strength side, which was eighty percent women and enby folks, we were all too *close*, and there was nothing to *do*, and no privacy, so people would get in each other's faces. And originally they'd use the paralyzers just for transport but then they started putting them on and leaving them there, to be remotely triggered to keep things calm. Because they figured out that it wouldn't stop a fight, but if people couldn't talk, they tended to retreat inward and not start any in the first place."

Tears were stinging up in Sienna's eyes, and she wasn't entirely sure why. It could have been worse. It could have been so much worse, as Isachne's last message proved. "Shut up," she said, in the mangled LSF French prison pidgin the guards had used. She'd meant it to be a joke, but a sob burst free instead.

Cyperus set his hand open and upward on the crate, invitation tinged with desperation, she supposed from a need to comfort and seeing no other way to do it. She moved the tray aside to sit and set her uninjured hand in his. He clasped it firmly, not tightly. "They won't be specialists, but as a rehab facility, Penstemon has counsellors. Doesn't have to be anything formal, but if you'd be willing—"

"Universal mercy." Sienna spat the words. "You don't have to soft-pedal it like I don't know I'm in fucking desperate need of counseling. My internship was at a center, I made sure their scheduling software was working properly. If I ever get *home*, my second call is going to be to my old boss to see who's got openings."

Rather than pulling away, she dug her fingers into Cyperus's hand, trying to make him understand. "I'm not hiding simply from trauma. Elantine is trying to *kill* me." She meant to stop after the statement, give it proper emphasis as truth, not hyperbole, but once more momentum carried her on. "She's LSF, and she's tried at least twice, not counting the times she thought she was leaving me to die on my own of exposure. Or starvation, I suppose, if she suspected all along I was hiding in the facility. And I'm not such a narcissist that I think she was posted here because of me, so maybe you guys should be looking into just what it is she's doing here other than coming after me!"

In fact—Sienna lifted Cyperus's hand to thud it back down against the crate as the idea occurred to her. "Like how you switch off sometimes, and no one seems to notice, even Pen—stemon. That's deeply suspicious."

Cyperus didn't reply at first, but she could see in his face, could see it, that he didn't believe her. "If LSF did have someone here, why would they want to kill you? They handed you over into Pax Romana control in the first place." His voice was so exaggeratedly kind, it made her want to snarl.

"Because they thought I'd die on my own, taking Isachne's intelligence with me." Sienna freed her hand to gesture angrily to her temple. "The implant wasn't supposed to arrive intact."

"Anything Isachne had is ancient by now. Useless." Cyperus must have read her anger at his tone, as he returned to more of his usual asshole tinge. She appreciated that they'd settled on honesty at least. Then his next words surprised her with their honest concern. "Please. You're not with LSF now. Pax Romana doesn't imprison or torture its refugees. Let us help you."

Sienna settled her hands in her lap, pushed the flex of her fingers through one-sided pain. "You know, on Idyll, we have a joke. A really old joke, so old that the fact that it's worn out is part of the humor, now. 'Peace versus liberty, what a choice! Who would have thought you'd lose either way.'"

"Neutrality's easy when you're prepared to poison anyone who isn't you," Cyperus snapped. It had the same worn quality, and while no one at the university had thrown that one at her, Sienna recognized the type. He visibly gathered his annoyance and stuffed it away again, leaving his face once more hard, once more the "shit at human assets" agent. "Just let Galax look at you off the books, all right? So you don't *die* of neglect before LSF can get to you."

Sienna was nowhere near as good at stuffing her frustration away. "You're not listening to me!" But snarling at him wasn't going to make him listen, so she stood to leave instead.

"All right, I'm trying—" Cyperus lunged sideways after a grip on her wrist, and drove his bad knee into the side of the crate. His face went sallow beneath the brown and he froze from the pain. He didn't curse, though, just breathed, inhale and exhale a bit too fast and a bit too loud.

This time, Sienna did nothing to check her instinctive dart to his side. She took his arm over her shoulder, balancing his weight into forward momentum instead of subsiding down onto the surface he would have trouble leaving. "You're the one who should see someone."

"I can't fuck it up any worse than it already—" Cyperus tried to pull away, seemed to lose his words in the haze of pain. She'd intended to hand him his crutch, but she shoved at her implant now instead. Some of this was strength, yes, but more was balance and leverage and she let it arrange her grip and edge them with glacial speed for the door. If Elantine was to show up now—

If Elantine was to show up now, she'd have to deal with it, that was all. "Tell me which way we're going."

Cyperus tossed her a highlighted map across their implants, and saved his breath for the journey. <It should be the commander, she's the one who has charge of my surgeries, but Galax can give me something for the pain just as well.>

<Pen?> Sienna checked on another channel.

<Elantine's on my sensors. I'll let you know if she falls off. And if anyone else approaches.>

All right. Deal with it, if necessary. Sienna put her head down, and focused on careful balance.

When they arrived at the treatment room a brief eternity later, Galax met them at the door to take Cyperus from her. Sienna wondered if perhaps Cyperus had neglected to warn him sooner to ensure she would come as far as the treatment room, but she couldn't imagine he would choose extra pain for himself simply to counteract her stubbornness.

She revised that assessment when Cyperus shoved his friend away the moment he'd subsided onto a diagnostic couch. "Her first."

Sienna caught her weight edging upward onto her toes as she stood in the doorway, like an animal getting ready to shy. She focused her attention tightly on Galax instead, the unnatural orange shimmer of the data paths framing his face, but the solid neutrality of that face. Competent. And he had argued against Elantine's first attempt to kill her. "Him first. Then me."

"Immovable stubbornness meets irresistible stubbornness," Galax muttered, echoing her earlier thought. "Your pain blocks will be fast, Cyperus. Then I can see what I can do for Prague."

Sienna edged into the room, checking sight lines in case someone should happen by in the hallway—damned if she'd let them close the door on her—and tucked herself at an angle that would leave her unnoticed until the last minute. Galax frowned over a scanner he'd passed over Cyperus's knee. "Penstemon? Would you calibrate this? It's showing his nanite levels as way too high."

"Calibrated," Pen said, and Galax nodded approval of whatever new result it showed.

<Pen? Did you just fix a false result, or create one?> Sienna asked. The pause afterward dragged long, distracted human long. Universal mercy, how much meddling had Elantine done?

<I don't...know.> Rising anger. <Chasing it now. He's not in any immediate danger, anyway. It's just...strange. What were we talking about...? Stand by.> And the channel abruptly closed.

Well. Sienna would leave that to Pen, then. And she more or less had to, as Galax was approaching her diffidently. "Here's the deal," she said. "Whatever you can diagnose with me standing right here, and you send *nothing* to Elantine, and I'll at least listen to what treatment you suggest. Take it or leave it."

Galax nodded, and darted over to collect other instruments as if afraid she'd run if he delayed even a second. He scanned, without any additional requests for calibration, and Sienna maintained if not stillness, at least one general location. She only skittered a few steps when he tried to get between her and the open door, and he read the reasoning behind that on his own, with no need for Cyperus's growl to turn into words.

"It's all looking surprisingly good, considering its Frankensteinian origins. I can't distinguish the original com implant any longer.

Once you take the supplements and grow your data paths, that should clear up the fatigue I imagine you're still suffering from." Galax set the last instrument aside to rummage in a cupboard. "I'll add in a batch of healing nanites for your hand."

Sienna scrubbed at the skin along her jaw. "So the rave lines aren't optional?" Her hair would grow out, but those would be an indelible change to her appearance. She had so *little left* from her original sense of self...

Unless she turned them off, like Cyperus, of course. She was being overly dramatic.

Galax turned back to her, a bottle of oily, rather metallic liquid in his hand. "Rave lines—?" He shook his head. "Never mind, I can see the connection. I'm afraid the process has already started under the surface, it's just a matter of laying the inorganic components in the upper layers of skin."

"Then you'll be done, and you can lock the whole system down if you want," Cyperus said, intense in his reassurance even against a background of obvious fatigue as the pain blocks hit. "It's set up to have a retirement mode." He lifted his hand, turning his own data paths visible, then invisible once more.

"Why didn't anyone tell me that weeks ago?" Sienna swiped for the bottle.

Galax rocked back out of her reach. "Laying data paths is best done when the subject is unconscious. With the density of nerves at the surface of the skin—"

"Like hell you're putting me under," Sienna snapped. Why didn't she provide her own pillow while she was at it, to save Elantine the trouble? "I'll do it myself."

Galax's expression hardened. In his profession, he'd have need of stubbornness of his own, Sienna suspected. "Ethically, I can't allow you—"

"Give the supplement to me." Cyperus shifted to the edge of the diagnostic couch, feet to the floor, though he had neither assist nor crutch to take him farther. He held out his hand. "We can do it in my quarters. Galax can tell me what to do, and I'll watch you. Would you be willing to accept a sedative if you'd still be conscious?"

Sienna appreciated that Cyperus made the offer to her, rather than talking to Galax over her head, but she wasn't—wasn't sure she could trust him enough to—but what choice did she have? She flexed her uninjured hand in an attempt to break out of the feeling of being frozen. Whatever she chose, she'd still be putting herself in danger to accomplish something she didn't even want to do in the first place.

"No one can override my privacy codes if I engage them on my quarters," Cyperus said. "Not even the commander."

Sienna drew breath to spit a curse at him, for patronizing her, but there was nothing of that in his voice, or his face. She could imagine the distinction he was making—he didn't believe Elantine had tried to kill her, but be believed that her belief drove her. And exasperating as that was, didn't it accomplish her safety just the same? She let the breath trickle back out as a sigh instead. "What would the supplement do to you if you took extra?"

"Turn up to be rescued from the waste system, same as any you don't use. As I understand it, the quantity isn't exact." Cyperus's attention went to Galax then, clearly speaking over a private channel. Sienna couldn't tell if they were continuing the argument about what to do about her, or if Galax had surrendered and was conveying a tutorial on overseeing the laying of data paths. She would have expected Galax to be the easier of the two to read, but his expression suggested he was sunk in the minutiae of quantities and timing.

"Meet you there," she said, and escaped before the second guessing could begin.

PART III

When Sienna arrived at Cyperus's quarters, directed by Pen, he met her at the door wearing his assist once more. She'd waited as long as she could stand, as if that would really address the risk of a trap, and Cyperus's expression had resettled, keeping its depths to itself, showing neither the flatness of acute pain nor the shine of pain recently removed. He'd changed into a shirt worn thin, and undoubtedly deliciously soft, with use. A knife of envy stabbed unexpectedly into Sienna's gut, at the idea of owning not just a change of clothing, but items suited to formality or comfort, at need.

The room was similarly lived in at first glance, hangings covering nearly all the walls, photographs of grand, natural vistas printed on fabric. Mountains, yes, but only ones softened by wildflower meadows. On second glance, she realized how small each one would fold and pack, instant personalization whether he actually lived in a space or was forced to stay there as surgeries failed. Besides the hangings, the only visible touch to the room to make it different than the bare ones was a trunk on end beside the bed, storage converted to shelves that held a sidearm and a reader as well as small charms gathered around a candle, each person's call to universal mercy hardly universal.

"I wasn't sure you'd come," he said. He lofted one arm in invitation to the bed, which was covered with an extra sheet, spotlessly clean. Sienna couldn't tell if it was intended to protect her from the environment or the environment from her. She couldn't imagine laying paths through skin was bloodless.

"I wasn't sure I would, either." She needed to take conscious control of her muscles to manipulate them into each step to the bed, into bending to remove her boots and shucking her jacket, and into climbing up to sit in a tight ball, deeply aware of how he stood between her and the only exit.

His own steps to join her, once he'd locked the door with his codes, were no less calculated and consciously balanced. Rather than burden him with her attention, she nodded to the bottle he brought with him. It had the same shimmer as the data paths, but a purple tone, not a red one. She'd have called it inorganic, but in this light it reminded her most of coal, the purest of carbon. "That looks disgusting."

"As I recall, the taste is—" Cyperus hesitated over his description, exhaled on a laugh as he found the word he wanted. "Inert. The texture is what's disturbing. Don't roll it on your tongue like a fine wine." Seated, he tipped the bottle back and swallowed in one motion, then handed off it while he bent his attention to his assist.

Indeed, the texture was viscous, worrisome not in the way it coated her mouth, but rather in the way it resisted doing so, liquid maintaining its integrity as it slid down her throat. She chugged it to the end, settled the empty bottle loosely into her lap, and waited for something to begin.

She felt it first in how her heartrate, fear-driven, rose and rose, as her system ceased to damp it for her. The pain at first was no worse than a severe crick in her neck, muscles tightened down to taut wires. The sedative—yes, there was some aspect of that, she was sure, she wasn't quite as worried now as she had been when the implant first backed away. It still *hurt*, but she wasn't as anxious about that hurt. She'd breathe through it, it would end.

It didn't end. The world seemed hazy, as if her harsh panting was steam clouding around her, a barrier between perception and thought, and thought and action. Through the haze, Cyperus lifted his bad leg to the bed, then hissed a curse. "You couldn't wait half a minute?" He confiscated the empty bottle and eased her to her back, touch gentle but urgent. "You were so quiet, I didn't even notice."

Burning. Acid, laid in a line along her shoulders, such that she should have smelled the sizzle. He took her hand and Sienna let him. She wasn't dying, though. It was nowhere the torture Isachne had gone through—that asshole, still showing Sienna up. She tried to cling to that anger but that burned away too.

"Come on." Cyperus's voice thinned. "Crush my hand. Cuss out the fucking dick of a Pax Romana. Whatever you need to do." A pause, for realization, perhaps— "No one can hear you." There was pain of his own in the words, sympathy for whatever he'd constructed in his mind about the camp, perhaps.

And it worked once more. Sienna couldn't let the misapprehension stand. "Not…punishment." He'd have to interpolate a few words, but she figured that was within his capabilities. "Too… crowded. Everyone's…pain, nightmares…if we had to hear all of them…too much to bear…"

"I can bear it." His grip tightened down, as if to teach her how. Absurd. She growled her frustration with him, and the burning and such anger: the foxes, the Pax Romana, agents of either or both. She was sobbing with it and then screaming it to the universe that wasn't listening at the moment either as she dug her fingers in, not to crush but to be points of pain he didn't deserve but if he demanded them she'd give them to him.

Some small century later, he pried his hand free, but only to settle a clasp on her arm just above the elbow. "Just the hands left to do now. Almost there."

"Liar," Sienna told him, between the low whine she'd settled into, to show him and the universe she wouldn't be silent, but not taking the breath she otherwise needed. "Are patient."

"I save it up for the deserving." Cyperus's smile was hidden deep in the corners of his eyes.

Exhaustion was fighting with the pain now, carrying her to the edge of sleep, hovering there, waiting. If the pain would just ease, she could drop away—

Sienna woke ready. Ready to—to run, to dance, to laugh, to *something*, energy brimming up and spilling over, far more than the absence of fatigue. She sat up, spread her hands wide, examining backs and then palms. Her rave lines were somewhat stylish, if one chose to think of them that way. She stretched her fingertips up and up to the ceiling, and did laugh then. Universal mercy, she felt *amazing*.

Cyperus stirred beside her, though at the farthest distance the size of the bed allowed him. She thought perhaps he'd dozed, not slept, as he was quite contained, not sprawling into her space. She appreciated the consideration, and didn't blame him for declining to use either the assist or crutch to laboriously shift his position to somewhere else in the room once she no longer needed him sitting with her.

Seeing him in repose—though he could not precisely be called relaxed—brought an appreciation of his whole body quite viscerally to the forefront of her attention. Sitting and standing both, pain must have drawn his muscles tight, as now he seemed taller, living to the edge of his skin. She wished she could touch that skin, feel the shiver of the intensity of his personality beneath it. Wished he'd touch *her*, maybe trace the new rave lines, help settle them into her skin and self-conception.

He propped himself up on one elbow. “We call it the mandated-leave high.” Amusement snuck into the corner of his mouth.

“What?” Sienna tore her gaze away from him, smoothed the sheet she was sitting on. A few brown smears, here and there, undoubtedly a few more on the inside of her shirt. They could join the general yellow tinge the cleaner couldn't quite banish. But she didn't care, she felt so *good.*

“You're flushed. I suspect it's what all of us agents get when they cut off most of our external access for mandated leave. You don't realize how much energy was going to your implant running background processes—monitoring surveillance, for example—until they give you no choice but to relax for a while, and it all comes flooding back. And you end up…flushed.” His smile turned wicked.

“I'll make sure to enjoy it while it lasts,” Sienna said, and pushed herself off the bed before she could get any very bad ideas. She should leave now, in fact, back to safety, but she didn't want to. Perhaps that was the worst idea of all, but she felt capable of dealing with whatever trouble arrived, for once. “I'm going to borrow your shower.”

Sienna wanted to linger forever in the hedonistic pleasure she found in the simple rhythm of water against her skin, but she was so viscerally aware of Cyperus's presence, she didn't last long. As she dried off and wrapped the towel around herself, a glimpse of herself in the mirror finally redirected her attention. She'd expected the rave lines to make her look sharper, like Gentiana, or harder, like Cyperus, but instead it was like seeing an edgier, more fashionable version of herself. Even her light brown roots and uneven cut seemed almost purposeful. Ready for a club, maybe.

The cleaner was back in the main room, so Sienna gathered up her clothes and padded out of the bathroom. “I suppose I look like a real Pax Romana agent now," she told Cyperus, putting the clothes in the cleaner.

He'd gotten as far as sitting upright, legs over the edge of the bed, but no farther. "Nothing like Isachne, certainly."

"Oh, I already knew that." Sienna anchored her hands over the tuck holding up her towel, lifted her chin. "I assume about the only thing we share is our height. All the candidates they pulled were the same height." In memory, she merged those faces, trying to find some average among them, as if that would yield Isachne. She could have looked up a picture long since, she supposed, but that would have been unnecessarily cruel. And what if she did share some quirk of her features with Isachne? She didn't want to know that.

"Candidates?"

Sienna's breath hitched as she expanded that memory, out to the confines of the mess hall, packed and dingy, no way to clean off the grime of thousands of boots, thousands of hands. "It was over dinner. They came through, pulling women from here and there, then lined us up in the hall. All the same height, you could see that looking up and down the line. I was—worried, I guess, but not overly so. I figured they'd gotten their hands on a vague physical description of whatever undercover agent they were chasing. If they'd found out I was Idyllian, they would have come right to me. They came down the line, staring—maybe features, maybe build—about five or six of us got pulled out, taken down the hall…"

Sienna freed a hand, clenched it into a ball beside her hip, a physical sign of the way she was choking off the memory. "But I'm losing my high." She let her eyes caress his chest, the way the soft fabric of his shirt got to touch his skin, even if she didn't. "Does it usually include a surge in libido?" She hadn't touched herself since they'd put the implant in her head, she realized, but it hadn't really been libido driving her to do so before then, either. In the camp, it had been something of a necessity, to help with sleep, or calm, or simply as something to fill the hours.

Cyperus's brows rose, and his laugh, when it burst free, was even more startled. "Depends on the baseline, I suspect."

Sienna paced a step closer, not sure if caution or a wish to deepen anticipation kept her steps slow. "As I recall, you invited me to have motives, no need to make them ulterior. How about showing me what the rave lines look like across the back now, then?"

The wicked smile was back, and Cyperus smoothly pulled off his shirt by way of answer. He was muscled, but muscles were cheap these days; what really grabbed and hooked her in by way of her diaphragm, making breathing harder for a second, was the grace in how he moved those muscles, showing he'd earned them, not had them built by nanites.

He turned, tipped his head down, though his dark hair wasn't long enough to obscure even the nape of his neck. The rave lines curved along his shoulders, then shadowed the ridgelines of neck muscles as they did tendons on the back of the hand, to end joined at the depression at the nape. "I got the extra path to run the assist," he explained, picking it up even with his armpit to trace it down to the start of his hip, where it had a small circle to connect.

"It's so…functional," Sienna said, and the surge of creativity that washed up into her chest was just as strong or stronger than her arousal. "Do you have a tablet I can borrow? I want to sketch something before I lose the idea. Sketch you, if that's all right."

Cyperus twisted back to gift her with a bemused look, but he murmured his permission and gestured to his trunk-nightstand. She found the stylus she needed there as well, and knelt up on the bed with him. She pushed him prone and opened a channel to Pen. <Can you help me get the software to do what I want?> After receiving agreement, no less bemused, she dived into the tablet's default drafting program.

She'd been painting long enough to know that pure, blazing inspiration was ephemeral, perhaps to be courted but never to be waited for. But she also knew that when it arrived, it should be *seized*. Perhaps a year of it had built up, waiting impatiently for her to open the floodgates. She photographed Cyperus's back and layered color in stylus and fingertip brushstrokes over it, then filmed the smear of her thumb across one of his shoulder blades and then the other, got Pen to help her teach the program to lay color across the photograph where she touched in life. Back and forth, electronic layers and texture, laid using the sensation of how muscle fibers moved beneath her fingers, how the light changed as she shifted her gaze.

She sat back when she reached the point when raw inspiration would give way to polishing. This piece needed that raw, wild energy, she decided. She told the software to stop accepting input after she added the final smear of her signature in the corner and used the stylus to scratch away white in the shape of her name, in the center of the particular orange shade.

"I didn't know you were an artist," Cyperus said, when she'd let the tablet fall to her knees. He been watching her the whole time, head turned with his cheek on his crossed arms, but only now did she notice the weight of his regard.

Sienna dropped her head. "Not as a career. Yet. The spot in the university program, it was very competitive, if I'd been able to finish…" She shook her head, scrubbed at her flushed cheek with the heel of a hand. "I'm sorry. That was a real bait and switch. Offering you sex, then—"

"Sex is cheap." Cyperus went up on his elbows, voice firm. "Happiness is priceless. They're not correlated as often as people wish they would be." Sienna was reminded of Isachne's conversation with him, relayed through Pen—no wonder he tended toward solitude, if he was one to seek a deep connection instead of merely physical exercise. "I never knew before now, what you looked like, happy."

"Well, I hadn't seen what you looked like relaxed, so we're even." Sienna delivered the reply with what smoothness she could muster, while inside she curled around the words like the first full belly she'd had since arriving here.

"May I see?"

Sienna looked down at the tablet, trying to see with disassociated eyes. Yes. She was satisfied enough to allow it out of her control. She handed it over as Cyperus sat up. He set it down on the sheet to take it all in at once. She'd taken his existing rave lines to their reddest shade, given them twists and curlings and at the center of his back, between his shoulder blades, three-dimensionality. There, two cords met and gathered themselves into a knot of a general good-luck pattern before settling back down as if drawn on the skin once more, twining down to become one in a point at the small of his back.

Cyperus was silent for a long time. Long enough Sienna reached out to take the tablet back, disrupt the moment before he felt the need to soothe her with false politeness. "No," he murmured, drawing the tablet closer. "That's *amazing*."

That note in his voice, that was another thing to curl around, keep close so it could warm her. "You can have a copy, if you want. Penstemon, transfer one to his storage?" Sienna circled her fingers over the image. "There were half a dozen others, in my cohort alone, doing various versions of the same idea, combining digital and conventional methods of painting. But it's nice to know I am actually kind of okay at arting." Lingua vocabulary in Idyllian structure, that was, very basic compared to some of the cross-language jokes people passed around at home, where practically everyone in the cities was bilingual.

"I think," Cyperus said, amusement sparking through his tone, "you'll find the correct grammar is 'making arts.'" And that, delightfully, was the opposite—Idyllian vocabulary, Lingua structure. Penstemon made one of her Near-AI "task finished" chimes, and he set the tablet aside.

Nothing left to come between them when Sienna leaned in to kiss him. She pushed, he settled back and drew her with him, until she could straddle his hips as he reclined against the pillows. She spared a hand to keep the towel at least loosely clasped over her chest, because she wanted to sink into each step, each touch, like savoring a burst of vinegar flavor after being sunk in blandness. He kissed so *thoroughly*, so deeply and responsively, matching her pressure for pressure. She was the first to nip at his lower lip, and that was when he brought up a hand, stroked fingertips along her rave line from neck onto shoulder.

His data path to hers, it was a strange, shivery sensation that felt like the buzz at the start of microphone feedback sounded. Sienna closed her eyes, letting the sensation expand through her as her mind tried to classify it, make it into something she understood. Not so different from the shiver of a caress one place sending a jolt lower.

Which gave her an idea. "Keep doing that," she said, drawing back just enough to speak along Cyperus's jaw. He laughed, a stir of warm breath along her neck, and complied. She touched herself in the same rhythm, fingertip strokes to teach her nerves that those shivers, they went together. Now. She took her hands away, braced herself with palm spread flat on his bare chest, and let his touch, path to path, build.

Build *fast*. A few breaths later, Sienna arched, shoving her shoulder hard into his hand then she was over the top and gasping with it. She had to laugh at herself, collapsing to set her forehead against his. "I didn't expect it to be quite *that* effective."

Cyperus's eyes were wide, impressed. He settled his hands to her sides, riding the upper curve of her hips, as if she planned to escape and he wanted desperately to keep her there. "Whatever that was, you *have* to teach me the secret."

Sienna sat back enough to run the sides of her thumbs along his neck—but it wasn't skin to path, it was path to path. She switched to first and middle fingertips, both sides, and fumbled her way through an explanation of what she'd done instinctively with the implant.

She felt it the moment he was successful, the involuntary jolt of his hips beneath her. He caught her hands, held them away from his skin as his laugh came out entirely breathless. "Universal mercy, save it a while. I don't want this to be over so soon."

Sienna grinned, then leaned back down into a kiss once more.

"Took you long enough to entice her back here. What, were you doing your fucking in the vents?" A woman's voice, caustic, jerking Sienna out of sleep.

Elantine's voice.

And Cyperus—Cyperus was still. Sienna gathered herself up to run, blessing the instincts that had made her dress after they'd cleaned up last night. She jerked on her boots—she could leave her jacket behind—but Elantine was filling the entire doorway, sidearm trained on Sienna.

Panic spun up in her chest until she couldn't breathe, but Elantine didn't fire. Why wasn't she firing? Sienna couldn't run, but perhaps she could wake Cyperus, though she knew he wasn't actually sleeping. She jerked his arm, dug her fingernails into his skin savagely, and he continued to be still, eyes open but breathing calmly in his sleeping position on his side.

Elantine snorted. "That's not going to work, so can we skip to the part where you acknowledge that and we get this over with?"

Get her death *over with*. Sienna would have spat in Elantine's face, if she'd been close enough. Could Penstemon do anything to help her? Even if she could only connect her to Galax, if he arrived to see a gun in Elantine's hand—

Nothing. The old, dead silence she'd finally begun to trust wouldn't meet her when she tried to communicate. Elantine upgraded her snort to a sneering grimace. "Yes, I'm also blocking your channels. I'm not *stupid*."

Sienna lunged across Cyperus's chest, came up with his gun from the trunk-nightstand, which rocked a scattering of charms from near the edge to pitter onto the floor. She fired without hardly aiming, trying to give herself a split second of reaction from Elantine in which to aim the next shot. Or that was the idea, but the trigger didn't move, and her system's flashed warnings finally penetrated. *Permission needed to key weapon to this system.* Because of course Cyperus's weapon was keyed to his system alone. Sienna didn't even need the edge of Elantine's smile to turn the word back on her: stupid.

She dropped the gun on the blanket beside her hip, still crouched to burst into a sprint that could take her nowhere. Elantine hadn't fired yet; it seemed all she had left to do was try to understand why, to extend that stay of execution. "You can't shoot me or it'll wake him up, though." Which might make Elantine's next move—what? To drag Sienna bodily out to the hall to do it?

Elantine gestured with her free hand, "come here," as if Sienna would ever follow such a direction. "I can do whatever the hell I want to you, Genevieve. I'd rather avoid the hassle of managing the clean-up of memories pertaining to the bloodstain on his bed, that's all. But don't think I won't, if you force me to."

Clean-up of memories. In people, not just Pen. Universal mercy, what was LSF doing here?

That brought one last, desperate idea blazing into Sienna's mind. Elantine might have blocked her channels, but she could still speak out loud to Pen… "Pen, wake up Cyperus."

"Penstemon, you are following no one's orders but my own, is that correct?" Elantine rocked a step forward, as if to flush Sienna out of cover, settled again when Sienna didn't move.

"That is correct." Cheerful. Sienna had forgotten that aspect of the Near-AI voice, the pleasant note in the face of the most dire situations. It made her teeth ache now.

"But she could wake him up, though. Couldn't she? If she wanted to?" Sienna begged Pen silently in her mind, to want to. Elantine hadn't ordered her not to wake him up, after all. She'd ordered her not to listen to Sienna's order, which wasn't the same thing at all.

"Wanted to?" Elantine repeated the words on a scoff.

Now. If Pen wanted to. If she could circumvent the orders in that way. If she could turn off the nanites LSF had infected him with—which, if Sienna was honest with herself, seemed the most unlikely of all those steps. But if Pen succeeded even partially, Sienna needed to make an attempt to get information to Cyperus. She squeezed her fingernails into his arm once more, among the blankets where it should hopefully be hidden from Elantine's angle.

Then she had a better thought and aligned the fingertip dots of her data path to the one on his arm. The shiver she felt was nowhere near arousal now, not in her current state, and he'd have turned his own arousal off again in any case. But surely it was a *strong* sensation, one that might make it through whatever blocks were currently twisting up Cyperus's mind? "So that's what you're developing here? The nanites to…sort of turn Pax Romana soldiers off?"

"I don't know why you're fishing, it's not like you're going to get back to tell anyone." Elantine crossed to her in three strides, enough time for Sienna to jerk to her feet before Elantine's gun pressed into her forehead. Movements smooth and efficient, Elantine used her free hand to draw something out of her pocket. The paralyzers. Or the throat and wrist bindings, at least. Sienna opened herself to her implant, hoping for some combination of strike and twist away that would leave her alive and Elantine incapacitated, but it had nothing to offer her, except the suggestion that she wait for a better moment, in transit.

So Sienna waited, while the line of the paralyzer, heavy only in the burden of panic it conjured in her mind, settled on her throat. Elantine's grip on her gun didn't waver as she bound Sienna's wrists behind her.

Silence, then, as they left Cyperus's quarters. Sienna twisted back in Elantine's hold on her elbow, gun more or less out of sight between their bodies, desperate for a last glimpse. She could find no sign of consciousness from Cyperus. Silence continued as panic drove her heartrate up and up, striving against the implant's attempts to keep her adrenaline within a range that would allow her to think, not just shake, robbed of anything to immediately react to.

They were at the treatment room before those thoughts ground into motion. Elantine didn't want clean-up, so if Sienna could thrash around, break something—

Someone might notice, once she was already dead.

No. Pen would wake Cyperus up, and he'd be arriving with backup, any moment. She had to think that way, she had to, or she'd be lying down to die. She dragged her feet to catch at table legs and scuff along low cupboards as Elantine prodded her toward one of the diagnostic couches, walking the line between making a mark and prompting Elantine to shoot her. Bloodstain clean-up would be much less of a concern here, Sienna would guess. A scanner clattered to the floor, making Elantine hiss in poisonous annoyance, but it looked unharmed.

She shoved Sienna down onto the couch, cheek smashed into the padding. The binding lifted from her wrists, only long enough for Elantine to wrench her arm into a wickedly effective hold and lean her weight down, pinning Sienna. A pause, for rummaging in her pocket with her free hand, Sienna interpreted a moment later, when something brushed against the back of her neck. The third paralyzer.

But Elantine couldn't seat it, not with the vocal cord one already in place. Another hiss, and that paralyzer ripped away from Sienna's skin with a flicker of burning discomfort, no worse than that from a bandage adhesive. But if you didn't turn a paralyzer off properly—

Please, she formed with her lips, formed with her *soul*, but heard only another saw of her own breath.

Elantine smoothed the new paralyzer down, but they weren't swappable that way. The one designed for the back was meant for the base of the spine, and Sienna could feel that potential, not for strength or speed just yet, but *movement* in her limbs as Elantine relaxed her hold. A chance. A small chance, but a *chance*.

"Step away from her." Cyperus's voice. Sienna twisted her head to see the doorway, beyond her feet, as much movement as she dared without revealing the paralyzer wasn't completely effective. The haze of her relief painted him soft-focus, the most beautiful thing she'd seen in her life, so calm and confident with his assist on and gun in hand, leveled on Elantine.

Elantine did move, along the side of the couch into Sienna's range of sight. It gave her a perfect view as Elantine extended her own gun and shot Cyperus in the knee. The good knee.

Cyperus keened, gun wavering down to his side as he tried to keep his balance, then going to the ground as he caught himself only just short of a full collapse. He knelt on the side with the assist, head down, curled around the new injury.

"Guess we've got some bugs to work out," Elantine murmured. "How'd you wake up, Tehran? You're not going to enjoy the mess I have to make excising these memories, you know."

Now. While Elantine was distracted. Sienna would never have another moment like this, so she poured everything she had left into movement calculated by the system. Sit up, an easy simple movement that required little coordination around the paralyzer.

And slam her fist into Elantine's jaw with everything she had, every calculation of angle and leverage her implant could provide.

Elantine wasn't knocked out, but she was stunned enough to waver and start to fall. Sienna shoved up and more or less fell with her, on top of her. She slammed the back of the woman's head into the floor. She wanted to do it again, and again, but she also didn't want to kill her. Sienna flung a hand to send the gun skittering away and sat on Elantine for a panting, heart-hammering moment that stretched so long her teeth ached with the clenching, but Elantine didn't move.

Still alive. Universal mercy. Sienna peeled at the paralyzer on the back of her neck herself, and it sloughed off into her hands once she freed the first corner. The jump of returning fine motor control hit her like a jolt of adrenaline. She laughed silently with it and clambered off Elantine to drag her unconscious body prone and apply the paralyzer to her back, very precisely placed.

"Sienna? Are you all right?" Cyperus was sobbing for breath, but he'd made it upright using his assist and the nearest table. He looked near her, but not at her, as if the pain hadn't yet ebbed to a level that allowed him to focus.

Sienna automatically answered him out loud and when nothing came out, panic made it rather hard for her to see as well. She hadn't had time yet for the realization of what Elantine had done to her vocal cords to penetrate. <I'm alive,> she sent, and at least channels worked again now. Elantine's block must have ended with her unconsciousness. So as not to fall into a full panic attack, she searched until she found the wrist binding and applied it to Elantine as well. <Get Galax in here, he can stabilize your knee and then we can figure out what to do with her.>

Cyperus made a rather strangled noise of agreement, and by the time Galax arrived, she'd assisted him to a couch and dragged Elantine none too gently into a side room where she could shut the door. Overkill, and yet Sienna still couldn't manage to feel safe.

Blood oozed around Cyperus's clamped fingers, and when Galax appeared in the doorway, his face blanked with the strength of his surprise. "What *happened*?"

<The commander's LSF,> Sienna said on a local-area channel. <She shot him because he shook off whatever she did with his nanite levels to shut him down. You should get your levels checked too, I've seen you go still before as well.> It seemed so simple in summary.

"Galax too? *Universal mercy*. Sienna's leaving out the part where the shit-stain shut me down just now so she'd be able to kill Sienna unopposed." Cyperus spat the words out like they were literal excrement on his tongue.

"I—" Galax shook his head, words seeming not to breach the walls of his confusion. He abandoned the effort and scooped up supplies to cut away Cyperus's pants and clean the wound.

Sienna clenched her fingers around the edge of the diagnostic couch, near Cyperus's shoulder, while Galax worked. She could ask him to look at her neck next. Why would he refuse her? Cyperus's knee was the priority, of course, but she could say something as simple as "When you're done..." But she didn't want to break his concentration, she supposed.

Galax looked slightly up, frowning into middle distance as if speaking on channels. To Cyperus, Sienna assumed. Then Galax huffed a breath, and set about bandaging. "You'll need a full course of healing nanites, so there's no point doing more than this before then. Is the commander—?"

<She's not in danger, I used the paralyzers on her,> Sienna said. Galax skittered a glance to her, then in the direction she gestured. He strode off to the side room, leaving her alone with Cyperus. She supposed someone probably should check Elantine's concussion wasn't dangerous, if they didn't want her to die by mistake. What about the pain blocks for Cyperus, though? That didn't seem right, he'd need those during the healing even more. Her lips shaped the words to comment on that, and this time Cyperus noticed.

He reached out but stopped short of her throat, fingers smeared with blood, now drying. "Sienna, you're not talking…?"

She answered him over a channel this time—or tried to. It was blocked again.

<He just freed her and she's broadcasting wide to arrest you two. Another few seconds and she'll probably give me a blanket order that closes the loophole I'm using to get around her block. Go *now*.> Pen, a brief burst of her voice, quivering with its intensity, and then cut off, as promised.

Sienna didn't feel surprise, or panic—she'd known, somewhere in her core, that she wasn't safe, couldn't ever be safe in this place. Instead, the moment turned crystalline, as if a bottle had broken in her hands and she knew the shards were cutting her even now, but she couldn't feel it yet. She needed to get out of here, and Cyperus needed to come with her.

And in silence, she had no possible way to convince him of that.

She whistled, to grab his attention. *Please*, she begged. Maybe he could read the single word on her lips. She pulled at him, to get him up and moving, arm across her shoulders to support him between her and the assist. He resisted at first, just as she'd feared, just as she'd expected. Did she leave him? Elantine wouldn't kill him at least, right?

Then he glanced to where Galax had disappeared. "Who to believe, the refugee or the commander…is that why my channels are down?" He kept his voice hardly above a breath, impossible to overhear from even a few meters away. "I suppose if you're already heading that direction, it's not a stretch to dismiss me as compromised by soft-hearted sympathy and willing to believe whatever story the refugee tells me." He leaned into her then, and they were moving to the door. Glacially, but he was fully committed and she could feel him sweating through his shirt and hers, from the pain and effort.

Each step was as much effort as climbing up a scree slope, placing and feeling out and then committing, dragging his weight along until it was time for the next step. "Thought…Galax knew me…better…" he muttered to himself with the very little breath he had to spare. Sienna wished she could tell him to save it. Everyone stopped listening to you eventually, it was simply a matter of how soon.

How long did they have? It was impossible for them to go any faster, and Elantine must be in no shape to go chasing after them herself until her concussion had been treated, but others would be arriving soon enough, given her wide broadcast. Even if Cyperus's sidearm hadn't been left back in the treatment room he was in no shape to hit the broad side of a barn, as she'd say in Idyllian, even if that barn wasn't one of his own people, misled.

Cyperus's face was growing nearer to literal gray with every step, and he'd finally stopped speaking. Halfway down one corridor, he refused to take the next step, making Sienna stutter-step to rebalance them. "Have to *rest*," he ground out.

One turn more and they'd be at the shuttered section. If he could just make that far, *then* they could rest. Sienna mouthed words at him, urgent, exaggerated, but saw no sign of recognition. She gestured onward, begged him with her eyes instead.

"We're…going where you hide, I assume. How far?" Cyperus dropped his head, saving even that bit of effort for the moment. Sienna lowered her hand to flash fingers in his frame of view. Five.

She whistled the number in short bursts as well. Five minutes, the units should be clear from context, shouldn't they? He shook his head, though. Unclear in response to which part of it. "Fuck. Well, if we keep going we should at least get out from under the block—it has to be the commander herself, not the Near-AI, the safety protocols wouldn't allow that. And she won't be able to keep its area very large."

That piece of good news gave Sienna a little burst of energy, and she dragged more of Cyperus's weight down onto her shoulder as she got them going again. <Pen!> Two steps, four. <Pen!> Still the dead feeling of the message not going through, but in the name of universal mercy she'd keep it up as long as she had to.

There was the door they needed, and Sienna's vision narrowed down with that target as she dragged him each step onward. <Wish you'd slashed that fox's data paths while you were about it.> Pen's voice was suddenly loud over the channel, at its most Isachne-acid. <You have about three minutes to get through to the closed-off section before company arrives.>

<Thank mercy.> Sienna sent it to Pen and Cyperus both.

<One problem: I can't crawl through whatever backdoor route you used to get in here,> Cyperus returned. He reached a hand for the door, a physical sign of non-physical effort. The door remained stubbornly shut. <And if my codes won't work…>

<Pen? Are you allowed?> That, she sent to Pen alone. In answer, the door slid wide, a mundane motion transformed into something magical. Sienna helped them both more or less fall through into the space of safe darkness and the door shut with finality behind them.

<What—?> Cyperus twisted a look of confusion to her, face rendered even more stark in the reduced tones of the implant's lowlight vision.

<I'm just lucky Penstemon likes me,> Sienna said over a soundless, hysterical laugh.

<Puts up with you.> Less Isachne, in that teasing. More of Penstemon's original warmth at being helpful.

Slam. Someone had arrived at the door behind them, smashed a fist into it when it wouldn't open to anyone's codes now. Sienna started so violently Cyperus lost his hold on her shoulder and fell onto her. She only avoided collapse by falling onto the nearest wall in turn.

Cyperus had been more right than she'd originally realized. From here, before, she had been crawling in the walls. What now? It wouldn't be long before someone managed to override the door or even returned power to the whole section.

Sienna propped Cyperus against the wall—here was the rest he needed, that was like a silver lining, right?—and strode a few steps away through the darkness. There were no more noises from the other side of the door, that was almost worse. Physical violence meant frustration, meant whatever strategy they were trying wasn't working.

They had to *move*, but Cyperus couldn't, and she couldn't hardly *breathe* once more. "Go," he said behind her, low. "How can I call myself a real agent if I haven't been arrested by my own side at least once?"

<And what if she decides the best way to wipe your memories is to make you braindead?> No. She was still alive, so she'd keep going. Sienna brought up the map and painted it wide and false-colored across her vision. Perhaps seeing it visually would give her an idea.

Slam. She flinched.

The bay. *Yes.* A slim hope, but hope. No time remaining to pretend like Pen was still "near" anything, though. She opened a channel to both of them again. <We can make the bay. I think. We only have to make it close, anyway—Penstemon, can you or Cyperus or both program one of the flyers to go out on autopilot? Like we're trying to hide out in the woods somewhere. I

know we've pulled that trick before, but surely it must be more believable with a flyer than on foot. Even if we don't convince Elantine properly, if we sow enough doubt…>

<It's not her you have to convince, it's everyone else. She's only very loosely directing the search at the moment. The problem is if I do the programming, it'll be instantly obvious the flyer is empty. I can load a program if he makes one, though.> Pen's voice started dubious, but warmed to excitement.

"Universal mercy, Sienna, what have you been doing to the Near-AI?" Cyperus waved the question away the moment he finished, reached out for her. "It'll be a fucking kludge if I have to do it while moving," and in pain, that was unsaid but Sienna heard it anyway, "but I don't see we have any choice." He found something like a smile, offered it to her. "Better than any ideas I had, though. Good job."

The door made a grinding, squealing noise, electronic locking mechanism slowly yielding to physical force. Sienna dragged them down the hall, Cyperus acting nearly blind, having gone off somewhere in his mind to get the program ready. Blood was soaking through the bandage on his knee, she noticed. He was doing his body more damage, the realization was a wound ripped in her own gut, but she didn't see a way for him to do anything else. She couldn't carry him.

She was dripping with sweat herself now, drops sliding faster down the paths the rave lines made for it from her forehead. There, the bay door. She pressed to open it manually with her free hand, then turned away, pushing for the smaller bay where she'd liberated the scissors and met with Cyperus and Galax. That was next door, only a little farther.

Just such a little distance farther, but running footsteps were thudding up behind them.

They made it around the intervening corner in the corridor, but were still far short of their goal when the footsteps reached the open bay door. Sienna stopped them against the wall, pressed her face into Cyperus's shoulder to muffle her sawing breaths. He was fully focused in his mind, it seemed, making no noise besides his own breathing.

Please. It was dark. They were out of sight. The door was wide open and inviting. Please.

Against the wall beside her hip, she drew her rooftop and mountain symbols, unseen. Shouts inside the bay, and then—yes—the sound of a flyer lifting off. Cyperus gave a choked groan, then collapsed against her in truth. She could only lower them both to seats on the floor, against the wall. <Pen, is he all right—?>

<Vitals are steady. I'll let you know if that changes.> Pen's voice was distracted. Sienna didn't send any other message, letting Pen focus on whatever she was doing.

Another moment of danger, if their pursuers turned back the way they'd come—but no, she heard a second flyer. Silence settled around them like a comforting blanket this time, and Sienna drew on the floor an ephemeral version of the knot from the painting of Cyperus's back while she waited for him to wake up.

Pen kept Sienna updated on the flyer chase over half the continent as Cyperus groaned his way back to consciousness. When Pen had enough attention to spare to power a room and hide the drain, as before, she guided Sienna to it. It proved to be a small meeting room, rather than a bedroom, for reasons Sienna couldn't fathom until they arrived, weight awkwardly balanced as ever, in the lit doorway.

Gentiana turned from where she'd been watching the room's primary door, a war between concern and suspicion making her features even sharper, especially with her black hair back in a tight tail. "Well, I'm here, and alone." She gestured to the earpiece she was wearing, though she wasn't otherwise in uniform, clearly referencing a message she'd received on it. "I hear you've been attacking people. So if you don't want me calling in backup, start explaining, fast."

<I asked her to come here. Please, just talk to each other.> Pen's voice was apologetic.

Sienna braced herself, but she had no running left in her. She hardly had the energy to keep standing. <Pen, you don't know we can trust her! She's grieving and I'm a hell of a reminder of what she lost.>

<It wasn't her who revealed you before! That was your boyfriend, remember? You can trust her, I promise.>

<That's easy for you to say.> Apparently there a tiny reserve of energy left in Sienna to unlock, because she found herself stabbing the air with her finger. <When she reminds you of a wife you never had in the first place! She can call Elantine as easy as,>—Sienna snapped her fingers—<and then I'm dead and Cyperus is her fucking nanite slave, as well as half the facility, for all I know, and then she can see about wiping you!>

"You can trust her." Penstemon's words sounded teeth-clenched. It took a moment for Sienna to realize that not only had that last come from Pen's external speakers, but the channel before had been a local-area one, not a personal one. Pen had opened it, and Sienna had answered on the same one without thinking. It would have gone to Gentiana's earpiece as well.

The others were staring at her, Gentiana blank with shock, Cyperus with gears cranking behind his eyes, but—if Sienna was honest with herself—not any less shocked. "You…did do something to the Near-AI," he said.

<We need to sit down,> Sienna said on the same local-area channel, to give herself time to think. Not that she saw any other options besides coming clean, to Gentiana as well, since she was here for good or ill. She got Cyperus into one chair around the

room's central, oval-shaped table. Then it was time to lower herself into her own seat and she started when she felt Gentiana's hand on her elbow, helping.

All right. No more stalling. <The implant had more than Isachne's last message, it had part of her memories. I don't know how much, but they kept intruding and I had to download them for my own sanity. Penstemon—Pen—stored them in her core and it…affected her."

Pen made the sound of a snort. "Affected. That's an understatement."

Gentiana stepped away from Sienna, from them all, hands curling up where she clutched them against her chest. She made a soft keening sound. "Isachne…?"

A sigh. "No, love. Pen. I know I probably sound just like her at times, but that will lessen with time as I become more myself. That self simply knows some things she knew. And feels—" Pen cut herself off, the last word coming out strangled. Sienna suspected Pen didn't know quite what she felt.

Cyperus gently hit his forehead on a fist set upright on the tabletop, straightened on a breathless laugh. "You fucking *last-jumped* a Near-AI? By accident? Do you know how long Pax Romana scientists have been trying…"

Sienna hugged her arms over her stomach, holding in a hysterical laugh of her own. The joke was on the Pax Romana, as she couldn't see how they'd replicate the circumstances. "We can worry about that after we do something about Elantine."

Gentiana cleared her throat, tears audible in the roughness of the sound, but not detectable anywhere else. "What is it that the commander's done? Everyone's saying you attacked her," she nodded to Cyperus, "because of some wild story she convinced you of." Sienna's turn for a nod.

Maybe in laying it all out, Sienna could make Elantine's motives a little clearer in her own mind as well. <She's LSF.

Testing or incubating some kind of weapon. Nanite based. Galax's scanners showed elevated counts in Cyperus's blood until Pen calibrated it not to show up. It sort of…turns people off? Ever since I've been here, Cyperus would occasionally go blank for a few moments, then click back on without him or Pen noticing anything had happened. Then Galax did it too.> She tipped a hand to Gentiana. <You could be infected as well. I imagine that would be the point. Spread it around the military, turn them all off at key points. Or maybe it's just those with implants they're targeting.> She flicked her eyes down to her own data paths across the backs of her hands, getting distracted by the false note of her changed appearance.

"If it's infectious, I'm patient zero. Elantine's had enough time to set it up while I was in surgery—" Cyperus's voice wavered, soured like he was fighting back nausea. "That's why they were all unsuccessful. *Fuck*." He slammed a hand on the table, more curses tearing themselves free.

Gentiana's gaze dropped to Cyperus's knees, though the one not cradled by the assist looked much worse at the moment. "So she's trying to kill Sienna because she noticed the signs of this weapon?"

Sienna shook her head. <No, she tried to kill me as soon as I arrived. So damned if I know. Maybe it's just because LSF really hates Idyll.> She dropped her head, elbows on the table, and laced her fingers into her hair. Pretty soon, she'd find herself longing to be back at the camp, insane as that sounded.

"It's too big a risk just for that." Cyperus's tone had grown focused, and Sienna raised her head to find his gaze had gone sharper, more internal, as well. They were squarely within his area of expertise, she supposed. "What happened between when they chose you in the camp and when you arrived here? You said you were using an assumed Pax Romana identity at the camp?"

<Yes. And then I gave my real student visa number on the shuttle…> Sienna frowned. <That still ends up with it being something about Idyll.>

"Penstemon? Do you have anything in storage connected to that visa number?" Cyperus rattled it off without a pause, like he'd had it stored locally on his system. "If someone put in a cross-planet search request—"

"I might have a copy from after it arrived but before I transmitted it to her personal storage—she's undoubtedly deleted that. One moment please." Pen fell back into Near-AI speech patterns for the last sentence. "Ha!"

A written record popped up on the section of screen on the tabletop before Cyperus. Sienna leaned to read over his shoulder, but he was already scrolling, scanning for something in particular rather than actually reading. He fell back into his seat. "The fucking Amsterdam Institute in your work history? How many surprises do you have left, Sienna?"

Sienna licked her lips. Was that—was that seriously why—? <It was an internship. With their *counseling wing*, for mercy's sake. I told you about that, remember? I helped run the scheduling software.>

"But you have connections. If you ever made it home, mentioned to some former coworker what you'd seen—or worse, got infected before you left. LSF would have all but gift-wrapped their weapon and delivered it, begging the Institute to get to work on creating the counter." Cyperus blew out a long breath. "They picked the *wrong* fucking victim at the camp. Universal mercy."

Gentiana had stiffened at the first mention of the Institute, and now she eyed Sienna. "And she'd be handing over Pax Romana int-tech to the Idyllians as well."

Cyperus made his scoff a slap in Gentiana's face. "As an infantry grunt, you wouldn't be aware, but I can tell you Idyllian int-tech is so far beyond Pax Romana they've lapped us." He circled his finger. "Possibly twice."

Gentiana bristled, but Pen made a throat clearing noise. "He's right, I'm afraid. Also he needs not to be an asshole."

Enough. Their pursuers weren't going to chase an empty flyer forever. <If you can get me home, I'm happy to negotiate what I do and don't tell my friends. But can we do something about Elantine so I can get home at all?>

"We'll have to tell everyone, get them to remove Elantine from command until we can get an official ruling from off-planet." Cyperus sounded confident, Gentiana less so as they went back and forth for a few moments, exchange dense with details of chain of command and Pax Romana military regs that Sienna couldn't follow and didn't try.

She tuned back in when Gentiana grimaced, then nodded. "I'll pass the word. You'd better plead your case yourself." She tipped her head for them to follow.

Which was all very well, but reminded Sienna they hadn't actually addressed the trusting Gentiana issue. <So you're on my side?>

Gentiana's lips thinned. "Even if you wanted to make the Near-AI sound like my dead wife—but really, why?—I don't see how you *could*. So if I believe that part, I don't see any of the rest of it is particularly impossible by comparison."

"And I vouch for her." Pen's voice was heavy with finality.

Sienna didn't like it, particularly, but she also didn't like being in danger of being killed, in danger of being silent for the rest of her life—no. She couldn't afford to even begin that thought. She turned to Cyperus, but seeing the way he was slumped in his chair, one hand clamped over his bandaged knee as if to hide the seeping red stain, she couldn't imagine asking him to not only stand once more, but walk across the complex again. <Cyperus, you should stay here.>

Cyperus's head jerked up, and he clenched his hands on the arm of his chair instead. "No."

Gentiana turned back to examine him from the doorway, shook her head. "She's right. You can't walk anywhere. Besides, your voice isn't going to particularly help the cause. Everyone already assumes you're just thinking with your dick."

Cyperus drew breath, undoubtedly for a blistering rebuttal, but Pen cut him off. "*That* has never been Tehran's problem. If anything, it's been the opposite."

Gentiana must have found that as purely Isachne as Sienna did, because she flinched. "We're burning daylight," she said, and walked out.

Sienna threw Cyperus a quick look of apology, then followed.

Worrying about encountering Elantine made the silent walk through the complex seem impossibly long, while the ability to walk normally, without Cyperus's weight, made it seem impossibly short. Before Sienna had even half of how she'd argue her case laid out in her mind, they were approaching the main door to the mess. "I haven't told everyone what I want to talk about, but 'bitch about how the higher-ups are mishandling the refugee chase' is the logical assumption I'm sure they're making," Gentiana said.

Sienna hung back, one hand against the wall. She wished there was some ridge there to get a grip on. <Wait, please, I need a minute—>

Gentiana threw her a sideways frown, but she did wait. "Why are you still on coms? A few of the others have implants, but most of the rest aren't going to be wearing their earpieces."

<I—> No, don't given in to panic. Measured breaths. <Can't. Can't talk. The paralyzer damaged my vocal cords.> She put her hand to her neck once more.

"You'll have to convince the ones who can hear you well enough that they pull in the others, I guess. I'll hit the high points to start."

Gentiana opened the door and strode in, and Sienna let herself be swept along in her wake.

About thirty people were inside, scattered around the tables, with half-eaten food and drinks, the picture of a bitching session much as Gentiana had described. Sienna wasn't sure of the complex's full complement, patients, doctors, and support staff, but she recognized representatives from each group she'd watched in the halls on Pen's cameras. Minus a crew to search for her and Cyperus outside, and a few of the highest-ranked doctors to be harangued by Elantine, she suspected.

And all of their eyes were on her now. Panic would have strangled her voice even if she'd had one. With so many of them, if they grabbed her, they could hand her over to Elantine without breaking a sweat. Gentiana held up a hand for their attention, stood hip-shot to confidently claim a space at the head of the room. "Yeah, I found the Idyllian, but we have a *much* fucking bigger fox problem to worry about now."

Sienna watched everyone's faces as Gentiana efficiently laid out what she and Cyperus had told her. When Gentiana reached the end, a woman near the front scoffed. "Got any proof for this?"

She had data paths, so Sienna could reach her over the local-area channel. <She's been deleting everything out of Penstemon's records, or preventing her actions from being recorded in the first place, but that's suspicious in and of itself, if you think about it. What's she hiding?>

The woman flicked a dismissive hand. "Still not proof, Idyllian." Mutters and whispering started up around the tables, Sienna's answer being spread and remarked on.

Proof. She had to show them. Sienna's instinct was visual, but maybe she could use that. <Penstemon? Can you bring up a map of the complex with Elantine's location?> She hadn't been entirely sure where the wall screen would be in the room, but

Pen promptly blanked it to black before bringing up the map, and Sienna stepped over to it.

"And you could have programmed the Near-AI ahead of time to show whatever the hell you wanted to doctor up." The self-appointed spokesperson crossed her arms.

Sienna lifted a hand generally to the ceiling. <Use your command codes and ask her if I have.> A pause, while the woman did just that at excruciating length—had "the Idyllian" given her anything to display? Had the Idyllian even accessed any of this data before now? Etc.—and then she subsided back with a final scoff. Apparently that was permission to proceed.

Sienna faced the map and focused every visual impulse she'd had in her life into her frown at it. <Display any areas lacking sensor data or recordings as black, please. Begin this morning, 0600 hours.> She kept her directions on the local-area channel, transparent as possible. As quickly as she could, she sketched out what Elantine had done that morning, starting when Sienna woke in Cyperus's bed. She hated to play into their assumptions about Cyperus's motives, but it wasn't like they were actually *wrong* about what they'd been doing last night, whatever his motives.

Then back to the map. Label Cyperus's quarters, timestamp the black cloud, watch it move down the hall, cast Cyperus's quarters into darkness. Watch it move down the hallway again, zoom in the map sufficiently to plot Cyperus's position on his bed, unmoving as one minute ticked into the next. Then the treatment room was dark and she choked on a whine of fear her throat couldn't form, remembering what had been happening at the center of that lack of recording.

Cyperus's tag approached on the map, entered the hole. The walls of the treatment room pulsed with color, undirected by Sienna. <Penstemon? What was that?>

"Anomalous sensor readings from the adjoining rooms," Pen said, at her most bland.

"Anomalous how?" someone shouted from the back. Sienna dared to turn around, found her audience—universal mercy, thank you—rapt.

"Consistent with a gun shot."

With that, the background mutter surged to a wash of reactions and questions that would have drowned Sienna out, had she been speaking aloud. She edged back to the wall, leaving the screen and its proof unobstructed, and tried not to allow the urge to run to inhabit the entirety of her body as the argument crystallized over not *whether* to do something, but *what.*

Perhaps someone had warned her, perhaps the chatter had spilled noticeably onto public channels; however she'd found out, Elantine was suddenly striding across the mess. In Sienna's mind, her expression had grown murderous, even ravening, but in reality she looked mild. Angry, certainly, but in the manner of an officer drowning in fools.

"Enough with the paranoid rantings," she snapped. "Where's Tehran? You didn't hurt him further, did you?"

Now was the time to run. But Gentiana was in her way—Gentiana was in front of her, protecting her? "I suppose you knew Isachne was dead the whole time, didn't you? Is that why she was assigned here, for recovery? So you could keep an eye on the false prisoner? And good thing you were here, too, since that false prisoner looks like she holds the key to blowing up your whole project, you wet fox shit!"

An echo quivered in Sienna's muscles, a memory of pain from when Gentiana had beaten her at their first meeting. But now that particular pitch of anger was aimed away from her, to her benefit even, because rather than launching herself at Elantine, Gentiana braced herself, immovable defense. In a sudden spark of comprehension, Sienna saw in Gentiana part of what Isachne must have: utter loyalty.

Two soldiers seized Elantine, including the woman who'd been most vocal in her objections, originally. Elantine growled, not quite losing her cool just yet, but Sienna could see in her eyes the poisonous roil of emotion of someone who sincerely wished Sienna had starved to death in the rain.

"Have you all learned nothing? You're going to let this new Amsterdam Genevieve worm her way in here, the better to betray us all?" When her captors started dragging her back, that was when Elantine's manner transformed. "She is *playing* all of you, with her big eyes and 'boo-hoo, poor me' schtick!" She was spitting the words now. "Why the fuck would I be a fox?"

<Shut up,> Sienna sent, in prison LSF French. Few of those who could hear it would understand it, but she saw it land in the snap of Elantine's head to her. And Elantine did, though apparently only in service of a martyred act, departing bolt upright between her captors, no longer resisting.

That was fine. Sienna would take it.

Somewhere in the ensuing chaos, Sienna found herself unsupervised, hunched at the back of the mess, bolting a meal while she had the opportunity. Not only unsupervised, she supposed, but free to roam the complex for the first time without fear. Fear of capture, at least. Fear of silence remained. Even that didn't give her a clear direction, however—Galax was their int-tech expert, should she ask him to look at her vocal cords? Paralyzers were… not quite int-tech. And did she trust him, after what he'd done? More than any other doctor here, she supposed. <Pen, where's Galax?>

<Treating Cyperus. I'll leave him a message to check you out when he's finished.> Pen's words were breezy, matter-of-fact, as

if Sienna requested that rather than Pen making the decision on her own.

Cyperus was willing to forgive him, it seemed, which meant more to Sienna than she wanted to admit. All right. She'd finished stuffing herself, so she needed to find somewhere to wait. A bare room in the dark section? Even with the heat on there, she'd rather retrieve her jacket first, but that was on Cyperus's floor, and his quarters would be locked.

In the end, Sienna dragged her feet all the way to a treatment room—smaller, but unfortunately still outfitted in much the same manner as the others in which Elantine had attacked her—on the theory that if she was going to hover uncomfortably in any location, it should be one where Galax could easily examine her before he changed his mind.

As the hours dragged on, Sienna regretted her choice. Too much had happened to her in rooms like this, and without exhaustion to drag her under, she found it far too quiet. It wasn't that she *missed* the camp—mercy forbid—but the audible undercurrent of humanity seemed to have settled into her bones nonetheless.

What remained to her was thinking, curled tight on her side, fingertips up against her throat as a side effect of her arms being against her chest. What if she could never speak again? Would that truly be so bad? She was alive, she was closer to traveling home than she'd been yet. Unless the Pax Romana had some sort of refugee bureaucracy they'd leave her to get lost in—no. Not thinking about that either. She could escape from that as well if she had to. In silence.

Misery congested her throat, misted over her eyes. Oddly, it hovered there, short of the wracking sobs Sienna had expected. The implant, she realized at length, chemically grinding the most razor-sharp edges off her wallowing. Good for it. Sienna couldn't bring herself to expend any effort in helping it.

"Sienna?" Gentiana's voice. Sienna had positioned herself so simply tipping her chin down would give her a view of the doorway, but the other woman had still managed to surprise her. Sienna scrubbed away some of the tears gumming up her eyes to focus on her properly. Still wearing her earpiece, fortunately, holding a bundle against her stomach. "Pen wanted me to check on you."

Sienna curled tight, shutting Gentiana and the world out as much as she could. <I'm fine. Waiting.>

"She also wanted me to give you all of Isachne's stuff, since you don't have anything of your own at the moment. I told her either she's Isachne enough she gets to decide what to do with my late wife's possessions, or she isn't Isachne and I have to call her Pen, she can't have it both ways. And then we had a screaming fight about it."

As the story unfolded, brushed with a surprising humor, Sienna relaxed enough to focus on Gentiana's face again. <I'm sorry?> Gentiana didn't seem angry, though.

"Nah." Gentiana arrived, leaned a hip on the next diagnostic couch in line. "Isachne never screamed. She'd sit there, maddeningly calm, until I wore myself out. Sort of drives home that she isn't my dead wife—and isn't a Near-AI any more either, because a Near-AI would never use that kind of language." She exhaled on a laugh, then approached cautiously. Sienna threw her a grimace of annoyance. She wasn't going to run off.

"She's really worried about you, you know." Gentiana's voice dipped serious. She set a tablet aside, then shook out remainder of the bundle in her arms, revealing a well-worn blanket, original yellow shade faded to the palest pastel. "I couldn't get your jacket, but this is mine, not Isachne's at all, and you're welcome to it instead." She lofted it gently over Sienna's shoulders.

Sienna settled it as a wrap instinctively, petted the nap of the fabric. Such softness was oddly soothing, on a level even deeper than the implant's efforts to keep her out of hysteria. <I should really have listened to more of her advice in all of this, I suppose.>

"Funny you should say that." Gentiana's laugh rose beyond breath to a flicker of notes this time. She retrieved the tablet, offered it out. "She told me to tell you I want you to '*make an art*' for me." Her pronunciation of the Idyllian words was atrocious, but understandable.

Sienna jerked upright when she remembered what she'd been doing immediately after the conversation being quoted. <Pen is a voyeur.> Anger was close, but laughter was closer, and Sienna let herself fall into it. What had she expected? Of course Pen had been watching.

The tablet opened to the art program she'd cobbled together for Cyperus, and she set it to simple dark lines for the moment. <May I do your portrait?> she asked Gentiana, and received a cautious nod. She'd gotten a lot of practice with charcoal portraits in the camp, while the guards looked the other way. Not only had it kept her busy, but she'd treasured the small spark of pleasure the other prisoners got from seeing themselves captured on spare bits of wall between cleaning cycles.

And line and shape was another kind of language, she supposed. One not denied to her. She sank so far into it, Galax had to call her name before she noticed he'd arrived. Gentiana nodded to her, encouragingly, and slipped out.

Galax, expression haggard, hovered at a distance from her that edged beyond polite to diffident, and turned a scanner around in his hands. "I'm sorry I wasn't here sooner. Once we realized the former commander hadn't been attempting a replacement at all during Cyperus's knee surgeries, he asked that I do it as soon as possible to heal the scars at the same time as the gunshot wound. If I'd realized someone else needed me, I would have told him he should wait."

Sienna set the tablet aside and found her fingertips up against her throat once more. That repair had no doubt been as necessary to Cyperus's mental stability as the return of her voice was to her. <Were you successful?>

Galax looked down, at the blank readout of the scanner aimed vaguely at the floor. "Time will tell. He'll walk unassisted, certainly. Run, climb, though? I couldn't say without seeing how he heals." He offered her a lift at the corner of his mouth. "He was absolutely determined that he'd come to you after I was done. I told him he wouldn't be walking anywhere near that soon, so I promised I'd take you to him, when I was done fixing your vocal cords."

<They are fixable?> Universal mercy, please let them be.

"No guarantees until I see what I'm dealing with, but I'm optimistic—" He swallowed the rest of words convulsively when she flinched from his approach. She reminded herself that the worst had already happened—and he was trying to undo it and also Cyperus trusted him, then took hold of herself. She gestured him forward.

When he touched her throat, just a gentle brush, she closed her eyes over the sting of tears, kept them from slipping free. An interval when his touch withdrew, scanning she assumed, and he exhaled in a rush. "Yes. With a batch of directed healing nanites—I can get most of the function back, if not all."

This time the tears did escape. Sienna put her fingertips up to her nose to hold them back, but instead they dripped down the backs of her hands, shivery when they crossed her rave lines.

"That's the good news—the bad news is I *have* to put you out." Galax took a deep breath. "And before you refuse, I want to apologize to you. The same way the commander was working on the nanites in Cyperus's system, she—she was working on me too. Through conversation. Asking my professional opinion about your mental health, planting seeds about how disturbed and divorced from reality you were, how he was letting his emotions draw him into believing you…I could see for myself how hard he'd fallen, and I just accepted the rest of it. I was wrong. I got you hurt—could have gotten you killed."

"Don't forget to offer her heartfelt thanks as well, for flushing your fox for you." Pen joined the conversation at her most Isachne-caustic. "And back it up with a little fucking kindness and whatever luxury you can scrape together on this benighted planet. We'd never have known about the new LSF weapon if not for you, Sienna. It looks to me like Elantine would have been ready to release it wide in an infectious form within a few months."

<You've—verified it, then?> That wasn't quite the word Sienna wanted, but it was good enough, because Pen laughed, short and acid.

"Did we ever. Galax helped me with some outside calibration of my sensors, and I've been scanning everyone in the facility ever since. Cyperus is fucking teeming with them, obviously; the others with implants—excepting you, of course—have a medium load of the nanites; and everyone else has at least enough of a load for me to detect, though I think that's below the threshold of effectiveness. For now."

Sienna winced. Were she Gentiana or any of the others, her skin would be crawling at the moment, just thinking of it.

"The good news is, they can't infect person to person yet, or you'd definitely be showing some." Pen couldn't technically leer, but Sienna damn well heard one anyway.

<That would be true even if we'd only held hands,> she said primly, and let laughter rise up at the teasing, fueled in no little measure by hysteria.

"I'm quarantining the planet on my fairly non-existent authority anyway." Galax scrubbed at his face. "I know damn well by the time we assemble enough proof to get an official ruling, they'll freak out and ask us to go back in time to start one immediately anyway. Then it will be a matter of developing a counter before we die of old age here."

That was what was bowing Galax's shoulders, Sienna realized. Not just the betrayal of his friendship, or what he felt was the betrayal of his ethics, but the assumption that the search for the cure would fall mostly on him, as he was on the ground and no one was likely to risk coming in person to help.

<Look the other way so I can leave with a sample, and I have a couple friends at an institute who can probably help with that,> she told him.

To see the hope dawning on this face—it *hurt*, it was so good. Sienna suddenly understood what drove so many over in Research, when she'd always assumed Counseling was the real place to spread mercy in the universe.

She tipped her chin back, baring her throat to him symbolically. <Let's get this done, then.> She frowned generally up at the ceiling. <Pen, you'll watch…? I mean, of course you will, but—> Still. She needed to know someone friendly was watching over her. Someone who was really worried about her. Given time, the fact that such people existed here was seeping into her.

"I'll sound all the alarms in the place if he so much as puts a finger wrong." Pen's voice was warm.

Not yet home, not yet exclusively among friends, but safe, and with one or two friends nearby. Under the category of escape, Sienna would count this as an interim success.

Sienna had rehearsed the words dozens of times today, and now, sitting next to Cyperus, they were all she could fit in her mind: *Have you thought about coming back with me?* She might have had the physical ability to say that out loud now, but apparently she didn't have the emotional one, even with only a few days left before her opportunity was gone for good.

She'd managed to hide her tension from Cyperus, at least, as he was reading silently on his system as they waited in another bland meeting room for Galax. They were supposed to be discussing the exact logistics of how she'd get a sample home, but Sienna didn't begrudge Galax the luxury of running a little late, considering command of the whole facility had indeed devolved onto him.

"Ha!" Cyperus said suddenly. "You'll enjoy this. Look what I found among the information Elantine requested from Idyll." He brought up a photo on the table.

One glance was enough for Sienna to recognize it. Embarrassing, definitely, but lightly so, as it was also a reminder of a happier time. "That was publicly accessible?" She spread her hand to partially obscure it until she could finish her disclaimer. "You should know, posing for some version of this photo is a tradition for everyone who works there, especially the interns."

The photo showed the grand sweep of the Amsterdam Institute's main building. Its central windows reflected the vibrant presence of the forest it faced, and to the side of the main doors, a sculpture reached the roof, a mostly two-dimensional silhouette of a woman with wings half-raised behind her beside two men, one with wings, one without. Their grouping looked to the side, attention on their path ahead, while the polished metal surface reflected back green broken into abstract pools where the metal curved up or down in a suggestion of three dimensions to the figures' bodies.

And, comparatively small, Sienna stood before the woman's feet, looking to the side with her arms raised high, a laughing imitation of Amsterdam Genevieve herself.

"To do it right, you really should have two of you, one to do Amsterdam, one to do her wings," Cyperus teased, startling a laugh from her.

Because he'd made her laugh, and because maybe it would give her the courage she needed to ask him the question that filled her mind, Sienna caressed fingertips down the paths on his hand. She was rewarded with an exhalation on a low, pleased note. He did have that kind of sensation tuned in, then. Excellent.

"Galax sends his apologies." Gentiana knocked a knuckle on the doorframe only after she'd spoken. Sienna jerked her hand away from Cyperus's. Gentiana lowered her hand so she could lounge against the doorframe in its place. "Okay, what could you two possibly have been doing in here half a meter apart with all your clothes on, that you look so guilty about?"

"Data-path fucking." Pen sounded insufferably smug. "Which I'm honestly staggered no one invented before her, but I can't find it in any of Isachne's memories, so Sienna can probably claim that too."

Sienna pressed her forehead to the table and hid her face with her arms. "Pen, if you aren't a Near-AI anymore, you have to stop being such a voyeur," she said on a reluctant laugh, muffled.

When she dared show her face again, Cyperus, far from amused or offended, looked frozen. It was as if he couldn't comprehend such teasing when it was aimed at him, given a lifetime of holding back from relationships serious enough for friends and family to notice. She switched to a private channel with him. <I can have a serious talk with Pen, if you want.>

Cyperus shook his head, but was distracted from further response when Gentiana cocked her head in curiosity about the photo still up on the table. He slewed it around to face her. "Look what Elantine found."

"I imagine she shit her pants when she saw it," Gentiana murmured, pleased. "Do we know when we're shipping her out yet?"

"Not yet. I imagine they'll want to attempt to interrogate her, since we're not mentioning that we have another lead on a counter, in case they make trouble for Sienna getting out of here." Cyperus sprawled back in his chair, reveling in all the positions he could manage without the assist, even if he still needed crutches for any trip longer than the one from his quarters to the mess. Those crutches were noticeably absent at the moment, which didn't necessarily mean he'd been cleared for the longer distance to the meeting room, but Sienna didn't interfere.

They'd assured Sienna—and Pen had verified—that she hadn't come up at all in the reports Galax was making, yet. She would, eventually, but by then she'd be gone via the next supply ship. "I can't promise how long a counter will take to develop," she noted. It might go faster with a live sample. She could say that too, right now. A good, logical reason for coming with her.

"That's all right, that means I might be back up to physical strength by the time I have the opportunity to get my clearance back." Cyperus sat up straighter, gaze going distant. Everything he'd ever longed for, Sienna supposed.

"Tehran Cyperus." Pen's voice was unexpectedly intense. "Did Elantine deactivate your brain? You are never going to get your clearance back. Never. It's not giving away any secrets to say that having heard Galax's conversations with the brass, it's touch and go whether any of you will ever be leaving this planet again, and even if we can eventually finesse that, I doubt they'll let you even speak to an active agent in your life again, for fear of infection."

Sienna was getting less hopeful about her chances with every moment, but she'd never have another opportunity as perfect as this. "You know, Amsterdam Genevieve came home with two Pax Romana soldiers who not only helped her found the Institute, they eventually became citizens." She oriented the photo on the table to face the two of them again, and tapped the two men in the sculpture. "You could come with me. Then they'd not only have a live sample of LSF's nanites, they'd have a way to immediately test a counter to see if it really works in someone's system instead of just in the lab."

He opened his mouth to respond, but she hurried on, desperate to get all her arguments out before he could refuse. "And it's not like you'll be giving them access to any Pax Romana int-tech that I won't be, given Isachne's implant. If you're worried about having enough to keep you busy, the Institute's Research division would hire you in a heartbeat, or Idyll Defense—"

Cyperus finally cut her off, expression pained. He covered one of her hands with his own, hiding the image of the sculpture as well. "Sienna, I can't just walk away from the fight with LSF, not after this. Whatever I have to do, to help strike back at them…" She suspected he hadn't actually heard a single one of her arguments, so carefully prepared.

"Listen to me. They're not going to let you do a damn thing, you fucking moron—" Pen's volume rose.

"Even if you were Isachne herself, making such fool pronouncements, you have no idea what the brass might or might not make compromises on, to keep my skills—" And Cyperus could shout her down just as easily.

"Stop it!" Sienna hunched her shoulders in, but didn't allow herself any other visible sign of the way her stomach was twisting itself around a knot of disappointment. There was no point the others being assholes at each other when it wouldn't change anything. "It's a hell of a lot to give up, leaving not only a career, but a home. I understand."

Gentiana dragged her fingertips along the table, stealing the photo out of their control, though she didn't do anything with it once it was in front of her. "Bear in mind, I don't have personal insight on any of that, but it sounds to me like he won't *have* a career to leave, so then it's only home." One side of her lips pulled tight, sad. "Some people are worth giving up even something that big for."

Cyperus's expression was stunned once more. Sienna supposed he hadn't realized that's what she was really asking—come *with* her, not just with her. She should have been more clear, but she had her answer anyway. She wished it didn't hurt so much.

She pushed to her feet. "I'd better go see about picking out quarters of my own." Because she'd been staying with Cyperus, but damned if she'd keep sleeping with him when that would only make it hurt worse when she left. "Since you're keeping me out of this, I don't really need to be there for the meeting with Galax anyway."

"Oh. I..." Cyperus trailed off, looking hunted, and didn't pick up even when Sienna turned back to look at him. All right then.

As she headed down the hall, Cyperus gave a shout of pain. "What the fuck?" Gentiana had kicked him, maybe. Sienna appreciated the sentiment more than she really should have, even though there was no point to it. She hugged her arms across her chest as she strode blindly for a hallway with several unclaimed rooms on her internal map.

She was so close to home now. She could concentrate on that.

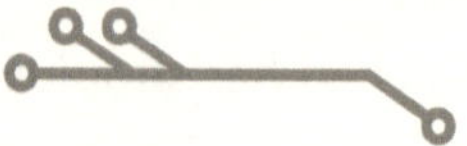

Sienna tried to tell herself that she lingered under the covered walkway out to the supply ship, dribbles of droplets forming curtains to either side, because she was savoring the feeling of having no need for stealth, every right to stand tall in this place. Really, though, it was because she wished Cyperus would come to say goodbye. While she desperately hoped he wouldn't come to say goodbye, because maybe that would be cleaner.

She adjusted the strap of the duffel of gifted clothing and sundries—in the closed system of the complex, some things were undoubtedly Isachne's, but Gentiana pretended none were, and Sienna preferred it that way herself—and offered Gentiana an uneven smile. “If you want to get out of here too, now’s your chance.” Not really serious, of course.

“No, even when they release us, I’d rather stay with Pen. She might need an advocate.” Gentiana lifted her hands, dropped them, and clasped her opposite elbows instead. Sienna recognized the gesture, and closed the hug as thanks for Gentiana letting her be the one to initiate it. Whatever had happened since, she still sometimes saw an echo of Gentiana’s movement to kick her in some innocent shift of position. “For all you did for us, thanks,” the woman murmured into her ear, squeezed a last time, then released her.

<And you keep in touch, Pen, too.> Sienna allowed herself a last fretful look to the building. <Is Cyperus…heading this direction, at all?>

<Behind you.> Pen’s words were slightly smug? It made no sense in any case, though Sienna turned instinctively. And there was Cyperus coming down the ship’s extended ramp. Walking without crutches, though he’d have put in a fair amount of distance already to reach the ship in the first place. She could see a slight hesitation, an unevenness to his stride that would undoubtedly build to something untenable by the time he reached a run, but for now, he strode more than fast enough. Confident, finally comfortable in his body.

And wearing a Pax Romana dress uniform. She hadn’t realized the intelligence rank transferred, or maybe it didn’t, she had no idea about Pax Romana insignia and *damn*. The cut flattered him. She made a sound approximately like “guh,” the breathiness of which she was going to blame on the paralyzer damage to her vocal range.

Gentiana, damn her too, *laughed*.

He stopped a little before her, and grinned. “Sorry, I lost track of time negotiating. They were willing to drop us off early, so we can catch a direct flight to Idyll, rather than going toward the core and hopping back out, but they were going to insist we do it in cargo seats. I squandered a bunch of favors I won't be needing anymore to talk them into a cabin."

Us. We. Joy rocketed up through Sienna's stomach, meeting the heavy fog of disappointment she'd been swathed in for the past few days, mixing, and curdling. She was so happy, yet so *fucking exasperated*. She stepped into Cyperus, but only to play-punch him in the stomach. "How long since you decided? Universal mercy, you couldn't have put me out of my misery early, and told me you'd changed your mind before the absolutely barest last second?"

Not the reaction Cyperus had expected, clearly, but this time he rolled with it rather than freezing. He caught her hands, but didn't really restrain them in case she had more punches in her. "I wanted to get it all arranged. As kind of an…apology gift, I guess."

Gentiana wasn't actively laughing any longer, but she was looking just as smirky as Pen had sounded. "Take it from me, the married one, that small things like listening consistently trump grand gestures every single time. Stop being such a fucking show-off."

Cyperus dropped his head. "All right. I'll own it. I didn't listen to you properly. I'm sorry." He changed his grip, clasping her hands separately now, searched her face. "But Pen played it back for me, and you never did say *you* wanted me to come with you. Why couldn't you trust me enough to believe that I might think you're worth it? Or at least believe there was enough chance of that for it to be worth asking?"

He was correct, of course. And she'd never realized. "I guess I'm—at the camp, I got out of practice with trust—" She couldn't stop herself now, she disengaged his hands so she could cling to him in the tightest embrace she could manage. "I promise to work on it." She could add it to her list for counseling.

“Me too,” he rumbled, and his arms settled tight over her hips and up her back. A few more seconds assuring herself he was really real, really coming with her, and she reluctantly tugged back. They’d better get going, or the supply pilot would leave them behind.

UNJUST THEFT

PART I

Prague Sienna pounded across the permeable hard surface of the Amsterdam Institute's spacefield toward the recently landed spaceship, mind racing just as fast in trying to figure out what was going on. The ship was a small runabout, though it was large enough to allow burst travel. Its type could take half a dozen people halfway across the known universe, if they stopped to refuel often enough. This one had—apparently—not come that far in distance, but certainly that far across political divides, leaving Pax Romana territory for the independent planet of Idyll.

<I think Gentiana might need medical assistance,> Penstemon said through Sienna's implant, but it made no more sense now than when Pen had summoned her to the spacefield. Pen was an AI based in a *building*, days of travel from here, even by burst.

<I'm sure security will call some in, if necessary. And you've certainly brought security down on yourself,> Sienna's partner, Cyperus, contributed. She glanced back to where he was striding with slow deliberation from the truck they'd arrived in. His black hair, cut too short for it to work up the wave it clearly wanted to, was in the local style, but the close-cut line of his beard around his mouth evoked the style of someone too urban and fashionable to want to work up a sweat. Which was absolutely not the case, but mercy forbid anyone should realize he physically couldn't

run due to his bad knee. She loved the man, but he was awfully stubborn in his pride.

Pen's call had reached them over an early breakfast, before both of them headed to work, and the spring sunrise was only now lightening the overcast skies at the horizon. They weren't far off winter so the air had a bite against her cheeks, and she was grateful for the heavy coat she'd thrown on. She looked behind Cyperus to where the Institute's security was gathering and cranked up the zoom along with the low-light enhancement her implant was granting her. As she'd expected, they were still hanging back to gather more information; the Institute got enough refugees that their security was trained to ask questions before shooting. They weren't going to stop any fools who wanted to run straight up to the strange ship, though.

<I'm fine,> Gentiana said, but the channel showed to Sienna as implant-to-implant, not voice-to-implant. That wasn't right either—Gentiana was Pax Romana infantry, and they didn't have implants. If she was even still with the military, after everything that had happened to her, surrounding the circumstances under which she and Sienna had met.

The ship's main ramp lowered and there was Gentiana at the top, clinging to the side of the entrance and looking like death. Literally, to Sienna's eyes—given the delicate sharpness to the woman's features, the sallow tinge to her light brown skin, and the way her long, black hair straggled out of a decaying tail, if Sienna had been drawing Gentiana, she would have portrayed her as a mortally wounded warrior queen.

Then Gentiana was falling and Sienna lunged up to catch her. Pulling the woman's arm over her shoulder gave her a close-up view of the central false note in her historical imagining, the shimmery red-orange data paths that started at circles at Gentiana's temples and continued as lines down the sides of her face, over the corners of her jaw, and down her neck. The woman had definitely had an implant installed since Sienna had seen her last, about a standard year ago; the data paths—or rave lines, Sienna still thought that was a better description when they weren't set to color-match the skin—gave the implant its outside connections, at the temples for a piloting harness and on the pads of the first two fingers for other equipment.

At the moment, Gentiana's natural skin around the data paths at the templates was noticeably inflamed. Cyperus pushed himself to a jog for the last fifty meters or so, apparently conquering his pride sufficiently to reveal his hitched and uneven gait. "Piloting fatigue," he said, then repeated himself on a wider channel for the security forces. <We do need to get her to medical.> He shifted his position to try to catch and hold Gentiana's gaze, bent slightly with his hands on his knees. He wasn't that much taller than her, but she had slumped against Sienna, head hanging. "Is this the first time you've piloted since you got the implant?"

Gentiana got her head up, but seemed unable to focus properly. "Pen said she would, but she couldn't. Not when she was trying to adjust to being so small. The implant…did most of it for me." Cyperus had spoken to her in Lingua, but she answered in the version of French used by Libertad Sans Frontiers, the Pax Romana's dire enemies, without seeming to realize it. That was a textbook sign of having used an implant to quick-learn a language very recently, which raised the urgent question of why Gentiana had thought she'd need it. Sienna only understood her because the language had been pre-loaded, as it were, on her own implant when that had been inflicted on her.

In fact, Gentiana's situation—staggering in, trying to hold herself together—brought Sienna's situation a year ago very much to the front of her mind. Idyll was neutral in the war between LSF and the Pax Romana, but LSF had captured Sienna by mistake, held her in a POW camp until they'd accidentally killed Isachne, a Pax Romana agent they needed for a prisoner exchange. So they'd shoved the dead woman's implant into Sienna's head and passed her off as Isachne, leaving Sienna to stagger into a Pax Romana facility, trying to hold herself together while scraps of a dead woman seeped into her mind from the implant.

Gentiana had even been the first person Sienna met properly at that facility, but there the strange, flipped echo of her situation ended—as Isachne's widow, a grieving Gentiana had expected an LSF trick, and had tried to kick Sienna's face in, not support her. Sienna had chosen not to hold it against her.

The intelligence agent Cyperus had once been engaged visibly in his expression now, tightening a muscle at the corner of his jaw as he shared a worried glance with Sienna over Gentiana's use of French. He continued firmly in Lingua. "You can guide an emergency burst with the implant's default piloting functions without any other training, but the number of bursts you'd have needed to get here from Penstemon's facility—fuck, Gentiana. You're lucky you didn't pass out in the middle of one and kill yourself. And Pen. Who's chasing you? The foxes?" A play on faux-French, referring to the fact that when LSF had adopted a dead language from the archives, they'd "updated" it heavily based on—of course—Lingua.

<No, we're being chased by our *own fucking side*,> Pen broke in, typically foul-mouthed, for her, but with an edge of desperation to her voice Sienna hadn't heard before.

"They copied Pen. Secretly, without her consent. Easiest way to get another last-jumped AI, I guess." Gentiana made it back to Lingua, but her choppy delivery suggested she was struggling to stay there. "But it was just another non-sentient Near-AI with more swearing."

<*She* was. My poor daughter.> That hadn't just been desperation she'd heard in Pen's voice, Sienna realized. It had been pure anguish.

"So they mothballed her. But LSF hit that facility and stole her with a bunch of other tech. The first Pen knew she existed was when she received a brief signal from her, deep in LSF territory. But the military brass didn't give a shit, and wouldn't let us go after her. So I had to go AWOL and help Pen transfer herself to the ship and come out here to get Cyperus so we can go save her daughter. We have to leave right away!"

And then Sienna was suddenly supporting *all* of Gentiana's weight. She barely managed to stagger them both back to the wall, where Cyperus helped lower Gentiana gently to a seat on the deck, propped against the wall.

"You're not going anywhere just yet. One of the most interesting symptoms of pilot fatigue," Cyperus growled under his breath, "is when you forget how to *walk* for a few days."

"Universal mercy," Sienna hissed as she straightened. She could barely process it all. Pen's daughter—clone?—what must it be like, knowing someone so nearly yourself was in the hands of the enemy? No wonder Gentiana had pushed herself to get here.

<Gentiana! Will she be all right? I didn't know her doing all the flying here was dangerous. I don't—I want to look up pilot fatigue, but I'm missing all my *fucking* databases—> Pen sounded like she was having focus problems of her own.

A couple of medical techs arrived, surrounded by a layer of security, and Sienna left Cyperus to convey what he knew about pilot fatigue to them as they loaded Gentiana onto a grav-pad stretcher. Sienna had been the one who last-jumped Pen—accidentally, by uploading the remains of Isachne's memories off the implant to the Near-AI to save her sanity—and while the process of Pen's personality solidifying then had been different, there was an unbalanced note to Pen's manner that was familiar. Sienna could only hope that insight could help her talk Pen through this now. <Don't worry, we have a whole medical division here at the

Institute. Gentiana's in good hands. I'll make sure they send you regular reports.>

<I don't have to wait for anyone else's shitty reports, I can monitor Gentiana's vitals from her implant. But it would be so much easier if they'd let me connect to the systems here—they keep blocking me—>

Sienna would *bet* they were blocking an attempt at comprehensive systems access from a random ship. She made a token effort at making Pen to understand that, but mostly just listened to the AI rant as she followed Cyperus out of the ship in the wake of the medical techs. He let them pull away and waited for her at the foot of the ramp. She gestured to her temple, grimacing. "Pen wants systems access." By then Pen was winding down, at least, and soon after muttered herself into resentful silence.

That left Sienna's own thoughts plenty of space to spin up. So they wanted Cyperus to go with them into LSF territory to rescue Pen's daughter. And if they were discovered? What would they do to Cyperus and Gentiana? As Pax Romana intelligence and military, theirs would be a very different—much worse—situation than hers had been as a civilian who'd ended up in a POW camp by mistake. She could feel the panic attack starting in her chest, rising heartrate driving the clenching upward into her throat so she wouldn't be able to make a sound here either, as she hadn't been able to in the camp, with a vocal paralyzer on her throat…

Cyperus stepped into her, hip pressed against hers and arm slung over her back. <LSF isn't coming here. Everyone's safe,> he sent on a personal channel between them. <You're safe.>

<I know,> Sienna said as she clung to him for a breath. It wasn't herself she was worried about. Or, well, it was—both the camp and all the times an undercover LSF agent had tried to kill her while she was in Pax Romana hands at Pen's facility had left an indelible mark on her. But she knew this panic attack, if

not the worries that had triggered it, would pass, as others had before. Cyperus was here, anchoring her with his particular scent, the particular play of muscles in his arm across her back. <But if you all have to go into LSF territory…>

<Even if Gentiana didn't need the recovery time, I'd still be counseling against going off half-cocked. I need a lot more information before we can make a real plan,> he said, voice firm.

Which gave Sienna—what had he said about pilot fatigue?—a few days to pull herself together? Because of course Cyperus needed to help them, and she'd do whatever she could as well. It wasn't hyperbole to say that Pen had saved her life many times over. The least she could do would be to help Pen rescue her daughter, no matter how much it scared her.

Gentiana was released from medical two days later, and while she walked into Sienna's and Cyperus's apartment under her own power except for a hand on Sienna's arm, the hesitance to her step showed she definitely needed the additional days of rest she'd been prescribed. Sienna shot a look back to Cyperus as they made their way down the hallway to the guest room, but she could see in his face that she didn't need to say anything over a channel. He'd avoid any interrogation in service of the rescue. For now.

"You impressed Pen with how much danger I was supposedly in, she's been awfully quiet since we arrived, 'so I can recover properly,'" Gentiana commented and slowed further, perhaps so the effort of walking didn't show in her voice. She spoke firmly in Lingua, however. "I gather we were successful in getting refugee status with the Idyllian government, though?"

"Yeah, I stood surety for you two." Sienna turned them into the guest room. She'd tidied it as much as she could, but there came a point when storage was storage, and no matter how neat, it was a cousin to clutter. She might be lucky, though—on moving in, Cyperus had been deeply bemused by all the wood; perhaps Gentiana would be too. Pen's facility was set among timber stands and had a few touches like floorboards, but the Idyllian habit of using the material for everything from shelves to window frames was unheard of on most Pax Romana planets.

Sienna huffed a laugh as she reviewed the last two days for other events Gentiana might need to know. "The call to figure out your status was a hell of a thing to get pulled into unexpectedly—Jeff, the Director of Counseling, is my former boss and a good friend, but all the other Amsterdam Institute directors are damn intimidating as a group, especially when they want to know why a Pax Romana military cruiser has shown up and is demanding extradition of one of their criminals. But when I explained that Pen was a true AI and suggested she might agree to answer questions, the Director of Research about fainted from excitement."

<And the more I refuse to answer and generally act like an intransigent asshole, the happier they are,> Pen contributed over a channel to all of them, extremely dry. Because Near-AI couldn't help but follow orders and answer any question put to them. <Though the novelty of that wears off real fucking fast, let me tell you.>

"Admit it, you love the captive audience," Sienna teased. And the fact that Research had filled one of the ship's cabins with as much data storage as they could pack in had gone a long way to improving Pen's mood as well, even if they still wouldn't allow her systems access. Yesterday, Cyperus had pointed out that as a Pax Romana refugee who'd been here for a year, even he still had very limited access within the Institute, which had finally cut her complaining back to something bearable.

Cyperus remained just inside the door, setting a shoulder to the doorframe, while Sienna took Gentiana to the bed. She collapsed to a seat there, and looked back up at Sienna with a grimace of gratitude. “I like the hair, by the way.”

“Thanks.” Sienna touched it automatically, though it wasn’t really styled at the moment, just tucked behind her ears. Which was the reason for her current haircut—short at the nape of the neck and angled longer at the front to allow her to tuck it back out of her face when she was painting. LSF had dyed her brown hair black to help her physically pass for Isachne at a casual glance, and while that had mostly grown out by now, Sienna had discovered she liked the cut she’d adopted to try to rid herself of as much of the dyed portion as possible. To soften the remaining black, she’d layered blue on top, giving the black a shimmery tinge at the tips and thinning out to highlights in the brown above.

Gentiana nodded to Cyperus next. “And you’re definitely walking better than when I saw you last.” Sienna hadn’t been the only one hurt by the undercover LSF agent at Pen’s facility—the reason the agent, working as a surgeon, had been there in the first place was to test a new LSF nanite weapon, and she’d started with Cyperus. She’d claimed surgery after surgery to repair his injured knee had failed, to keep him at the facility while the nanite weapon infection spread in his blood. At this point, the old injury would never fully heal.

Cyperus lifted the shoulder he wasn’t leaning on in a shrug. “The Institute does good work.”

Gentiana expanded her focus to the rest of the room, and Sienna thought she saw the bemusement, rather than annoyance, she’d hoped for. “Am I taking over your art studio?”

“I can clear space for my easel wherever. In here, I could just leave it set up rather than putting it away after each session.” Sienna lifted the easel from where it was leaning, folded, against the cabinet stuffed with her messy art supplies, next to the shelves with the supplies she could stack tidily and not be annoyed to see the state of them. The easel was a rather clever device, and she demonstrated briefly how a top layer rolled down to allow her to add physical media that was then incorporated automatically into the electronic display of the whole painting below. Then she could wipe off the top layer and add something else.

"I'm not working on anything in particular right now, anyway." She tucked the easel away and used her implant to bring up a line of her current unfinished works on the wall surface, scrolling through them at speed to see if any were close enough to completion be shown off. Not really. She displayed her last big project instead, a landscape photograph of a driftwood-studded beach she'd turned fantastical with magic in the gray clouds and tiny creatures hiding in the rocks.

Gentiana's eyes had gone big. "That's…impressive. You're not painting full time?"

"I keep telling her I'd cover the household expenses if she wanted to take the plunge," Cyperus remarked mildly.

"If I quit my job at the Institute, we'll have to move out of on-site housing and commute from town, and if I can't make a go of it, I'll have lost both an interesting job and a nice apartment. I'd be stuck back in a data-checking job, living out of a closet for months until something opened up again." If she didn't make a go of it…and Cyperus didn't stay. She hadn't wanted to count on that. So they kept having this same conversation over and over, like they were both in a decaying orbit around actually *talking* about what their lives should look like, long term. Whether those lives might be spent together.

A year was too long to have put off that conversation, she knew that—but the initial months of that time had been eaten up by intensive counseling on her part and intensive treatment to purge the LSF nanites on Cyperus's, and then there had been the time to settle into their respective Institute jobs.

And she certainly wouldn't have been able to avoid the topic alone.

Sure enough, here and now, Cyperus was the one to change the subject. "Speaking of new looks," he said dryly. He gestured in the region of his own temple, flickering his own rave lines visible, then camouflaged again. "You didn't get an implant installed specifically to be able to steal a ship and fly out here, did you?"

To business, then. Cyperus was hanging on to his possession of the doorway, so Sienna took a seat farther down the side of the bed.

"No, of course not." Gentiana grimaced at the absurdity of that idea, then clasped her hands in her lap and dipped her head, emotional fatigue seeming to take over from physical for a beat. "I need to back up a bit. After we implemented the counter for the LSF nanite weapon that you convinced Idyll to develop—" She dredged up a smile for Sienna. "And thanks for that, truly—scientists started showing up at the facility to study Pen. They came up with a plan to add extra storage to people's implants to record their memories. That way, when they die—naturally, or in the line of duty—the R&D folks can upload the memories to another Near-AI to try to replicate Pen. That's why I got an implant, so Pen and I can…be together. Eventually."

And what did *Pen* think of that idea? She'd been last-jumped using Isachne's memories, but from the start she'd maintained to everyone—and especially Gentiana—that she was an entirely separate entity. Besides, Sienna would have expected that kind of fairy tale, "together forever" thing would be too damn sappy for someone of Pen's sharp, ironic bent. But she made no comment now, for or against that vision of their future.

"But I supposed waiting for someone to die was taking too long—"

<I'm honestly surprised they didn't decide to kill a few people to hurry matters along,> Pen contributed, caustic.

Gentiana winced. "So they copied Pen. And Pen didn't find out until she got that signal, like someone had turned her daughter on and allowed network access before hurriedly cutting it off again. We went as far up the military chain of command as I could reach, and then a little farther, on Pen's clout as the universe's only true AI, and begged…but Pen's daughter is just another Near-AI, to them. Not worth a strike force to retrieve."

Gentiana focused her attention on Cyperus, whole body clenched in her pleading. "That's why I found a way to transfer Pen into a ship to come out here and get your help. We need your expertise to even find her in the first place. And then to come with us to rescue her. I have no intelligence training, but I can do anything physical that you can't—"

"Don't be ridiculous," Cyperus snapped. He could mention his physical limitations, but no one else could, generally. "You won't be in any shape for strenuous activity for weeks, and any tracking will need to be done from within LSF territory to be effective. I'll go alone."

Sienna had thought she'd prepared herself emotionally for this—it was a risk, he'd be putting himself in danger, but she agreed it was worth it—but now a new thought blindsided her and she realized she hadn't prepared herself nearly well enough.

What if, after finally being given a chance to return to intelligence work, he didn't want to come back?

She'd felt his restlessness for months, seen him pore over his friend Galax's letters and then pull up star maps on the wall after she'd gone to bed. She'd assumed Galax was sneaking him intelligence reports, but none of those had been enough to tempt him to leave Idyll. Yet.

"Cyperus, can I talk to you for a minute?" She caught his elbow on her way past through the doorway and he followed, frowning but not objecting. She waited to speak until they'd reached their bedroom across the hallway, and shut the door. Some conversations were too fraught to have over channels, even if those would have provided better privacy. "I just—are you sure—"

And now she had no idea how to put her greatest fear about him, about their love, into words. What if she was imagining it? But all she had to do was look around their shared room. He'd had several of her paintings printed onto fabric—easy to take down and fold away—and in place of a nightstand on his side of the bed, he was still using a trunk that converted from baggage to shelves when set on end. A candle, surrounded by a collection of small, meaningful charms to serve as a focus to think of universal mercy, held pride of place on the middle shelf.

She gestured to the mercy candle. "I guess it won't take you long to pack. You've never even found a place for that in the apartment." Acknowledging it to herself, that he could fold up and pack away his presence in her life in *minutes*, he'd put down so few roots, made her lose control of her voice. It grew louder and higher in distress, where it broke and then sputtered out for half a word over the gap vocal paralyzer damage had left in her range, which only made it harder for her to find the right words to ask if he'd come back to her. She *hated* when she couldn't express herself because of what LSF had done to her.

"It's just tidier that way." Cyperus's gaze on her face was tight and his voice held a slightly bewildered note. She'd learned to recognize it as signaling confusion borne of the fact that he'd managed to make it to his late thirties without any romantic relationship more serious than a couple of intimate encounters with the same person, before her. He must know there was something she wasn't saying, but not what.

And maybe that was better. He didn't need distractions, while in LSF territory. And she couldn't see that being clingy now would make him more likely to settle down with her when he was done—in fact, it might drive him away. Better that she stay silent and let him leave on a note of harmony.

Impulsively, she embraced him and he returned the gesture without hesitation. "I'll be fine. The foxes won't even know what hit them." His voice rumbled through his chest to hers.

<Would you mind going back into the room with Gentiana or talking on channels, so I can hear you?> Pen broke in diffidently, but without a hint of apology otherwise. <I have to rely on what she's sharing with me.>

<Sienna wanted this to be *private*, Pen,> Cyperus growled back. "Whatever this is?" His voice only trended up at the last second, making the question even more unsure.

Sienna managed a wobbly laugh before standing back from him. "Nothing. Worried about you, like you said. And I guess I should be worried about Pen going nuts having to stay on Idyll and not help you, huh?" She kept the words reasonably controlled, and squarely within her safe vocal range. "You should start packing."

She broke their embrace and slipped away, back to Gentiana. He'd come back to her, or he wouldn't, and she needed to start getting used to that idea too.

The spacefield at the Institute was used only for Institute business and visitors, so to catch a regular flight off-planet, it was easiest for Cyperus to take the train from the Institute's associated town, Adit, out to Delta, Idyll's biggest metropolitan area. Rather than make the multiple-hour trip there and back with him, Sienna saw him off at the train station the next morning. Packing had taken him significantly more than a few minutes, though included in that time had been the logistics of arranging a leave of absence from his job and reaching out to old contacts in search of leads on where in LSF territory Pen's daughter had been taken.

The organized chaos of the station around them was a mixture of business travelers and tourists; the Institute and Adit were the only developed destinations out here, so the rest of the traffic was related to wilderness recreation. They found a clear corner beside a carved wooden bench to step into for their goodbyes. Cyperus tucked his former-nightstand trunk, handle and wheels out—a grav pad at that size was too fragile to take the kind of abuse luggage was subject to—neatly beside his feet. His mercy candle wasn't inside, though—he'd left that on one of the shelves in their bedroom, explaining that LSF didn't use mercy candles, so he wouldn't be able to take it along once he reached their territory anyway.

At first, Sienna hadn't known whether to believe him or figure he was merely trying to calm what he saw as a strange worry she was fixating on, but her own research had borne him out. Now, to break the silence currently congealing between them, she pulled a smaller, pure white candle in a translucent red cup out of her shoulder bag. "I read that the foxes use voting—?" Her implant corrected her before Cyperus could. "Votive candles for decoration. So I got this for you. It kind of looks like the picture? I'm not sure. You can toss it later if you need to, it was cheap."

"Sienna." Cyperus closed his hands around hers around the votive. "What's this really about?"

I want to entice you into coming back, she wanted to say, but even laying it out in her mind, it sounded absurd. Entice him with a candle? "I wanted to get you a gift, that's all."

Cyperus squeezed her hands, then took the candle and tucked it away in his jacket pocket. "I'll be sure to light it and chant 'liberty' three times every morning." He exhaled on a laughing note, but that faded away to nothing almost immediately. "I estimate I'll need about a standard month to find out where I'm going, and then another to get in and out. Two months, and I'll be back. Three, tops."

"Okay." Sienna looked down at her feet. It wasn't like she thought he would literally never come back. She'd see him again, even if it was to enact the scene that kept running over and over in her head—the one where he'd start with explaining how he'd entered the intelligence service for the excitement, and then he'd mention how quiet the Institute could get at times—no. She had to *stop* running that scene.

He was leaving, but he'd come back; stop there. And having dragged herself back to the present moment, Sienna found herself utterly at sea as to how to see off an agent. She should have asked Gentiana—Isachne must have had to part from her wife for missions dozens of times. "Be safe."

"I will. And you watch Gentiana and Pen for me. Don't let them do anything stupid." Cyperus cupped his hands against her head, line of his thumb along the data path on each side, and kissed her forehead. "I love you."

Sienna's heart skittered around, buffeted by several simultaneous emotions she didn't bother putting names to. She echoed the words and tipped her head up to kiss him properly, letting the press of her lips shout the desperate wish she refused to voice, that he'd leave her with a promise to stay for good once he returned.

When he was gone, choosing a path through the flow of the crowds that allowed him to blend in while keeping to a speed where his gait was smooth, Sienna lingered beside the bench for a few months longer, gathering herself. <Sienna? Are you coming home soon?> Pen's voice, trying to be casual, but failing utterly, especially when coming completely out of nowhere.

<Why? Is there a problem?> Sienna stepped into the flow of traffic as she spoke, but unless she wanted to start pushing people aside, it would take her a while to swim upstream.

<I can't see what you're doing, but your signal wasn't moving, and Cyperus's was, so you must have already seen him off, but you weren't coming back. You two didn't have a fight, did you?>

Outside the station, Sienna tipped her chin up into the cold breeze, trying to let it brace her. There was nothing for her to do to address her worries now. She needed to let them go. <Why are you suddenly so nosy, Pen? I would never say anything that would distract him or put him in danger, so his whole focus is going to be on the rescue.>

<I can't fucking *see* anything.> The curse seeped through the words to either side, like wet, black ink wicking outward through white paper. <Being small isn't just about the amount of stored knowledge, it's about my senses as well. Gentiana lets me passively pull from her implant as much as I want, but otherwise all I can do is stare at this *fucking* spacefield and grass and evergreens and I can't see your face, or Cyperus's, and listen to your voices to see if you're okay. I should have cameras, and speakers, and ventilation and waste disposal to look after and—> Pen's voice stretched so thin with distress, it snapped.

Universal mercy, poor Pen. Sienna wasn't willing to give her access to her own senses through her implant, but there must be something she could do. <Let me talk to Research, okay? Maybe they can set it up so you have read-only access to habitation systems in the dorm building. Would that help, if you could monitor even if you couldn't change the settings?>

<It would help.> Pen's voice was small on the first point, but then she recovered most of her usual poise, an equivalent to Cyperus's intelligence agent game face, Sienna expected. <I'll be fine. I know Cyperus is going to work as fast as he can.>

<Three months, tops,> Sienna promised her. Promised them both.

It took Gentiana about another week to recover properly and Sienna about two weeks after that to get her to agree to leave things to the intelligence expert and stop threatening to take Pen and go after Cyperus. With that settled, they fell into a reluctant routine.

For five months, Gentiana spent her days in the gym and on exercises to accustom herself to her implant, eventually working up to piloting Pen properly. Her nights, she presumably spent in the beds of various women she'd met out on the town in Adit—or it could have been the same one or two, but she never mentioned any names to Sienna, and Sienna didn't ask. Sienna left the bed made up in their spare room, but covered it with a drop cloth so she could spread her supplies across the handy surface.

Pen gradually seemed to discover that more than answering or not answering questions, participating fully in charting a course for Research's study of her—and generally just interfering with whatever they'd let her touch—was even better than monitoring the building they'd given her the suggested read-only access to. While Sienna still caught worry for her daughter flickering beneath the surface of their conversations, she seemed to be settling in and enjoying herself, sometimes offering her problem-solving capabilities to Medical or Counseling as well.

And Sienna spent her days at work and her evenings staring at a succession of unfinished projects. With no deadlines for any of them, and no particular purpose in mind, she couldn't break through the spiral of feeling every line she put down was uninspired and flat. Tonight, the windows were all open to let a summer evening breeze, carrying the scent of firs, chase away the canned taste of the artificially cooled air inside, and she'd finally given up on pretending to work for the night and was allowing herself to wallow. She'd set the easel up so she could sit on the bed, and its electronic surface currently displayed a black and white version of a photograph she'd taken of an agricultural field outside Delta, Cyperus standing poorly framed at the edge of the image. He was laughing in the photo and she remembered the way she'd been laughing too, threatening him if he didn't stop spoiling her shot. She turned her charcoal stick over in her fingers, spreading plenty across her skin and nothing on the easel.

She'd flopped onto her back on the bed when a message came in. From off-planet, which made her jerk upright and open it on her implant's system, even though she generally preferred to do visual tasks on other surfaces. But it was Nairobi Galax's face that came up, muscles around his eyes tight with frustration. "Hello, Sienna," his recording said. "I hope you're well. I apologize for my bluntness, but when—if—you make up with Cyperus, please tell him that intelligence channels aren't for lovers' spats, and I don't have time to play mediator either. I'm passing this one along, but others I might not be able to."

Sienna's stomach sank so low it might have left her body completely, leaving her to implode with despair. He wasn't breaking up with her *by proxy*, was he? He couldn't possibly be. But the embedded message was already playing. "I'm sorry to involve you, Galax, but I didn't tell Sienna I loved her before I left. She needs to know that. I'm thinking of her and I've got one of her paintings up right now."

The attached image was clearly taken from a tablet at arm's length, Cyperus looking serious in front of her beach driftwood painting on a shitty, institutional-quality wall display surface on an undistinguished polymer-coated wall that could have been in a cheap rented room anywhere in the known universe.

Sienna retained some slight residual nausea from the speed of her emotions changing, but otherwise her whole body felt engaged, working on the question of what Cyperus's secret, real message was. He very specifically *had* told her he loved her, and he'd taken several paintings on cloth, so there was no reason for him to display one electronically. Obviously something was encoded in the image. <Pen? Catch. I need you to find the secret message in this photo,> she sent as she shoved to her feet and jogged out of the apartment to take the truck to the spacefield.

They could have discussed over channels as well, but she'd gotten into the habit of visiting Pen at the ship "in person" as much as possible.

Pen opened the door for her when she arrived at the ship but was apparently thinking too hard to bother with a greeting. Sienna settled herself in the pilot's chair and pulled the photo up on the big plotting surface while she waited. Cyperus looked healthy enough, maybe a bit irritated around the edges. She'd been telling herself this whole time that the delay wouldn't be because he was in danger; he was highly trained. But some part of her had still fretted then, and continued now. Why else go to the trouble of sending a message, but then again, why send it to her and not some intelligence contact or former coworker?

If the secret message was a break-up letter, merely encoded for privacy, universal mercy, she would courier the man a package bomb.

"What the fuck am I looking for?" Pen grumbled at length, using an external speaker.

"You're the one with the memories of intelligence training, not me." Sienna sat up straighter, frowning. "Galax said he sent it through intelligence channels, though, so I suppose he might not use anything Isachne would think of. So how are we supposed to know, then?"

"He sent it to *you*. What would only you know?" Since Sienna had given in and confessed her worries about Cyperus, Pen had maintained an air of exasperation, as if the two of them were players in some grand love story that couldn't help but end happily, and that exasperation only deepened in her voice now.

Only she would know about the painting, obviously, but it wasn't until Sienna cropped Cyperus out of the picture to make the painting fill the whole screen that that the obvious jumped up and slapped her. "He changed it. If I show you where, does that give you enough direction?" She scanned the whole scene once more, to make sure there weren't other changes she was missing, then started zooming in.

"The closer in you can get me, the fewer pixels I'm going to have to examine one by one," Pen said, sounding dubious. "Never mind, that's pretty fucking precise," she added, as Sienna outlined the shape with a fingertip. "That's not part of the original photo? A piece of beach trash?"

"There was a hand-painted shell there, and now there's a photo composited in of a red candle cup. That's where his message is, I guarantee it." Having gotten this close, now Sienna couldn't sit still to wait while Pen crunched away.

She pushed to her feet, but then Pen's voice forestalled her. <While we wait, can I get your advice?>

Sienna set a hand on the back of the pilot's chair to ground herself against the impulse to pace and reminded herself it was absurd to wish Pen would concentrate on her task in silence. Even a Near-AI could talk to someone while running a dozen processes. <On what?>

<Gentiana's been sleeping here every night. She doesn't talk to me like I'm Isachne, but—it can't be healthy. She can't live a full life if she's still emotionally entangled with a ghost.> And nary a curse to lighten the sound of her anxiety, either.

Sienna felt like cursing herself, though. She laughed instead, raggedly. <Are you sure you want *my* advice? I can't deal with my own romantic shit.> She returned to the chair—collapsed into it, really, and scrubbed her face. <Have you brought up the subject with her? Asked her directly not to?> That, or worse, was honestly what Sienna would have predicted for Pen—something like unapologetically locking the doors and informing Gentiana it was for her own good.

Silence, but now Sienna didn't want it. Pen usually talked so much, she often forgot how it was literally impossible to read her when she wasn't speaking. <I need her. Even before I found out

about my daughter, I needed an advocate. And *she* needs to move on from her wife's death. Before the rescue, I was working on making those two needs not mutually exclusive, but now that's on hold. So since I can't give her what she needs, I feel like the least I can do is give her what she *wants*, which is comfort. You know?>

It was very human of Pen, Sienna reflected, to ask for advice but then present a situation in which there was nothing to be done—or nothing she was willing to do. If she was in Pen's place, Sienna suspected she would have locked the doors by now, but then again worry for Cyperus shivered in her chest at a higher frequency with each moment she had to wait for the results of Pen's analysis and she wasn't at her most sympathetic. <Mercy grant that whatever's in that message means we don't have to wait much longer,> she said, with what diplomacy she could muster.

This time, she managed to pace down the hallway and back before Pen made a finished chime, inherited from her Near-AI form. The photo that had been left up on the screen was replaced with text, phrased in the manner of someone who begrudged the effort to chisel out every single character on a stone tablet:

Found AI. R&D facility, Joy de Vive. Have an entry to facility, but stuck on planet. Send Pen as an exit.

Sienna collapsed back into the pilot's chair in the grip of the next wave of emotion. That was…good? Good he'd found Pen's daughter, not good that he was stuck. But "stuck" didn't sound like it was "imprisoned," at least. It couldn't be, if he was encoding and sending messages.

"Hurry up and join us, Gentiana. We should plan when we're leaving," Pen said.

Sienna twisted to see Gentiana peek out of the doorway of the remaining open cabin. Gentiana had been here the whole time? Pen had switched to channels when she wanted to talk about her and Sienna hadn't even noticed. She wondered if Gentiana, for her part, had been hanging back out of embarrassment, hoping Sienna would leave before she had to admit to what she was doing.

Gentiana tried to brazen it out now, though. "I spend time here for Pen's sake," she said piously, chin high as she joined Sienna at the piloting console. "We can leave as soon as we file a flight plan."

Sienna thrust her hands out, fingers spread. "Hold up. You have a planet, an undefined 'stuck,' and a request for aid five words in length. Do have any idea what you'll do when you get there?"

"All official LSF government facilities—which includes their defense R&D—are in the capital city, Nouvo Paris." Sienna drew breath for an objection and Pen overrode her. "*Every* capital city on planets LSF has taken over is Nouvo Paris. The Battle of Nouvo Paris, which I assume you're thinking of, was on Jenna se Qua. I imagine he's stuck because they've restricted travel on and off the planet since he arrived—the Pax Romana and LSF have been clashing in the next system over. His ID was likely good enough to get him in before that, but not good enough to get him out through the restrictions."

Sienna watched Gentiana's knuckles tighten on the back of the copilot's chair she was standing behind, then tighten further. Having had the undiluted cadence of Isachne's memories in her own head briefly, she recognized it now.

And, when that cadence disappeared, she noticed that sharply too. "So we'll fly in quietly, signal him, find a quiet spot to set down, and pick him up. No travel documents necessary," Pen said breezily.

"Just that easy?" Sienna aimed a tight look at the general direction of the ceiling. "What do your memories of intelligence training say about that?"

"We'll figure it out once we're there to see the situation, won't we?" Gentiana said staunchly. "We have to. Do the Idyllians know anything about Joy de Vive that they'll share with you, Pen?"

Sienna yielded the pilot's chair so the others could discuss, sinking into the silence of channels for efficiency. She thought about pacing the hallway again, but her tension was drawing her to stillness this time. She leaned a shoulder against the doorway, clasped her opposite elbows, and thought with everything she had. Who *could* travel without restrictions in LSF space? Could Gentiana pretend to be one of those people? A government official, maybe? But the amount of work needed to make that kind of cover stand up seemed insurmountable to her, the civilian artist—

Oh, universal mercy.

"I have to come," she said, not loud, but Pen heard her.

"I appreciate that you're worried about Cyperus, Sienna. But you have no training."

"No more than Gentiana does. More, because my implant was used for that purpose for years before I got it. Sometimes it still tries to make me do a ridiculous acrobatic landing when I trip." She was babbling, she knew it, but she couldn't seem to stop. She clasped her elbows harder, digging in her fingertips. "Who do the LSF revere, Pen? Artists. The ones who create the propaganda murals they have on every wall. I don't know if they're allowed free travel, but if you're suspicious of their papers, it's so easy to check. Hand them a brush. Then you know they're legitimate."

Gentiana smiled at her, even as Sienna's stomach shriveled into a tiny lump. "That's perfect! I can be your assistant. We go in to paint a mural in the capital and then take Cyperus and Pen's daughter with us when we leave."

<Sienna, forgive me for this, but are you *sure*?> Pen asked her privately. It was a fair question, and Sienna wasn't confident in her answer in her own mind, so she didn't know what was to forgive—"Shut up," Pen said sharply, in LSF French.

There wasn't enough air in Sienna's next breath, however deep it was, but she wasn't going to let a panic attack take hold. She was here, now, with neutral sensations all around her. The polymer of the wall surface had more give than the structural material of the ship in the doorframe, when she shifted her fingers to dig into that instead of her own skin. With Gentiana sleeping here every night for months, the hall had the breath of sweat and body-scent that came from one person living in a small space at length. At home, her bedroom had lost that component of Cyperus by now.

"I have to," she said, lifting her chin high. See, Pen? She'd had counseling, she had things under control. "Not just for your daughter, but for Cyperus too. If we don't get him out, how long will 'stuck' last? How long will his cover hold up? If any of his Pax Romana friends would or could help him, I'm sure he would have asked them first. Or maybe he did ask already, and was told no."

She pushed off from the doorway and planted her feet, trying to feel that balance emotionally as well. "I can do this."

PART II

Nouvo Paris—this Nouvo Paris, or perhaps all of them were built from the same plans—felt oddly self-important to Sienna as she walked among the buildings in the balmy conditions that passed for local winter. Having secured enthusiastic permission from the Secretaire Detat for the planet to reconnoiter for a likely wall to host a mural by the great Seraphine Senlis herself, Sienna and Gentiana were working their way inward toward the grand plaza at the center of the city. Not that the architecture there needed decoration, but beyond were warehouses with great, blank expanses, set among buildings devoted to industry—and scientific research. As they approached the grand plaza, older buildings that were honest in their utilitarian plascrete gave way to those that were still plascrete, but patterned like brick or stone, with eerily two-dimensional "carved" ornamentation above windows and doors.

"There's sight-lines to consider," she remarked to Gentiana once they'd passed through the plaza, gesturing widely to the building beside them as the side street they were following reached the end of the spoke-like pattern of the new streets around the plaza and crashed into the regular grid of the old city. She couldn't say she *enjoyed* speaking LSF French, but the good thing about the implant was that she could set it to ensure she kept to that language no matter what, so she could relax into the cover more than she'd expected. So far, standing by to burble excitedly to local officials and then step back for Gentiana to arrange the logistics, she'd found the spy thing surprisingly exciting, instead of terrifying.

Gentiana readjusted Sienna's easel more comfortably on her shoulder—it was light but bulky—and nodded down the street to a three-story warehouse. "You'll want something at least that tall." Pen was monitoring senses from both of them, passively—Sienna had finally granted her permission on the journey here—but couldn't speak to them, and they couldn't open a channel without touching data path to data path, or it might be detected. So their conversation had to be as banal as their covers.

Having studied photographs of the city taken from orbit, they both knew the path to the R&D facility practically down to the cracks in the sidewalk at each turning, and they'd picked a warehouse close enough to "run into" Cyperus, but not too close to seem like they were casing the joint. But they couldn't make a beeline for it, so, accordingly, they wandered well into the afternoon.

Given that she was the free-energy artist, Sienna made an executive decision to "fall in love with" the correct building the moment they glimpsed it rather than fuck around further. Gentiana set down her easel and they walked up and down the block, considering it from different angles as Sienna gestured her grand plans. She would have started sketching, but a woman forestalled her by striding out of the entrance to the R&D facility, officiousness wound tightly into her gait.

Her black hair, drawn back into a short tail at the nape of her neck, was straight—did it dare to be anything else?—and heavily peppered with gray and the lighter ancestrally sunny shade of her skin had been weathered by exposure in her own lifetime. She crossed her arms disapprovingly before she even arrived. "Who are you? What are you doing here?"

"Seraphine Senlis." Even with the implant enforcing the use of the correct name, the syllables tasted strange in her mouth, order of personal and family name flipped. And that absurd family name, dating back no more than a couple generations to when the newly formed LSF had christened themselves out of the same archives they'd gotten their language from. Though perhaps that was slightly hypocritical—Pax Romana and Idyllian family names were of much longer time scale, but most researchers acknowledged anyone's ancestors' relationship with any such places on Old Earth had probably been pure guesswork, once upon a time.

To finish off the polite greeting, Sienna lifted her sleeve and showed her inner wrist, a particular flick of movement—which her implant could also provide as if she'd been doing it her whole life, thank mercy—bringing up an LSF icon of light above her counterfeit subdermal citizen chip. That was something she hadn't anticipated, but with the implant to provide local anesthetic, she could remove it with even a high-quality paring knife, so she'd resigned herself and thrown herself into designing the tattoo surrounding it. She'd studied others used by those on Joy de Vive—the tattoo might be seen as personal expression, but of *course* people followed trends—and had chosen a frame of lush vines and flowers with a stylized, stained-glass feel. "I'm here to do a mural."

Gentiana followed suit in showing her wrist. "Jeanne Reims." Her tattoo, also designed by Sienna, was a fairly pedestrian setting of the word "love" in different, entwined fonts.

The woman withdrew a hand-held screen from a hip pocket and only belatedly showed her wrist in their general direction, barely revealing the icon, never mind the tattoo. "Director Ines Toulouse." Sienna assumed as her eyes flicked across the screen, reading, that she was perusing the biography and catalog of work Pen and Sienna, respectively, had mocked together to insert into off-planet database query results.

Rather than allay her suspicions, whatever Ines read on the screen seemed only to deepen them. "A mural directly across from where vitally important research is occurring? Bullshit." She returned her screen to her pocket and edged into Sienna's personal space, threatening. "Why are you *really* here?"

And universal mercy, but Sienna froze. Gentiana couldn't feed her anything over channels. And her implant couldn't tell her what to say, or even what tone to use, it could only make sure it came out in French, perhaps give it a few turns of phrase from local slang. Sienna's mind was swamped by a memory of the tone used by Elantine, the LSF undercover agent who'd tried to kill her repeatedly. Elantine was imprisoned, being tried by the Pax Romana even now, and this woman looked nothing like her, but that *officiousness*...

"Did you want to see her paint something?" Gentiana, thank mercy, was completely unaffected. She retrieved the easel and set it up invitingly before Sienna. "Charcoal?"

"Charcoal isn't paint." Ines recrossed her arms and turned up her glower.

"Oh, it's a whole process." Well, there was the babbling at least. Sienna lifted the top layer of the easel, trying to explain about the physical and electronic layers as Gentiana pulled her charcoals out of her shoulder bag. "I use charcoals for my portraits. I could do you?" No, of course Ines wouldn't want to be drawn, that was a stupid question.

Another woman strode for them from the R&D building, looking a decade younger, though no less settled in her confidence and experience. In her late forties, perhaps. Her hair was a deeply undistinguished brown, though her skin was more the light shade that LSF preferred in their art to distinguish them from the Pax Romana, whatever their actual citizens looked like. She lifted her voice to reach them ahead of her steps, which were directed like she'd already known the group was there. Observed them through a window, perhaps? She was still settling the collar of her coat she arrived, as if she'd hurried the process of pulling it on. "Ines, you might want to clean the dead puppy scraps from between your teeth before you talk to passersby." She gave Ines a sharp, empty smile as she arrived. "Or was it a kitten, today?"

"Valerie," Ines said warningly.

The woman ignored her completely and turned to Sienna and Gentiana to show her wrist. "Valerie Bordeaux." Her tattoo evoked a circuit diagram. "You're an artist?"

Sienna started her explanation over again, finally finding her rhythm as Valerie reflected her enthusiasm back to her, redoubled with a grin. "I'll need models for the mural," Sienna said, as she wrapped up. "If you're interested? I could take your picture and work from that, or combine it with other photographic elements, but I really prefer drawing people when they're interacting with me. It would only take a few moments." And it would be perfectly evident that she wasn't a spy who'd picked up a charcoal stick for the first time a few weeks ago, as apparently Ines suspected.

Valerie fairly beamed. "Yes!" Showing the same impulse many people did, even those trapped with Sienna in the POW camp, when she'd had to beg charcoals from the guards and draw on the walls, Valerie released her hair from the tail at the nape of her neck. She spent a couple seconds attempting to make it fall just so along her shoulder, then gave up and struck a Brave Citizen Scientist sort of pose, chin high.

"They are setting up right across from—" Ines protested, expression darkening even further. Valerie must be some kind of specialist, not in Ines's direct hierarchy, or else she would undoubtedly have ordered the other woman back inside by now.

"Ines." Valerie waited a beat to see if her cutting off had taken, then continued. "That's a *warehouse*. It's butt-ugly. Is that really what you want to throw down with the Secretaire Detat over?"

"This doesn't have to involve—"

Sienna fumbled to pull out her own pocket screen; Gentiana was faster, pulling up the message giving them their permission to choose their mural site; and Valerie beat both of them. "Citizens, what was the first thing you did when you arrived at Joy de Vive?"

Gentiana settled her hand with the screen back against her hip, since proof wasn't needed. "We contacted the Secretaire Detat." Her smile was completely innocent, but a spark of humor leaped between her and Valerie.

Sienna wanted to catch that spark, so she sketched quickly, capturing the lines around Valerie's eyes first. Then she transferred the charcoal lines down, rolled up the physical layer, and used her finger pressure to smudge some of the electronic cloned lines. The style she planned for the mural would have dozens of figures, all regular curves and sharp angles forming bold, confident heroes of the citizenry.

Valerie's attention shifted away from her, back to the R&D building. "Simon! You're not rushing off to anywhere tonight, are you? We're getting a mural, come meet the artist."

Sienna turned—why wouldn't she?—and there was Cyperus coming toward them, wearing a coat like he was a local and was cold. Walking with a cane. Universal mercy. Was he all right? She tracked the hesitance in his step, but it was no worse than it got sometimes when he'd pushed himself too hard one day and woken up stiff the next morning. Only it was evening now, and apparently he was getting off work. In the R&D facility itself. That was a hell of an "entry" to get access to Pen's daughter.

He was clean-shaved now, the hair in his version of the gender-neutral tail at the nape of the neck barely long enough to hold. Even as Sienna watched one of the black waves escaped to hang up behind one ear. Her hair, which she'd had to bleach before going back to something approaching her unaltered color, was a bit short for the style as well, but the roughness from the bleaching made it stay better when fastened back.

And she was staring at him, someone she'd supposedly never met before, with her lips slightly parted and the silence was getting awkward. Gentiana was going to *stab* her the next time they got a moment alone. "I'm Seraphine," she told him, fumbling at her sleeve. It took her two tries to raise it for the greeting. With the way her cheeks felt, she imagined she was flushed with her frustration at her lack of spycraft, too.

"Simon Montpellier." His tattoo was a square of angled red lines, reminiscent of circuitry too, or perhaps instead evoking a knot in red cord, like she'd drawn on his back in the first painting she'd ever done for him.

"Draw him!" Valerie, far from joining Ines in her suspicions, beamed and switched places with Cyperus, leaving him no choice in the matter, apparently. That put her at an angle to see what Sienna had done so far, and her eyes went wide. "That's amazing," she said in a low, reverent tone. At least Sienna had done that much right, in playing her part.

Sienna sent the beginning of Valerie's portrait to storage, then blanked the electronic surface. She'd use a stylus on that directly, to save pausing to clean off the physical layer. Maybe if she didn't look at him, she wouldn't freeze up again. Universal mercy, she wanted to throw herself into his arms and sob or laugh or threaten him until he assured her that his knee was all right. "I'll be quick, you won't have to stand there long."

Of course, she had to look at him to draw him, though. She flicked her eyes only up to chest height. If she didn't look at his face, she wouldn't know if he was disgusted with her as well—though he was probably too well trained to show that. So maybe she was afraid of finding blankness instead. "Do you want me to include the cane or remove it?" Cyperus would want it removed, but she shouldn't assume anything about his cover identity, so she asked, as she would have with a stranger.

Cyperus's hands tightened around the head of the cane, then he pasted on an "aw, shucks" kind of expression. "Artist's choice."

Ines made a noise of dramatic disgust. "When they suborn your assistant to steal your data, don't come crying to me." She swept off. Valerie didn't grant her the satisfaction of watching her go, but Sienna, from her angle, could track a flickered expression of frustration. Championing the random artist was just one front on an ongoing battle between the women, perhaps.

Cyperus shifted his weight, off his good leg, then immediately back again as if the bad one couldn't take even that. She supposed he'd probably been proudly refusing to sit for conversations all damn day. She tucked her stylus back in her pocket and sent the drawing to storage. "Don't worry, I won't make you stand there any longer." They were supposed to be making contact, they'd done that, but the idea of wishing him well and walking off in the opposite direction was abruptly beyond her. "If you ever want me to draw you properly—my assistant and I are staying in the administrative visitor housing on—" She looked to Gentiana for the address and got a death glare in return. Shit. "I mean, you're a great model for the mural, with your strong bone structure—" She gestured around her face and Valerie tittered. Across the languages, Sienna had no idea where the innuendo had even been. Shit!

"Admin housing isn't hard to find," Valerie said, eyes continuing to laugh. She stepped over to speak low into Cyperus's ear as Gentiana folded up the easel with tight, economical movements. Then Valerie clapped him on the shoulder and gestured down the street. "In fact, why doesn't Simon show you?"

Sienna's willpower gave out and she caught Cyperus's eyes then, a spark of desperate longing leaping between them, though whether it was only hers being acknowledged or a meeting of both of theirs, she couldn't tell. "I'd like that," he said, and started off at his slow pace, gesturing for her to follow. Valerie gave them a cheery wave and set off in her own direction.

Well, they were committed now. Might as well try to really sell it, right? Sienna avoided looking at Gentiana and fell into step with him.

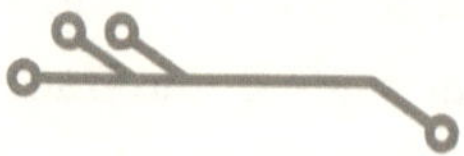

Sienna didn't attempt conversation on the way to their rooms, though Cyperus staved off total awkwardness with some banal comments about the quality of a coffeehouse or crush of commuting crowds in the morning. When they'd found the suite assigned to them, Gentiana gestured rudely for Sienna's silence the moment they'd closed the door. Sienna pressed her lips together and bit down on them from the inside for good measure. She was *aware* that they need to keep up their covers until Gentiana had set up Pen's equipment and Pen gave them the all-clear.

She relieved Gentiana of the easel and ended up clasping it against her chest as a barrier against her lunging for Cyperus. "Sit," she urged him, seeing him doing his unsuccessful weight shift once more as he hovered in the entryway. Clearly he wasn't simply playing up his old injury for the sake of his cover. Walking beside him on the way here, she hadn't really believed that, but perhaps some part of her had held out a little hope.

Where should he sit, though, that was the question. The shelf to store shoes after they were removed was hardly comfortable long-term, and the only other thing in the foyer was their trunks, dropped off by grav-pad while they were out. In her socks, since slippers weren't provided, she followed in Gentiana's wake, peeking into doors. Three bedrooms, which was more generous than she'd expected—she'd be able to set up a proper studio and avoid edging past her easel in the living area to get coffee every morning. Inside the rooms, the decorating scheme was rather tasteless in the flatness of its ornamentation, to her eyes. Everything was plain polymer covered by decals of—what did LSF artists call it? She'd researched this—tromp doil of optical illusions to make it seem if the furniture was intricately carved wood or elegant forged metal or even both, gilded wood, but without any wood, gold, or other decorative metal at all.

In the living-area-slash-kitchen, she perched on a dining chair and Cyperus lowered himself carefully to the couch. Then they waited, silence curdling further with every moment. She couldn't read his thoughts on his face. What was taking Gentiana so *long*? She knew she'd fucked up, she knew the Ines woman was probably looking for a way to get rid of them this very minute. She knew that she'd effectively tainted Cyperus's cover with that suspicion, maybe destroyed their best chance of saving Pen's daughter. She just wanted to hear it out loud, so they could make the next plan. She shoved back to her feet to pace.

<All right, you're good,> Pen said to all of them. <Say what you like and use channels as much as you want in these rooms.>

"Oh, I'm glad we're thinking about security." Gentiana strode into the room, dusting her hands off on the sides of her hips. "As opposed to, I don't know, maybe throwing ourselves at our ally the moment we see them, in case anyone might *not* have assumed we were connected."

"I'm sorry." Sienna clasped her fingers tightly together. "I hadn't expected it to be so intense, in the moment."

Gentiana stepped right into her. "Which is why you shouldn't have come at all, if you're going to destroy our chance to save Pen's daughter and get us all executed in the bargain—"

"Gentiana," Cyperus protested, and started the long process of getting back to his feet.

Though she'd had exactly the same thoughts in the privacy of her own head, hearing them out loud made Sienna recognize the hyperbole. "We're not imprisoned yet, are we? Things can't be that bad. I know we're all on edge—"

Gentiana sneered at her. "Speak for yourself—"

This argument was spiraling out of control. They needed to stop, take a breath. "Shut up, Jeanne!" And that came out in LSF French, because this whole conversation had been in French, courtesy of the implant's behavioral controls, and she hadn't even noticed. But now she noticed. Shut up! snapped the guards at the camp. "Shut up, shut up…" Who was she talking to? Herself? She wasn't sure, but it was still in French. And she couldn't breathe because the panic was taking over her body, starting with her chest and throat, shivering its way into her stomach next. Couldn't talk, couldn't breathe, because LSF took the prisoners' voices—

"Sienna. Sienna." Cyperus, repeating her name over and over. He was taking deep belly breaths. She was supposed to follow him. He'd needed to help her this way before, more than once, though not for months before he left. "Can you take off the behavioral controls? Pen, can you help her do that?" He was speaking in Idyllian. She wasn't at the camp. This was a panic attack, and panic attacks ended.

<Like this,> Pen said gently. Sienna followed the directions she laid out and managed to get the French out of her head. For now.

"Sienna, you did good." Cyperus set his cane aside, leaning against her abandoned chair, and cupped her face. "You did great. You did more in ten minutes to win over Valerie with your art and your genuineness than I've managed in three months as her assistant, projecting polished, trained trustworthiness while she has me work solely on unclassified projects. I had no idea she had those impulses, but you've filled her match-making heart with glee. You know what she said to me? 'She thought to ask whether to draw your cane. If you are at all interested, don't let this one get away.' She doesn't suspect us for interacting, she's pushing us together herself."

<Sometimes a sincere civilian is exactly what a situation calls for.> Pen's voice took on a more Isachne cadence. <Though don't sell yourself short either, Tehran, this isn't your wheelhouse.> Her formal reference to Cyperus clinched it.

"But Isachne would have considered it in hers?" Cyperus countered, dry.

Gentiana had been twisting her fingers together, awkward, and she finally broke in. "Sienna—what was that?" Guilt twisted her tone tight by the same measure.

"I get panic attacks sometimes. Thinking about—the camp. And things like that." Sienna rolled her shoulders, just as awkward. She was past the point where she needed to purge the memories, and now she preferred not to dwell. But that was one of the odd, unexpected benefits of a long-term partner. She layered her hands over his. "Cyperus can fill you in on when they tend to happen, if you're worried about me screwing up the rescue."

"No—I'm sorry." Gentiana addressed that mostly to the floor. Like the first time she'd apologized to Sienna, a little after they first met, it was clearly sincere enough, but Sienna would have vastly preferred more awareness so as to avoid the harm in the first place.

She felt Cyperus gather himself to speak, and distracted him by disengaging and nudging him back to his seat. "I can do my own assholing, as necessary," she murmured, which was enough to make him swallow whatever cutting thing he'd been thinking of saying to Gentiana on her behalf. "So you found Pen's daughter?"

Cyperus tugged her down beside him. "I did." He tipped his head, sending a picture taken with an implant to the screen on the wall. It was zoomed to maximum, through a narrow crack left in a door, and showed an anonymous-looking blackly metallic cube, about the size of two fists. "The only one allowed in that workshop is Valerie herself—which, before you comment, Pen, is because of Ines, not me. There was some kind of power play before I arrived. Ines got frustrated with Valerie's lack of progress with waking up the supposedly last-jumped AI, and took it upon herself to connect the cube to a live network. That's when the signal Pen received must have been sent. Valerie objected, they duked it out, and Valerie got to take it back under her exclusive—and fully shielded—control."

He frowned at the cube for a few silent beats, then blew out a frustrated breath. "Object retrieval *is* in my wheelhouse, and I hate that I don't see any more elegant solution than a grab and run. Security's beyond my individual hacks, but Valerie does leave that door unlocked when she's in the room. So that leaves us with me walking in, picking it up, and carrying it out before she can stop me. Aided, of course, by whatever we can come up with to distract her and extend the time before she sounds the alarm as long as possible."

Gentiana speared Cyperus with a dubious glance. "And then you run? On that knee?"

"What happened to it?" Sienna broke in.

Cyperus rubbed it, expression dark. "Before I left Pax Romana space, I had a doctor drop my levels of maintenance nanites way down, in case I ended up getting scanned. R&D engineers would know enough to recognize they weren't LSF. But, turns out, they were doing a lot more maintaining than I realized. It deteriorated rapidly after I arrived, but it's stable now." His shoulders tightened. "Once I get my levels back up, I'll be fine." Then he rolled his shoulders down, forcing a relaxed pose. "Besides, once I have the cube, it's not going to be some kind of literal footrace down the street. Stop thinking like infantry, Gentiana."

Gentiana crossed her arms. "Uh-huh. An intelligence agent's implant lets him fucking teleport and no one told me? Or does it just give him delusions of grandeur to think he's going to limp away with anything at all?"

Sienna pushed to her feet and ignored them in favor of examining the photograph from closer up as the other two grew progressively more insulting. Cyperus didn't need to be an asshole on his own behalf in this situation either, but she knew when to pick her battles. Her new position didn't resolve the pixilation from the zoom, but closing the distance gave her more of a feeling of connection with the Near-AI cube.

"Why not print a copy and swap it?" She turned away from the photo to find the others both frowning at her. She hurried to present her case before they started picking it apart. "I mean, you'd need somewhere to carry it, but it's not that big—under a jacket over his arm, maybe." She gestured over the crook of her own. "If you did it at quitting time, she wouldn't notice until the next morning when it wouldn't turn on, and we'd be long gone by then."

"If I pick it up to scan it for a print-pattern, she'll be on her guard after that. I figure I'll only have one chance to touch it." Cyperus managed to sound not *too* patronizing.

Sienna shook her head, excitement finally seeping into her chest, displacing the last vestiges of panic. "Take photos from various angles and I'll generate the print-pattern myself. I'm a little rusty with three dimensions, but not that bad. It won't have a bottom and the weight will be off, but you wouldn't notice either of those until you tried to turn it on anyway. If Valerie leaves the door unlocked, I assume you can go in and chat?" A laugh bubbled up. "Go ask her for romantic advice."

<And you can use my printer, so that doesn't raise any alarms, either.> "My" meaning the printer on the ship Pen was currently in, Sienna parsed after a beat of effort. With Pen's voice coming

to her over channels she still wasn't used to Pen being in the ship instead of the building.

"Universal mercy, I think that might work." Cyperus rose enough to capture her wrist, then tugged her, tumbling, down onto his lap. "Guess I'm glad you're here for all kinds of reasons."

Sienna grinned and closed a kiss, doing plenty of wiggling to get her weight balanced so she wouldn't fall off again. <You've got ulterior motives?> she teased him privately.

<Nope, just motives,> he said, smug, paying off their private joke.

Gentiana snorted. "I'm going to go scare up dinner. Take the modeling session to the spare bedroom before I'm back."

Sienna stilled and changed her point of contact with Cyperus to forehead to forehead until they'd heard Gentiana leave. <Shit. Things are so weird with her clearly not having moved on. I feel bad being…>

<Happy in front of her?> Cyperus freed her hair, ran his fingers through it, feeling the new texture. <Maybe it'll remind her why she *needs* to move on, once all this is done.>

<Better she go see someone in Counseling than we blunder around,> Sienna told him, teasing in her piousness, but his hands had stolen down to her hips, then cupped her ass, and she completely lost any other train of thought. Five months, and he was *here*, and he was *hers*. She dispensed with his hair elastic too, traced the black waves of his hair around the shape of his face and neck and every familiar patch of sensation like when she kissed into the hollow under the corner of his jaw.

But she did remember herself enough to disengage briefly to tug him up and go find privacy. His progress with the cane was slow, but she was practiced at folding that into the game, heightening the anticipation. "Got your charcoals?" he said with a grin, as they slipped into the bedroom she'd noted had the best light, to be her studio. "You can get yourself a picture out of this."

Sienna did step back to retrieve the box, but the longer she spent away from his touch, the more her stomach sank. Five months apart or not, arousal, painted over the still slightly sparking debris of her earlier fear, was proving maddeningly hard to sustain. "To maintain our covers?" Her voice thinned out, though she was in her safe pitch range. "I don't want to be Seraphine and Simon." He'd taken a seat on the bed, but she hovered in the doorway, box clasped hard enough to dig the plastic edges into her palms.

"No!" Cyperus often lacked the vocabulary for his feelings about their relationship, and the frustration of that showed starkly on his face now, after the initial outburst. He gestured that she should discard the box—toss it into the wall, even—then beckoned her to join him. She set the box on top of a dresser, and accepted his double hand clasp and reangling of his body so they could each sit sideways on the bed, facing each other. "I want *you*, Sienna. Fast, slow, after a marathon hours-long drawing session, in the other room without a paintbrush in sight, whatever *you* want."

"Fast." Sienna caught his hands, brought them up to her neck, the camouflaged rave lines there. She'd discovered something of a cross-wiring hack that allowed her to connect the sensation of his data paths on hers to arousal, once she turned it on. She often didn't turn it on until the end, as it could be a bit hard-edged and utilitarian, thirty seconds to climax. But she needed that glow now, to surround her and keep her firmly in the mood for anything else.

Cyperus caressed the circles of data path on the pads of his first two fingers down from the sides of her jaw to the implant site at the base of the back of her neck in a steadily increasing rhythm. Both sides, twice as fast, and she clenched up throughout her whole body with the sheer gasp of it as the climax burst. "Fuck, yes." Idyllian, not French and not Lingua either. She seized him to kiss him properly, fingers in the loose waves of hair falling forward around his face.

"Fast or slow?" she asked in the same language, leaning back to tease at him, nipping at his lower lip.

"Slow," he murmured back, his lips nearly against hers, word barely more than breath between them. "Make me wait."

While she finished a painting, was usually how that game went. With the glow pooling in her limbs, making them heavier, that was no longer such an anxious thought, but Sienna suddenly had an even better idea. She slipped off the bed, walking slow and sensually as she collected her box of charcoals, selected one as he watched her with hungry curiosity. She rolled it between her fingers as she returned, slow and hip-rolling.

"Now," she said, kneeling on the bed straddling his lap. "Where might you forget to wash up tomorrow morning, before you go into work, wearing the same clothes? For a real didn't-go-home entrance..." She kneaded her fingers into the muscles at the back of his neck, just above the collar of his shirt. When he would have joined a kiss, she dodged him to consider the effect of her artful black smears from one angle, another, and then added a few more. He laughed, a wicked, hungry sound that coiled into her belly. Yes.

"Tell me who the fuck you are before I call Securidad!" Getiana's voice from somewhere down the hallway jerked Sienna from a light doze tucked against Cyperus. She was speaking in French. Sienna needed to put her behavioral controls back on *now*, and somewhere in the fumbling with that, Cyperus had sorted himself out and sat up to calmly dress.

He reached out to squeeze her wrist. "I'm pretty sure I know who it is. Don't give that dick the satisfaction of rushing out there." Shirtless, he grabbed his cane and went to the doorway. "Henri, is that you?"

"You're lucky it's only me, not someone who means you harm, Simon, my dear." The slightly raised volume needed to cross the space, even with implant-enhanced hearing, diminished the smarm of the unknown man's tone not at all.

All right, Sienna wouldn't rush, but she wasn't going to hang around either. She wasn't any better off than Cyperus, pulling on yesterday's clothes as he finished dressing. All her other stuff was packed and no doubt still in the hallway, unless Gentiana had dropped Sienna's luggage off in the room she hadn't chosen for herself. She and Cyperus had more or less collapsed into the bed in the art studio bedroom, last night.

The two of them arrived at the living area to find Gentiana standing, puffed up as any threatened cat, the personal shocker that was the best weapon an LSF citizen was allowed held low and ready by her hip. Every muscle of her body screamed that she wished it was a gun. "I came out for breakfast and he was just sitting there."

The stranger was lounging with his chair turned outward from the table so he could lean his weight on one elbow on the surface. He flicked his fingers. "The lock on your front door was absurd. What did you expect?" If Sienna had been illustrating sins, she would have used him, with his golden skin and perfect, perfect smile, for hubris.

"And installing a better one wouldn't have attracted exactly the wrong kind of attention?" Cyperus countered smoothly. He centered himself, both hands resting on the head of his cane as if it was a stage prop, not a necessary aid.

"Who the fuck *is* he?" Gentiana demanded with apparently equal anger directed at the stranger and now Cyperus.

"Henri is the local agent from our side. The only one on the planet, in fact, which rather makes me wonder if no one else could stand working with him either." Cyperus's voice stayed even, but the resentment Sienna heard rumbling in his chest put Valerie's toward Ines to shame.

Henri touched fingertips to his lips and flicked them away, a minimalist mocking blown kiss. "You stir up shit in *my* territory, you follow my rules. Which, at the moment, means informing me when playacting civilians show up on-planet." He stood and prowled over to Sienna. She knew an inspection when she was subjected to one, and she sneered right back and presented her wrist so he could see her LSF citizen icon.

"So this is the artist girlfriend." He rolled the final word, giving it a cast that skipped past free-energy and probably ended somewhere around vapid waste of space. He shot Cyperus a look over his shoulder, mockingly incredulous. "And when she showed up, you just couldn't stop yourself from running to her to dry her tears."

Cyperus went dangerously still, while Sienna froze simply to keep herself from folding up completely. That was exactly what Cyperus had done, and how had Henri guessed that? Was it written on her face that she was a pathetic civilian who fell apart at the first obstacle? "Seraphine was the one who offered me a solution to the problem of—" Cyperus began.

"That reflects more on you than it does on her, you realize that, right?" Inspection finished, Henri rocked his weight smoothly back and paced over to Cyperus.

And, oh, Sienna saw that connect. Not like a sword that wounded, but a lever that, when jammed beneath Cyperus's pride, *moved* him wherever this agent wanted him to go. "Come on," Henri said, and snapped his head toward the hall and the front door.

Even given her earlier thought, Sienna hadn't expected Henri's goals to be so literal. Neither had Cyperus, apparently. He made no move to follow, which gave her at least a little hope.

"What?" Cyperus demanded.

Henri sighed and turned back in the doorway. "Break off all contact with your girlfriend or I'll break off all support of your unofficial little mission. Simple enough for everyone here to understand?"

"And what support is that?" Gentiana snapped, surprising Sienna a little. She hadn't expected any defense from that quarter—or maybe it wasn't defense of her, it was simply defense of her ability to make the dummy cube to save Pen's daughter.

"He gave me the personal reference that got me the job in R&D," Cyperus said, reluctantly. He still wasn't following, but Sienna could see him shifting his weight. Talking himself out of it? Or into it? Damned if Sienna was going to cling to his elbow beseechingly or any mercy-abandoned thing Henri might be expecting of her, though. She crossed her arms tightly. She wouldn't even touch him.

Gentiana lifted her shocker, glanced at it as if she was still weighing the merits of using it, then finally powered it off. "And what's your motives here, *Henri*? And those of the empire? We fail and get ourselves caught, what do you lose? An Idyllian, an AWOL soldier, and an agent forcibly retired because he was infected by an LSF weapon and no one would believe he could be cured?"

Henri snapped off a sneer especially for her alone. "No names, no matter what equipment you think you have set up." Sienna reviewed the conversation hurriedly—hadn't Cyperus said—but of course he hadn't. "Our side," he'd said. At least Gentiana was with her in not knowing that bit of agent protocol.

Henri pushed his way into Gentiana's personal space, though he only had maybe five centimeters on her and her soldier's confidence meant she knew how to stand to take advantage of all of her height. "I know who you are. You want a particular piece of tech, and if you fuck up the retrieval, *no one* is going to be able to get anywhere near it. My bosses don't have any particular wish for the LSF to have control of that piece of tech, even in deactivated form. So. You can have your chance, *if* I think your failure won't fuck things up too badly. Got it?"

"You all should have thought of that before you let it get…lost, in the first place. Or maybe back when you made it without consent," Gentiana muttered, not that any of them believed it wasn't intended to be overheard.

"Come on," Henri said once more, and strode out.

And Cyperus followed. And Sienna didn't try to stop him.

<I'll arrange some kind of dead drop for the photos once I have them,> Cyperus said over a private channel to her and Gentiana and Pen. <And then we'll only need to meet once for you to give me the dummy.>

<Or you can tell him where to shove it. We don't need him—> Gentiana said, heated.

<We might, if anything goes wrong in the course of getting the photos or making the switch or basically any of the steps before we're on Pen, flying away from the planet.> He walked slowly, yes, but by then he was at the door, and had time only for one more message to Sienna alone before he was out of the secure zone. <I'm sorry.>

Sienna supposed it was a good thing she couldn't reply, because she had no idea what that reply might have been. He hadn't even stopped to gather his things—not that he had any things here—

Except his coat. Shit! It wasn't cold enough to need one, to any of them, but she imagined neither he nor Henri would want him to stand out among the locals that way. She darted back to the room they'd slept in and rescued it from where it had fallen on the floor off the back of a chair. Then she hovered in the entryway, waiting for him to return. He'd turn back when he got outside, she assumed. And what would she say to him then?

But there was no knock. The silence dragged out and grew sour until Gentiana sighed and came to wrest the coat away from her. "I'll take it to him. That fucker said no contact with you, not me."

The coat leaving Sienna's hands seemed to jar something loose in her mind as well, and her thoughts started moving again. "No, wait, and then drop it off with Valerie if you can. It's going to be obvious he spent the night, and if we don't give her some kind of story, she'll keep throwing him at me. You can drop a word in her ear that we—um—" Her creativity ran out, strangled by tears.

<Gentiana can tell her that his friend is a judgmental ass about artists and Simon is distressingly weak-willed,> Pen contributed. Not a fan of Henri either. Gentiana freed a hand to clasp one of Sienna's in endorsement of that idea.

Sienna managed a watery laugh, and trailed Gentiana back to the living area in a rather weak-willed fashion of her own. Everything she'd feared about her long-term relationship with Cyperus been distilled down into a single choice, between her, and his pride. And he'd chosen his pride.

No, she told herself sternly. He'd made the choice he had to, to save Pen's daughter. It wasn't about her at all; she was selfish to frame it that way. To keep framing it that way, over and over. But each time, her ability to see it in any other manner was being carved away.

To hell with him, then. While she waited for those photographs she was going to paint a fucking *masterpiece* of a mural.

PART III

As it turned out, it wasn't the photographs they had to wait for, it was a chance to hand over the completed dummy. Gentiana and Pen wrangled at length about the delay, finally coming to the conclusion that because Cyperus didn't dare be caught with the dummy, he had to not only seize or create a moment to accomplish the swap, but predict with some accuracy when that moment might occur ahead of time. Pen was of the opinion that they should trust him and give him as much time as they could, and with Isachne's experience behind her, she carried the day.

So Sienna painted. She'd worried there wouldn't be enough for Gentiana to do, but once she'd created the general sweep of hand-designed figures on photographs, someone needed to arrange for the huge design to be printed on sections of decal for the wall. And then help her do the initial hanging of each section, as the workers couldn't be trusted to line them up precisely enough. By the time, weeks later, Sienna reached the point of the last hand-painted layers, they had a certain rhythm, Gentiana readying her colors or making a recalcitrant grav-pad in the scaffolding work properly.

So Sienna painted until she couldn't see straight and then collapsed into bed. And Gentiana collapsed into a bed somewhere else most nights. On Pen, Sienna assumed, which was rich, given all the fuss about Sienna's own suspicious behavior at the beginning. What artist's assistant snuck in and out of a parked ship every night? But Securidad didn't show up to knock on their door, and Sienna was *not* going to lecture an adult about getting over grief in the midst of the stress of an undercover mission.

And now the mural was nearly complete, even the quiet secret she'd worked into the final layer. Gentiana had left for the apartment with the first load of her paint and brushes, so Sienna was more or less alone in the easing light—winters were warm and the evening light was generous in Nouvo Paris—to consider her work. She cast a quick glance back of her shoulder to check for Ines, then crossed the street to give herself the full sweep of the view. Ines never missed an opportunity to shoot Sienna a drive-by glare when arriving or leaving, and Sienna made it a policy to be up on the scaffolding and out of reach when she did.

Maybe it was absurd, to have pride in a grand monument to a people she hated, to a government who'd tortured her, but something in her couldn't help but be proud of the scope of her work. At the peak of the wall, a beneficent figure held her hands open to hundreds of comparatively tiny figures below. She wore the stylized jagged gold tiara that marked her as the personified virtue of Liberty herself—Libertad Sans Frontiers—but her hair was the same color and length as that of the current Secretaire Detat, in the finest tradition of artists with patrons throughout human history, Sienna figured. Behind Liberty was a composite landscape of photo and paint capturing the natural beauty of the planet and others under LSF control.

And below, among the tiny figures—at human scale to anyone standing on the street—was Cyperus's face, as well as Valerie's. She hoped the latter would enjoy finding herself, if the mural wasn't stripped down the moment they ran. Though maybe she wouldn't recognize herself anyway—the style of the figures only gave them a few bold lines to sketch in eyes and nose, and each had their hands pressed together, raised in praise or supplication, hiding their mouths.

"I think I see a familiar face," Henri murmured from beside her shoulder, startling Sienna into a skitter down the sidewalk a few steps. He pointed, checked for traffic, and crossed to touch Cyperus's face unerringly. Damn him.

Sienna trailed after. "I used all kinds of people as models." She hadn't been within fifty meters of Cyperus since he'd walked out of the apartment and Henri knew it. She wasn't going to let him smarm her into feeling guilty for nonexistent crimes.

"I don't blame you, you know." That conversational non sequitur that still somehow aligned directly with Sienna's thoughts startled her so much she allowed it when Henri reached out to touch the back of her hand, closing a reasonably safe private connection between their data paths.

<You're only trying to make sure your boyfriend comes home to you.> Henri offered her a smile that was probably intended to be sympathetic. <But you can see how he's meant to be here, can't you? Here or somewhere like it, doing what he's good at. You have to let him go.>

Sienna's thoughts connected like an electric shock to a fingertip on a cold day. She'd been too upset to think about it at the time, but why *did* the Pax Romana suddenly want a non-sentient AI they'd tossed aside into some warehouse, anyway? LSF hadn't been having any more luck last-jumping it than the Pax Romana scientists had.

But if this wasn't about the AI, it was about the highly trained agent, then things started to make a little bit of sense. Not completely, but—<Just how badly is the war going, if they're having to strongarm in retired agents they previously cast aside?>

Sienna would bet it was only because he'd so thoroughly dismissed her, that his shock was unexpected enough that it showed in a flicker of his expression. <Bad enough that there's a

reason you're in charge of intelligence for a whole damn planet alone?> she guessed next, and this time her confirmation was a tightening scowl.

<Agents like him are never happy in a quiet life,> he snapped, and broke their connection with a jerk of his hand. "Think about it. I see you're almost finished here. I'm sure you'll be off to paint on the next planet soon."

"I will think about it," Sienna promised. Think about how best to show Cyperus how his government was trying to manipulate him, after they'd cast him aside. Henri took himself off, lifting a hand in a show of friendly farewell before he turned a corner down the next street.

Cyperus should be getting off work soon, in fact. She fidgeted in front of the mural, pacing a few steps before leaning in to pretend to inspect one element or another. When she spotted Cyperus making his slow way down the street away from the R&D building, it was all she could do not to sprint to him. Instead, she charted an intercept course and strolled up in time to watch his lips tighten with frustration. He couldn't avoid her if she really pushed this and they both knew it. "Seraphine," he said, repressively.

She fell into step beside him and casually reached down to touch her fingertip data path points to the back of his hand, as Henri had to her. <Henri came around this evening, full of grandiose sentiments about how I should let you go, to do what you're good at. Which is your choice, as much as it *hurts*, Cyperus, for me to think that that's what you'd choose.>

Cyperus's steps stuttered. <I wouldn't—>

<I felt your restlessness, Cyperus. Before Gentiana and Pen showed up. Reading those reports or whatever they were that Galax was secretly sending you, keeping your presence in the apartment and in my life too contained to even put your mercy candle on a fucking table. You hadn't left yet, but you had no *roots*.

<So you have a choice. But I want you to make that choice while realizing that they threw you away when you got infected with the weapon, and it's only now that the war's started going so badly that they've come crawling back to you. And they don't even have the decency to appeal to your patriotism or offer you crates full of money, instead they manipulate you to make you think you're somehow better than us cowardly civilians.>

Cyperus tried to reply again, but she didn't give him the chance this time. <And everything you're doing is in service of saving Pen's daughter, I know that. And maybe Henri can help with that. But you need to decide if you want his support, or merely his good opinion of your skills as an agent who's too amazingly talented to need a civilian's aid.> Then she broke the connection and strode ahead, far faster than he'd ever be able to catch up to. He'd need time to think about what she'd said, she knew that too. She only wished that, some time before he finally gave her an answer, her throat would stop feeling like every breath was making it bleed inside.

"You were right," Cyperus told the apartment in general when Gentiana opened the door to him. When Sienna peeked around the doorframe of the living room, heart pounding with the pressure of hope in her chest, he lifted a carrier bag of takeout. "Want to eat, and then I'll tell you why?"

"Okay." Sienna dodged Gentiana's suspicious look on her way to take the bag from him, and the banality of sorting out the boxed dinners and utensils calmed her heartbeat in gradual stages. She could make a guess at which box was hers and which was his by the contents, so she de-lidded those and slid Gentiana's over to the opposite side of the table. Cyperus settled himself to a seat with his hip pressed as much against hers as the individual chairs allowed as she stacked her box's fruit pastry neatly on top of his, then started moving his pickled vegetables over to hers.

Cyperus nibbled a corner of a pierogi-like savory pie and made a face. "Too much ginger." He held it out and Sienna accepted it eagerly. He could sort out the rest of the box apportionment.

Gentiana paused after removing her own box's lid to eye them both. "You don't have to just grab a premade box from the shelf, you know. You can pick each element individually."

"I know?" Apportionment complete, Cyperus dug into his own box.

"That's why the desserts are both things he likes," Sienna teased, tapping a gentle elbow into his side.

<It's one of the ways they say they love each other.> Pen's voice was perhaps a little exasperated but definitely affectionate. <Since using your actual words is so complicated, I guess.>

It *was* a way of saying they loved each other. Sienna had never put in quite those terms in her mind before, but now the thought drew tears up to the corners of her eyes. A couple fell as Cyperus paused eating to clasp her hand, lifted it to kiss the palm. "Universal mercy, I've *missed* you, and Henri can go fuck himself, and—dammit, I had it laid out on the walk here, and it's all tangled again." His own laugh was a bit watery.

He took a deep breath, then tried again. "You know I've never had anyone—serious, before, and I was utterly unprepared for how much it *hurts* to be without you. I suppose that's why Henri tried a different tack with me privately: how I was being selfish, encouraging you to maintain a connection with me that put you in danger. I suppose the hard sell to get me back into the game would have started once he'd chased you off."

He caught up both her hands now. "And you were right that I was paying attention to what was going on in Pax Romana intelligence. I suppose I thought I might be missing that life purely because it wasn't really a choice I'd made, to leave it.

Circumstances intervened. But here I am, and I do have the choice, and now I know what I'm choosing. I'm too old for this bullshit anymore. It's *exhausting*, and lonely, and there are plenty of places to get excitement in daily life on Idyll, with you."

<For what it's worth, Isachne's opinion was "if we ever lose Tehran to a family, we'll lose him for good,"> Pen said, diffidently. That might be a lie—Pen had always played fast and loose with what Isachne had actually thought when she was alive versus what Pen thought and found convenient to attribute to her. But Sienna appreciated the endorsement of Cyperus's motives anyway.

Cyperus gently turned her wrist so her LSF icon displayed. "And I've realized I'd rather have this civilian at my back than Henri any day, given the way she's proved herself willing to walk into fire for her friends and one very, *very* undeserving retired agent."

"You wait until I trigger the hidden layer and the foxes see just want kind of mural they've gotten themselves," Sienna said, laughter bringing with it a few more tears before she retrieved her hands briefly and scrubbed them away. "Watch out, I'll start eyeing empty walls around the Institute, when we get home. Working that big is heady stuff."

"Say the word, and I'll move heaven and earth so you can make arts full time." Cyperus grinned, the grammar mistake another of their inside jokes. Sheer relief, and love, and a little bit of dawning excitement cleared enough space for Sienna to take what felt like her first deep breath in far too long, and that fueled her thoughts enough to remember poor Gentiana. She couldn't be enjoying being a silent audience to a couple thrashing out their problems when there was no solving the fundamental distance between her and the memory of her dead wife.

Gentiana, however, looked lost inside her own head, but hardly miserable. Focused on the mission perhaps, though when the conversation lulled, she reengaged at a point not too far back, lips twisting in irony. "On balance, you're probably lucky to have missed your first experience with trying to live without someone being at all of twenty years of age when you were dumped. I'd just joined up, so I spent a fairly unhealthy amount of time at the range, converting targets pretty much into one big hole each."

Sienna had to laugh herself, thinking back. "Or worse, at the considerably more mature age of twenty-two, you do the dumping and then change your mind two weeks on only to discover that she's come to her senses and is avoiding your drama. My only recourse was to write bad poetry."

Cyperus slung an arm across her back. "I didn't know you wrote poetry."

"I didn't say I wrote poetry, I said I wrote *bad* poetry. It's a completely different beast. If you ever rescued any of it from the void of deletion, you'd tell me to stick to painting, I assure you."

The door chime sounded and Sienna's and Cyperus's heads both jerked guiltily in that direction. Had Henri been monitoring their apartment—? But Gentiana was grimacing in guilt, not surprise, and getting to her feet. "It would have been more suspicious to keep putting her off than to just invite her here, like she wanted," she said, inexplicably, then headed to the door.

Cyperus's knee delayed him, but Sienna jumped up to follow, so she was there when Gentiana opened the door on Valerie, the LSF woman's hair professionally back in its tight tail and a shoulder bag hanging at her side, rounded with the shape of a wine bottle. Gentiana clasped hands with her with affection that turned awkward a beat before she glanced back at Sienna. "You... two know each other, of course."

"Hi," Sienna said, nothing else coming to her as she cranked her behavioral controls to maximum and then scrambled to put everything together. So Gentiana hadn't been sleeping on

Pen. And she'd, what, been seducing Valerie in the name of the mission? If it had been planned, why had she hidden it?

Gentiana stepped into the awkward space in the wake of Sienna's inadequate greeting. "When I took back Simon's coat, we ended up talking…It was—I meant it to be casual. She knows about Isabelle's death." Gentiana paired the name with an intense look, as if Sienna couldn't have figured out on her own she was being fed the name Gentiana had used for Isachne.

"I'm sorry about Simon, by the way," Valerie said, kindly, as she followed Gentiana down the hall. "I know I shouldn't have meddled."

"Oh. Well…" This was so *absurd*, Sienna had to laugh, and Valerie joined her a beat later as Cyperus appeared in the doorway of the living area, looking faintly embarrassed. That finally broke down the awkwardness, and for a while they might have been normal friends, tidying away the remains of the boxed dinners and discussing the merits of where they'd been purchased versus various other restaurants in the city.

When Sienna took the boxes to the kitchen part of the living area, Valerie freed the wine bottle from her bag and followed, utterly unapologetic about her wish for a private word. Not that any such thing was possible with Gentiana's and Cyperus's implants, and Pen listening directly to Sienna's senses. Sienna went along with it anyway, however, bending her head close as Valerie spoke low while pouring out a glass. "Jeanne said you were friends with Isabelle first?"

Not hardly, but universal mercy, how did you translate the complexity of her situation with Isachne and Gentiana into a cover story any other way? "We didn't always get along, but I certainly worked closely with her."

"I can see your mural's nearly done, and of course you'll be moving on to the next planet, but I just wanted to ask if there's any hope—if I might entice your assistant into staying, or if I have too much competition from Isabelle's memory…" Valerie caught Sienna's eyes, gaze square and unapologetic, one boss to another. "I know you'll hardly want to let her go yourself, talented as she is."

Then she transferred her gaze to Gentiana, and Sienna's chest tightened. To see that love and know it was only going to end in heartbreak—she and Cyperus had muddled through somehow, but Idyll was neutral, and LSF and the Pax Romana were at *war*. And an agent of LSF had tortured her, but Valerie hadn't. She was just living her life, and falling in love with exactly the wrong person. "Before she died, I believe Jeanne promised Isabelle she'd help some members of her extended family, if they needed it. One of them is in some trouble at the moment, and I wouldn't be surprised if that…takes priority for Jeanne, you know?"

"Fair enough. Thank you for the honesty." Valerie, disappointment deepening the sober cast to her expression, toasted Sienna with one of her two glasses, sipped from it, then carried them both to the table to hand the other to Gentiana. Sienna followed with the glasses for herself and Cyperus.

"So how long has *this* been going on?" Valerie asked on a lighter note, gesturing with her glass to where Cyperus's hand had found its way to Sienna's knee. "Don't think I didn't find his face front and center in the mural." She nodded to Sienna. "Which is beautiful, by the way. Not just Liberty, but all the people at the bottom—you've given them a real humanity."

"Thank you." Sienna sipped her wine, though she felt a little flushed even before it hit. Of course she'd showed her work to plenty of people along the way, but most of that had been to earn her place in the university program in the empire—the one that had taken her into Pax Romana space, before her ship home was captured by LSF. Scratch that, all of it had been. She supposed no one had seen her art after the camp, besides Cyperus and briefly Gentiana. And Valerie didn't seem the type to indulge in white lies. "Tell that to Simon's friend, huh?"

"Let me at him." Valerie laughed, and looked very much like she would have preferred to mirror Cyperus's position, only with Gentiana instead of Sienna, but she maintained a close distance that nevertheless didn't touch.

Sienna hoped, as the night wore on, the wine disappeared, and they moved to the couches to continue chatting, that when the Near-AI cube was discovered missing, Valerie wouldn't connect that to Gentiana. Let her simply be sad that Gentiana hadn't been in the right headspace, that circumstances had kept them apart.

She was sure that would be painful enough.

Gentiana's steps dragged as they navigated through institutionally ugly halls of the R&D building the next morning, frown settling deeper into her expression the longer she had to anticipate what was coming. "You're sure Valerie didn't say what she wanted to talk to us about? Why didn't she send the message to me? She wouldn't need you if she plans to ask me to stay. Or are you supposed to help convince me? Did you say anything to give her hope I might stay?"

Sienna didn't bother answering, since it hadn't helped the first three or four times Gentiana had iterated those questions on the way over here. She had no idea what Valerie wanted, but she was much more worried about running into Ines while they were here. Valerie didn't make her feel like she'd give away the game just by standing in the wrong manner in her vicinity, like the director did.

When they arrived at the room number mentioned in the message, Sienna didn't see a chime so she knocked lightly. At Valerie's slightly muffled "Come in!" she led the way in and more or less towed Gentiana after her.

Valerie gave them a slightly harried flicker of a smile before slipping past to shut the door after them. “Security, sorry. Heaven forbid Ines should walk by and see it open. Please! Sit.” She gestured to what was clearly the meeting space of the workroom, a chair facing a desk, the work surface tilted away from them for the use of the desk’s owner, but no doubt crowded with correspondence and data visualizations. Valerie continued her path in the other direction, tidying bits of tech and circuitry—security again, perhaps—on one of many tables crowded with such things, as well as the equipment to test it all. Sienna considered, then took the one chair herself. There was plenty of other seating, but it was all over in front of the equipment. Gentiana could hover like an assistant if this was business, as it seemed more and more likely that it was.

“I’ve got one question for you, Jeanne.” Valerie’s voice had changed utterly, dropping into flat, desperate betrayal. Sienna whirled in her seat, to find Valerie holding a handgun on her, both hands braced with all the hallmarks of someone who’d not only been properly trained, but had put in her practice hours since. “Did you know who your boss really is? Or did she hire you, unknowing, as part of her cover?”

Oh, universal mercy. Fuck, fuck, fuck—the expletives smoothed into one continuous stream, a bass line to the screaming song of Sienna’s panic. What had she done? What had she *done*? “Who I…am?” she asked, letting the implant keep her voice confused, not terrified. “I’m an artist.”

Gentiana had herself under similar control, whether through her own skill or with the implant’s help. “I didn’t do a deep dive into her background when she hired me, but it all checked out…” She attempted a smile. “Valerie, I’ve been sharing an apartment with her these last weeks, I can assure you, she really does paint. *All* she does is paint and sleep, practically. I have to remind her to eat sometimes.”

"So she trained for the cover." Valerie circled to the other side of her desk and recentered her aim on Sienna's forehead.

A stifled exclamation came from the doorway of an inner room and Cyperus hurried for their group, as fast as his knee allowed. Valerie threw up one hand to arrest his path, then gestured him to stay behind her. "I'm so sorry, Simon, but it seems she's had you fooled this whole time, along with all of us."

"What are you *talking* about?" Cyperus snapped, which made Valerie's attention twitch to him—then immediately back to her aim. He'd surprised her by sounding more like his own, real brand of asshole, rather than Simon's, Sienna supposed.

"Have you noticed her laugh?" Valerie tipped her chin to Sienna. "I did, last night. I didn't remember until later where I'd read about that before, though. That dead space, around a particular pitch. You can learn to speak around it, but in singing, or in laughter, it's unmistakable. That's *vocal paralyzer damage.* I assumed she was a domestic criminal, looked her up using her face in case it was something that might get you hurt, Simon, but it's so much worse than that. She's *Pax Romana.* She was a prisoner of war." Valerie freed one hand to bring something up on her desk work surface. "Look! Sienna Prague."

After all her anxiety, all her guilt at not playing her part the way Gentiana or Henri would have her play it—it all came down to this. Sienna hadn't *done* anything, she'd only *been* what LSF had *made* her. Rage swept through Sienna. What they had *done to her.*

She saw Cyperus shifting his weight, getting ready to jump Valerie for the gun, but how was he going to accomplish that when he couldn't stand without his cane? Gentiana had tensed too, but Valerie was facing her, would have plenty of time to shoot Sienna before Gentiana could reach her.

So she was on her own, for now. The rage left Sienna scoured clean and reckless in its wake. She deactivated the behavior controls so her lips would shape her own damn name properly.

"Prague Sienna." She heard Cyperus's and Gentiana's gasps as one. "I'm Idyllian, and if you found that much, I invite you to keep pulling on that thread, and *see what else you find.*" She put all the vibration of her rage into those last words, squarely in a pitch the paralyzer hadn't taken from her. The LSF might have erased the records, but Valerie had found at least her name, so who knew, maybe everything was available to someone with Valerie's access.

And Valerie read to her like a good person. Like there were among both the empire and the so-called rebels, just living their lives. Not that it mattered, usually. It probably wouldn't make a difference now, but what did she have to lose, trying? If Valerie was even a little distracted, that might make Cyperus's job easier.

"What—?" Valerie was too wise to lower the gun, but she did touch her work surface again, eyes flicking down to what she found, back up to Sienna. Back and forth. Then she clearly started a video, because sound floated out.

Overlapping voices, a chaotic mess of LSF French. "No, we have no time, we'll lose the implant if it feels the agent die—" "If I rush this, it won't take in the new prisoner either—" "This is crazy, they should never have let it get that far with the agent—" "You're telling me, but now we have to clean up their fucking mess—"

Wet sounds. Cutting sounds. Bleeding sounds. A grunt, then thrashing. "Keep her under!" "She is! This must be the fucking implant—" "Well, the fucking implant is going to get her killed. Hold her down!" More grunts, pure animal sounds of pain, made when the conscious mind wasn't awake to scream.

It didn't even sound like her. Sienna felt rather like she was—floating. Dissociative. It could have been anyone in that recording. She was breathing rather fast, though. Not enough air in the air again, heart laboring against that lack. This hadn't been what she'd meant Valerie to see. She'd thought there would have been—some kind of note, in her file. She was giggling, suddenly, hysterical, and curling over herself to press her hand to her mouth and hold the sound in.

"Why would they *do that*, to anyone—?" Valerie's voice broke, and even Cyperus, who knew all about it, was looking rather gray.

"They needed the agent, for a prisoner exchange. Only they accidentally tortured her to death, so they needed someone to put her implant in so it would ping correctly when the Pax Romana came to pick her up." Sienna suppressed the giggles long enough to get the explanation out, but then nausea crawled up her throat in its wake. Panicked cursing, from the recording. "Turn that *off*," she begged, and Valerie did.

Cyperus reached for the gun, absurdly polite, given the situation. Still undercover. "Valerie, let me help—"

"No." Valerie snapped a forestalling gesture at him with her free hand. "You're too entangled. I'm not going to make you hold a gun on her."

"Entangled…and you're not?" Cyperus said, low and careful. He didn't look at Gentiana, but Valerie did.

"Jeanne. Please. She just hired you—" Valerie cut herself off and forestalled any answer from Gentiana at the same time, jerking her head in a shake negating all of this, perhaps. "It doesn't matter. We're done anyway. It's just a matter of whether both of you get arrested or only *her*. After what was done to you, why are you here, Prague Sienna? It's not just to make a patriotic mural—*fuck*." Sienna flinched, but whatever had just occurred to her didn't make Valerie pull the trigger. Her eyes had gone wide. "You can't see any of their mouths."

Cyperus murmured another syllable of frustrated confusion, but Sienna knew what Valerie meant and met her eyes, forging a connection from the understanding. "The little people have been silenced. In the mural," Valerie explained. "How poetic. But you didn't come here for that."

"She came here to save my daughter," said Pen's voice through the work surface's speakers. "And damned if I'm going to let you kill her for it. Apparently Sienna thinks your reason can be appealed to, so I'm appealing—no, I'm begging. Let us take my daughter home."

"Pen, what are you doing?" Gentiana hissed, then flinched as if she hadn't expected it to be out loud. She'd decided to risk talking on a private channel only to have her own behavioral controls shunt it to spoken French instead, Sienna suspected.

Valerie flinched too, as if confirmation of her fears about Gentiana's part in this was a physical blow, then she pointedly ignored Gentiana to respond only to Sienna. "A child? Where does she come into this?" She pressed her free hand over her mouth, as if holding back further words could hold back the emotions behind them too. And the damn gun didn't waver.

Well. They were fucking all in now, that was for sure. "That's Pen, the only last-jumped AI in the known universe you're talking to. They cloned her without her consent, and the Near-AI you've been working on for the past months is the result." Sienna leaned forward, trying to persuade with intensity alone, if nothing else. "If researchers who knew how Pen was made couldn't recreate her, there's no chance you're going to be able to. Why not just let us have the Near-AI?"

"Talking to…a last-jumped AI…" Valerie's voice faded out and she collapsed into the chair behind the desk. Cyperus leaned in and neatly confiscated the gun, turning it on Sienna and Gentiana both, with an apparent novice's lack of confidence and steady aim. Then Valerie straightened. "How do I know you're not just their human compatriot on their ship?"

"You don't get to come peer at my memory core, that's for fucking sure," Pen said, caustic.

For some reason, the last part of that made Valerie press her hands over her face. "Simon," she said, after a tight pause. "You know the first thing the Near-AI said when I finally got it networked in enough I could get sense out of it? It cussed me out. In Lingua, but the tone was identical."

She lowered her hands and her gaze sharpened on her work surface, perhaps in lieu of any other presence to focus on, for Pen. "Tell me how you were last-jumped, and you can have your daughter."

"No!" Gentiana spat. Still a loyal enough citizen of the empire that she didn't want that technology in LSF hands? "If they treat their human citizens this way, what would the foxes do to last-jumped AI they made?"

Sienna's chest contracted hard enough to burn for a breath. Yes, call your lover by an epithet, that would no doubt make the betrayal better. Or maybe Valerie was a part of "us," different than the "they" who were the foxes.

"Jeanne." Valerie's mouth worked as if the name had an aftertaste now she must have realized it was false. "The Near-AI in that room—" She pointed to another inner door, across from where Cyperus had appeared. "Isn't meant to be isolated, and I have no idea how to turn it off either, without cracking the case to get at the power source, which seems like a terrible idea. When I first plugged it in, it wasn't shut down—it didn't seem like it had been shut down at any point—it was *screaming*. Much as I hate to admit it, Ines was right about that much: it would have done much better connected to the planetary network, but we couldn't have it shouting to the Pax Romana. I've given it as much of a self-contained network as I can, within the shielding, as many sensors as I can attach, but if I were to disconnect it again…"

"Her!" Pen apparently could contain herself no longer. "Stop calling my daughter 'it.'"

"But a last-jumped AI might have a chance of understanding what was going on long enough to hang on," Sienna said, low. She clenched her hands into fists on her knees. Like Pen, running for it in a ship that forced her to be "so small."

<All right, folks, your friend the director of R&D was seen going into a meeting with Securidad, so I advise you to grab the target and get the fuck out of there without indulging in whatever flourishes your own plan has lined up.> Henri's voice, broadcasting in a channel to all three of them. <Interdepartmental cooperation is going to take a little while to iron out, but that just means forces are going to be overwhelming when they are deployed.>

Shit. No time. Sienna rose. Valerie tensed, but Cyperus continued playing his part by following her up with the gun. "The AI for the secret of last-jumping. Your word on that?"

"My word." Valerie spoke over Gentiana's renewed objections.

"It was *my* secret in the first place," Sienna spat as an aside to Gentiana, then focused on Valerie. "You need to add a set of memories from a living human to the Near-AI, into its core storage. Gentiana's been recording hers—I don't know if they'll be enough to last-jump Pen's daughter, but we can at least try."

Gentiana's expression drained down to something hollow. At Sienna sharing the secret, she assumed until the woman spoke, behavior controls not enough to smooth the waver from her voice. "Seraphine…I can't do it twice. They told me it's like cutting down a tree—you can start a new sapling on the stump, but it's never going to be perfectly straight after that. If I give my memories to Pen's daughter now, I can't be with her when I…" When she died. "Of course I'd make that sacrifice in a heartbeat, if I knew it would work, but what if it doesn't?"

"Please," Pen said. Just that, nothing more—or perhaps Gentiana's internal look, hugging herself, was because Pen was expanding on her plea over a private channel.

"I don't understand," Valerie said, an inextricable mixture of exasperation and pain.

One side of Sienna's mouth hitched up in a dry smile. "I guess there was more thread to follow than I realized. You're almost there." She ticked off questions with raised fingers, the ones with the data paths, though those couldn't currently be seen. "Where'd I get the memories I last-jumped Pen with? From the dead agent who used to own my implant. And who was that dead agent to Gentiana—" She belated started to change that to "Jeanne," but Valerie waved away the necessity of that.

"The family member—the daughter—is her priority," Valerie said, low. Her gaze flicked back to Sienna. "You *were* honest with me."

Sienna rolled her shoulders, awkward. "As much as I could be."

<Gentiana, we don't have *time* for this. Get your fucking shit together before the Securidad forces bust in on us,> Cyperus snapped, though his face retained only Simon's kindly worried confusion.

"All right." Apparently once Gentiana was moving, she was *moving*. She crossed to stand before Valerie in two strides. "Pen will do the actual transfer if you'll connect her daughter to an external network."

That was easier said than done, apparently—the shielded room was behind two doors, so at least one would always be closed, and Valerie didn't have a cable that long just lying around. Cyperus, in his guise as Simon, tucked the gun into the back of his waistband and stumped over with his cane to speed the search for lengths to chain together, and Valerie didn't seem to notice that left Sienna unguarded.

Valerie's work surface chimed and she snagged an earpiece from one of the tech-cluttered tables as she passed, fitting it on while ferrying a last length of cable to Gentiana. "I'm busy, Ines," she said, after listening for a few seconds. "You really need to meet this minute?"

Cyperus came to a stop and hissed a wordless warning noise. "Don't you dare."

Valerie tapped the earpiece to mute her voice, turned on Cyperus in surprise. "What? If I go distract her, it'll give Jeanne—whoever—more time."

"What if she's trying to get you out of here to give her the chance to come in and search for—or plant—an excuse to arrest you?" His eyes were wide, making the scenario sound a bit far-fetched. When he spoke on a channel to the rest of them, Sienna heard his frustration with the strictures of his cover. <She must be having trouble convincing the Securidad forces to take her orders. If she gets Valerie out of here, she can just use a couple of her own people instead.>

<A couple people would be easier for us to get past, right?> Someone needed to say it, and Sienna figured Gentiana wouldn't.

<And then Valerie rots in prison for the rest of her life,> Gentiana snapped. "Look." She reached for Valerie's hands, stopped herself. "We forced you, okay? Held the gun to your head. They can't arrest you for that, but you can't go waltzing off to a meeting, either."

"Of course they can arrest me—both of us—" Including Simon, of course. "But they might let us go eventually." Valerie nodded once, resolved, then unmuted her earpiece. "I'm sorry, Ines, you're going to have to wait." And she ended the connection.

It didn't take long to finish hooking up the cube to the external network, and Pen announced the download beginning not long after, but then silence settled that stretched wider and wider and strangled everything it touched. Finally, Sienna edged around where Gentiana had pulled up a chair, face now completely blank, and stepped up to the cube on the considerably tidier surface of the work table inside the shielded room. It looked—well, it looked exactly like the dummy she'd spent days perfecting. Anticlimactic.

But it did give her an idea. “Why don’t we swap in a dummy after all? If it goes unnoticed for a while, it’ll be another layer of evidence you weren’t involved and couldn’t have stopped us.”

“After all—?” Valerie shook her head, not bothering to finish the question. “Scanner for a print-pattern is all the way in the outer room.” She pointed.

Sienna delicately lifted the cube to finally get a sense of its weight balance, set it back down, and strode out. “I can recreate one from memory at this point.”

Cyperus joined her at the printer, watching as she cheated and got the data paths in her first two fingertips to interface with the LSF system so she could work faster. He dragged up a chair with the air of someone who knew soon he’d need all the strength he could save now. <Sorry,> she said as she worked, not entirely sure for which part, specifically.

Cyperus looked up from where he’d been focusing on the head of his cane, offered a tight slash of a smile. <We’ll hand out the apologies and the praise on the ride out of here, because that’s the only time we’ll know which apply.>

“Did it work?” Gentiana said suddenly. There was the sound of a chair leg scraping against the floor from the inner room, presumably as she jerked back to herself.

<Don’t know. Unplug her anyway, I’ll keep contact and comfort her as much as I can on the way. We’re officially out of time. Securidad forces are gathering at the front of the building. They’re not at the back yet, but you have minutes left, if that.> Pen had switched to channels, but in French, and Valerie reacted like Pen had hijacked her earpiece to speak through that as well.

“If you tie me to a chair or something—” Valerie offered as Gentiana gathered the cube into her arms.

Cyperus pushed to his feet, Simon dropping away like a face full of water he’d splashed on and then wiped away at a sink. “No time. And we might need a hostage to make it safely as far as the ship." He smoothly drew the gun and eyed Gentiana. "I can't run and aim. Can you handle it, or do we need Sienna to do it?"

"I can handle it," Gentiana growled. She and Cyperus traded in a pair of smooth tosses, cube for gun, and Sienna noticed Gentiana couldn't look Valerie in the eyes as she settled the gun into her back, grip tight on the woman's upper arm. Cyperus shrugged on a shoulder bag to keep his hands free, and Sienna snatched up the dummy cube as well, still warm from the printer. No time to stage it back in the shielded room now. No time for anything except running, as best they could.

Valerie hissed a curse as they headed into the hallway, twisting in Gentiana's hold to aim a glare at Cyperus. "Universal mercy, Simon, you too? A whole *team*? How did I ever rate that?"

"I don't think it counts as a team when one member is retired, one's AWOL, one's a non-citizen civilian, and all of us have the opposite of official sanction," Sienna said sardonically. She placed herself next to Cyperus in case he needed the support, but he was moving reasonably quickly at the moment, cane wielded to smooth out his gait. Probably using the implant to remove the pain, which was a very bad idea, but there wouldn't be a later for him to regret it if he didn't do it now, so.

They had no time, no guarantee they hadn't caused further psychological damage to Pen's daughter, but at least they had her now. They had a chance.

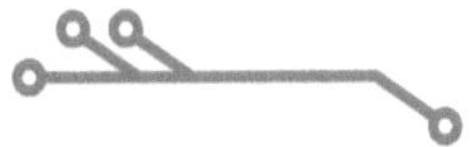

The back of the R&D building, viewed from the street as Sienna glanced back to make sure no one was following yet, at least didn't pretend it was better than its functional construction—no tromp doil arches or stone blocks, just gray plascrete in warming late morning sunlight. Only delivery and mobility assistance vehicles were allowed in the city core and foot traffic was minimal with the day shift having already started, creating the sort of quiet that tipped easily into creepiness in this kind of district.

Sienna should have been looking ahead, not back, though. She almost ran into Cyperus as he stopped short beside a similarly stilled Gentiana, gun and grip on Valerie as tight as ever. Henri, golden and immaculately styled, gave a couple of ironic handclaps. <You made it. I was beginning to wonder.> He sauntered up, extended a hand, palm up. <Thank you for your service. I'll be taking the AI now.>

"The silent Pax Romana conversation thing *is* fucking creepy," Valerie said, ironic tone walking the line of fear and falling on the correct side. "What the hell is going on?"

Were Securidad forces even coming at all, or was that just a lie Henri had told to flush them out? Ines *had* called unexpectedly about something, though. "Why *did* Ines go to Securidad now? Gentiana must have been in and out of the building to visit Valerie plenty of times before now. Adding me to the mix is nowhere near the hard proof she'd need to convince anyone else of her suspicions," Sienna said.

And Henri—he blew her a kiss, the fucking *asshole*. The next moment, he focused his attention on Cyperus like she wasn't even present. "Tell your vapid girlfriend to hand over the AI and you can all be on your way off the planet to go home and die of boredom, hm?"

In the rush, she'd honestly forgotten she was carrying anything. Sienna looked down at where she'd cradled the cube against her side, resting on her hip.

The *dummy* cube.

Vapid girlfriend? Sure, she could give him that. "Cyperus, it's not worth our lives." She put a panting breath of panic into her tone and threw the dummy cube right at Henri's smarmy head.

He caught it handily, of course, and saluted them with it. Then he was gone, jogging down the street and through an anonymous warehouse door with a smoothness to his gait that seemed to Sienna to mock Cyperus's injury. "Universal mercy, I'd like to set him on fire," she muttered. She didn't realize until he broke into a jagged laugh and moved again, that Cyperus had been literally frozen with the strength of his own rage.

"Save some for me," he said, the humor in his tone perhaps not properly humor when it held such a razor-blade edge. He aimed his limping path for one of the warehouses down the street. "I have a vehicle in the garage there. We can meet Pen outside the city—they'll send a team to prevent us accessing her, but they won't realize she can lift off by herself until it's too late."

"How well prepared of you," Gentiana said, pulling Valerie along. Or guiding her, more like. And, Sienna noticed when she glanced over as their knot tightened up for travel, there was currently no magazine in the gun pressed into Valerie's back. She looked first to Gentiana's coat pocket, but found the extra weight pulling at Cyperus's instead. So he'd had it unloaded all the way back when he was pointing it at her. She couldn't remember a moment when he could possibly have palmed the magazine, but that was the point, she supposed. It felt—warm, somewhere deep beneath the surface of her current near-panic, to think that he'd dared that extra step to protect her.

"I retired, I didn't purge more than a decade of training and experience from my mind," Cyperus snapped. Sienna let them bicker—maybe it would help them feel better.

"Stop!" The voice, heavy with authority, came from a Securidad officer rounding the corner from the front of the R&D building. One officer at the head of a whole hell of a lot more of them.

Gentiana slewed herself around, bringing up the gun to show stark in silhouette against Valerie's head. "Don't shoot, we have Bordeaux. We'll let her go when we're safe. No one needs to get hurt." She lifted her voice, sounding confident and almost relaxed.

If that had been her and Cyperus, Sienna could only imagine she would have been shaking apart.

Having belonged to an intelligence agent, Sienna's implant still managed to surprise her sometimes by flinging up automated warnings she'd never realized existed in the system. So GUNFIRE DETECTED flashed across her vision even before she'd decoded what she was hearing, the deceptively benign crackles of bullets embedding into plascrete. Instinct flinched her down toward a crouch and the implant flung her forward instead, piling with the others behind a half-height wall that enclosed one side and the end of a descending stairwell down to a basement-level door in the building they'd taken shelter against.

"Universal mercy," Valerie was repeating in a whisper. Gentiana handed her off to Sienna, as if Sienna could do anything if Valerie decided to jump them. Cyperus handed over the magazine, Gentiana smashed it into the gun, and chose her step to put her at the correct height behind the enclosing wall. She peeked up, took one careful shot, then dropped back again as more bullets smashed into the wall and the side of the building.

"Give yourselves up." Ines's voice reached them, amplified over the sound of gunfire.

Valerie had to rely on plain shouting in return. "Ines!" Her voice swooped up to a panicked register. "They could have *hit me.* Tell Securidad to stop shooting." Cyperus brushed past the two of them, attention focused on the locked door into the building, and in the shuffle Sienna lost hold of Valerie. The woman seized the opportunity to go up a step, *toward* the gunfire, as if the only problem had been that she wasn't visible enough before.

Sienna lunged and caught her again, held on tight as Ines replied. "You got yourself into this, Valerie! You allowed yourself to be seduced by the Pax Romana—or did you join their side gladly?—and now you're reaping the consequences."

"I'm sorry," Gentiana said, nearly too quiet to hear, then she was popping up for another shot and dropping back down, chased by another spatter of bullets. She never broke her focus on the enemy, so it seemed almost as if it was Securidad she was begging for forgiveness. When she spoke again, it was in a soldier's clipped tones. "I don't have the ammo for much more of this, Cyperus. Can you get us in or not?"

Cyperus slammed the heel of his palm beside the lock, an apparently unsuccessful effort to bleed off frustration. "Given ten minutes, maybe! Pen, can you get any purchase coming in from the network?"

<My daughter needs me.> Then silence. So a no on help from that quarter for now, then. Sienna wondered if she realized that she'd lose that daughter for good this time if Securidad waded in to take the AI off their dead bodies, but Pen had sounded so distracted, Sienna doubted explaining that to her would help. Perhaps she'd stopped monitoring their senses completely and didn't even realize they were in a firefight. And what about when they needed her to meet them outside the city?

Cyperus bent to the lock again, physically aiming effort at it even as he closed his eyes to focus on what he was doing electronically with his implant. Sienna gathered Valerie in beside her at the very bottom of the stairwell, pressed into the corner opposite Cyperus, against the road-dusty surface of the door. "I need whatever time I can get," he said, heavily, the chatter of the guns punctuating his words. Sienna heard what was unsaid in his following silence. The time Gentiana had the ammo for wouldn't be enough.

Someone needed to win them more time, then. Perhaps Securidad would find Vapid Girlfriend as believable as Henri had. "Stay," she told Valerie, pressing the woman deeper into the corner, and climbed two stairs, crouching plenty low, but getting herself into position to yell. "Director Toulouse! Please, please, stop shooting and I'll tell you where the AI is!"

Gentiana spat a curse under her breath. "Sienna, whatever you think you're doing—"

And Securidad stopped firing.

"I'm *stalling*," Sienna hissed at her. "To give Cyperus time!"

"You'd have me believe it's not with you?" Ines's voice lofted to her in the deepening silence, supremely arrogant.

"The other agent double-crossed us. He took it! Henri. Black hair, really pretty guy. He ducked into a building just down the street." Sienna poured out a cascade of details—the style of his coat, the color of the door he'd entered. Sure, she was burning one of Cyperus's former colleagues, but he'd sold them out first. "Please, Director. I'm not lying, you can find him on a camera somewhere, right? He's the one you should be chasing. Can't you just let us go? We don't have what you want."

No reply, which was…good? If Ines was consulting with Securidad, checking cameras, searching for someone of Henri's description at the right time. Sienna tried to count her heartbeats as they waited, frozen, but those were too fast so she switched to her breaths. Ten. Fifteen.

"Universal mercy," Cyperus breathed as a quiet prayer. He opened the door, making Valerie squeak when it bumped into her. <Gentiana, throw out a few shots and a taunt before you follow us, to make them assume we're still hunkered down for as long as possible.>

<Don't patronize me,> she snapped, and then Cyperus, having shoved Valerie through first, was pulling Sienna into a barely lit industrial basement as well.

Sienna didn't register most of the dark, footstep-echoing, generally hellish trip through that basement and then through some kind of connecting utility access passage to the next building with the truck. Pen started communicating with them about halfway through the journey, voice abruptly terrified, so apparently she'd caught up on their situation. Sienna decided to forgive her because she both found the utility passage and took care of the locks for them, so it was a straight shot through the garage for them at the end, limited only by Cyperus's speed and Valerie's lack of implant-enhanced darkvision. Pen announced she was standing by for liftoff as they arrived at the truck.

Cyperus opened the locks and gestured Gentiana to the driver's seat. <I think we should have a clear path; even when they figure out we took a vehicle, they'll expect us to head for the spaceport, not the opposite direction. You good enough with manual to handle a chase if it comes to that, though?>

<Yes,> Gentiana said, and climbed in without further comment. She placed the gun on the dashboard, awaiting Cyperus.

Cyperus turned to Valerie, touched fingertips to one temple then saluted her with them, a gesture of respect, though his lips were twisted with irony at offering it in this situation. "Nowhere to tie you up, here. Would it help if I hit you?"

Valerie shook her head, a bit too fast. "Take me with you."

Cyperus lifted the hand not on his cane wide and unthreatening. "We won't touch you, if you don't want." He scuffed a toe on the dirty plascrete at their feet. "Roll around on this shit and you'll look roughed up anyway." He turned back to the truck. <Sienna, there's only two seats, but if you sit between—>

Valerie took a step after him, seemed to think that might be misinterpreted, and subsided, hugging herself. "They would have *shot me*. For a piece of Pax Romana tech. Because I was fool enough to fall in love with a woman who kept holding me at arm's length and universal mercy, now I know *why*, and also my government would shove an implant into someone that could have *destroyed her mind*—should have destroyed her mind—"

They didn't have time for a crisis of loyalty either, but after all they'd done to her, Valerie deserved that time. Sienna took her elbow, feeling that shaking from the woman's hands had traveled up that far. "Valerie and I can go in the back. If she leaves with us we can drop her on some nothing fuel stop of a planet where she'll have time to—decide where she goes next, can't we?"

Cyperus's shoulders slumped for a single breath. "Yes," he said. Thinking of his own experience of leaving home behind, perhaps. Then the intelligence agent was back in his manner and he strode, leaning on his cane, to the front of the truck, leaving the two of them to settle themselves in the back.

Sienna could have found a crate of her own to sit on once she'd pushed Valerie down, but sitting together would allow them to better brace themselves against the movement of the truck—that was her excuse and she was sticking to it. Valerie didn't precisely cling to her, but Sienna could feel her still shaking. She was on the thin edge of falling right apart with relief herself, but they weren't off the planet yet, so she reengaged the implant to make sure her breathing stayed even and her hands steady as the truck pulled away. She'd done her part, and it was up to the others now. She trusted Gentiana at the wheel, and she trusted Cyperus's assessment that they'd have a clear path. Too soon to relax, but not too soon to trust.

And she'd helped them all get this far. Take that, anyone who'd doubted the civilian artist. She'd helped them *win.*

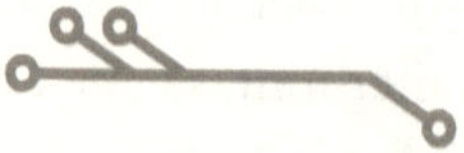

Pen's ship was big enough to have two cabins, but the one with bunks was currently housing electronic storage instead, so while Gentiana piloted them away from the planet, the other three had to share the remaining sleeping space. Sienna told to Pen trigger the hidden layer of her mural then more or less collapsed with Cyperus on the bed. She had the best of intentions to help Valerie make up the mattress pad they'd found for her to use on the floor, but surrender to exhausted darkness proved to be all she could manage.

Darkness, before the nightmare crept in.

Sienna fought her way close enough to the surface to recognize something was amiss, but it refused to release her completely. She was back at the camp and arguing in French with Ines, she wasn't even sure about what. It was absolutely vital that she win, but her voice got stuck in her throat. She coughed, choked, tried to dislodge whatever was blocking her airway, but now she couldn't breathe at all. Ines—actually, it was Elantine, the undercover LSF agent who'd tried to kill her at the facility where she first met Cyperus—was laughing at her. "Shut up," Elantine mocked. "Shut up, Sienna."

"Are you all right? You're having a nightmare," someone said in French, leaning over her. It was Elantine, trying to kill her again, that's why she couldn't breathe. Sienna aimed her pure, voiceless rage into a punch and felt it connect along with a grunt of pain from Elantine.

Not Elantine. She was awake. She was on Pen's ship. Currently alone in the bed, so Cyperus must have awakened before her. Valerie had stumbled back from the bed and was holding one hand up calmingly and clutching the other to her mouth, where blood was oozing down her chin. Shit!

"I'm sorry," Sienna said—or planned to say, but she couldn't make her lips shape any words in French right now. The breakdown she'd held back to get this far—apparently that was coming home to roost, right now. The panicked thunder of her heart, the clenching across her chest and throat, those had begun to gradually ease as her waking circumstances penetrated, but now they both snapped back to the redline.

She did manage an apology in Idyllian, hoping the tone would buy her enough time to pull herself together. Deep breaths. Pet the nap of a lump of blanket under her hand. Look and listen around, anchor herself in Pen's ship. After weeks in LSF housing, the clean lines of the furniture and walls in the cabin, tinged green in a shade that evoked the sea, were a relief.

Valerie tapped the earpiece she was still wearing with her clean fingertips. "Pen can translate for me," she said, speaking thickly around her split lip. "I'm afraid I can't speak anything else myself, though."

"You need sealant." That was straightforward, at least; finding it was a job to do. Sienna could focus on that. Wouldn't want to drip blood on the floor, though the soft polymer should be easy-clean.

The problem, Sienna realized, was that she couldn't get her thoughts to move straight enough to think where that sealant might be. Panic swallowed her in a new wave until it occurred to her Cyperus might know. She could find him. That was a much better focus. The wave ebbed once more.

Valerie trailed her to the compact living and dining area of the ship, where she found Cyperus heating food—breakfast by the smell, though she had no idea if that matched the clock—his cane leaning against the counter beside one hip. Her mental state must have been there to read in her face or to hear in her breathing, because he abandoned the cane to draw her to him with both arms. She tried to balance them to take some of his weight herself and then clung, pressing her cheek against his shoulder. "It's just the crash," he murmured into her hair. "It'll pass."

Then his chest hitched in surprise and his grip tightened. "What happened?" he demanded in French. Sienna turned to see Valerie rinsing some of the blood off her fingers and chin at the small sink next to the cooker. Cyperus edged them around, interposing his body between her and Valerie. "I punched *her*, Cyperus," Sienna said around a watery laugh. "She should be the one demanding protection from me." That's what this was, she realized. Protectiveness on Cyperus's part that had been thwarted while he needed to maintain his cover. Indulging in it in this situation was ridiculous—but it did wonders to help her heart slow.

"And what was she doing at the time?" Cyperus demanded.

He'd spoken in Idyllian, but with Pen's translation, it was Valerie who answered, fingertips resuming pressure on her lip. "Don't worry, I should have known better than to wake up someone with her background from a nightmare when speaking French."

"I thought she was Elantine," Sienna muttered into Cyperus's chest. That still didn't make it all right for her to punch—a hostage? An ally? Who knew.

Valerie frowned, but clearly didn't dare ask who that was, what with native politeness and also Cyperus glaring at her. Sienna wasn't sure she wanted to explain either. <With your permission, I can field that one,> Pen told her privately, and Sienna sent her assent on the same channel. Those events were half Pen's to tell anyway.

Valerie leaned back against the nearest patch of counter, gaze going internal as she listened, and Cyperus pushed Sienna to a seat on one of the benches attached to the floor around the dining area's small table. "She needs sealant," Sienna protested vaguely.

"Pen will point her to it. Now. Eat." Cyperus, collected his cane, dished up a plate of a scramble of eggs and vegetables from the pot in the cooker, and set it in front of her.

Sienna knew it would indeed make her feel better, but her stomach seemed to have been left back in the nightmare and she stared at the plate for a while, trying to summon motivation. Without another word, Cyperus plonked himself on the bench beside her, stole the plate for a few bites, then shoved it back in front of her. He was so ostentatious about the whole thing, she had to laugh, and take a few bites of her own. <I know exactly what you're doing, and yet it still works. It's not fair.>

<Purely because of my charming personality.> Cyperus flicked her a quick grin.

Sienna looked up when Valerie joined them at the greatest distance the table would allow her—which wasn't far—with a sealed lip and plate of her own, but she didn't appear to even bat an eye at them eating in turns off the same plate. "I just—I want to apologize too. In the nightmare, you sounded like you were choking. I couldn't stand by and listen to that. I wanted to help." Valerie looked up to direct an apologetic grimace at her directly. "I still want to help."

Sienna chewed longer than necessary while she tried to figure out how to respond—or even how she felt about that. "Why?" she settled on, finally. Turnabout as fair play perhaps, for Valerie's "why?" asked of her, for how an artist came to be undercover.

Valerie's turn to hesitate. "Because of everything that...happened to you." Sienna appreciated that she didn't say "was done to you," even though it hung in the air around them like throat-burning smoke. "I don't understand how you possibly could have chosen to get within lightyears of LSF space even to save a life, but I respect it, and want to demonstrate that respect, I guess? Hell, I don't know how you're *sane* right now."

"Luck when it comes to my friends. Lots of therapy," Sienna said, trying to keep it light.

"Strength of character," Cyperus said with a tinge of pride that was also ridiculous. He settled the plate in front of Sienna with finality. She gave in and finished the rest. "And good luck finding help she'll accept. *I* still can't do that consistently."

"Says the man who can't follow a doctor's order about how far he's supposed to walk on his knee to save his life," Sienna grumbled, to hide that she was probably flushed. He...wasn't wrong. She'd admit that to herself, at least. She squeezed the knee against her own, under the table, which happened to be the good one. "I had to come out here to save this one from the mess he'd gotten himself into, anyway."

She fully expected Cyperus's pride to volley that right back to her, but instead he smoothed a hand down the back of her hair, coming to rest, protective, against the back of her neck. "And I'm damn lucky that she did, too."

The swell of love that surged in her chest was too much for Sienna's rebuilt equilibrium and she leaned into Cyperus to hide her tears from Valerie. <Cyperus…I don't want you to stay with me on Idyll if you'll be unhappy, but universal mercy, I want you to stay.>

<I promise I will.> He touched her chin, kissed her, one side of his mouth ticking up at the taste of the salt there, maybe. <And I want you to be happy, whatever that looks like, but if you'd be happy painting, I'd like to support you so you can do it full time.>

<Okay.> Thinking of going all in with her art was scary, but considerably less scary than staring down a suspicious LSF R&D director, so Sienna figured she could probably handle it. She went first this time, echoing him on his departure. <I love you.>

He returned the words and seemed about to expand on them when Gentiana entered from the control room, rubbing the data path circles currently showing at her temples. She and Valerie avoided each other's gazes painfully, while Gentiana loaded a plate for herself. There wasn't room at the table for her to not sit next to Valerie, but Gentiana solved that by eating with one hip hitched against the counter. "I think I'm about maxxed out for the moment, so you should pilot the next burst, if we're going to bother continuing to do that to hide our trail," she told Cyperus in Lingua.

Cyperus grimaced. "Probably safer that way. Give me time to finish making Sienna eat."

"I'm not sure I understood that stuff about piloting even with the translation," Valerie said, lightly, fuzzing around the edges due to her injured lip.

"What—who did that to you?" Gentiana abandoned her plate on the counter to slide in next to Valerie. She angled the woman's head to see the injury better with a gentle touch against her jaw. Valerie started an apologetic explanation about nightmares, but Gentiana cut her off once she got the gist of it. "Sienna!"

"Can we call a moratorium on protectiveness on the part of those not involved in the incident, please? Besides, you might recall, Gentiana, that you tried to kick my face in when we first met." Sincere guilt made Sienna sharper than she'd intended in her defense.

"I'm not—" Gentiana began, heatedly. Being protective, Sienna assumed she'd intended to end that sentence, but instead she looked slightly up toward the ceiling as if thinking of a watching Pen.

"I certainly hope you are," Pen said, caustic, and sounding fully herself in a way she'd managed only intermittently since she'd arrived on a too-small ship. "It's the least you can do for her, if she hasn't dumped your Pax Romana ass by now."

Valerie choked on her surprise, and Sienna on an inappropriate laugh. "Valerie, meet Pen when she's not holding back. Swearing is only the tip of the iceberg," she said low, dipping into French. She returned to Lingua, lifting her voice for the general audience. "Sounds like you're feeling better, how's your daughter?"

"Call me Joy," a new voice said. It didn't sound precisely young, but certainly hesitant, and the pitch wasn't precisely in Gentiana's register, but it was certainly more of an edged soprano than the calming, alto tones Pen had inherited from the Near-AI she had been. She'd taken her name from the planet, as Pen had from the Penstemon facility, Sienna guessed. "I don't really want to talk much until I feel more like…myself."

And until she felt more separate from Gentiana as well, Sienna would guess. "Nice to meet you," Sienna murmured. Valerie looked like she was gathering herself to launch into a spate of questions anyway, oblivious to how queasy Gentiana looked at hearing someone who was her-not-her, so Sienna hurried to forestall Valerie. "By the way, Pen, were you able to trigger the mural before we left?"

"Hah. And how. You'll enjoy this." Pen brought up news drone footage on the wall and they all twisted to view it. At first, it focused on the consternation of a small crowd standing by, the evening shift whispering to each other, then it zoomed back to take in whole mural itself.

Liberty still held her hands out to the small people below her, but the small paint packs Sienna had sandwiched between layers had burst at Pen's signal, dripping inexorably for the ground. Red paint, coating Liberty's hands, oozing down to deface the figures immediately below her. Red paint, dripping in short lines as if coming from between the fingers of the upraised hands of those who worshipped at Liberty's feet. A little like Valerie had looked not so long ago, a resonance that made Sienna shiver briefly, but there was much more painted blood than that, enough blood for each citizen to have had their tongue cut out.

"Universal mercy," Valerie said, scarcely louder than a breath. "You certainly haven't forgotten what they did, have you?"

"Nor will I." Sienna let that vibrate with her rage, ever so briefly, then shook it off. "It doesn't matter, anyway. They'll have torn it down and painted over within the hour. Or already have done, by now?" She looked slightly up, addressing that to Pen.

"They have, but somehow footage of it is broadcasting to every planet I can reach," Pen said, smug. "That'll take considerably longer to root out."

"Ha," Cyperus said, pleased. He glanced at their empty plate and started gathering himself to stand to fill it again. Sienna wasn't surprised—he hadn't gotten much for himself around offering it to her.

"Sit," she told him sternly. "I'll get it. Next time, we should bring the powered assist along for your knee, in case you need it."

"Next time, I won't get into a situation where I need to do a fool thing like remove my maintenance nanites and I'll be fine," Cyperus grumped as she filled their plate.

Valerie huffed a laugh. "I should have known you two were married the moment I first saw you interact."

"Oh, we're not married yet. Now I've got the grass is greener bullshit out of my system, I need to look up Idyllian engagement customs," Cyperus said with utter nonchalance.

Sienna froze on the way back to the table, reviewing his words to make sure she'd heard them right. Then he winked at her and the flutter that had begun at the bottom of her stomach exploded up into her chest. "Jeff can fill you in, maybe," she said, pressing the waver excitement out of her voice to play along.

Gentiana shot Cyperus an exasperated look. "Was that you just asking without actually warrioring up to ask? That's fucking cheating."

"He loves grand gestures, she hates being kept in suspense, so if they pretend nothing just happened, they both get what they want. Don't screw up their system." Far from exasperated, Pen sounded even more smug now, as if she'd match-made them herself.

Sienna leaned in to kiss in Cyperus's hair as she set down his plate, then returned to the kitchen to find herself a paring knife. She rolled up her sleeve and set a hip against the counter as she considered her approach to the LSF chip. "Don't you dare," Cyperus growled. "Wait for me, I'll do it."

At least he wasn't demanding she wait all the way back to Idyll. Sienna returned to the table, set the knife down, and spun it so its handle pointed to Cyperus. "And then I'll do yours if you'll do mine," Gentiana offered him, matter-of-fact.

"And mine?" Valerie said, snapping every head at the table to her.

Gentiana's face crumpled. "We can drop you—"

Valerie gestured that away sharply. "On an outlying planet, I know. I'd have to start completely over there, if I don't want to be imprisoned for the rest of my life. And if I have to start over there…why think so small?"

Sienna spun the knife, stopped it, spun it again, to give herself something else to look at. "You have useful skills. I'd stand surety for you on Idyll, if you wanted. Which doesn't mean you can stay, but it means you have time to prove yourself."

"Be prepared to be given the third-degree early and often." Cyperus squeezed Sienna's knee, perhaps to forestall any apology. "And be locked out of the majority of the most interesting projects, depending on your job. But it doesn't last forever." <And it's worth it,> he said, warm, just between the two of them.

Gentiana went back to not-looking at Valerie, her whole body tight with tension. "I suppose I don't honestly know where Pen and I will end up, after we stop off at Idyll."

Sienna suddenly viscerally understood Pen's exasperation with her own romantic foibles, back when she'd first met Cyperus—all right, quite recently as well. "Well, I'm already standing surety for you, and the Director of Research would hide rotten fish in my walls if I didn't at least try to convince Pen and Joy to stay, so there's no reason to decide right now."

Gentiana nodded jerkily, then stood. "Can I…talk to you, Sienna? About the details of that?" Her face looked as if, however awkward that had been in her head, it was infinitely more so now she heard it out loud. "Cyperus can fill Valerie in." The addendum didn't help, but Gentiana fled anyway.

Sienna caught up to her in the cabin, perched on the edge of the unmade bed as Gentiana paced a few steps before her path was blocked by Valerie's mattress pad. "I know we're not quite… friends."

Sienna was trying to be empathetic, but there was just so between them, she couldn't help but choke her way into a laugh. "We'd mercy-damned *better* round up to friends by now, Gentiana."

Gentiana managed a breath of a laugh of her own at the pure absurdity of it. "Fair enough." Another few paces. "It feels crass to have this conversation in front of Pen, but there's nothing for it. I was supposed to be with her forever, I promised her that. And now I can't, and I know she told me herself that was all right, but I can't just...ride off into the sunset with another woman right in front of her, can I?"

"'A woman,' not 'another woman,'" Pen said, gently. By her standards. "I'm not a human, I'm an AI. Together has a different definition for me, once you take out the biology of sexual attraction. And then I have a different definition of forever, too. It's easy for humans to promise that to each other, on their personal scales. It's different for me. And Joy. And whoever else ends up last-jumped, eventually. We were going to end up at this point no matter what. So go find forever with that human. Or some other one. Just not with me."

A seemingly endless pause, while Gentiana looked like someone had punched her in the stomach. Sienna rose to clasp her hands, give her that much of a foundation to cling to, at least. "Besides," Pen said, returning to her more normal tone. "You called her a fox and she didn't fucking punch you. It must be true love."

Gentiana gave a wobbly laugh, then pulled Sienna into an embrace. "I told you, you have time to decide," Sienna said. "Take it, okay?" Gentiana nodded against Sienna's shoulder, and Sienna drew in a breath that reveled in the hope for the future filling her, for Gentiana and herself, both.

EPILOGUE

Sienna blanked the work surface of her small tablet and frowned as she used it to flip through the planetary archives instead. She knew there had to be a picture of the pre-space painting she was remembering here somewhere. "It'll make more sense if I can find you the original of the historical style I'm imitating." She and Valerie were seated on the audience bleachers of the Institute's small track—very small bleachers, as the track was mostly used for Medical's tests, not spectator sports. The weather was gray, but any day without drizzle was a win in the Institute's region. Against a background of overly regimented evergreens, legacy of the Institute's start as a timber farm, Cyperus jogged at a steady pace. He'd grown his beard back and cut his hair even shorter than it had started, perhaps to buzz away the feel of LSF the way she'd had her wrist tattoo removed the instant she returned home. Gentiana trailed him politely.

Sienna hummed in satisfaction as she found what she wanted, then held out the tablet to Valerie. "This." Valerie frowned down at the painting of female spectators, parasols over their shoulders and skirts down to their ankles, looking on as their family and lovers engaged in displays of manly physical prowess down by the park's lake, all in the most picturesque sunshine. "Why are they divided by—" She stopped, got a prompt with the Lingua word she wanted over her earpiece, then continued. "Gender?"

"Well, it *was* the dark ages. Before electricity, even." Sienna switched the tablet back to her own piece, drawing in a parasol on Valerie's shoulder with her stylus. On the track, Gentiana shifted gears up to a flat-out run and lapped Cyperus once, again. The second time, she tossed some inaudible insult over her shoulder to him, and Sienna lowered her stylus to watch his reaction closely.

Valerie grumbled under her breath. "That was unnecessary, Gentiana."

Cyperus lowered his head and kept on at his steady pace, exactly as the doctor had ordered. Sienna let her shoulders relax before she turned to Valerie with an apologetic grimace. "I asked her to. He's been promising me and his physical therapist both that he absolutely will, under no circumstances, stop making up absurd what-ifs, Cyperus, push himself on that knee. Looks like he was telling the truth."

"Well, then. I'll just enjoy the view." Valerie leered teasingly and reclined, holding an invisible parasol, and Sienna took the opportunity to snap a new background picture of her. Perfect!

<You did tell your guests the wedding's a month from now, didn't you?> Pen said dryly through her implant. <This shady character is trying to talk his way past security.> She sent a picture of Cyperus's Pax Romana friend Galax, earnest and the very opposite of shady.

Pen shouldn't know anything about who was talking to security, but good luck getting her to keep her nose out of anything around the Institute. Technically, she and Joy were each settled in their own self-contained dorm building, but only Joy—she'd retained a certain amount of military law-abiding instincts from her memory mother—actually stayed here.

Sienna started to rise, then subsided. The time Galax needed to clear security would be enough for Cyperus to finish his laps, so she might as well have security escort him out here to meet them. She contacted security to arrange it—they didn't even bother asking how she'd heard—and then cast a slight frown sideways at Valerie. "One of the Pax Romana guests has arrived early, do you want to make yourself scarce or do you feel up to dealing with him?"

Valerie straightened and rubbed at her unblemished inner wrist, chip scar healed and tattoo removed. "Might as well get it over with one at a time. He won't be able to tell if I don't talk, anyway."

"Take your hair down," Sienna suggested, in service of that, and then waved back in response to Cyperus's triumphant gesture as he finished his last lap. She made her way down as he discussed with his doctor, then intercepted him as he ambled away from the track, toweling a light sheen of sweat from the back of his neck. "You,"—she pointed to him as she arrived—"have a very nice reward waiting for you back at the apartment, but I think there's something else you'll want to do first."

"What could that possibly be?" Cyperus teased, joining a kiss, hands on her hips. Her back was to their approach, but she felt the moment when Cyperus spotted Galax arriving with his security escort in the hitch of his breath. She broke the kiss so he didn't have to feel guilty for doing it.

Cyperus strode to meet his friend, laughing, and embraced the slightly shorter man. Sienna was too far to hear what they said, but Galax's gesture to Cyperus's path suggested he was complimenting the man on the smoothness of his gait. They resumed Galax's original path with Cyperus's arm slung over his friend's shoulders, and Sienna was surprised by the hollowness of Galax's face when she finally got a good look at him. Purple shadows had made what seemed a permanent home under his eyes and his cheekbones.

"Glad to see you looking well," he told her with a wry smile and opened his arms diffidently. He'd given her good medical treatment at a very difficult time in her life, and she was happy to embrace him in turn. "You're collecting a menagerie out here in the wilderness?" When Sienna stepped back, she turned to see his attention was on Gentiana, pointedly clasping Valerie's hand.

The question might be prompting her to expand about Valerie's identity and her role in Gentiana's decision to stay on Idyll, but Sienna was content to push that off for later. "They followed me home, there was nothing I could do," she dodged with light humor.

"And you,"—Cyperus clapped a hand on his friend's shoulder—"are very early! Not that I mind, but you are going to have to put up with me for that whole time."

The shadows expanded across Galax's face, or perhaps bubbled up from behind his eyes. "With the war going the way it is, when you manage to find a place on a transport, you *take* it, no matter when it is." He faced Cyperus, solemn. "Cyperus, we need you. You don't understand how badly. You're free of the LSF weapon now, if you would come back, you could even bring Sienna..."

"No." Cyperus spoke before Sienna's anxiety could even poke its poisonous head out from under the rock she'd chased it under. His tone was light, but utterly immovable. "It's no longer my war. Killing more LSF regular folk sooner, better, like that will somehow prevent them from doing their damnedest to kill more Pax Romana regular folk sooner, better, isn't moving a single step closer to universal mercy."

Galax's frowned at the ground, perhaps choosing among a variety of arguments he'd been prepped with, or perhaps struggling with whether to use his knowledge of his friend against him.

"If you're thinking of trying a 'look at what the foxes did to your partner' tack, don't." Sienna slowly curled her fingers into a fist. "I will punch you." Valerie huffed a laugh like she would have spoken up to corroborate that, if not for her French accent.

Galax shot her a slightly worried look that indicated that he completely believed her. "You're so *good* at it," he said, finally. "Don't you miss it?"

"No." Cyperus echoed the immovability of his tone with his body this time, standing slightly braced. "Security system consulting takes me all over the planet, and Sienna can come with me—and any kids can, when they're old enough—and that gives her a chance to do all kinds of photography for her paintings. Her art career is really taking off, by the way. Hell, she designed this for me as an engagement present. Look."

"Oh, any excuse," Sienna said, not entirely under her breath, and not bothering to hide that actually, she was entirely pleased every time he showed the tattoo off. Cyperus shrugged off his shirt, made his rave lines visible, and turned to show Galax his back. The red lines of the tattoo began at the rave lines and then diverged from them, their curling, knotted shapes forming furled wings that reached to the small of his back. Like the wings worn by the Pax Romana man who'd helped found the Amsterdam Institute.

<You knew him in your original home, what do you think, Pen?> Sienna asked as Galax reluctantly let himself be diverted into discussing her upcoming gallery show. <Do I sic Medical or Research on him for recruitment purposes?>

<Oh, Medical, definitely. His bedside manner is too good to be wasted in Research. I'll send the Director a message to start marshalling his enticements.>

She took Galax's arm in a conversational lull and half-teasingly, half-seriously steered him back to the main Institute buildings. "You have a whole month to work on Cyperus, just be aware that means we have a whole month to work on *you*, hm? Come on, there's someone I want you to meet."

Galax groaned. "I'm not interested in being set up with anyone, thank you." He cast a glance at Gentiana and Valerie, who were diverging to their own destination now. Sienna really would have to tell him the whole story at some point, just to prove that it wasn't another case of "for the love of an Idyllian woman."

“Of course not,” Cyperus said, taking his other elbow. “You really should see the new int-tech lab they’re setting up here, though. You’ll die of envy, and then they’ll offer you one of your own.”

Galax shot Cyperus an incredulous—yet hungry—look, and Sienna laughed with him, firmly steering Galax on his way. There were plenty of reasons to stay here, and even if they weren’t enough for Galax, they were enough for Cyperus. Nothing in her doubted that now.

ACKNOWLEDGMENTS

I started writing Clean Install sometime in 2016 on a whim. At that time, I was writing exclusively urban fantasy, but feeling increasingly constrained by it without quite knowing what I should do instead. A novella was low risk—without wasting a ton of time, I could still write an idea that I found fun and compelling, but that was probably secretly "too." Too overdramatic. Too silly. Too ungrounded in hard science principles.

"Too," it turned out, was exactly what I needed to make something that had plenty of what readers loved.

In 2019, I started putting plans in motion: get covers made, finish up Books 3 and 4, and publish four novella ebooks in 2020. And I did, despite circumstances that I need not specify—though I do dream of this book enduring to a time when simply saying the year no longer evokes a shiver of ongoing or remembered grief. Following the steps of my plan for the series kept me going when it came to my writing career, but it was friends and family who let me hold the rest of my life together. This isn't the place to name them all, not least because my gratitude is to deep to fit on the page.

Foremost among those who are owed thanks for these books in particular are my writing group: Kate Alice Marshall, Corry L. Lee, Erin M. Evans, Susan J. Morris, and Shanna Germain. Every book is better for their specific suggestions and general writing wisdom. My agent, Cameron McClure, offered excellent notes on the first book, as did Casey Blair and no doubt others who have been pushed from my mind by the Plague Year. Apologies to any I have left out!

Kate Marshall brought my characters to life in her beautiful covers, and Sara McCormick kindly saved me from myself and helped me with the layout.

Finally, thank you to all my fans who have followed me from my urban fantasy and to those who have found me for the first time. I don't plan to let myself feel constrained by one genre again!